LION'S HEAT

LORA LEIGH

BERKLEY SENSATION, NEW YORK

THE BERKLEY PUBLISHING GROUP
Published by the Penguin Group
Penguin Group (USA) Inc.
375 Hudson Street, New York, New York 10014, USA
Penguin Group (Canada), 90 Eglinton Avenue East, Suite 700, Toronto, Ontario M4P 2Y3, Canada
(a division of Pearson Penguin Canada Inc.)
Penguin Books Ltd., 80 Strand, London WC2R 0RL, England
Penguin Group Ireland, 25 St. Stephen's Green, Dublin 2, Ireland (a division of Penguin Books Ltd.)
Penguin Group (Australia), 250 Camberwell Road, Camberwell, Victoria 3124, Australia
(a division of Pearson Australia Group Pty. Ltd.)
Penguin Books India Pvt. Ltd., 11 Community Centre, Panchsheel Park, New Delhi—110 017, India
Penguin Group (NZ), 67 Apollo Drive, Rosedale, North Shore 0632, New Zealand
(a division of Pearson New Zealand Ltd.)
Penguin Books (South Africa) (Pty.) Ltd., 24 Sturdee Avenue, Rosebank, Johannesburg 2196,
South Africa

Penguin Books Ltd., Registered Offices: 80 Strand, London WC2R 0RL, England

This is a work of fiction. Names, characters, places, and incidents either are the product of the author's imagination or are used fictitiously, and any resemblance to actual persons, living or dead, business establishments, events, or locales is entirely coincidental. The publisher does not have any control over and does not assume any responsibility for author or third-party websites or their content.

LION'S HEAT

A Berkley Sensation Book / published by arrangement with the author

PRINTING HISTORY
Berkley Sensation mass-market edition / April 2010

Copyright © 2010 by Christina Simmons.
Excerpt from *The Demon in Me* by Michelle Rowen copyright © by Michelle Rouillard.
Cover art of man by CURA Photography/Shutterstock.
Cover art of lion by Svemir/Shutterstock.
Cover design by Rita Frangie.

ISBN: 978-0-425-23380-1

BERKLEY® SENSATION
Berkley Sensation Books are published by The Berkley Publishing Group,
a division of Penguin Group (USA) Inc.,
375 Hudson Street, New York, New York 10014.
BERKLEY® SENSATION and the "B" design are trademarks of Penguin Group (USA) Inc.

PRINTED IN THE UNITED STATES OF AMERICA

10 9 8 7 6 5 4 3 2 1

"Lora Leigh delivers on all counts."
—Romance Reviews Today

continued . . .

HARMONY'S WAY

"Leigh's engrossing alternate reality combines spicy sensuality, romantic passion and deadly danger. Hot stuff indeed."
—*Romantic Times*

"I stand in awe of Ms. Leigh's ability to bring to life these wonderful characters as they slowly weave their way into my mind and heart. When it comes to this genre, Lora Leigh is the queen."
—*Romance Junkies*

MEGAN'S MARK

"A riveting tale full of love, intrigue and every woman's fantasy, *Megan's Mark* is a wonderful contribution to Lora Leigh's Breeds series . . . As always, Lora Leigh delivers on all counts; *Megan's Mark* will certainly not disappoint her many fans!"
—*Romance Reviews Today*

"Hot, hot, hot—the sex and the setting . . . You can practically see the steam rising off the pages."
—*Fresh Fiction*

"This entertaining romantic science fiction suspense will remind the audience of *Kitty and the Midnight Hour* by Carrie Vaughn and MaryJanice Davidson's *Derik's Bane* as this futuristic world filled with 'Breeds' seems 'normal' . . . [A] delightful thriller."
—*The Best Reviews*

"The dialogue is quick, the action is fast and the sex is oh so hot . . . Don't miss out on this one."
—*A Romance Review*

"Leigh's action-packed Breeds series makes a refreshing change . . . Rapid-fire plot development and sex steamy enough to peel wallpaper."
—*Monsters and Critics*

"An exceedingly sexy and sizzling new series to enjoy. Hot sex, snappy dialogue and kick-butt action add up to outstanding entertainment."
—*Romantic Times*

For laughter, love and freedom.

∙ P R O L O G U E ∙

Jonas Wyatt, Director of the Bureau of Breed Affairs, and a Lion Breed with secrets that could destroy him, stared at the door through which what was sure to be his greatest weakness had just stepped. He then turned to the mated wife of the Feline Breed leader, the Prima, Merinus Lyons.

She should have been showing her age, Jonas thought critically as he focused on her unlined face, her clear dark brown gaze and the youthful curve of her lips. There wasn't a single strand of gray in the fall of long, dark brunette hair, nothing to indicate she was nearing forty with two children and a life that would have had any other woman in therapy.

Jonas knew for a fact that she hadn't aged a day, physically, since the moment she had mated with the Feline Breed Pride leader, Callan Lyons, twelve years before. As far as her body was aware, time hadn't passed.

She may not have aged physically, but Jonas could attest to the fact that Merinus had definitely grown in strength. Perhaps not in wisdom if this latest stunt was anything to go by, but there was no doubt she had developed a backbone of steel.

Only steel would have her sitting across from him, that victorious little smile tugging at her lips as she arched a brunette brow back at him challengingly.

If she weren't already mated to his Pride leader, she would have been a woman Jonas would have definitely been interested in. At least, before today.

"She's pregnant." The words slipped past his lips in a frozen statement of disapproval. Not for her pregnancy, per se, but that Merinus would consider hiring her to work with him in her current condition. That she would bring a woman with such vulnerability into his life, into any Breed's life, and expect her to survive it.

"Really?" Merinus's brows arched as though in shock. "Why Jonas, I must have missed that. Do tell how I could have been so neglectful as to have not noticed."

He didn't wince, though he had watched Merinus's husband mate, Callan, do just that whenever she got that tone, warning him to tread carefully. Jonas knew this woman for the subtly dangerous adversary she could be. She could make his life extremely difficult if she wanted to; she was his superior, at least in the hierarchy of the Pride. Which, on most days, was truly the only thing that mattered.

Jonas liked to tell himself over the years that her power didn't reach here, to the Bureau, though. Based in D.C., the Bureau of Breed Affairs was his baby, his playground, his hobby and his lover. He'd tried to pretend she would never dare stick her too-curious, too-scheming little nose into the day-to-day running of the political law enforcement machine Jonas had built over the past ten years.

He had been so very wrong. And that knowledge had the power to prick his already testy temper.

Leaning forward, Jonas placed his arms on his desk and stared back at Merinus with cool determination. It wouldn't do to let her see a weakness.

"She won't work out, Merinus," he informed her. "I'll have her in hysterics in an hour. I don't want to deal with another overly emotional little girl, especially one so close to giving birth. And what about once she has that child? This is not a damned nursery, nor is it a nine-to-five job."

He had to force the words past his lips. He forced his tongue to push them from his mouth even as he felt the tiny glands at the side of it itch in impending disaster.

Not just disaster, but mating heat. A catastrophe in the making where his life was concerned.

Already he could feel the rage brewing inside, the knowledge that another man had created life within her. That she had belonged to another. That perhaps, even now, another man shared her bed.

All that stayed the power of his rage was the fact that there had been no other man's scent on her delicate body. There had been no mating mark, no hint of male possession spoiling the sweet, delicate woman scent of her.

Could he have borne it if there had been?

"She can deal with you." Merinus rose to her feet as she stared back at him regally despite the ragged jeans and T-shirt that gave her the appearance of a teenaged waif. "What's more, I'm fairly certain she can do so without a display of hysterics."

Jonas swore he could feel his hands getting ready to shake to his Prima. A sense of certain panic began to fill him, tightening in his throat and threatening to steal his power to speak.

He'd never been frightened in his life. Hell, he had no idea what true fear was until Merinus turned her back on him and began walking to the door.

"Why?" The question was a subtle, feral growl that had Merinus pausing in offense before turning back to him slowly.

Jonas snapped his teeth together before a tight grimace contorted his face and he forced himself to turn away from her. She deserved the same respect he would give his Pride leader, and that growl had been the furthest thing from respect that he could come up with.

"Why?" Her tone was lethal now. "Because, Jonas, I'm sick of watching perfectly good secretaries become neurotic head cases because of your complete disregard for civility. I know Rachel. I know her abilities as well as her temperament." Merinus's triumphant smirk had his guts twisting in terror now. "And I know Rachel can handle you. If she could handle my brother Kane at the tender age of sixteen and actually keep his finances as well as his schedule in order, then I have no doubt she can put up with your diabolical, manipulating personality and perhaps even manage to lend a measure of respectability to the Bureau before you destroy the last shred of civility that it could possess." She walked to the door before turning back to him with a mocking look of accomplishment. "Consider it a favor of sorts. And remember, Rachel is one of my dearest, best friends in the world. Hurt her, Wyatt, and it's no different from hurting me."

With that warning firmly in place, she pulled the door open and left the room. The panel closed behind her with a gentle click, sealing Jonas into the cool silence of his office as the murmur of voices could be heard in the other room.

She had just ensured that he couldn't yell at Rachel, he couldn't fire her. Merinus couldn't have forced his hand more with that statement than if she had simply cut it off. She had made it clear he was stuck with his new secretary.

Jonas sat back down slowly. He laid his palms flat on his desk and took a deep, hard breath. He was a Breed. Grown men trembled in fear of him. Hell, his own species trembled in fear of him. He'd made certain of it. He'd worked to instill that fear, that driving wariness that wouldn't allow for any possible rejection of any demand he made.

It seemed, though, that he hadn't impressed upon Merinus just how dangerous he could be. That, or she really didn't give a damn.

He wondered if it was too late to rectify that small detail?

A light knock at the door, a subtle, gentle scent that sliced through his senses and had him stiffening as the door opened.

"Mr. Wyatt, if you'd like to take a moment to discuss your itinerary with me, then I could get started."

She stood there, the slight mound of her stomach smaller than he would have thought for the stage of her pregnancy. At five months, that little mound should have been larger. Long, long dark red hair was pulled up in a bun at the nape of her neck; delicate glasses were perched on her nose. Deep, deep green eyes stared back at him with chilling intensity.

Well-fitted black pants were paired with a white blouse, which flowed over the mound of her stomach to her hips. Flat, conservative black shoes covered tiny feet.

She was a fairy, he thought. A whimsical creature that no man dared touch for fear of inviting the wrath of some unknown dark force charged with her protection. That dark force being Merinus Lyons, the wicked ogre of his life, as far as he was concerned.

"Mr. Wyatt?" Her tone was even, polite. "Your itinerary, sir."

His itinerary. Of course she would want that. How else could she effectively destroy his world unless she knew how he moved through it?

"Don't worry about the itinerary," he growled, not bothering to hold back the deep-throated rumble. "I'll take care of that myself. Just . . ." He waved his hand toward the outer office. "Do the filing or something."

A dark, winged brow lifted slowly.

Then she did the most amazing thing. She closed the door softly, all the while holding his gaze as she moved to the front of the desk.

Jonas watched her as he would a cobra preparing to strike. Hell, she was more dangerous than a cobra.

"Mr. Wyatt, I am not some glorified clerk who you need to patronize," she said. Sweetly. So fucking sweet her voice dripped with honey while those wild green eyes glittered with a dare. "You will give me your itinerary, and you will do so in time for me to make sense of it, as well as to make any adjustments needed. All appointments will now go through me, as well as all scheduled business trips and meetings. As I understand it, the last finance meeting at Sanctuary was a farce. Pride Leader Lyons and his Prima have ordered me to ensure the next one actually contains some viable numbers that at least come close to the amount used from the Bureau's accounts. We can do this the easy way." Her smile was gentle, benign. "Or we can be difficult about it." That smile turned to ice.

Jonas rose slowly to his feet, his hands remaining planted on the desk. He ensured that he towered over her as he glared down at her.

"Good luck." He kept it short and sweet, more because she had his tongue tied in so many fucking knots that he could barely think, let alone speak.

As she stood there, he closed the laptop he used, slid it into a protective case along with the slim external drive that contained the files he needed.

Rachel watched silently as he snapped the case closed, gripped the handle and strode from the office.

She felt as though she should be taking a deep, much-needed breath as the tension that filled the room slowly eased away. But with his departure was a strange sort of emptiness as well. As though the life had been sucked from the office. It was now no more than a shell.

Her lips quirked at the thought before she shook it off and strode back to her own office. Merinus had given her a new lease on life with this job—if she could stick it out.

She laid her hand on her stomach. She had to stick it out, she didn't have a choice. Jonas might be the scariest man she had ever met, probably the most dangerous. With those quicksilver eyes and that hard, corded body that screamed sexy and lethal, he was by far the most fascinating man she had ever met.

Short black hair was just long enough that it lay against his scalp, giving the hard, sculpted planes of his face a savage, diabolical appearance. And those eyes.

Quicksilver. Mercury. Eyes that saw into a person's soul.

Eyes that seared.

Eyes that had nearly mesmerized her.

If she wasn't very, very careful, Jonas Wyatt would end up owning her soul, as it appeared he owned everyone else's.

And that just wouldn't do. She had a feeling Jonas might be a little bit spoiled. Which meant she was going to have to definitely break the habit.

Striding to the desk, she took her seat and called Merinus.

"He's on the run," she reported.

She could almost hear the smile that curled Merinus's lips. "That's okay. I know where he's running to. Pack a bag and bring your laptop. It's time to show Jonas the power of the Breed cabinet. And I can think of no better time than now."

Rachel wondered if Jonas would ever look back and realize that Merinus was trying to save him, rather than piss him off. According to the Prima of the Feline Breeds, Jonas Wyatt was on a path of self-destruction where the Bureau was concerned.

"Do you think discussing this with him would do any good, Merinus?" Rachel asked, her tone wary now. Jonas didn't seem like a good man to piss off.

"Callan and Dash have talked to him until they're blue in the face." Merinus sighed. "He can fight with them; that instinctive code of honor he has nearly dictates that he does. If he doesn't stop stirring suspicion where the Bureau is concerned, he'll be voted out of it. That's something I don't want to see happen. No, Rachel, we're the only ones that can get through to Jonas now."

"We are?" Rachel rather doubted that.

"You are," Merinus amended. "Just treat him like you treated Kane. Trust me, he won't know how to combat it. Jonas has always been the one doing the bulldozing. To my knowledge, no one has ever used the same tactics on him that he uses on others. Let's see what happens when they do."

"He takes a chunk out of their ass?" Rachel asked, a vision of those lethal canines flashing before her eyes.

To which Merinus's laugh was soft, and suspiciously knowing.

"Now Rachel, do you really think he would bite you?"

"Only if I get close enough," she murmured.

"Then don't get close enough," Merinus advised her with a heavy hint of amusement. "Be very careful, Rachel, not to get close enough."

Three Months Later

"Did I ask you to set up a meeting with Senator Racert?"

Jonas Wyatt stepped out of his office, coldly indignant to face the icy composure of his secretary's porcelain face and frozen ocean green eyes.

There was a heartbeat of time when his entire system froze, his control shattered and the animal that lurked just beneath the skin jumped free. A single moment out of time when every cell in his body clamored to claim his mate.

Just as quickly he reined the animal back, jerked at the ragged edges of his control and fought the hunger tearing through his system.

As always, the battle was nearly lost in the face of Rachel's perfect, mannequin-like composure. He had had more than one fantasy regarding breaking that composure.

Unfortunately, each time he thought about giving in to those fantasies he came smack up against the ripe appearance of motherhood. She was with child, but it didn't stop him from wanting her, needing her. It didn't stop him from doing everything he could do to make her life easier, to make her job easier, to give her the man he was inside—at least as much as possible.

He was gentle with her while he was harsh with others. He made a place for her in his life while he held others at bay. And still, she seemed as cool, as unemotional, as she had the day she began working with him.

"Actually, Senator Racert asked for the meeting," Rachel answered with icy disdain. "You've put him off for over six weeks now, and he does control the Bureau's governmental purse strings as well as carry significant weight in the Breed Appropriations Committee."

"Their governmental purse strings couldn't concern me less." He leaned against the doorframe as he crossed his arms over his chest and attempted to glare at her.

It was damned hard to glare at one's mate, especially when the child she sheltered so protectively was listening, and reacting so closely to every word he said.

He could sense that. The girl child she carried paused whenever she heard his voice, just as she would pause when she heard her mother's. No others. She flat out didn't give a damn if anyone else spoke. Hell, he couldn't even curse anymore. And that had been damned hard to do anything about. But he ensured that the child stayed calm. If the child was calm, then that meant the mother was calm. Keeping her settled during her pregnancy to ensure the child's continued good health and, therefore, the mother's happiness, was all that mattered to him.

"Senator Racert's voice is important to the Breed community as a whole." Rachel rose from her chair, still graceful and exquisitely beautiful as she moved across the room to the file cabinet.

He followed. He couldn't help himself. The damned file cabinet was taller than she was.

He reached it before she did, pulled the top drawer free, then plucked the file out of her fingers and inserted it in its proper place.

He was more than aware of the look of narrow-eyed suspicion she shot him as he pushed the drawer closed before following her back to her desk.

"Cancel the appointment with Racert," he demanded as she retook her seat.

There was an edge of suspicion in her gaze as she looked up at him.

"Stop hovering over me." Ice dripped from her voice, as though his presence did nothing to affect her.

He may have believed it if the child, a perfect barometer for the mother's feelings, didn't choose that moment to let out a silent whimper of distress. Her mother was clearly upset, off balance, perhaps even frightened. Because whatever emotion her mother was feeling, so then was the child feeling.

Jonas backed up with three deliberate steps, waiting tensely for the child to regain the calm he wanted the mother to feel.

It happened slowly. One step at a time. Rachel turned back to the computer and that impossible itinerary she was working on.

"Racert is double-crossing us," he finally told her, careful to keep his voice quiet. "He's after information."

"Which you give so rarely and with such perfect manners," she mocked him.

He grunted at the comment. He would tell her anything she wanted to know; she only had to ask. Racert, however, was another thing entirely.

"Cancel the meeting," he ordered her again.

"No." There was pure stubborn refusal in her voice.

His lips thinned.

"Fine, I'll leave the office." He stalked back to the doorway.

"Go ahead." He heard the shrug in her voice. "I'll handle the meeting myself. I believe the meeting involves the latest projected budget, which you haven't yet turned in. I'm certain I can handle that."

Jonas assured himself he wasn't paling at the very thought of Miss-Financial-Tight-Ass creating his budget.

A growl slipped free before he could hold it back.

Rachel's brow arched as disdain filled her expression. But from the child, he felt something far different, something he was certain he should at least protest.

Amusement. The baby was amused, which meant her mother was much more amused.

"Are you laughing at me?" He paced back to her desk, flattened his hands on the dark wood and leaned forward. Close enough that he could smell her unique scent. Close enough that the hunger ripping through his guts sharpened to a dagger's stroke. "Be careful, little girl," he warned her softly, holding her gaze, watching the wild green become darker, wilder. "Or you may well get far more than you're bargaining for."

The amusement drifted away and something far darker took its place.

Jonas eased back. He forced himself from the suddenly reckless anticipation that poured from the woman, despite the composed features, the iron will and stubborn determination. Slowly, he straightened, turned and forced himself back to his own office.

There was desire there, in the sweet scent of her, in the tension that tightened between them each time he went near her. There was hunger. The scent of it was like a soft summer rainfall. It was fresh, tinged with the scent of the earth itself, and a sweet moisture that he knew could become addictive as hell.

The woman was everything he could have wanted in a mate. She was the dream he'd never allowed himself to wish for. Because it was the greatest danger he could bring to his life, and the future of the Breeds.

This was a temptation he knew he could never allow himself to weaken to. It was a promise he had made to himself. It was a vow. And this small woman was shredding his determination one look, one word, one breath at a time.

His mate would never know mating heat.

· CHAPTER I ·

For the first time in her life, Rachel Broen was terrified. It wasn't fear. It was soul-destroying, mind-numbing, silently screaming terror.

She couldn't scream aloud, it would draw notice. Notice that her tears and ragged sobs wouldn't draw, weren't drawing as she slid her unassuming little Civic into the deserted parking lot of the Bureau of Breed Affairs.

The night guard on duty at the gate had taken her pass without much notice. He knew her car, had seen enough of her to know who she was. It wasn't unusual for her to leave late, or to arrive early if she was commanded to do so by the autocratic Bureau director, Jonas Wyatt.

The guard had easily accepted her hasty excuse that she'd forgotten to update his memos and his morning schedule, and that it had to be done tonight.

He hadn't noticed her torn blouse or the jacket she wore that covered it. He hadn't seen the bruise she could feel spreading across the right side of her face, or the swollen condition of her right eye.

The blow had been carefully delivered.

Jumping from the car, she felt the rough asphalt bite into her bare feet as she stumbled before racing to the door. It took two attempts to get her electronic card pass to activate the doors and release the locks.

A thin sob tore from her chest as she nearly fell through the door and ran for the stairs that led to the third floor and the private offices of the director, Jonas Wyatt.

Jonas. The manipulating, calculating bastard. This was his fault. He'd played too many games. He'd pushed the wrong people and had so erroneously believed they would come after him.

She tripped, her knee slamming into a step, the skin breaking as a ragged scream of rage and pain tore from her lips.

She was paying for it.

Oh God. She was paying for it. She was paying for her stubbornness, her determination . . . No, she wasn't paying for it. The bruises, the agony tearing through her leg, the ragged pain in her side from the fist she had taken earlier, the bruises on her face, they were nothing. She would suffer that pain a thousand times over. She would suffer the fires of hell if only her child was safe.

Jonas. He was here.

A strangled scream tore from her lips as she fought to breathe, to race up the second flight of stairs. One more flight. Dear God, she was almost there.

Jonas was here. She knew he was. He had warned her that evening not to come to work tomorrow. He had known his enemies were tracking him. He'd known, the son of a bitch, he'd known and just as she'd warned him months ago, when they struck, it wouldn't be him they went after.

She had never believed they would come after her child.

"Jonas!" She tried to scream out his name as she fumbled with the electronic key at the door to the main offices.

Sliding it again, again, and still it wouldn't work.

"Jonas, please . . ." she screamed out again, terrified he would ignore her, knowing he had to hear her.

He was a Breed.

The lock released, the heavy steel door flew open, nearly pitching her to the floor as the door to Jonas's office jerked open across the room.

He was there, and he wasn't alone. She barely saw the others though. She saw his face, hated and yet adored. His eyes, alive in his bronzed face, swirls of silver mercury as he jumped to her, barely catching her before she fell to the floor.

"You bastard!" An openhanded slap to his shocked face as sobs tore from her, tears making her vision cloudy as terror choked her, ripping the breath from her body. "I warned you! I warned you they wouldn't strike you!"

"Rachel!" A horrible rumble of sound in fury, a muted roar left his lips as he gripped her arms, his fingers tight around her flesh as he gave her a firm shake.

"They have Amber!"

The strength left her legs, her body. Collapsing against his chest, she clawed at his arms, desperate for the strength she knew he possessed, fighting for sanity in a world that had suddenly exploded around her.

"They want those files. They'll kill her." Wild, terrified, she knew he would never do it. She knew he would never save her baby. "Please, Jonas. Give me the files. Save my baby. Oh God, save my baby."

Jonas felt the life leave his body. For the first time in his life, Jonas Wyatt felt pure, unadulterated terror washing through him.

His unflappable, cool paragon of a secretary, the mate he refused to claim, stared up at him with tear-drenched dark green eyes, her pale face so horribly bruised.

The scent of her terror and her injuries were an affront to his senses, the knowledge that the child he had claimed as his own so many months ago was in the line of fire, had the animal inside him screaming in rage.

"Chimera." His head jerked to the side as the Jaguar female stepped from her position in the office behind him, moving past the three men that were quickly pulling weapons from a once-hidden vault and strapping them on. "Take her."

He pushed Rachel to the female Enforcer, seeing in the other woman's clear, predatory gaze the need to fight rather than stand back.

"No! Jonas, no!" Rachel clutched at him, ripping his heart from his chest as the agonizing fury in her voice tore through his mind.

A scream of rage tore through his head, only years of patience, of strength, years of conditioning held back the instinctive response as his mate fought to be strong, fought to hold on to her sanity in the face of the danger her child now faced.

"Rachel, listen to me." He shook her again, gently, staring into her beautiful dark green, velvet eyes. "I'll get Amber. I swear to you."

Panic filled her eyes. He hadn't believed her face could become whiter, but it did. The scent of her terror tore through him like a ragged blade as her sobs ripped through his soul.

"They'll kill her," she tried to scream, but the hoarse desperation in her voice came out as a ragged plea. "I don't have time." She jerked at the hold he had on her. "Give me the files. Please. Oh God, please Jonas."

"Jonas, we have to move." Dane Vanderale, the son and heir of the Leo, the strongest Lion Breed ever created, moved to his side. "We have a location. Brandenmore's limo is parked at her house. I have a unit heading there now."

"Back off." Jonas jerked around, snarling at the man whom genetics tied him to as a brother, as the other man made plans—not to save Amber, but to take the enemy instead. "Call your team back. Too many will be dangerous." He turned to the men he knew he could trust. "Rule, have the Blazer brought around." The specially modified city SUV would hold the team, as well as weapons. "Lawe, Mordecai, go ahead, recon only."

The men moved out as Dane cursed behind him.

Jonas held Rachel as she pleaded. Her rejection of a team moving out was a ragged litany of desperation as she begged him to just give her the files.

"Chimera, the files are on my desk."

He'd been waiting for Brandenmore's men. The files had been in place, the information the bastard wanted lying in clear view as they'd laid the trap for him. A trap Brandenmore thought he could use a child to escape.

"Rachel, enough." Her sobs were destroying him as she tried to pull away, to gain the files and escape with them, even though she knew he would never allow it.

"No, Jonas." Her tear-drenched, bruised face destroyed him as her gentle voice, so often cool and yet tinged with amusement was now filled with rage. "You won't play games with my child's life."

So many months she had worked for him, with him. Still, she hadn't seen beyond what others called the games.

Releasing one of her arms, he let his fingers trail down her unbruised cheek. His throat was tight with the agony that this one person, whom he had been slowly allowing into that inner core of himself, still saw only his outer surface.

"Give me the files," she begged, though he saw the fury in her eyes, the knowledge that he could never do that.

"Jonas, the files." Chimera stopped at his side as Dane, Rule and Mordecai moved into place at the door, fully prepared, weapons stowed carefully under jackets and in the duffel bags they carried.

"Come on." He made the decision quickly, his hard gaze connecting with Chimera's in a silent order that he knew the other woman would understand.

She had sole responsibility for Rachel's life once they arrived at the small home where the baby was being held. Jonas would move in with Dane and the others to secure the baby, to ensure that those who threatened her never threatened another living soul.

"Jonas?" Rachel stumbled again, only to find herself lifted into his arms, his broad, muscled chest beneath her, his hard, savagely hewn expression more animal than man at the moment.

There was rage swirling in the living depths of those

quicksilver eyes. Like a beast, separate from the man, raged inside him now.

"The files won't save the child." His voice was a hard, rasping growl. "You know it as well as I, Rachel. They'll kill her, and they'll kill you. I won't allow it."

She knew it. In her mother's heart, she had seen it in Phillip Brandenmore's eyes each time he struck her, his fist brutal, his gaze reflecting pleasure—and anticipation.

"He doesn't know you were waiting on him." She forced the words past her lips. "I didn't tell him, Jonas."

But she had known. Jonas hadn't told her either, but she had gotten to know the man she worked for over the months. She'd learned to anticipate not just his needs, but also his actions, and to prepare accordingly.

"I know you didn't tell him, Rachel." They moved along the hall to a side door, inaccessible except for the highest level of security.

"We need to know what we're driving into." Dane Vanderale's normally mocking, amused voice was now steel hard, icy with death. Rachel could almost believe he was a Breed as well, as those eerie emerald eyes of his narrowed on her. "What happened?"

The nightmare of the night thickened her voice as she told him.

She had gone home. Her babysitter wasn't there. Amber had been crying. She was only three months old. She was hungry, she was wet and she was frightened. Rachel had heard the baby's screams the second her feet hit the small back porch.

She hadn't thought; she had reacted. She had rushed to get to her baby, and she had met the merciless eyes of the men who had been awaiting her instead.

"Is the baby unharmed?" Jonas questioned when she finished relating that evening's horror, rushing from the elevator as it deposited them inside an underground garage she hadn't even known existed.

"She was when I left." Her voice quivered.

Jonas had never said Amber's name. It was always "the child," or "the baby."

"She's hungry," she whispered, staring up at him. "And cold. They took her blankets. I know she hasn't been changed."

She was dying inside. Amber was such a good baby. She never cried unless she was cold or hungry. She loved to watch the world; she loved to watch her mother. The few times Rachel had defied Jonas's orders and brought Amber to the office, the baby had always seemed mesmerized by his voice. She listened. She watched. And now she was alone, without warmth or comfort.

"I can't stand it, Jonas." Her stomach cramped with pain, both from the blow she had received earlier, as well as the knowledge that her child was hungry and cold. Confused. Frightened. "Please, Jonas, don't let them hurt her."

"No one is going to hurt her." He stepped to the SUV and deposited her in the backseat.

Chimera jumped in the other side as Jonas slid in beside Rachel, cushioning her between them as Dane took the wheel and Lawe rode shotgun.

"Weapons." Lawe turned, an opened bag at his feet as he pushed the weapons to Jonas.

Rachel watched, terror building inside her as she saw more than the lethal laser and explosive ammo–contained weapons Jonas strapped on.

She saw a small army preparing for battle, and her child, her three-month-old baby, so defenseless, so tiny, was going to be smack in the middle of the war.

"Jonas, please." She couldn't breathe. Her chest tightened with panic, with a sense of terror so overwhelming it threatened to cut the air from her lungs.

His head turned, those eerie silver eyes flashing with living rage as he stared back at her.

"I put that child's life above my own," he suddenly stated,

the growl in his voice a horrible thing to hear now. This was the animal she had heard whispers of: the Breed, whom so many feared.

Looking down, she watched as he quickly checked his weapon, his statement reverberating through her head. Jonas placed too many people above himself, she had often thought. He was a manipulator, he was calculating, but there was nothing cold, nothing cruel about him other than his demeanor.

"How many are there?" Dane Vanderale's tone was harder, if possible, and colder. Rachel hadn't imagined anyone could be harder and colder than Jonas, but Dane had him beat.

"There are four. Phillip Brandenmore is with them."

Silence filled the vehicle for long moments.

"Lawe is in place," Rule stated into the silence. "There are four men inside. Brandenmore has the child in a carrier next to him."

"He's prepared to take the baby with him," Dane stated.

"Shut the fuck up, Dane," Jonas snarled, and Rachel knew Jonas understood the implications of the report.

Rachel felt herself shaking from the inside out. She knew enough of the Breed history, the labs and the scientists to know that her baby would become no more than a research project.

Pain tore through her abdomen at the thought. A sob tightened in her throat, nearly choking her.

"Look at me." The harsh sound of Jonas's voice had her gaze lifting to him. "No one will hurt that child. Do you hear me?"

"Jonas." Dane's voice was warning. "Let's concentrate on doing what we can."

Don't make promises that couldn't be kept. She heard the underlying message as Jonas held her gaze, his eyes terrifying as the color shifted and swirled.

"No one will hurt that child." His eyes raked over her, his expression turning savage as he reached out, a single finger whispering over the bruise on her face. "And they'll die for this."

The bruises on her face were an affront to the animal crouched and snarling within him. He could feel the beast, the savage wildness that he had always fought threatened to rise to the fore.

This was his mate. No matter that he hadn't claimed her. No matter that he had no intentions of taking her. She was his, and God help the ones who had dared to lay a hand on her.

He could smell the scent of her blood, her pain. Even now, her body was drawn tight with the physical agony that raced through her system.

"Call Sanctuary," he ordered Chimera. "Have the heli-jet waiting close to fly us home. I want Ely and the medical staff prepared and ready for us to fly in."

Chimera gave a quick nod of her head.

"Lawe, Dane, give the order." Dane glanced back at Jonas in the rearview mirror. "The child's life is priority," he ordered them. "Nothing else matters."

Surprise flickered in Dane's gaze before he turned back, just as Jonas felt it emanating from Chimera and Lawe.

He had been attempting the capture of Brandenmore and his cohorts for years now, before they had ever been aware who, or what, was stealing information from Sanctuary or why. For the past year, nothing had mattered but capturing the bastard, alive, in the act of attempting to steal the information he wanted.

They needed him alive. They needed the chance, the opportunity, as well as the reason to place him under Breed Law during interrogation.

The interrogation mattered little in the face of the child's life.

His child.

God, how he wished that child was his rather than another's. How he wished he had been the one to sire the babe, to hold Rachel, to bring her pleasure.

If the world were a different place, if he were a different man. If there wasn't more risk in taking what was his than there was to maintaining a distance from it.

"We're moving in," Dane stated quietly.

"Jonas, please." Rachel's voice was ragged, her fingers gripping his arm, nails biting into the black sleeves of the black combat uniform he wore. "Please, Jonas, don't let them hurt Amber. Please."

Amber. The babe. His soul ripped apart at the thought of that child in danger.

"Stay in the vehicle, Rachel." He glanced at Chimera once again and received a quick nod in reply.

Rachel's life was in her hands. Her only responsibility was the protection of his mate.

The SUV drew to a stop, and Jonas let the animal free where he normally kept it leashed.

To every Breed there were two sides, alternate parts of their psyche that often worked together. But in certain instances, one became more dominant than the other.

The Lion that raged inside him now demanded dominance. His mate had been attacked, harmed. The child the animal and the man had claimed so many months ago was now in danger.

Not a single man would walk from that house without spilling precious life blood for his part in the bruises that marred his mate's flesh. For his part in the fear that even now, Jonas could scent raging from the child.

Moving into the small yard, he used the shadows that reached out from the houses surrounding it. The block Rachel's home sat on was small, quiet. Families lived and worked here. Children laughed, and parents watched after them.

Sliding in along the window that looked into the living room, Jonas caught a glimpse of Phillip Brandenmore, the owner of Brandenmore Research. The man who was determined to use the Breeds to create a drug that could decrease aging and could be sold for millions per user sat in front of the flat-screen television, a frown on his face as the babe whimpered at his side.

Amber was tired. The animal scented her weariness. She

had cried until she had exhausted herself. She was cold and hungry. No one had fed her. No one had changed her. No one had placed a blanket over her fragile body to block the slight chill in the room.

Her mother kept the house warm. The first thing these strangers had done was turn the heat down, taking away the warmth. Then they had stripped her comfort, her security.

The animal inside Jonas sensed Amber's fear, and crouched with predatory intent inside him.

"They have a Coyote with them." Rule spoke through the communications link at Jonas's ear. "He's currently in the kitchen with a pot of coffee. Stupid bastard."

Coyotes could be lazy. They were savage in battle, merciless in a pack, but those that stayed with the council or moved into the less acceptable areas of the world were downright lazy.

"Take him out first," Dane ordered as Jonas eased along the window, checking Brandenmore and the child's position before pulling back.

"I'm going through the window," he told the others. "Brandenmore is alone in the living room."

"Coyote's in the kitchen, we have a sentry on the front porch, we have one in the bedroom upstairs," Rule reported. "They're not expecting trouble."

They hadn't expected anyone at the office tonight. They had thought they could send Rachel back, force her to do their dirty work, then kill her. And only God knew what they had planned for the child.

"Jonas, he'll use the baby." Dane's voice was matter-of-fact, regretful, but realistic.

"The child is priority," Jonas repeated.

"There's no way to get to Brandenmore before he gets to the baby," Dane stated. "Think about it, Jonas."

Jonas glanced in the window again. Brandenmore's gun hand was within inches of Amber's head, the small, snub-nosed laser elite in his hand.

The animal inside him was screaming. From the first moment that Jonas had realized Rachel was his mate, he'd had a connection to the child. Defenseless, and yet confident of her place in her mother's world. She'd known no danger, no fear—until now.

Now she was experiencing sensations she should have never known. Exhaustion. Hunger. Drugs.

Jonas inhaled slowly. The baby was tired, but she was quiet because she had been drugged as well.

She was frightened.

He heard the tiny mewls, little squeaks of sound as her fists clenched and released. She wanted to cry, but she didn't have the strength.

"Dane, if this child is harmed, we're going to have problems." Jonas heard the growl in his own voice, felt the hidden claws as they parted the tips of his fingers, shifting beneath the regular nail beds and tearing forth.

Blood tipped, curved and sharp. His fingers flexed, his senses became sharper, edged with the hunger for blood and vengeance.

The problem had already arrived. The Lion, always kept so carefully leashed, had slipped free. In a moment of weakness, an awareness of the danger the child—his child—faced and it was there.

A snarl molded his lips, canines flashed in the darkness, a growl rumbled in his chest, deep-throated, predatory.

"Boss, we're in position." Rule knew the sound. "I have the Coyote, Lawe has the sentry in front."

"Dane converged on Brandenmore," Mordecai, the Coyote team member, gave the final order as Jonas, man and animal, moved into action.

The Genetics Council that had created the Breeds had one purpose in mind: the ultimate killing machine. The Breeds were created, enhanced, and trained for any and every situation that could be conceived.

They hadn't been created to save lives. They hadn't been

trained to care, to mate or to love. But what they hadn't been trained for had made them better, faster, stronger.

It had made them the most dangerous creatures on the face of the earth.

The ultimate weapon.

✦   ✦   ✦

Glass crashed, shattered.

It had taken precious minutes, patience Rachel had never believed she could have before she had the chance to tear open the door and fling herself from the SUV.

She made it to the side of the house, no farther. Hard, restraining fingers latched onto her arm, dragging her back as she watched the dark, snarling figure throw itself into the living room window.

The sound of glass breaking and an animal's snarl were the only sounds in the night. A shadow moved on the front porch, and silhouettes twisted and churned against the curtains covering the kitchen window.

It was the broken glass that held her horrified attention.

Shards, dark tipped with blood, were jagged in the frame. There were no sounds, not even so much as a child's whimper.

"Let me go." Her voice was reed thin, hoarse as she felt the tears falling once again.

"He'll kill me." Chimera's tone was regretful. "I've risked enough letting you this close."

Rachel's head jerked back to the other woman. "This close?"

Eerie green eyes glanced toward the house before coming back to rest on Rachel. Chimera's shadowed features tightened with some unnamed emotion. "She's your daughter. You have the right."

As the final word passed Chimera's lips, all hell seemed to break loose.

A roar, unlike anything Rachel had heard in her life, shattered the silence of the night.

❖   ❖   ❖

Jonas went through the window. He felt the glass biting across his shoulders, felt the animal rage that surged through his body, and went for the enemy.

Brandenmore hadn't expected an attack. Rather than thinking to grab the child, he came to his feet instead. The weapon aimed and fired, the minute burst of explosive energy barely missing Jonas's head before Brandenmore jumped for the door.

A roar tore from his throat. A sound Jonas knew had never escaped his body as the full scent of the child hit him then.

Jumping between the babe and the door, Jonas faced the other man, his own weapon ready, held firmly in claw-tipped fingers as he snarled back at Brandenmore.

His faced creased with cruelty and age, Brandenmore smiled, a cold, mocking sneer that had Jonas's finger tightening on the trigger. Brandenmore held his weapon aimed in the direction of the babe.

"So much information." Brandenmore shook his head with a cluck of his tongue. "So many experiments. We've learned a lot since you escaped, Alpha One."

His eyes narrowed on the other man.

"That baby." Brandenmore nodded to the too-silent babe. "She's a test, no more than you were a test. No more than any other has been. It doesn't take a lab to create an experiment, now does it, Alpha One?"

He'd shoot him, but the slightest movement of Brandenmore's finger on that trigger and the laser burst would destroy Amber despite Jonas's attempt to protect her.

"I'll kill you," Jonas promised him, staring into the cold, merciless cruelty of the other man's gaze.

Brandenmore smiled again. "You've been trying for a while now, Alpha One. You haven't succeeded yet." He glanced to the cradle, which held the child. "And you won't succeed now."

Before Jonas could jump for him, Brandenmore dove through the doorway.

A roar of rage tore from Jonas's lips. Adrenaline and pure animal fury had him starting for the door before he stopped, turned and went for the child instead.

Pulling the tiny body from the cradle, Jonas tucked her close against his chest. He launched himself through the window seconds before fire and heat exploded behind him, catapulting him through the air as the night seemed to go to hell around him.

· CHAPTER 2 ·

SANCTUARY, FELINE BREED HEADQUARTERS
BUFFALO GAP, VIRGINIA

The Breed heli-jet touched down in the main estate yard, an almost unheard-of occurrence. Teams of Breeds—Feline, Wolf and Coyote—surrounded the area, hard eyes, weapons ready as the outside entrance to the labs was flung open just as the doors to the heli-jet slid open.

Jonas Wyatt jumped from the black jet, his clothes singed, his dark face smeared with soot and blood as he clutched a small bundle to his chest and raced for the labs.

Behind him, Feline Breeds Lawe Justice and Rule Breaker stayed close on his heels, each gripping a fragile arm of Jonas's secretary, Rachel Broen.

Tears and soot streaked down Rachel's face. Her dark red hair was no longer in its carefully arranged, precise little bun. It flowed around her face, long waves cascading to the middle of her back as she was pulled into the bunker beneath the main house.

"I want Elizabeth and Ely immediately," Jonas shouted as they raced through the steel- and cement-lined corridors to the main lab.

"They're waiting in the labs." Pride Leader Callan Lyons raced at his side as head of security Kane Tyler and Sanctuary's Enforcer commander, Mercury Warrant, brought up the rear. "Elizabeth was still on-site when you called. She and Ely have everything ready."

"Jonas, what's going on?" Rachel could feel the dread tearing through her system.

The hair-raising ride from D.C. to Virginia hadn't taken more than fifteen minutes in the heli-jets. It had raced to Sanctuary at full power with Jonas yelling at the pilot for more speed as Amber lay lax and limber in his arms.

He wouldn't let her hold her child. Amber hadn't whimpered, she hadn't cried.

"Here's the syringe. It was beside her in her carrier." Jonas slapped the small pressure syringe that Rachel hadn't even noticed in Callan's hand. "I want a full analysis from Amburg ASAP."

Callan passed the syringe off to Mercury, who took a quick turn down another corridor and disappeared.

Jeffrey Amburg, the scourge of the Breed community. He had been known as a butcher in the Breed labs before the rescues twelve years earlier.

Moving ahead, Kane Tyler, his dark hair cut military short, his icy blue gaze frozen with fury, flung open the doors to the main level of the labs where two women raced from a nearby office.

"We have everything prepped and ready." Elizabeth Vanderale, her dark hair tied back in a close ponytail, a white lab coat flying out behind her, pushed open another door as Ely Morrey, the Breeds' main scientist, moved quickly to an incubator set up in the middle of the room.

"Jonas." She was pulled to a stop just inside the room, watching in horror as Amber's small gown and diaper were pulled quickly from her before she was laid inside the incubator.

"We need blood, saliva and tissue samples immediately," Elizabeth was barking out as she and Ely began to move quickly.

"What's going on?" Jerking away from the two Breeds holding her Rachel latched onto Jonas's arm, fury and fear tearing through her as she stared into the living fury that brewed in his gaze. "Damn you to hell, talk to me. What did that bastard do to my baby?"

Terror was tearing at her mind, digging into her soul. God help her, if anything happened to her baby, she couldn't survive it.

She'd been begging Jonas to talk to her since the second he had rolled to his feet, just ahead of the fiery blast that had taken her house to the ground in an explosion of flames.

"Rachel, give him room." Kane gripped her arm to pull her back, only to face the snarling, animalistic fury that Jonas turned on him.

Rachel almost stepped back herself as Jonas's head lowered, his lips pulling back from his teeth to flash the predatory canines at the side of his mouth. One hand clamped on her arm, and Rachel jerked her gaze down in time to see the lethal curve of sharpened claws that had sliced from the flesh beneath his fingernails.

She lifted her gaze slowly. "Jonas, please. Tell me what happened."

A growl tore from his throat.

"Miss Broen, my son is primal at the moment. He can think, he can react, but the beast is currently controlling the man."

Rachel jerked around to face Leo Vanderale. He was a near replica of Callan Lyons, or perhaps it was more accurate to say Callan was a replica of the other man.

Long, flowing tawny hair was streaked with blacks and reds. Fierce features framed golden eyes, and power seemed to exude from his very pores and give lie to the civilized cut of his dark gray suit.

Jonas snarled back at Leo, only to receive a flash of canines as the other man came slowly forward.

He stopped and stared into the incubator for a long second

before turning to Jonas. "Will you trust me to oversee her safety as you oversee the child?"

Jonas's jaw clenched. "No!" The sound was a rumble of rage.

Leo's lips tightened. "Do you really want to take me on tonight, whelp?" he growled. "Or make this woman hate you?"

Jonas growled again as he finally allowed Rachel to jerk away from him.

"Get them out of here, Leo," Elizabeth barked out at him as she moved back to the incubator with a syringe designed to draw blood.

The pressure-activated vial was quick, painless, but at the moment, it looked like a tool of death as it neared her baby's tiny arm.

"Jonas, please." Her nails dug into his arm as she gripped him. Anger and fear latched onto her with an inhuman grip. "What's wrong with my baby?"

"Brandenmore," he snarled down at her. "He injected her with something, Rachel. We have to find out what."

The words were barely human. The implications were a nightmare.

She released him slowly. Rachel pressed her hands to her stomach as it cramped with a spasm of horror, threatening to heave what little contents she had taken in that day.

Her gaze flew to the unconscious form of her child as she began shuddering, shaking with such fear now that she wondered how she managed to stay on her feet.

Amber looked so tiny in the incubator. She'd been born underweight, not sickly but her slight weight had given Rachel months of worry.

Now she lay pale and unmoving, her mop of red-gold curls laying limp along her tiny head as Rachel slowly released Jonas's arm and backed away from him.

"Amburg is testing the syringe," Kane reported, a finger pressed against the small communications bud at his ear. "He expects an initial report within thirty minutes."

"Five minutes or he dies." Jonas turned on Kane, his dark face so much more savage than normal and filled with predatory mercilessness. Rachel had no doubt he meant what he said.

Coldly, Kane repeated the order.

Evidently, Amburg didn't argue.

"Why?" Rachel turned to the only man willing to give answers, the man who had called Jonas his son. Rachel had no idea that Leo Vanderale was a Breed until this moment—until she had seen the wicked incisors at the side of his mouth that he normally kept hidden. "Why would he want to kill Amber?"

Leo shook his head. "I doubt seriously what he's done was done with the intent to kill her. Anything Brandenmore does is done with the intent to experiment, nothing more. He simply doesn't care if she lives."

Jonas snarled at Leo again.

"Why?" Rachel cried again, her voice rising as terror began to steal her senses. "Why would he do it?"

"Because certain tests have proven that you, as well as your daughter, are viable Breed mates." It was Callan Lyons who answered her, despite the rumble of fury that came from Jonas. "Brandenmore managed to steal certain information from Sanctuary last month, Ms. Broen. That information contained the results of several tests done for Breed mating. Your tests."

Rachel shook her head. Breed mating was supposed to be nothing more than a rumor, though she had wondered at the truth of it often enough.

She stared at Callan. Neither he nor Merinus appeared to have aged in the twelve years they had been together. And Kane. She had once worked for Kane. He was in his midforties, but appeared to be a decade younger.

Good genetics; she had heard that given as an excuse.

There had been a multitude of reasons thrown at the press, as well as scientists who had questioned the phenomenon. No Breed had ever admitted to mating heat though.

"Tests," she whispered as she tried to control the nausea welling inside her. "I was tested?"

"The blood, saliva and vaginal samples you were asked to give were to test for your viability as a mate with any Breed that you would come in contact with." Callan nodded shortly as Jonas snarled silently before turning his back on them all. "You tested positive in that viability, which led us to suspect that Amber would be viable as well as she grew older. It was a precaution we had to take, Rachel."

She shook her head slowly, denying the truth. Merinus hadn't warned her of this. Surely she would have warned her if anything like this were possible.

"I need all of you out of here," Elizabeth snapped, as she was forced to move around Jonas.

Blue eyes flashing with ire, she glared up at Jonas. "You and the mother can stay, but get the hell out of my way. The rest of you, clear out. That means you too, Leo." Her tone brooked no refusal.

Rachel turned her head, stared at Jonas and suddenly the implication of those tests hit her.

"They think we're somehow mated?" she asked as he kept his back to her.

"If you have questions, then get out with the rest of them," Elizabeth ordered as she attached electrodes to Amber. "I can't save this child if I have to listen to you berate Jonas at the moment."

Rachel clamped her lips shut, but the look she directed at her boss was a promise. The questions would come, and once she had answers, then she would decide exactly where she and her daughter would relocate to.

She wouldn't trust another Breed, not as long as she lived. She had trusted Jonas; she had trusted Merinus and Kane.

As the heart monitor began to beep, Rachel latched desperately onto the noise. Blood pressure and heart rate monitors, as well as several machines she'd never seen before in any hospital, began a life-saving symphony of sound as they surrounded the incubator.

Elizabeth Vanderale nodded slowly at the readings as she attached a nearby comm set to her ear and began to talk quietly into it.

"Rachel, we'll be outside if you need to talk," Kane promised as they passed her. "Merinus is on her way back from Colorado now. She flew out immediately when Callan called her with the report. We'll answer what questions we can."

The large lab emptied as Rachel crossed her arms over her breasts and fought back more tears as she stared at her daughter.

"She's innocent," she whispered. "You should have warned me she would be in danger."

She would never forgive Jonas or Merinus for neglecting that warning.

"We had no reason to believe she would be in any danger." Jonas's voice was still an animalistic rasp. "We had no reason to believe you would be. It wasn't the tests of viable mates that Brandenmore needed. It was the tests of current mates and certain hormonal shifts that occur with mating that he was interested in. There was no reason for him to go after potentials, because it's been proven that those tests aren't always reliable."

Rachel rubbed at the chill that invaded her arms as she focused on the machines once again.

Elizabeth Vanderale was still talking softly. Jonas glanced her way several times, his more acute Breed hearing picking up the conversation when Rachel most likely couldn't.

"Amburg has initial results back," he told her softly as her lips parted to question him. "The syringe held certain Breed hormones, but in his estimation, nothing that should be harmful to her."

"She's not moving," she whispered painfully.

Jonas jerked as though in pain before rubbing his hand along the back of his head. She'd seen him do that often over the past months she'd worked for him. The gesture normally indicated a sense of frustration.

"He believes it reacted as a sedative," he related. "If so, then in a few hours, she should awaken her normal self."

"If so, then we're leaving . . ."

"Dream on." The look he turned on her was almost terrifying. Or would have been, if she hadn't already faced such an influx of fear in the past hours. Her system now seemed immune to his fierceness.

"I won't stay here." She shook her head fiercely.

"You won't be leaving until I know for a fact that you and that child are safe." He paced closer, his head lowering until her vision centered on the roiling mercury of his eyes. "Understand that, Rachel. If I have to place you under twenty-four-hour guard, you will go no place, make no move, not take so much as a breath that I don't know about first."

She stared back at him, shock winding through her system first before pure rage took over. Before she could stop herself, her hand lifted, flew, smacking open-palmed against the hard contours of his face.

Everything in the room seemed to freeze.

Elizabeth and Ely stared at them in shock, their expressions wary as they watched Jonas.

He could have stopped her. He was fast enough, instinctive enough that he could have prevented the blow. Instead, he stood still for it. He took it, his expression never changing, his eyes boiling with currents of emotion she couldn't make sense of.

"That changes nothing," he rasped. "Where it comes to you and that child, my word is law, sweetheart. Trust me on that. There's not a man or a woman in Sanctuary who would dare defy me on this."

"Kane . . ."

"Won't risk his life for it." His smile was tight, confident.

"Merinus won't let you . . ."

"Merinus wouldn't dare interfere," he snarled.

"They won't let you hold me here." She shook her head, certain they would never betray her to that depth.

"Tell me, Rachel, the mating tests that were ran—who do you think they were run with?"

She couldn't breathe now. She could feel her chest tightening with panic at the knowledge she hadn't wanted to face.

"It doesn't matter—"

"Oh, but it does," he cut her off again. "It does matter, Rachel. Those tests were run against my samples. They wouldn't dare interfere because they know the hell they'll face. You're my mate, Rachel. And I will protect you and my child with every last ounce of blood I possess. No one, but no one will do anything to harm either of you again. If I have to lock you in these labs to assure you don't leave, then I swear to you on all I hold dear that is exactly what I'll do."

◆   ◆   ◆

Hours later, Jonas glanced at Rachel where she sat in the small chair beside the baby's bed.

She hadn't spoken since the promise he had made to her, since he'd revealed exactly whose mate she was. She'd backed slowly away from him, her expression never changing, the scent of her fury never abating.

At least he hadn't scented her fear of him, he thought mockingly. That was the last thing the beast prowling inside him needed to sense.

The animal.

He rubbed at the back of his head, where his lab number and birth ranking had been tattooed into his skull. He hadn't been branded as many of the other Breeds had been. He'd been tattooed instead while the woman who claimed to be his mother had looked on in pride.

His *mother*. What a job that bitch had been. Madame LaRue had carried him to term, but it hadn't been her egg or the sperm of the male scientist that had created him, as she and the lab reports had claimed.

According to those reports his DNA had been enhanced with that of the first Leo, but that wasn't entirely true. Just as

it wasn't true that Callan Lyons was more the son of Elizabeth
and Leo than he was.

He let them believe it. Callan, Leo, Elizabeth. Dane. He let
them exist in that comfort zone they had that the bogeyman of
the Breeds wasn't really related by blood to any of them.

Not that they would believe it without proof. He didn't
carry their familial scent. His DNA had been fucked with too
many times; his scent was unique, with few of the markers
that other Breeds possessed.

There was just enough tint of the Leo's familial scent that
they had been assured Jonas carried his DNA, but nothing
more. And he was certain the Leo wanted it no other way.

And Elizabeth.

He glanced at his mother. Hell, she stared at him as though
he were an aberration most of the time. A puzzle she couldn't
quite figure out, and wasn't certain she wanted to know.

That was how most people, Breeds and humans alike,
stared at him.

Except Rachel. The few times he'd been able to draw any
emotion from her at all, it had been colored with desire and
laced with amusement. She tolerated him better than most.
But then, she was his genetic mate. What else could she do? It
wasn't as though she could hate him. Not with any amount of
true strength anyway.

Breathing out wearily, he paced the lab, his gaze going
between Rachel and the child.

His child. He had claimed the babe, though he had no
basis for it. He hadn't helped create that life inside her. Over
the months, he'd done nothing but attempt to watch over them
both, and he'd failed miserably at that.

The beast inside him claimed the mother, and in turn
claimed the babe.

Damn, Amber was too small.

He'd thought that the first time he'd seen her in the hospital, just after her birth. She'd been so small, underweight and
yet feisty as hell. She'd screamed in rage each time the nurses

had taken her from her mother, demanding with everything inside her tiny body that they return her to the safety and security of her mother's arms.

Unless Jonas had arrived.

How many times had he gone to the nursery and sworn the nurses to silence as he held her? Too many times for him to count.

Unlike adults, children's emotions were an open book. He'd connected with the babe while she had still rested safely in her mother's womb. The beast that was so much a part of him had bonded with the child. That animal sense reaching out on a plane that was mostly reserved for mother and child alone.

He had known the moment he'd seen Rachel Broen that she was his mate. The second he'd sensed she was with child, he had staked that claim as well. A solitary claim that he'd had no intention of informing Rachel of. And a claim he'd no intention of doing anything about.

What the hell was he supposed to do now?

"Blood pressure and heart rate are normal." Elizabeth's gaze went between the monitors and the incubator, one hand propped on her hip. A frown marred her brow as she turned to watch Ely, who worked silently on the samples of blood and saliva that had been taken.

"Initial blood readings are normal, as is saliva. There are no hormonal abnormalities thus far." Ely turned back to Elizabeth, avoiding Jonas's gaze before returning her attention to the tests results. "Everything is in range of the readings taken at birth."

Jonas's jaw tightened as he watched Rachel straighten, alert, rising slowly from the chair she had just sat in.

"What readings were taken at her birth?" Accusing eyes turned on Jonas.

"It's normal, Ms. Broen." Elizabeth's smile was comforting as she moved to Rachel to lay a hand against her arm. "You work within the Breed society; that makes you a part of our world as a whole, as it does your daughter. It was simply a precaution as well as a courtesy. You have the best doctors in the world overseeing your baby."

That was such complete BS Jonas almost snorted. He had ordered those tests. He had fought the Breed ruling cabinet for them to ensure that this baby had the best start in life, health-wise, as possible.

Rachel was less than convinced. She watched Elizabeth and Ely suspiciously, while all her senses were held captive by Amber.

"Jonas, Callan needs to speak with you." Kane stepped inside the lab, his icy blue gaze filled with a warning, a silent message.

Jonas turned back to the babe and mother, torn between staying to protect what belonged to him, and accepting that they were safe while he took care of the business waiting on the other side of the door.

He could smell that business. Dr. Jeffrey Amburg had a particular scent, was tinged with blood and Breed. How the hell the man had managed to become infused with Breed scent without Breed DNA, Jonas hadn't yet figured out.

He turned and stared at Ely, waiting until he caught her eye before glancing at Rachel. He was leaving his mate in Ely's care, none other.

Ely's gaze shifted with uncertainty before she gave a short, quick nod, allowing him to stride quickly from the room to the small glass-walled meeting area that looked into the lab.

Amburg waited. He stood still and silent as he stared into the lab, a frown on his face, his arms crossed over his chest as he seemed to glare at the mother and child.

Jonas stepped into the room, closed the door behind him and waited.

"I'll need fresh blood, saliva and urine samples," Amburg stated. "You'll want to ensure that the child stays here at Sanctuary for a while, and under close observation."

"What was in the syringe?"

Jonas would kill Brandenmore for this night, he swore it. He would never have the chance to harm another child.

"I don't know, Wyatt." Amburg shook his head as he breathed out wearily. "Initial tests are showing sedative qualities, but I know Brandenmore. He's a fucking genius when it comes to developing new drugs, and whatever he's been working on where the Breeds are concerned has been going on for a while. You can't trust him, you can't trust that it was no more than a sedative. That would be foolish."

"What was he working on?" Jonas had asked Amburg the same question for months.

"I wasn't told what he was working on." It was the same answer he had always given. No matter how Jonas tortured him, no matter the threats he made, Amburg always gave the same answer. And Jonas had smelled the lie on him each time.

Jonas stared into the lab; the two-way glass gave him the opportunity to watch Rachel where she was unaware of his presence.

"Then she's safe? There's nothing to worry about?" Jonas asked.

"I didn't say that." Amburg turned to him, his gaze heavy but clearly shielding his concern. It didn't matter, because Jonas could sense each emotion on him.

"Then what are you saying?" Jonas leaned back against the door, crossed his arms over his chest and watched the scientist narrowly.

Amburg's gaze flickered. "Just what I said. Where Brandenmore's concerned, you should worry, and worry a lot. For the moment, it appears the child is fine. There was nothing more than a sedative in the syringe. I just want to be certain."

And that was the truth. Jonas could accept it, though he knew there were still things he wasn't being told. He could wait. For a short while.

"Return to your lab if that's all you have." Jonas moved back from the door. "Let me know if you learn anything further."

Amburg nodded shortly before moving for the door.

"Jeffrey." Jonas stopped him as he reached for the doorknob. "Betray me, and you know what I'll do."

Amburg swallowed tightly, his gaze flickering in fear. "She has nothing to do with any of this, Jonas. She's innocent."

"So were the Breeds, once," Jonas countered. "Did that help us?"

It hadn't.

Amburg lowered his head before pulling the door open and leaving the room. He would find the answers Jonas needed, assured that if he didn't, his granddaughter would pay the price.

Jonas looked into the lab once again. Amber lay still and silent, her mother beside her, pacing, uncertain. Frightened.

Her fear dug sharpened claws of emotion into his soul, and left him questioning himself and decisions he had once felt were set in stone. It had him questioning the danger he had allowed into his life, and the danger he knew would now, always, be a part of it.

Rachel and Amber had become his life, and now he wondered how the hell he was ever going to protect them.

CHAPTER 3

Jonas forced himself to leave the small room more than an hour later. Amber was waking, groggy and hungry. Blood tests were showing no abnormalities or anomalies. She appeared to be as healthy as she had been before her ordeal with Brandenmore.

Jonas knew he wouldn't know more until he could slip into the room himself and hold her. The ability to connect with her through her mother had disappeared after her birth. Now he found that only when he held her did he sense any problems she might have.

Moving through the steel-lined corridors of the medical bunker, Jonas stepped into the meeting room where Kane, Callan, Lawe and Rule awaited him.

"You're already getting weird on us." Lawe flicked him a disgruntled look as Callan and Kane watched silently. "I swear, this mating shit has to be contagious."

There was an edge of bachelor fear in Lawe's voice, as well as in his brother Rule's expression.

Not that Jonas could blame either man. Mating was

damned scary when a man had no idea how to proceed. Heeding the animal's demand that he take her now, that he mark her immediately, wasn't going to work. He'd be damned if he wanted his woman to come to him because hormones forced her to do so. He wanted her to want him because he was a man willing to love her, to care for her and to ensure that her child was protected.

"What have you found out?" He ignored Lawe's previous comment as he turned to Callan.

"Mordecai is trailing Brandenmore." Callan leaned forward, laying his arms on the polished surface of the meeting table. "He had a heli-jet waiting several blocks from Ms. Broen's house. He flew immediately to Iran."

"He has a research facility there." Jonas nodded.

"And neither America nor the Breeds has an extradition treaty with them," Kane stated. "Our hands are tied unless Mordecai and his men can catch him outside the facility and manage to grab him without being seen."

If anyone could do it, Mordecai could.

"Dog was spotted in Iran just hours after Brandenmore landed," Rule reported. "He and his team were about a mile from the research facility and there's a rumor Brandenmore called them in."

Brandenmore had made a major mistake if he had thought to hire the mercenary Coyote unit Dog commanded. Dog might play the bad-assed mercenary, but Jonas and Dog knew whom he owed his loyalty to.

"I want Brandenmore." He turned to Callan. "This is Breed Law, Callan. It's no longer public. It's no longer a matter of bringing him to the humans' idea of justice. He's mine."

And he would suffer.

"Justice was your idea, Jonas," Callan reminded him as he sat back in his chair, his golden gaze somber. "You were right. The Breeds will gain more power, more approval, if Brandenmore is brought to justice publicly."

"He'll never be prosecuted." Jonas shook his head; that had been proven in the past year. "I once thought the political backing the Breeds had found would make us stronger. I agreed with that. But all they're doing is patting us on the fucking back and kissing the asses of men like Brandenmore. I'm not willing to see another Breed die by his hand."

"We knew it wouldn't be easy, Jonas." Kane Tyler leaned forward, his icy blue eyes concerned now. "We have the backing in the Senate, no matter how it appears. We have to have the proof. They can't move without it. And getting proof, when Brandenmore keeps acquiring Breed spies within Sanctuary, isn't going to be easy."

Breed spies. Select Breeds were turning against their own, destroying the tribe's home of freedom by selling information to their former jailors.

"Jonas, we could have an edge here. Let's use it." Lawe stepped forward, planted his hands on the top of the table and stared back at Jonas intently.

"And that edge is?" He had a very bad feeling he knew exactly what it was.

"Rachel and her child," Lawe stated quietly. "Brandenmore was taking that baby with him; that means he had plans for her. And Rachel can identify him and testify to his actions tonight. She has a solid reputation, just as her parents had before their deaths. She's proof that Brandenmore attempted to steal sensitive Breed information. She's your ace in the hole."

He was right, and Jonas knew exactly what Lawe considered an ace in the hole.

"You've learned too well, Lawe," he growled. "You expect me to use my mate."

"As you used Lance Jacobs to save your sister. Just as you've used every weapon, every asset you could find or steal in this battle we're fighting," Lawe agreed. "But Rachel has something no one else has: She has you, Jonas. The best strategist ever created to ensure her safety."

Jonas grunted at that. "Compliments will only piss me off, Lawe. Now I know how my Enforcers felt each time I used their mating heat to my own ends."

Not that he hadn't always sensed how they felt. Not that he hadn't regretted the choices he'd had to make, even before he'd put them in effect.

Breathing in deeply, he ran his hand over his hair, always aware, always sensing the tattoo hidden beneath his hair: F2.07.

He was the only Breed to ever carry an *F* rating in his lab designation. Most Breeds were *A*, for Alpha designation. His was *F*, for the very fact that he had been created to breed. To father hybrid Breeds. It was a designation that had never worked for the scientists who had created him. His sperm had never been viable with the Breed females they had paired him with.

It was only in recent years that Ely had managed to figure out why his designation had been a failure. It wasn't a Breed female that would be compatible with the Breed sperm. Nature had twisted the genetics the scientists had used. His Breed sperm—the genetics programmed into it, the Breeds it would create—needed a human female to be viable.

And now he had the perfect female to create the hybrid Breed the scientists were so certain would be the most dangerous Breed ever created.

Turning away from the other men, he exhaled tiredly, finally feeling the bone-deep bruises he'd acquired in the explosion.

"He'll come after her," Jonas stated, knowing Brandenmore would put everything he had into killing Rachel now.

"The spies he still has here, in Sanctuary, will be activated," Lawe agreed. "He can't have many left. We watch, and we wait. Pretend we're unaware that we know he still has those ties here. We catch them, then we ensure their cooperation in providing proof against him."

They could do that. The Breeds weak enough to fall in with Brandenmore were easily intimidated. They could never be trusted again, but they could be used.

"Assemble Ghost Team." He turned back to the group as he gave Lawe the order. "You'll be in command. I want

Rachel and the child completely covered. They are the team's main concern. No matter what, Lawe—especially if I can't control the mating heat. Nothing else matters."

He hadn't assembled Ghost Team since the first months out of the labs during the worst of the protests against the Breeds. Separately, the Breeds in Ghost Team were highly effective and lethal. Together, they were a nightmare against the enemy.

"The Prime family are primary concern, Jonas," Kane reminded him as Jonas's gaze met Callan's.

Callan knew the truth, and he understood the order.

"No, Kane," Callan murmured. "Not in this case. If Jonas doesn't control mating heat, and I fully suspect he won't, if Ms. Broen conceives, then nothing else matters but that child."

Because that child could destroy them all.

◆   ◆   ◆

"Rachel, I believe Amburg was right. Your baby has only been sedated." Elizabeth Vanderale sat on a stool on the other side of the incubator as Rachel held Amber and gave her the bottled formula that had been provided for her.

Amber's gaze was still drowsy, but she wasn't pale any longer, or lifeless. She stared up at Rachel with those bright blue eyes as she gripped the bottle with tiny fists and sucked hungrily.

"He escaped." She stared down at Amber, somehow sensing her daughter would never be safe until Phillip Brandenmore was dead.

"He'll be found." Elizabeth didn't seem concerned. "Trust me, Jonas won't allow him to remain free for long."

No, there was a hungry volcano waiting for Brandenmore, she thought. She had seen the obscurely worded reports on other missing Breed enemies, just as she knew the private flight plans Jonas had logged with the Breed Council just after their disappearances. Those flights had gone right by a very active, stone-melting pit of pure lava that had once welcomed human sacrifices with a greedy embrace.

"Brandenmore believes Jonas has information on the Breeds that involves an aging phenomena." She lifted her gaze back to Elizabeth. "Mating heat changes the aging process, doesn't it?"

Elizabeth's lips firmed.

"You're Callan Lyons's mother," Rachel stated. She knew the other woman was also the wife to the man they called the first Leo. The first Lion Breed ever created.

"Elizabeth can't answer your questions, Rachel, but I can." Rachel whirled around to find Jonas entering the room.

Rachel felt her heart leap, as it always did during that first moment when he entered a room. It was all she could do to maintain her composure, to be certain her body fell in line with the emotions she wanted to project rather than what she felt.

He wore the same clothes he had worn when he went after Amber. Black. Black mission pants, a long-sleeved shirt that was torn and bloody, and combat boots, which laced over his calves. The string of one boot was fraying. The left knee of the mission pants was torn, exposing reddened and bloodied flesh.

"Jonas, have you been checked for your injuries yet?" Elizabeth moved to the tray of digital and sterilized instruments next to the incubator.

"Ely takes care of me, Dr. Vanderale," he answered coolly. "If I need it."

"And of course, you don't need it," Elizabeth murmured. "How like the Leo you can be."

"And I'm certain the Leo is just as tired of hearing that as I am," he responded mockingly. "As the whelp he barely claims, I can tell you, it gets old."

Rachel heard the thinnest vein of some underlying emotion in those words. Resentment? Hurt? She couldn't imagine the steel-edged Jonas hurting over anything. But she had learned over the past months that there was a lot Jonas hid from the world and the people around him.

Elizabeth chuckled. "Why do you believe he calls you a 'whelp,' young man? Could it be because you're so like him that he's not certain whether to feel pride or to shoot you and put the world out of its misery?"

"I think he's just as happy over the fact that his DNA was used against him as I am." Jonas shrugged and turned back to Rachel. "We have a cabin ready for you. I'm sure you'd like to eat and get some rest now that Elizabeth has finished her examination of you."

Merinus had warned her when she first agreed to work for Jonas about the Breeds' incredible sense of smell and intuition. She had warned Rachel that the least weakness would be perceived by Jonas as a weapon, nothing more. That he would use it against her, would poke and dig until he managed to find a way to get her out of the office.

"I'd like to finish feeding Amber first," she stated with a calm composure she didn't feel. "I rather doubt Phillip Brandenmore had the consideration to do so."

The small rumble of danger that sounded in his throat would have been worrying if Amber hadn't chosen that moment to emit a small, distressed whimper.

"Calm yourself, Jonas." Elizabeth moved across the room to one of the myriad machines that lined a counter. "I've warned you that children sense emotions much better than adults do. You'll upset the child."

Rachel was surprised to see the grimace that tightened Jonas's face, but within seconds Amber calmed down once more and proceeded to finish her bottle.

He did that a lot, she realized: backed off when at other times she was certain he would have pushed for dominance in a given situation.

Setting the bottle aside, she lifted the baby against her chest. Patting the baby's back, she smiled softly when a loud, definitely unladylike burp came from the perfect, cupid's bow lips.

"We can leave now." Pulling a small blanket from the

table by the incubator, Rachel wrapped her daughter snugly, then turned to Jonas.

He was staring at Elizabeth, his expression tight, almost angry. Glancing back at the other woman, Rachel saw the same expression mirrored on Elizabeth's face.

These two were so much alike that it astounded Rachel that they weren't related.

"Let's go then." Stepping back, Jonas allowed her to pass before turning in behind her and following her to the door.

"Jonas. Rachel."

They stopped, glancing back.

"I'll need the two of you in for tests in the morning," she informed them. "Please be here before breakfast. It's rather important that it be done before you eat."

"That what be done?" Rachel asked.

"Mating tests," Jonas informed her, his voice cold. "Never let it be said that mating a Breed is easy."

Rachel glared back at him. "Never let it be said that I agreed to any of this. Forget the tests, Jonas. I haven't decided I'm your mate. Therefore, no tests are needed."

She pushed through the lab doors, determined not to show a weakness either in expression or emotion. For all Jonas knew, her heart wasn't racing in excitement, and her thighs weren't ready to clench in arousal.

She was immune. At least, that was the image she presented. The truth was a far different matter.

She watched as his expression seemed to change. It became emotionless, almost lifeless. Bronze, savage features tightened until they seemed carved from stone as his eyes boiled like heated mercury.

"Rachel, simply because you refuse to accept it doesn't make it so," Elizabeth ventured cautiously as she stepped closer, her hands sliding into the wide pockets of her lab coat as her dark blue eyes softened in understanding. "Mating heat is not a choice, my dear."

"I beg to differ." Rachel shifted Amber in her arms, her fingers rubbing against the baby's back in a comforting motion, despite the fact that Amber was sleeping peacefully. "I'm not an animal, Dr. Vanderale. Neither is Jonas, despite his attempts to convince me differently over the past months. I'm not ruled by my hormones, nor am I ruled by Breed hormones. Rest assured, should I decide to accept whatever anomaly dictates *your* mating heat, then I will submit myself to your tests." She stared back at Jonas. "Are you ready, or do I need to see about finding a hotel for the night?"

◆   ◆   ◆

It was his luck. Jonas entered his cabin, stood aside and watched as Rachel walked in, knowing that every curse, every ill thought his Enforcers had had concerning his turn at mating were most likely coming true.

The sight he'd seen in the medical facility had made his cock harder than it had ever been. She'd lifted her head with an arrogance that still amazed him, looked down that little button nose of hers and informed Elizabeth Vanderale that she was not mated because she hadn't accepted it.

It would have been amusing had she been another Breed's mate. Unfortunately, she was his, and though he'd had no intentions of fulfilling the mating promise, in that second, nothing else had mattered to him but mating her.

It was the Breed genetics, he told himself as she toed her shoes off and moved into the large living room and looked around. It was the challenge—the steely eyed certainty that she could deny him—and the fact that she was attempting to deny what he knew couldn't be denied.

It was the fact that she belonged to him. She was his. And she had dared to stand in front of the one woman he would never show weakness to and state that she was not his mate until she decided it was so.

It was enough to make a Breed consider relieving the ache of the mating hormone torturing his tongue, in a kiss that would burn them both straight to the tips of their toes.

"This is your cabin." There was an edge of accusation in the statement as she turned to him.

She had attempted to restore order to her hair, but still, it fell from the clip at the top of her head, long red strands cascading to the middle of her back as she flashed ire-filled neon green eyes at him.

Her face was scratched; her stockings were ripped and barely covered her flesh. The dark gray skirt she had worn the day before was torn along one seam, flashing a pretty section of thigh. The matching blazer was stained with oil, the cuffs frayed in several places. Her once-pristine white shirt was now gray with soot and dirt. And nothing in the world had ever looked so damned pretty to him.

"So it is." He shrugged as though it didn't matter while removing his boots and setting them alongside Rachel's black low-heeled shoes.

Padding along the hardwood floor, Jonas walked to the other side of the room and opened the door to the bedroom he'd added on once he'd realized she was his mate.

It was meant to be Amber's bedroom. The large, airy room was connected to a full bath, which separated the master suite from the child's room.

It would now be Rachel's room, he thought with a sigh as he turned on the lights.

The queen-sized bed had been installed as he'd ordered just after arriving to Sanctuary. A crib bed sat along one wall, a mobile of lions, tigers and fairies attached to the headboard while a soft baby-sized comforter covered the fairy sheets.

This would have been Cassie Sinclair's work, he thought with a spurt of amusement. The girl was a fairy herself, he often thought, as he stepped inside and allowed Rachel to enter the room.

The large bed was a romantic creation. The sleigh design of the bed frame was tall and heavy. Thick pillows were piled along the headboard, while a heavy blue-and-white quilt covered the mattress. His lips quirked at the sight of the small bed stool at the side of the bed, which made it easier for one of shorter stature to get into the bed easily.

"Surely there is another empty cabin." Her tone was weary, resigned.

"Sorry, sweetheart, this is it." Jonas crossed his arms over his chest as he stared down at her. "And you'll be safer here than you would be anywhere else. As will the baby."

She flashed him a hard stare. "Safer? With Brandenmore in custody . . ."

"Brandenmore escaped." Imparting that information wasn't easy for him. "He managed to make it to a heli-jet awaiting him several blocks from your home. He arrived in Iran several hours ago."

"Iran." Her eyes closed for a brief second and she turned from him. "One of the few places where Breeds can't touch him."

"Unfortunately, yes," he agreed. "The Genetics Council made an agreement with several countries such as Iran at the onset of the Breed rescues. That, combined with their radical views where the Breeds are concerned, have left little negotiating room with such countries."

Rachel moved across the room to the crib, where she turned on the small table lamp next to the child's bed. Then she glanced at Jonas.

He turned off the brighter overhead light and watched as she tucked Amber in.

Next to the crib was a line of bottles; beneath the stand that held the light were stacks of baby diapers. The shelf above the diapers held wipes and lotions, medicated diaper rash salve as well as a small case of baby first aid paraphernalia. Anything a mother could need to take care of her child.

The dresser at the bottom of the crib held clothes: sack gowns, pajamas and tiny outfits as well as socks, little headbands and assorted baby girl accessories. Jonas had been specific when he'd ordered the room prepared. The exclusive baby store in Buffalo Gap had opened its doors at three in the morning to ensure that the child was provided with everything she would need.

Moving efficiently, Rachel stripped the child, cleaned her with several wipes, then diapered and dressed her in a clean gown in a matter of minutes.

As he watched, Jonas felt the glands at the side of his tongue tightening, filling with the mating hormone as they began to itch and ache. The need to mate her, to mark her, would eventually make him insane, he believed.

"The closet has clothing for you." He nodded to the large walk-in closet on the far side of the room. "I sent one of the Coyote females who's currently assigned to Sanctuary. They seem to be more girly than most of our Feline females. They assured me that you have everything you need."

"Tell me you didn't send Ashley." Rachel turned back to him, a look of almost horror on her face.

Jonas hid his smile. Ashley was the scourge of the entire Breed society. Sociable, so girly it gave a man a toothache, and able to kill with a smile. The woman made friends left and right, bought enough clothes to fill a small house and could talk all day about shoes and purses.

"It was her sister, actually." Her younger sister wasn't much better, but Rachel wasn't aware of that.

"Where did the whole genetic profiling go wrong with those women." Rachel shook her head. "They'll slice your throat for causing them to break a nail."

That wasn't far off the mark.

"They were coddled." Jonas shrugged. "The lab that had these girls in Russia was secretly attempting to aid their escapes or rescues. They had complete control of the Breeds there with no oversight, mostly because the Council was unaware there were Coyote females. They were allowed to develop traits that other Breeds were never given the chance to find within themselves."

And they were still spoiled. The five Coyote females were given the funds for their pretty clothes, their shoes and purses by the Coyote leader and his Coya. They were still coddled and still protected in ways that other Feline females scoffed at.

And still, they were just as tough, just as merciless in battle, yet quicker to smile, to make friends and to endear the human population to the Breed cause.

"I'll shower, then, and head to bed." The look Rachel gave him was firm. It was time for him to leave.

Jonas nearly growled in frustration.

Patience, he warned himself. He'd spent so long assuring himself that he could control the mating heat because they shared few intimacies. He could keep from taking her, he could keep from destroying her.

That was no longer an option. As she had stated earlier, he wasn't an animal. Well, he was, but there was a side of him that was more than instinct as well. There was the strategist, and soon, there would be the seducer.

No battle was won purely with a show of strength, he told himself as he left her room, closing the door quietly behind him. Every battle won was done so with the right strategy as well as the proper weapons.

He simply had to determine when and where to begin the first skirmish.

As he set the alarms on the cabin and retired to his own bedroom, he found himself almost smiling. If he wasn't very careful, then he might actually have fun seducing his little mate. As dangerous as he knew claiming her would be, it could perhaps be even more dangerous *not* to claim her.

· C H A P T E R 4 ·

Ghost Team moved into Sanctuary late that evening, as Rachel and Amber slept soundly. Called back from a mission that was only partially finished in Guatemala, they were flown into the compound under the dead of night under condition "Alpha." Complete secrecy.

Jonas knew the second they entered his cabin, that sixth sense when it came to the team he had put together himself and commanded for ten years now.

Stepping from his bedroom, he checked the door to Rachel's bedroom, secured it to ensure she didn't step into the room, and faced the six-member team standing silently in the living room.

Ghost Team was the best. They were the most silent, most efficient, killers ever created, and they were also the best-kept secret the Breeds held outside of the truth of the mating heat.

Standing front and center was the team commander, the Black Jaguar Breed, who had excelled in killing at the tender age of five when he had sliced a trainer's throat for daring to backhand him. He was merciless, cold. He was as hard as diamonds and, often, just as cold.

"Your mate?" The commander nodded to the secured bedroom door.

Jonas nodded. "Brandenmore made his move on the files he believes I had. He used the baby against her and attempted to force her to steal them for him."

Fierce black eyes glanced toward the door once more before Jag shook his black head in resignation. "We should just kill him."

"We need to capture him if possible," Jonas reminded him. "But I have a larger problem. He attempted to kidnap Rachel's child. The baby was injected with what Amburg believes was a sedative, but there's a scent to the child now that wasn't there before. Whatever he's doing, it now involves her. I want a net around Rachel, the baby and the other hybrid children here at Sanctuary. I don't have a good feeling about this."

He could feel that odd twist in his guts, the premonition that something was building, that Brandenmore had a plan that they hadn't yet foiled.

"Indigestion," Jag quipped. "Brandenmore inspires it."

That was the damned truth. At this rate, Jonas would be the first Breed to develop an ulcer.

"We came in along the east border of the compound," Lobo, Jag's second-in-command, stated from the shadows along the far corner of the room. "There was a scent marker there, and signs that someone had used the ravine there to make their way into Sanctuary. We followed it until it disappeared along the main road."

"Were you able to detect the scent marker?" Jonas kept his voice low, his senses tuned to the next room.

Jag shook his head. "There was a faint hint of human scent, but it was too old for the trail we found."

"Too old or deliberately laid." The Coyote Enforcer, Loki, stepped forward, his gray eyes dark, the thick black lashes surrounding them looking almost too soft, too seductive, for the most elite killer the world might ever know.

"What did you detect, Loki?" Jonas asked.

Loki shook his head, the thick, straight strands of his devil's black hair feathering over his forehead and along his shoulders. "Don't know, Jonas. There was something odd about it though, as though the scent had been deliberately altered in some way."

Jonas turned to Jag, Lobo and the other members of Ghost Team.

"The rest of us didn't detect that, but Loki's ability to detect scents is better than ours." The other Coyote, Angel, growled the information, which was no less than Jonas had expected.

Watching Angel closely, he noticed the other man watching the bedroom door closely.

"Is there a problem, Angel?" Jonas asked softly, his tone dropping dangerously.

Angel shook his head, his black-and-gray hair shorter than Loki's, but just as silken and straight.

"I've no interest in your woman, Jonas," Angel assured him.

"Then why the interest in the door?"

"He likely senses what I smell." Loki stepped forward.

"And that is?" Jonas's head swung around.

"Your mate is awakening," Angel growled, drawing their attention. "That's what I sense. She'll be out in moments, and I'm certain you don't want us seen."

No one had ever seen Ghost Team other than Jonas. Jonas doubted the six men had ever faced another Breed or human without some sort of camouflage.

"If you see anything, if you learn anything, then let me know." Jonas nodded, still watching Angel closely.

There was no detecting a lie with these Breeds. Like Jonas, they had been taught how to use their emotions to trick other Breeds or animals. How to lie, to manipulate and deceive.

They nodded quickly before disappearing. Between one blink and the next, they were gone. Silently, blending in with shadows, moving quickly, taking advantage of the slightest weakness—that was what they were trained for before escaping into the pre-dawn darkness.

Moving quickly to the bedroom door, Jonas removed the electronic lock just as the doorknob turned and Rachel pulled the door open.

"Good morning." Jonas arched a brow at the glare she gave him.

"Amber will be waking soon." There was an edge of concern in her voice. "I need more formula and diapers before the day is out, Jonas. Elizabeth promised they would be here by time they were needed."

"And so they are. They arrived several hours ago." He nodded. "Her formula is on the counter; the sterilized bottles are beside it."

She moved away from him, the large shirt and even larger men's sweatpants she wore bunching around her small frame as she walked.

"I need a phone," she stated as she moved into the kitchen. "I need to contact my sister."

Jonas grimaced. "Diane is still overseas." He'd met her sister once. The woman was a Breed without the genetics. She would make a man think of suicide if he had to stay around her for long.

"Get me a phone, Jonas, before she has to come looking for me," she warned him as she moved for the bottles after checking out the rather large bag of diapers the Vanderales had had delivered.

"A secured sat phone will be delivered today. It was already arranged." There was no sense in delaying the inevitable. "Baby furniture as well the office will be delivered later today. There's a spare room that leads through that door." He nodded to a door that at first glance could have been a pantry door. "We'll be running things from here for a while."

"What about your schedule?" she questioned him. "You have several appointments this week, as well as the Hampton party you're scheduled to attend."

"That's why I have my own heli-jet." He shrugged.

Hell, there were days he almost wished he wasn't a steel-hearted Breed. Days when he wished he could sort through and understand the emotions that were pricking at him now. Emotions that had been building in him since the first day her sweet scent had wafted through his senses.

She made him . . . different. There was no other way to explain it. She made him want to be different when he knew it was the most dangerous thing he could do.

"Then we'll be running the office from here?" She fixed a bottle quickly. Using the purified water that had been provided and the powdered formula, the bottle was prepared within seconds. Next came a diaper and from the bag beside it, a pack of pre-moistened wipes and a tiny blanket.

"I have a list prepared," she told him as she glanced back. "Amber is going to need at least some of her things replaced. Whoever took care of outfitting her dresser did exceptionally well, but there are still some items missing."

"Taken care of." He leaned against the heavy post that formed the doorway into the kitchen. "Everything will be here before nightfall."

She paused for the slightest second as the heated tint of anger scented the air.

"Well, aren't you just on the ball?" There was just enough of a sneer in her voice to have his hackles rising.

"I have to admit, I think I did rather well," he stated mockingly.

Rachel's lips thinned. The look she shot him was heavy with irritation.

"You're not her father." The words were brisk, decisive, when she spoke again.

Jonas tensed. He knew what she was referring to. A slip of the tongue, no matter how slight, could be deadly in his world. He'd made a hell of a slip the night before.

"Now isn't a good time to push me, Rachel," he warned her as he straightened from the post, his body tightening as he fought back the need to go to her, to mark her, to force her to accept the desire that he'd known for months raged between them.

"Don't push me." Armed with a diaper, wipes and a bottle, she glared at him as though they were her battle armor. "You've drawn me and my daughter into one of your vicious little games . . ."

"You think I'd pull a child into this?" Incredulity rushed through him. She'd accused him of it the night before, but he hadn't thought she'd meant the words. "You think me so heartless, Rachel, that I'd use my mate and the child I've already claimed as my own in this battle against Brandenmore?"

"I believe you'd use whatever weapon you could grasp," she bit out, though she knew a part of her didn't truly believe that. She'd fought with herself over the months where Jonas was concerned, always certain that she would be safe, that Amber would be safe, simply because no one truly wanted to piss him off.

They wanted to kill him, and they often tried, but they never tried to piss him off. They knew better.

She watched as he stepped closer, suddenly more nervous where he was concerned than she had ever been.

"Don't touch me, Jonas." She stepped back quickly, knowing the few rumors, the whispered warnings she'd heard about Breeds when they took their mates.

He stopped quickly. His brow furrowed, the silver color in his eyes flickering and roiling like a storm coming to a head.

"Do you think I'd harm you?" His voice deepened and rumbled as she watched him nervously.

"I think you'd do whatever you needed to achieve your own end, but I don't think you'd harm me." She couldn't allow him to think otherwise; her sense of fair play went too deep. "That doesn't mean I want to tempt that hormonal funky stuff you have going on."

"Hormonal funky stuff?" There was a note of surprise in his voice though his expression became more brooding. "It's called heat, baby, and we call it that for a reason."

She gave a small snort, curiously ladylike, and so damned

hot his cock throbbed with a hunger he had never experienced before.

Jonas could feel his teeth grinding together as he fought to pull back, not to touch her, to force her to admit that she was burning for him.

Curiously, she wasn't. There was desire, strong, heated desire. But it wasn't heat. He hadn't touched her. He hadn't kissed or marked her. She was saved from the torturous need that was suddenly afflicting him.

The glands in his tongue were swollen to the point that the tongue itself was thick and heavy. A slight taste of cinnamon and cloves tempted his taste buds and urged him to share.

God, he wanted her lips wrapped around his tongue. First his tongue, then his dick. His eyes narrowed on the luscious curves of her mouth as he fought to hold back the hunger, the absolute craving to fill her mouth with the same tastes that filled his. Her body with the same lusts that were tearing him apart.

"It's called a woman's nightmare," she informed him tartly. "I can't imagine anything worse than being so tied to a man that you can't exist without him."

His gaze slipped to hers as she turned from him.

Merinus had told her about mating heat. In that moment, Jonas knew that the Prima had broken the strictest law of the Breed society. Mates were forbidden to reveal the mating heat to any unmated Breed or human. It was the only protection they had.

"I've yet to see a mate who considers it a nightmare," he snapped as he forced himself to turn from her. "But the subject is moot. If I had intended to follow that path and tie you to me, then trust me, sweetheart," he turned back long enough to spear a hard, cool look in her direction, "you would be tied."

He didn't wait around for her reaction. At that moment, the sound of Amber's protest that she had waited too long for her breakfast echoed through the house as Jonas stalked to his room and closed the door softly.

He felt as though he was going to break apart. Parts of him were shattering on the inside as the animal part of his psyche clawed and roared in protest at being jerked from his mate.

Mark her, it urged.

Tie her.

God help him, that was the last thing he should do.

He'd seen his Enforcers locked in mating heat. He'd seen how it compromised their abilities to maintain control and focus on their assigned missions.

There was something about the hormonal, super-charged aphrodisiac that spilled from a Breed's tongue that made that tie impossible to deny.

It formed a tie that bound him to her, despite her unwillingness to be bound in return.

But wasn't this what he wanted? he reminded himself. He had denied the heat for months. He had forced himself to hold back, deny the instinctive need that ripped through his senses.

Now, in a matter of hours, he was ready to bed her for a single touch.

He was screwed. It was that simple, and he knew it. Just as he knew that there wasn't a damned thing he could do to stop it.

❖   ❖   ❖

Rachel stared at her shaking hands before breathing in roughly, collecting the items she needed and moving back to the bedroom and to Amber, who fussed for her bottle.

She checked Amber's diaper, changed it quickly and all the while reminded herself, more than once, of all the reasons why she wasn't going to allow herself to touch the man. He was such a fascination to her that she could barely keep her mind, let alone her hands, off him.

And now there was the added complication that he thought she was his mate?

Oh, she knew about the mating. Merinus had been kind enough to go into detail—explicit, amazing detail—before

Rachel had taken the job. That was just after Rachel had been asked to sign a confidentiality agreement that didn't just affect her own life, but any heirs she may come to have, and a very subtle warning of the grief family members could suffer if she ever divulged the information. But even if her friend hadn't given her those details, Rachel would have still suspected the truth of the rumors that circulated.

Mating heat. Forced desires. Breed sexual virus. The gossip rags were full of names for it. Merinus's description was kinder. Natural selection, she had called it. God had chosen the perfect mates for the children He had allowed the Council to create bodies for.

Merinus was nothing if not a great believer in a higher power.

So where did that leave Rachel?

As she placed Amber on her shoulder, cuddling the child close to her and rubbing her back soothingly, Rachel began to pace the floor.

Jonas fascinated her too much. That was her problem. That had nothing to do with hormones, pheromones, or anything chemical or biological. It was simply an attraction she had learned to accept.

It was now a complication she was going to have to deal with.

After burping Amber and laying her down for a nap, Rachel let herself linger long enough to smooth her fingers over her child's red-gold locks, and to once again be amazed that such a perfect creation had come from her body.

It wasn't often that she allowed herself to become sentimental or find any regrets in her life. She tried to live in a way that ensured she had as few regrets as possible. But as she stared down at Amber, she wondered if she had made a mistake in informing Amber's father of her birth.

Devon hadn't been perfect, but she had felt he deserved to know about his child, whether she thought he would be interested or not. Now it was something she might regret though. Devon was so firmly against the Breeds that it was hard telling what he would do once he learned where Rachel and Amber were located. And finding her wouldn't be hard. The explosion at her home had been all over the news, as well as reports that Rachel and her child had been flown to Sanctuary. It wouldn't be something he would do out of love for his child, but rather out of pure spite.

Unfortunately, that was Devon's personality.

Breathing out wearily, she leaned forward, kissed her daughter's cheek, then turned on the monitor system beside the crib before leaving the bedroom and venturing to the front porch of the cabin.

The large, single-story structure sat on the hill overlooking the main estate house. The three-story mansion had once been home to one of the labs the Genetics Council had created.

Beneath the historic home, a sprawling cement-and-steel structure had been built. The labs, confinement cells and soldiers' barracks had been completely hidden from the citizens of nearby Buffalo Gap. The mountain had provided a perfect training location, while the area had been a strategic location for the Breeds to come and go from their assigned missions.

Stepping to the railing of the wraparound porch, she crossed her arms over her breasts and fought to hold back the chill working down her spine.

"She's sleeping again?" Jonas stepped out as Rachel turned to him in surprise.

"I thought you'd left." For the barest second, her heart raced, breathlessness assailed her chest and her thighs tried to clench in response to his presence.

He was, quite simply, total male perfection. Savagely hewn, exceptionally built. And those eyes. Staring into his eyes was like staring into a maelstrom of hunger.

She had seen that hunger the first time they'd met, and it had never abated.

"Not yet." Pushing his hands into his slacks, he moved closer and leaned against one of the porch's huge support columns. "I was on the sat phone arranging the packing and delivery of the office here. Everything should arrive in a few hours."

"I'm certain it will, if that's what you ordered." Few people, let alone Breeds, defied Jonas.

His gaze flickered at the irony in her tone.

"Ely called while you were gone. She's hoping that if she adds her plea to Dr. Vanderale's, you'll come to the lab for testing in the morning."

Rachel tilted her head as she stared back at him. "If I have none of your mating heat signs, Jonas, then why should I do that? My time is rather valuable, as I'm certain you know. There's quite a bit that has to be caught up with at the office. Now that you're transferring said office here, there will be only additional work. I doubt I'll have time to pamper Ely or Dr. Vanderale in this matter. But should I change my mind, I promise you'll be the first to know."

Her mocking little speech produced much more of a reaction than she anticipated. For months, she had been throwing out the cute little asides in a particularly cool voice, and for months, Jonas had pretended to ignore them.

He wasn't ignoring it now.

Before Rachel could move to evade, his hands gripped her arms, turning her to face him as his head bent, bringing his lips much too close to hers. Too much temptation, much too close. That's what it was.

"Do you believe this is nothing more than a game?" The rough frustration in his tone scraped over her senses and sent heat coursing through her body.

Backing down would have been the wisest course of action, Rachel thought distantly, but, as her sister had always claimed, backing down just wasn't part of *their* DNA.

"If I thought it a game, then I would have brought my scorecard," she retorted, her chin lifting, bringing them almost nose to nose. "Now let me go, Mr. Wyatt. I did not give you permission to touch me, nor did I give you permission to berate me."

His gaze narrowed, the liquid silver boiling as a subtle mask of male lust seemed to descend upon his expression.

The look did something to her. It caused her stomach to jump, her womb to tighten. This time, her thighs truly did clench as she fought to hold back a response that seemed more instinctive than hormonal or forced.

"You're giving it to me now," he assured her, his nostrils flaring as he seemed to inhale.

Rachel felt heat flare in her face, both from arousal as well as embarrassment.

"How dare you . . ."

"I dare because I've spent too much time watching you flip around my office like some ice queen that no man dare touch, even after you had Amber. I dare because you know what the hell you're doing to me and you stand there in all your indignation and do it anyway."

And he was right. That damned sense of fair play she felt kicked in and made yet another situation more uncomfortable than it should have been.

"Why shouldn't I do it?" She narrowed her gaze on him, her jaw tightening in anger. "I've watched you fuck your way through Washington as though it were your own intimate little playground. What the hell makes you think I want anything to do with a man that so many other women have already had?"

That wasn't exactly the truth, but what the hell. She was getting mad now. The rules didn't apply with the same strength when she was mad.

"Oh, you want me." A tight smile curled his lips. "You can deny it until hell freezes over, sweetheart, but we both know you want nothing more than my hands on you."

Oh, she hated that arrogant confidence that seemed to ooze from his very pores.

Fighting back the arousal that had slipped past her control wasn't easy, but she managed it. As quickly as the blood had thundered through her veins and rushed to the sensitive bud of her clit, it was settling, easing back into its normal pace.

She'd had to learn how to control herself and her responses

so many years ago. She and her sister both had learned the danger of ever giving rein to their desires versus locking them down.

She pulled back slowly.

"Nice little trick." His head lowered farther, his lips so close to her own that she stilled just as quickly, terrified of allowing her own to brush against them.

Merinus had warned her about the potency of a Breed's kiss and the hormone that filled the small glands beneath the Breed's tongue.

"What trick." She didn't dare lick her lips, not yet, not even to soothe their nervous dryness.

"Stilling the desire, the needs that claw at you." Before she could evade him his head lowered, his cheek brushing against hers, much too close to her lips. "Tell me, Rachel, do you truly think you can deny me if I share my kiss with you? If I allow you to taste the hunger that's ripping my guts to shreds?"

Lust. It was no more than lust, and Rachel had sworn to herself that she would never be the object of any man's lust again.

She wanted love, not just desire, or mating heat, or forced hunger. Whatever the description, she didn't want it without his heart.

She didn't want to be bound to a man who she knew would feel no more than an overwhelming responsibility to keep her alive.

"Do you have any idea how much I've wanted you?" Curiously gentle, his voice seemed to wrap around her senses, to stroke them with sensuality rather than lust.

"Let me go, Jonas," she whispered. If she felt the warmth of him surrounding her much longer, she might not be able to hold back the need to experience the taste of that kiss he was threatening her with. "Let me go, now."

He released his hold on her slowly, one finger at a time, reluctance filling each move, before stepping back.

"Do you think running away from it is going to help?" he growled, his voice dark, heavy with hunger.

"Immeasurably," she assured him as she moved away from him. "Trust me, Jonas, it will help immeasurably."

At least, it better. As far as Rachel was concerned, it was the last defense she had against her desire for him.

Mating heat, her ass. As though this could be forced without some kind of hormonal kiss. This was *desire*. The kind her sister had warned her years ago that she never wanted to know, and never wanted to regret.

It was the kind of desire that ended up breaking a woman's heart and scarring her soul. Rachel had no desire to have her world destroyed by a man as Diana had had her world destroyed once.

"Rachel." The sound of Merinus's voice had her turning and facing the woman who had been her dearest friend for most of her life, despite the gap in their ages.

Merinus Tyler Lyons still looked no more than twenty-four years old. Her skin was unblemished, unlined, her brown eyes still bright and filled with youth.

There was something eternally different about Merinus, though, an aura that she hadn't possessed before, a confidence and sense of power that Rachel had sensed the past year when Merinus had called her to take the job with Jonas.

Merinus had saved her life. Rachel had been in a strange country, alone, newly pregnant and fighting for survival after Devon had deserted her in Switzerland.

She had had to fight to survive those few weeks alone in Switzerland after losing her apartment, her job and her passport. She attempted to convince the ambassador there to provide her a ride back to the States. She was certain she could have eventually convinced him to do so without the night spent in his bed, as he was demanding, but things hadn't been looking good.

She had tried to call Kane, but he had been unavailable. She'd lost touch with Merinus and her brother years before, but she'd been unable to reach her sister and had no idea whom to turn to.

Within hours of the message she'd left on Kane's phone,

a Breed heli-jet had landed at the consulate and three Breed Enforcers had informed her they had been sent to escort her back to America.

That was friendship, she thought as Merinus stepped up to the porch, her expression hesitant, slightly guilty.

"How did you know?" Rachel asked, certain that Merinus had to have known that she would be Jonas's mate.

Merinus swallowed tightly. "Remember the blood and saliva tests that were requested before you were allowed to land in Sanctuary on the flight back from Switzerland?"

Rachel lifted a brow. "The ones to ensure that I wasn't carrying the flu or some infection that could affect your precious Breeds?"

Merinus's lips twitched at Rachel's acidic tone. "Yeah, those." She nodded as she came closer before taking a seat in the padded chair that sat against the side of the house. "Actually, that is truly what the blood was for. It's standard procedure to run the mating test against any Breed you may come in contact with, though. Jonas was here at Sanctuary when you called, so the test was run against his." She rubbed at her nose thoughtfully. "I actually thought perhaps Diana would be a better match myself. You surprised me."

Merinus was amused. Why didn't that surprise her?

"Diana would have castrated him," she informed her friend as she leaned back against the railing and faced the Prima of the Feline Breed species.

"She would have." Merinus nodded with a smile before sobering. "What about you, Rachel? Will you kill him, or will you love him?"

"Does it matter?" she asked, knowing that Jonas wasn't a very well-liked person among either Breeds or humans.

Surprisingly, Merinus nodded. "It matters very much. You can be his salvation or his destruction. Jonas is one of the most intelligent of the Breeds, and definitely one of the most dangerous. His very nature is his own worst enemy."

"And you think I can save him?" she asked incredulously. "Merinus, when did you lose your mind?"

A rueful smile curved the other woman's lips. "Let's say I've been warned by someone who cares a great deal for him. If Jonas doesn't learn to temper himself, then he'll self-destruct and we'll lose him forever. Win or lose, stay or go, the only thing that's going to temper him is his mate. Tag, my friend, you're it," Merinus finished with the childhood rejoinder.

"It was my turn last time," Rachel argued. "Remember? When I took on your brother's temper and that mess he called an office?"

Merinus bit her lip to hide a smile, but Rachel caught the merriment in her gaze as she responded. "Oh yeah. My bad."

"Your bad indeed." She crossed her arms over her breasts and glared back at her. "He's a pain in the ass."

"I'm sure he can be." Merinus nodded with no attempt to hide her amusement now.

"He makes me crazy, Merinus."

"He'll make you crazier," her friend promised.

"I refuse to accept this mating crap."

Merinus sighed then. "It doesn't matter if you accept it. You're here; that's all he needed. Like I said, win or lose, accept or reject, it doesn't matter. Whatever Jonas has to face with you as his mate is what he needs."

"You sound as though you've been looking into crystal balls or something." Rachel snorted.

"Perhaps I have," Merinus responded soberly now. "But really, who needs to? You've seen him. You've worked with him. I knew him before he laid eyes on you, before he sensed that you could belong to him." She leaned forward intently. "He's never known love. He's never known a caress that didn't involve some sort of payment, or a kind word that he didn't suspect didn't come with strings. And I know you, Rachel. I've watched you. You might not love him, but you care for him."

"I lust after his body," Rachel griped. "He's seriously ripped. That doesn't mean I want to risk my sanity for it."

"You care for him." Merinus shook her head in denial. "Don't lie to me. We both know you do."

"He's not completely hateful." She shrugged. "He's tolerable. I don't hate him."

"Are you in love with him?" Suspicions suddenly clouded the other woman's eyes.

"Indeed not." Rachel's eyes widened. "I haven't lost my mind yet, you know."

"Give it time." Merinus waved her hand negligently as though losing her mind were a foregone conclusion. "You haven't lived with Jonas yet."

"And you have?" Rachel questioned the confidence in her tone.

"Not on a bet." Merinus laughed. "Not even for the world. This is one time, my friend, I do not envy you the adventure."

Just what she needed, an adventure Merinus wasn't willing to fight her for.

"You're going to owe me," Rachel promised her.

"And as always, I'll pay up." There was blissful unconcern.

Rachel had a bad feeling, a very bad feeling, things were going to get very, very complicated.

And unfortunately, she had yet to see a time when her bad feelings didn't pan out.

She had a feeling it might have been more prudent to have stayed in Switzerland.

CHAPTER 5

The office was set up on the far side of the cabin, a vacant wing that Rachel had learned had been added only in the past year in case Jonas was forced to attend to business from his cabin in Sanctuary rather than the Bureau's offices in D.C.

The three-room wing boasted a large outer office for Rachel, a larger inner one for Jonas and an attached nursery for Amber complete with a Breed nanny to oversee her while Rachel was working.

What more could a personal assistant ask for?

Outside the wing was a large parking area, a sheltered yard with a toddler play set that Amber wouldn't be playing on for quite a while, if ever, and a Breed guard.

All the benefits of the D.C. office complete with additional security. There was no chance of meeting Brandenmore after dark any longer. Nope, all she had to contend with now was Jonas.

After a week of dealing with Jonas in his mating mood, Rachel was starting to wish she simply had to face Brandenmore. She doubted the other man was as completely arrogant as Jonas on a bad day.

"Rachel, if you schedule another appointment with Racert in D.C., we're going to have words." Jonas stepped from the office first thing that morning and glared at her with the promise of retribution gleaming in his eyes.

Rachel lifted her brow once that first breathless, sensually weak feeling that always assailed her when he walked in the room had passed.

"Racert is important to the funds that Senator Tyler is attempting to get approved through the Senate, Jonas, you know that," she reminded him as she kept her attention on the file she was currently adding information to. "I would be more than happy to deny the meetings he requests once you get those funds."

"You're going to begin denying them now," he informed her. "I have an assistant director, you know. Pawn the bastard off on him."

Rachel turned and stared back at Jonas with an expression of mocking disapproval. "We need to discuss your idea of an assistant director. Brim Stone isn't exactly the most tactful choice you could have made. I think his attitude may even be worse than yours. He growled at a congressman's aide yesterday and caused the man to wet himself."

No one ever accused the Breeds of failing to use intimidation to get their way.

"Pawn the damned meeting off on him," Jonas ordered.

"No." Rachel turned back to the file despite the sudden jump of her heart as she made the denial. It was never, ever easy to challenge Jonas Wyatt.

"I know a volcano hungry for a sacrifice," he muttered behind her. "You'd make the perfect candidate."

"Hungry volcanoes only accept virgin maidens," she informed him tartly. "That leaves me out of the running."

She almost grinned at the disgruntled growl that sounded behind her.

"Fine. Pack a bag. You're going with me."

Rachel froze.

She turned to him slowly once again, her fingers still poised on the keys of the electronic display board.

"Excuse me?"

Jonas moved closer, the lean, powerful shift of muscle holding her gaze even as she fought it. Hell, fighting it was becoming harder each day.

"I said, pack a bag. You'll be going with me. For the meeting as well as that insane embassy party you scheduled for me. Afraid to have me at home, mate?"

She swallowed tightly. Actually, she was. She wanted him out of the cabin, at least for a single night—long enough to rebuild the defenses she could feel weakening against him, despite his arrogance.

"I can't leave Amber . . ."

He snorted at that. "Merinus was taking Amber tonight anyway. Did you think Callan wouldn't inform me of that? What did you think you were going to do, Rachel? Get rid of me so you could rid yourself of the desire plaguing you?"

Actually, that had been her plan.

Her lips thinned mutinously. "I have no idea what you're talking about."

"Do you think I don't know about those very intimate toys that you picked up when you went shopping with Merinus last week? For God's sake. Those Breed guards on your ass don't take their eyes off you, Rachel, no matter what you think."

Mortification flamed in her face.

She'd been so certain she had managed to slip her purchases past the guards who had trailed after her and Merinus as they shopped several days previously. After all, she hadn't even bought the items herself. She'd convinced the sales clerk to take care of everything and then slip her the bag.

"Let me guess." His voice dropped to a husky, sexy croon as he flattened his hands on the top of her desk and leaned forward. "While the cat's away, the mouse thinks she's going to play?"

"That was the general idea," she gritted out. "So go away so I can play in peace."

She had no doubt in her mind that those ultra-sensitive ears of his would pick up the sound of a vibrator.

"Forget it." He straightened with a snap, his silver eyes like dark flames raging in his face as he glared down at her. "Now pack. You're going with me."

"I will not." Rachel came to her feet now, anger churning inside her at the complete arrogance of the order. "I am not required at either the meeting or that insane party being held for the ambassador to Switzerland. He's a jerk."

"Yet you thought I wouldn't mind attending?" he asked with carefully banked sarcasm. "How kind of you, Rachel. Pack a bag before I pack it for you."

Hadn't Merinus said something about Breed males enjoying spoiling and giving in to their mates?

"Come on, Jonas," she tried another tactic. A sweet smile. She batted her lashes at him. "You don't really need me there, do you? You know I hate these parties. You've always let me out of them before."

Amazing.

She watched his expression, and for the briefest second, she thought she was actually going to get away with it.

"You know," his voice dropped, became harder, "I'm certain that sweet little act would work if you were actually sharing my bed. But since you aren't"—he flashed those wicked incisors at the sides of his mouth—"pack that fucking bag."

Rachel flinched. She hadn't heard him curse like that in all the time she had worked for him. Her eyes widened as he turned on his heel and stalked from the office, the door slamming hard enough that her gaze shot to the room where Amber was sleeping, fully expecting to hear her disgruntled cries.

She slept on.

Breathing out hard, Rachel turned back to the door he'd just about slammed from its hinges.

Now, was that a Feline hissy fit or what?

Did she dare not pack to accompany him?

She grimaced. Hell, she had a feeling if she didn't pack, he would do just as he threatened and pack for her. Then he'd likely throw her over his shoulder and cart her to the heli-jet like a damned war prize or something.

Now wasn't that just what she *didn't* need: Jonas in a snit.

It looked like it was going to be a while before she was allowed to play with her new toys after all.

◆　　◆　　◆

Jonas stalked from the cabin, his control shot, and he fully admitted if he had stayed in that office so much as a heartbeat longer, then he was going to jerk her from her chair and kiss those pretty lips like the hungry Lion he was turning into.

The glands beneath his tongue were swollen to capacity now. They throbbed like a son of a bitch and the taste of cinnamon and cloves filled his mouth like a particularly forbidden sweet.

Sweet Lord have mercy, she was making him crazy.

Jumping into the Raider he kept parked in the driveway, he signaled to the two hidden members of Ghost Team that he was riding out, started the vehicle and backed out of the smooth parking area.

It was time he had a talk with Merinus. The meddling she had done in his life was becoming dangerous. He was poised on a razor's edge here and it was going to begin affecting his job.

Even Brim Stone, the Coyote Breed he'd elected to cover for him in D.C., was becoming frustrated with Jonas's lack of tact, which was worse than normal.

According to Brim, he was like a Lion with a sore paw, and if someone didn't dig out the splinter, then he was going to do it himself, with a knife.

Jonas had dared him.

It was never a smart thing to dare a Coyote. God knew most of them didn't have the power to turn away from a dare. They were fucking insane like that.

Pulling the Raider into the circular drive in front of the estate house, Jonas jumped from the vehicle and strode quickly up the marble steps to the double doors.

A Breed guard opened the door for him. Jonas expected to come face-to-face with part of the Pride family, but instead came to a stop at the sight of Cassandra Sinclair as she sat at the bottom of the staircase, staring up at him.

The eerie blue of her eyes could be disconcerting, to Breed as well as human. Her innocent face was somber, the long, heavy curls of her hair flowing around her like a thick, black cape.

Dressed in jeans, a light sweater and sneakers, there was still no way to pass this particular Breed off as anything but what she was. A very preternatural woman-child.

"How is your mate?" Cassie propped her arms on her knees before laying her cheek against them and staring up at him inquisitively.

This was the same young woman that the year previously had stood in front of the Breed tribunal and argued, quite successfully, that the female mate of the Coyote leader had the right to deny her mate. That she could indeed live apart from him, as long as she submitted to close protective supervision. That Breed Law had no right to interfere in free will and a woman's right to choose, and that the Coyote leader, Del Rey Delgado, had unfairly and with deception mated the woman against her free will.

All of that might well be true, Jonas had argued. But the Coyote leader had rights as well. It was he who would have to know when his mate suffered. It was the male who would have to bear the burden as well as the guilt should anything happen to her once she left his care.

The Breed tribunal hadn't heeded his arguments. Hell no. Instead, they had stood fast and followed the very skillfully presented argument this child had presented.

At nineteen, most Breeds were considered so fully grown that the majority of them had been killing for more than four years. Breed children were sent for their first kill between the ages of ten and fifteen.

Cassie, barely nineteen, had yet to take a life. And with her mix of Coyote and Wolf DNA, she might possibly be more dangerous than any of them.

Because Cassie sometimes saw ghosts, and because she often knew things she should never know.

"You're worried," she stated as she watched him too closely with those odd blue eyes. "What's wrong, Jonas?"

Unfortunately for him, Cassie was one of the few people he was fond of. She had practically been raised in Sanctuary. Her Wolf Breed stepfather had come to the Felines for help while trying to save her and her mother's lives. Because of that initial call for help, Cassie was now a part of them.

"I rarely worry, Cassie," he assured her with a slight grin as he took a seat next to her on the stairs. "Let's just say this hasn't been one of my better days."

"Because your mate is still denying you?" Playful humor glinted in her gaze as her lips quirked with a charming smile.

"Because my mate is a stubborn woman," he argued.

Cassie leaned back to rest against the step behind her. "Perhaps it's not stubbornness so much as it is fear," she stated then. "You would be a very hard man to walk into a mating with, I think."

"Ah, Cass, I thought you loved me." He chuckled.

She didn't smile back. Instead, she turned and gazed thoughtfully at the door for a long moment before turning back to him.

"Do you ever hate your life, Jonas?" she asked.

"No." He shook his head decisively. "I don't hate my life at all, Cassie. Though sometimes I must admit I hate those who attempt to destroy the life I and those like us have the right to live."

She nodded slowly again. "That's why you fight so hard for us. It's why some of us love you so much that we would do anything to see you happy and to see that you never regret your life."

Jonas frowned back at her. "Okay kid, you were waiting here for a reason. What was it?"

She nibbled at her lip for a moment as she considered her next words.

"Many Breeds don't like me. Do you know that, Jonas?"

He reached out and mussed the top of her hair a bit. "I love you, squirt."

The gesture didn't bring the usual smile from Cassie.

"I frighten them," she said softly. "I'm not one of them, yet I am. I know things I shouldn't. And they fear what I could mean to their lives. Do you fear what I could mean to your life, Jonas?"

He tilted his head and stared back at her with a sense of understanding. Cassie wanted to feel accepted, and sometimes, that was the last thing she felt.

"You don't frighten me in the least, Cass. Though sometimes, I am afraid for you."

She nodded. Sometimes, Cassie seemed to be a magnet for trouble, even more than she would normally be.

"Do you trust me, Jonas?"

And here was the kicker. "I trust you, Cass." He sighed. He did, though he didn't always follow the advice she gave him.

"Then don't berate Merinus for what was my fault," she warned him softly. "I told her a friend would call Kane, and that friend would be in dire need as well as important to all that we are."

"Enough, Cass." He laid his finger gently against her lips, amazed that there was no discomfort in that light touch. Mates normally found it entirely distasteful to touch anyone, in any way, of the opposite sex during the first stages of mating heat. "I know where this is going. It doesn't matter why Rachel came to me, or who played a part in it. I berate Merinus or she thinks she can make a habit of poking her nose in my business. It's that simple."

Cassie shook her head. "Nothing is ever so simple." She sighed. "No ill will come of berating her, but as you said,

she will give a second thought to her actions for a while."
Cassie stood slowly to her feet. "And really, Jonas, you don't
want her to do that."

She didn't say anything more.

Turning, she ran up the stairs, leaving him to watch after
her. He shook his head in resignation. He'd be damned if he
couldn't have drained some of the frustration eating him alive
if he could have tested his wits against Merinus's rapidly
growing will.

Cassie paused at the top of the stairs, turned and frowned
curiously. "Jonas?"

"Yeah, brat?" He rose to his feet and stared up at her with
a patient scowl.

"Why did you tell Rachel she thought that while the cat
was away the mouse would play?"

He didn't answer.

Stifling his curse, he turned on his heel, jerked open the
door and raced to the Raider.

Damn her. He wouldn't allow it. He had no relief. There
was no way to still the lust tearing at his guts and no way to
ease the hunger eating at his soul. He would be damned if he
would allow it.

◆   ◆   ◆

She did it, she did it.

Rachel was still doing the little internal chant as she sat
across from Jonas in the heli-jet hours later, the powerful
motor flying them quickly to their destination.

All he'd had to do was leave the cabin, something he hadn't
done in a week. At least, not while she had been awake.

But he had stomped out earlier, gotten in the Raider and
driven off. Rachel had rushed to the bedroom, locked the
door and pulled the toy free of her dress for one of the most
intense orgasms of her life.

Damn, that shouldn't have been possible using fantasy alone.

She peeked over at Jonas through the cover of her lashes
and wanted to let out a small laugh.

He was still furious. She didn't even care that he knew what she had done. The fact was, she had achieved it, and she felt great. Like a new woman.

How long had it been since she had found relief? Nine days? Yeah, she remembered the last time: the morning before Brandenmore had decided to invade her life, before going into work.

Jonas had been at the office every waking moment, it had seemed. Frowning. Growling. He'd even insisted on sitting beside her at her desk while she went over the figures for the new satellite system Vanderale Industries was donating to the Breeds.

That night, she had tossed and turned, and burned for him.

That next morning, she had made certain she hadn't gone to work in the same state. Breeds could smell arousal.

"I can smell the scent of your release on you, and it offends me," he suddenly growled.

Uh-oh.

"Really?" She smiled back at him. "The smell is offensive?"

She rather doubted it.

"Don't play games, Rachel," he warned her, his voice tight. "They could come with consequences."

She was intimidated, but showing it would be a really bad thing.

Instead, she leaned forward against the security harness that held her in her seat and stared back at him defiantly. "Just because you're my boss doesn't make you my keeper," she informed him. "I've been taking care of certain things all by myself for a long time now. I don't have a problem continuing to do so."

"Then I'll assume Devon Marshal provided little pleasure the night Amber was conceived," he stated, his tone flat and to the point.

Rachel sat back. "Devon has nothing to do with this conversation. Please stop being mean, Jonas. It doesn't become you."

It didn't become him, but he was so good at it. She cast him a narrow-eyed glare as her lips thinned in disapproval.

"Being mean definitely becomes me," he assured her. "Haven't you heard? I enjoy being mean."

There was the faintest note of resentment in his tone. She couldn't blame him. He was called the bogeyman of the Breeds on national television on a regular basis.

"I like you better when you're being polite," she pointed out calmly as she forced her body into a more relaxed state.

"I'm certain you do," he growled. "It's much easier to get away with things you know you shouldn't do then, isn't it?"

She shrugged. "It's easier to ask forgiveness than to beg for permission," she reminded him. "Isn't that one your favorite sayings?"

She knew it was. He said it often—whenever he broke the rules himself.

"In this case, not asking for permission could be dangerous. I'm about a second from that kiss you've been avoiding all week like the plague, Rachel. You don't want to push this."

She widened her eyes in mock fear. "I'm so sorry, Jonas. I promise to never do it again." She batted her lashes for effect.

She was slipping into a mood she was certain would get her into trouble. It never failed to make Diana crazy when Rachel set out to irritate her.

Of course, if her sister would find that sense of fun she used to have, then Rachel wouldn't have to irritate her so often.

"I can smell a lie too, remember?" He was so obviously controlling himself that for a second Rachel wondered what it would be like if he lost all that cool, calculated reason that was the backbone of his being.

This mood was all his fault, she decided. If he had just left her alone, if he hadn't somehow managed to draw her and Amber into one of the complicated games he was forever playing, then he wouldn't have had to worry about that troublemaking streak she fought to keep subverted.

Jonas watched her, eyes narrowed, his senses fine-tuned as he opened the primal part of his genetics and allowed it partial freedom.

His hearing, acute anyway, became more so. His sense of smell became deeper, nuances easier to detect. The pores of his flesh seemed to open as the claws beneath the human nails threatened to flex free.

She was good. She had a control over her responses that normally only Breeds possessed. She was able to convince her body to follow the commands of her mind, but only to a certain point.

The arousal she was fighting was on the edge of slipping free, and he could sense the fiery, spicy-sweet taste of it against his tongue as he drew in the scent of her.

She hid it well; he had to give her that. There were no external signs of arousal. Her nipples weren't hard, she wasn't flushed, her breathing wasn't in the least labored. The arousal was shielded, pushed back, but definitely there and waiting to break free.

As he kept his senses focused on her, she slid the electronic planner she used free of her leather briefcase and flipped it on with a smooth motion of her slender fingers.

The screen lit up as she pulled the stylus out of its holder and began to work on whatever she had brought with her.

"Senator Racert has sent you several emails," she murmured as she glanced up at him, her green eyes barely hiding the mischievous glimmer that he could sense pushing at her control. She was dying to test his limits, he could feel it.

He'd had no idea the playful little thing she could be.

"Racert is always sending emails." He shrugged. "It's one of his failings."

A quick little frown pulled at her brow. "Did you know this afternoon's meeting is going to involve several other senators who aren't part of the Breed Appropriations Committee?"

"That's normal." Jonas shrugged again at the question. "Racert likes to show us lowly Breeds how undeserving we are and make his attempt to convince us to turn over portions of the Breed funds to their little pork barrel projects."

They sickened him. Racert was one of the worst. He was convinced Breed intelligence was so far beneath humans' that taking the funds awarded to the Breeds would be simple. Ten years, and still the man was certain he could convince the Breed portion of the committee that they were receiving funds they didn't deserve.

Money they used to build Sanctuary and the Wolf base, Haven. Funds used to defend and protect the communities they were building to ensure the safety of their own species.

Most of the countries of the world paid into those funds. Predetermined amounts were set aside and deposited on a yearly basis into a multinational fund in Switzerland, which the Breeds had access to.

There were limits to the money, though. One was the appropriations committee, which had been created to oversee the larger amounts that were paid out. The committee had been created as a protective measure to ensure that future Breeds never used those funds to build arms against the countries that paid into it.

"The senators meeting with you today are there to attempt to convince you to use the funds for something other than Breed-designated projects, then?"

"Of course." His brows lifted at her surprise. "Surely you didn't think we haven't had to fight to keep that money, Rachel. You know your government better than that."

"True." She inclined her head in acknowledgment before turning her attention back to the electronic planner.

"Which toy did you use?" Jonas allowed the question to slip free, his curiosity getting the better of him.

She froze. He sensed her forcing her emotions as well as her response to him deeper inside that shielded parted of her psyche. She had no intentions of giving in to him any more than she had to.

"Excuse me?" She lifted her gaze back to him.

"Which toy did you use to achieve release?" His body was tight, his control was shaky. Jonas could feel the need to touch her tearing through his system now.

Evidently, she sensed the danger inherent in answering him. He watched as her tongue swiped over her lips nervously. She inhaled slowly, deeply, fighting back the need to tease him, perhaps? He wished she would tease him. For a moment, he would have given anything if she would have pushed at the fragile thread of control that held back the beast determined to mark her.

"Jonas, this is not a conversation I want to have."

He watched as her face flushed a delicate, rosy hue. Her green eyes flashed with undisguised desire, and slowly, temptingly, his senses filled with the sweet, spicy scent of feminine need.

She was losing control—over her body, at least. He could sense the sensual weakening, feel it rushing through him as it simultaneously pulsed through her body.

He had to clench his teeth, force back the claws determined to push free and hold back a growl of hunger that he feared could terrify them both.

"It's a conversation I want to have though," he assured her. "I want to know what you thought about, Rachel. Who was in your imagination when you came? Who was taking you as your body arched and your breath caught in pleasure?"

A fine shudder raced through her. Any other man would have missed it. Most Breeds would have missed it. But Jonas felt it. He swore he could feel the vibrations as the sensation tore through her body.

His cock was so damned hard he swore it was in danger of bursting. His balls drew up tight to the base, blood pulsed and shuddered through the heavy shaft.

In his entire life he had never wanted, never ached for anything as he did this woman, his mate.

His woman.

Nature had created her for him alone. God had gifted him,

and holding himself back from her was the hardest thing he had ever done in his entire life.

"Please don't." The plea in her voice was heavy with her own battle to deny him.

" 'Please don't,' " he murmured. "Such a delicate little plea for something we both want so desperately. Tell me, Rachel, how much longer do you think we can continue to deny it?"

He wasn't going to make it long. The taste of the hormone filled his senses, dug sharpened claws into his control and shredded it further.

"As long as we have to." She breathed in hard, deep. "I don't need a mate, Jonas. I don't need a man, period. I want my life back, and I'm certain you do as well. Giving in to this is only going to complicate both our lives."

"You think you can walk away then?" The animal instincts that were so much a part of him roared out in denial. He would never, ever allow her to walk away from him.

"I know I can." In her eyes he saw her belief in that statement. "I have no choice, Jonas. Neither do you. When this is over, Amber and I will leave. So I would suggest looking for a new assistant while you can."

He was in her face. Even before he realized it, he leaned forward, his palms flat at the sides of her seat, his nose almost touching hers, his eyes locked with hers.

"Never." The rumble of sound that tore from his throat bore little resemblance to the voice of a man. "I'll never let you go."

"And I won't allow you to hold me. Tell me, do you truly want a mate who wants nothing more than to escape?"

"If that's the only way I can have you, then I'll take it and be content," he promised her with a snarl. "Think about that, Rachel. Believe it. Keep pushing this, keep pushing me, and I'll show exactly how easy it will be to hold you."

Before he lost all semblance of the man he was, Jonas jerked back in his own seat and fought the need. God, he fought. He wanted to feel her against him. He was dying for her touch. Anything to ease the tightness in his flesh, the ache for the warmth of her touching him rather than reaching out for him.

He had lived through hell. He had been created to kill and to breed. Now, nature was pushing, demanding, overriding his control and creating a path he hadn't meant to take.

The plans he had made over the years were now falling by the wayside in favor of a life he had promised himself he wouldn't attempt to live.

Fate had stepped in, and Jonas could now only pray that she had some idea what the hell she was doing. Because he was damned if he knew.

· CHAPTER 6 ·

Her sister, Diana, had once told her that there was nothing worse than a determined man. Rachel hadn't clearly understood what she was talking about until she had seen the pure, undiluted determination in Jonas's gaze.

Seeing it wouldn't have been near so terrifying if the instant response that whipped through her body hadn't been so impossible to control.

And he'd known it. He'd sensed it. He'd scented the quick, rapid flow of moisture that filled her vagina, he'd glanced at her breasts to see the hardened tips of her nipples pressing against the thin material of the white blouse she wore.

Arousal—blazing, uncontrolled and rapid—had rushed through her, nearly breaking her own determination to deny the primal response she couldn't seem to control.

Thankfully, Jonas seemed wary of the edge they were suddenly skating on. He'd pulled back, remained silent and allowed her the chance to get her body, as well as her imagination, under control.

The imagination part had actually been harder. All she

could think of for precious seconds, all she had seen, had been Jonas rising over her, his expression savage, dark, as he took possession of her. For an instant, her pussy spasmed in need at the thought of him pressing inside her, filling her, working his cock into the sensitive, snug muscles between her thighs.

She'd felt her body's hungry desire for his touch in places where she had never known such need before. On her tight, hard nipples, the moist heat of his mouth sucking her. Along her hips, the swollen bud of her clit and deep in the aching center of her body.

Remnants of that hungry need still assailed her if she didn't keep a close watch on the control she'd fought to maintain for so many years.

Now, sitting too close to him during the luncheon Racert had requested, Rachel found herself fighting to keep her eyes averted.

She'd always had a slight attention deficit whenever Jonas was around, but now it was worse. Significantly worse.

"Jonas, you have to admit, the Breeds have an account that could pay off the national debt." Racert was still arguing his point, nearly two hours into the meeting, as Jonas sat back and simply regarded him with apparent lazy interest. "You can buy public opinion, you know. Hell, politicians do it every day." His laugh was one of forced cheerfulness, his wide smile seemingly sincere. "You could easily make several hefty donations and the Breeds would never miss the money. Hell, it's not as though you need all that damned money at the moment. The U.S. government is lining your pockets damned well with the fees your Enforcers charge for the specialized missions they do for the military."

Rachel watched as Jonas tapped one finger against his temple as though he were actually considering the idea, when Rachel knew full well the explosion that could be coming.

Using the electronic planner's stylus, she pulled up the fiscal file she kept on hand, laid the electronic pad on the table, then leaned forward.

"Senator Racert, I believe this luncheon is concluded." She smiled politely to the four men who accompanied the senator before directing a lesser smile in his direction. "We've been here for nearly two hours now and as I'm certain you know, the party for our esteemed ambassador to Switzerland begins in less than three hours. We do need time to prepare for it."

A frown checked Racert's brow. "My dear Ms. Broen, I don't believe you speak for the Bureau director here." He nodded in Jonas's direction. "Why not be a good little thing and not interfere where you have no knowledge."

Rachel saw Jonas tense from the corner of her eye and heard the tiniest vibration of a growl emanate from his chest.

"I have full knowledge of the Breed security fund in which you are currently attempting to convince the Bureau of Breed Affairs to approve an amount you'd like to use for your own purposes." She smiled sweetly. "And if you may have missed my title somewhere, it is personal assistant to the director of Breed Affairs. I'm fully knowledgeable when it comes to that security fund. Just as I'm certain you're aware that we're possibly skirting unlawful activities in even considering such a maneuver."

"There are ways around anything." Racert's plump lips flattened in barely concealed anger.

"There is no way around the Breed security fund, Senator Racert," she assured him.

Racert turned to Jonas. "She's a mouthy thing, Wyatt. You should consider a replacement."

Before Rachel could consider a comeback, Jonas rose slowly to his feet.

"Let it go," she advised him softly.

"Like hell." There was the faintest French accent to his voice as he stared at Racert, his gaze icy. "A report of this meeting will be turned in to the Breed Appropriations Committee," he informed the senator as Rachel rose to her feet. "And I would highly advise if you need to discuss Breed affairs that you contact one of the Breed cabinet members besides myself."

Racert rose to his feet as well, a glare slicing to Rachel before he turned back to Jonas.

"Come on, Wyatt, you don't want to say no to this deal." His eyes narrowed warningly. "I'm on that committee. I approve those funds . . ."

"You don't approve jack shit," Jonas stated coldly, insultingly. "Don't pretend you do. And the next time you address my assistant with such malicious disrespect, I'll rip your throat out."

There was no doubt he meant every word. The slice of frozen mercury that his eyes became sent a chill racing over Rachel as well as the senators who now stood, facing an animal in danger of losing its appearance of civility.

"Rachel, we're leaving." His fingers curled around her upper arm as she quickly grabbed her pad and briefcase.

A second later, he was leading her from the table and through the restaurant. He didn't stop to pay for the meal, nor did he make the polite attempts not to burn this particular bridge. Not that Rachel blamed him. Racert was asking Jonas to not only steal from his own people, but to do so secretively and selectively.

"That might not have been wise," she stated as he escorted her to the limo waiting at the entrance.

Sliding into the interior of the vehicle, she watched as Jonas took his seat, the door closing behind him as the driver, a Coyote Enforcer, began to pull out.

Slowly, the glass partition between the seats rose, sealing them into a quiet, intimate atmosphere that she could have done without.

"He insulted you," Jonas growled. "Right there to your face."

"He's not the first." She rolled her eyes at his anger. "I get insulted every time I refuse to allow someone who believes they're my superior to talk to you. Get over it."

The next growl that rumbled in his throat had her watching him warily. Her gaze slid from his, to his arms, to his hands. Swallowing tightly, she watched as he slowly curled his fingers into fists to hide the primal claws that had torn through what at first appeared to be scars in the tips of his fingers.

"I will not get over it," he rasped, the icy silver of his eyes unthawing to boiling mercury. "I should have torn the bastard's tongue from his throat."

Rachel's brows arched. "Why? Because he was an asshole? Good Lord, Jonas, when did you decide you were my keeper?"

"The day you walked into my office and I realized you were my mate," he snapped back.

For a moment, the normally suave, calm Jonas was the animal she had always sensed lurking beneath the carefully clothed exterior. His eyes raged, his body was tense with the need for action, his expression shifting between sensuality and fury.

"I'm not your mate . . ."

He was on her. That quick. Rachel found herself lying back along the seat, his large body straddling her, the feel of his cock, heavy and hot, through the material of his slacks as his hips pressed against hers.

"Jonas." Her gasp was part protest, part sudden pleasure.

How the hell was she supposed to control herself when he did this? When the forceful dominance he was displaying was the stuff of her fantasies?

"Never deny me again." His hand gripped her wrists, pulled her arms back and secured them above her head as he stared down at her.

The position lifted her breasts, made them appear fuller, more alluring. Her nipples pressed against the blouse where her jacket had fallen open, as the soft lace of her bra showed clearly through the pale material.

"God, I want to feel your nipple in my mouth." The words sent a punch of sensation straight to her womb. "If I touch you with my mouth, with my tongue, everything you don't want is going to come crashing down on you. You know that, don't you, Rachel?"

She knew it, and still, the sudden ache for it was almost more than she could bear.

"Touch me," he groaned. "Just once." He brought her hands to his chest. "I swear to God I'll control it. Just once."

Jonas found he wasn't above begging. He'd spent a lifetime in those fucking labs and never begged for anything, but now, he would go to his knees for a single touch from the delicate hands pressing against his shirt.

"This is dangerous," she whispered.

"Not touching me is more dangerous," he snarled. "Do it, damn you. You're killing me."

The need for it was ripping him apart.

Slowly, staring up at him, her eyes locked to his, she slid her fingers to the buttons of his shirt and slowly undid them.

She surprised him. He could feel the need in her, smell it. She wasn't trying to hide it. He hadn't expected her to actually touch him, but there was no doubt she was going to do just that.

The only question was, could he survive it?

As she spread the edges of his shirt apart with deliberate slowness, Jonas had to fight just to breathe as her fingertips raked over his hairless chest.

The fine hairs that covered his body lifted to her fingertips as a ragged groan tore from his body. Just the tips of her fingers were like flames as they stroked over the flexing muscles, rubbed, caressed, rasped his flesh with her small nails.

Jonas felt his claws sink into the leather of the seat by her shoulders. Never had he lost such control. Only during moments of rage did the lethally sharp bonelike matter flex from beneath his flesh.

But never had he known such pleasure, or need, either. It was burning inside him, stealing control, making him so hungry for her kiss that he had to clench his teeth to keep from begging for it as well.

"Your flesh is tough," she whispered as her fingertips rubbed against his pectoral muscles.

"Yours is like silk." And he wasn't even touching her. He knew what it would feel like, sensed it from the touch of her hands.

"Jonas, this is so very dangerous." Her voice was husky, filled with arousal.

Shifting his hips, he moved until he was pushing her legs apart, her skirt rising, allowing him to slide into place. Only the clothing they wore separated him from the sweet, wet flesh of her pussy.

"Shh," he soothed. "No danger here, baby. Just touch me. Just for a minute."

Her fingers curled against his chest, two little nails scraping over the flat, round disc of one nipple.

His hips jerked, instinct rushing through him as he fought to bury his cock inside her.

The gasp of her breath as the hard, covered flesh of his dick raked against her clit was nearly his undoing.

"Can I taste you?" The question had pure pleasure exploding through his mind. "Just once."

She wanted. He could smell the want pouring from her, a want he had promised he wouldn't take advantage of.

"Taste me," he whispered. Hell, he had no idea if it would hurt or not. There had been instances that even the tiny hairs on a Breed's body contained minute amounts of the mating hormone. But it was rare. So rare.

Her head lifted to him as he bent to her, expecting to feel the touch of her lips on his chest. Instead, her head lifted farther, and he felt the stroke of her tongue against his neck, the rasp of her teeth.

Goddamn. He was going to melt. Fire raced along his body, tore through his balls and melted his brain. Impulse and instinct were the only things left. He had enough thought process left to thank God that his animal instincts had enough honor to not force the mating heat on her.

"Cinnamon," she whispered. "You taste like cinnamon and cloves, Jonas."

"God. No." He tore himself from her.

Jerking back, he forced himself to his own seat, his head falling back as he ran his hands through his hair and fought for control. Just a little control, enough to keep himself from taking what he so, so desperately wanted.

"What, Breeds aren't allowed to taste like cinnamon and cloves?" There was an edge of frustrated amusement, almost playfulness, to her voice.

Jonas breathed in roughly. "That mating hormone: It tastes like cinnamon and cloves."

"Merinus said it tasted like a rainstorm." Confusion filled her voice as he heard her sitting up.

"Merinus has a big mouth," he muttered as he felt the claws slowly retract and control return by minute increments. "It's different sometimes. It's according to the Breed."

"So Callan is stormy and you're hot?" That was definite amusement. Damn her, she was laughing about it when he felt as though he were going to explode.

"Or something." Lifting his head, he stared into her laughter-filled green eyes.

"Just think of the tabloid stories I could sell with this." Her brows wagged playfully. "Bureau director tastes of cinnamon and cloves, Feline Breed leader tastes of water and sulfur. What surprises will the Breeds come up with next?"

"You have no idea," he growled.

"Tell me, Jonas, do you think if we ever get around to having sex that you'll do the barb thing, or do you think you can convince it to stay hidden a time or two, just until I decide if I want to actually experience it?"

Someone seriously needed to instruct Merinus on the value of keeping Breed secrets *secret*.

"I don't think it works quite that way," he groaned, torn between amusement and frustration. Damn, where had his ice princess gone? The mischievous imp staring back at him now was going to make him crazy.

"Ah well, too bad. That barb thing sounds rather intimidating to me." Straightening her skirt, she licked her lips, her expression shifting as though some taste there pleased her.

Damn, if he actually had the chance to taste her, he would do more than relish it. His tongue would be buried so deep inside her pussy that she wouldn't know where she ended and he began.

As for the "barb thing," as she called it, he had to admit he was looking forward to it. The whispers he'd heard of the pleasure it induced made it sound like a sexual nirvana. A pleasure that radiated to every cell of the body and left a Breed shaking and begging for more.

Blowing out another hard breath, he narrowed his eyes and watched as Rachel licked her lips again. Her nipples were still hard and the sweet scent of her pussy still infused the air, just as the darker, richer sent of her arousal tormented his already starving senses.

She was his buffet, and he was starving for her.

Pulling the electronic pad free of its case, Rachel frowned as she used the stylus to pull something up on the pad's face.

Her forehead tightened as she began to read.

"I need to skip this party tonight," she murmured as though it didn't matter to her either way. "We have information coming in from China concerning several companies there that Brandenmore and Ingalls have contacted. They suspect they've sent in genetic information to those companies. I want to follow the trail."

"Forget it. Put Brim on the trail; his contacts there are more extensive and he has the time for it. You don't."

He could almost feel her frustration now. He knew exactly why she was trying so desperately to get out of that party. She had obviously brought one of her toys with her and intended to use it.

That wasn't going to happen. He smiled at her, one of those slow, easy smiles that he knew her response to. It came instantly. Suspicion darkened her green eyes as they narrowed and her lips thinned in irritation.

Jonas leaned forward slowly. "Do you really think I'm going to allow you the chance to achieve release without me? Consider me your personal shadow."

Her lips parted as pearly teeth tightened in a charming little grimace.

"That's not fair, Jonas. You can find release without making a sound," she pouted.

"Can I?" He leaned back, wondering why Merinus hadn't apprised Rachel of this particular drawback of mating heat. "It does a male in heat no good to attempt to masturbate, sweetheart. It only makes the need worse."

She blinked back at him. "You're lying."

"Call Merinus and ask her about it." He snorted. "She hasn't been able to keep her mouth shut about anything else."

She crossed her legs, drawing his gaze to her slender thighs silhouetted beneath the short skirt she wore. "Merinus really didn't say much. She simply didn't answer specific questions."

She was lying through her teeth.

Jonas shook his head slowly. "Don't try that lie with any other Breed," he advised her. "As sweet as your lies smell, they're still lies."

And that cute little smile peeked through once again. It was impish, filled with warmth, and it threatened to drown him in his own fucking need. Damn, he needed her.

"We're here." The driver's voice came through the intercom between the two sections.

"Pull into the main entrance," Jonas ordered as he pressed the button to activate the speaker beside him. "Mordecai and Rule should be waiting for us."

"I see them at the entrance now," he was told.

The limo drew to a stop in front of the two-story brick town house. The building had been donated to the Breeds by an eccentric older couple who had lost their son when he was killed by Council soldiers in the Breed rescues.

"I assume you've had a room reserved for me at the nearest hotel?" she asked sweetly, though the chill underlying her tone was readily apparent.

"I guess I didn't," he assured her as Mordecai opened the door and stepped to the side. "Let's go, Rachel. We have little time before the party tonight. Your things are in the guest room waiting for you."

"As is the hairdresser the Prima ordered," Mordecai informed them as he glanced inside. "She called me herself to verify the arrival."

"I don't like this," Rachel muttered as she cast Jonas a highly suspicious look.

"What am I going to do with all the damned Enforcers assigned here?" Jonas asked her as he helped her from the limo. "The place is like Fort Knox when I'm here."

That wasn't necessarily the truth, but it sounded damned good, Jonas thought as he tugged at her hand and pulled her up the stone steps to the wide double doors that Lawe guarded diligently.

"Somehow, I'm not reassured," she told him as they stepped into the house.

"Somehow, I didn't think you would be." He chuckled as his hand settled at the small of her back while he guided her to the curved staircase. "Come along, sweetheart. I'll show you to your room, then we'll see about making it through that boring-assed party you thought I should attend."

"The party is hosted by Drey Hampton, a personal friend of Horace Engalls and one of the Breeds' more secretive contacts," she reminded him. "This was the only way he could get information to us that we were hoping he'd learn concerning Brandenmore's plans once he was out of custody on bail."

"Refresh my memory," Jonas drawled mockingly. "Didn't we warn the judge he would run?"

"Just as you were warned that the judge was going to set bail despite the arguments presented by the prosecutor," Rachel reminded him.

"He argued really hard too, didn't he?" Jonas growled as he opened the door to her bedroom.

The prosecutor had more or less sat back and allowed Brandenmore's attorneys to run the courtroom. It was sickening how many times Brandenmore had easily bought favor since his arrest. The judge was ready to throw the case out before Jonas had sent the paperwork in for his extradition and re-arrest based on Brandenmore's threats against Rachel and Amber.

"I warned you that you needed to check more diligently into his background," Rachel pointed out as she stepped into the bedroom.

She had argued with Jonas over this one. Jonas believed the prosecutor would fight with everything he had to make good on the promises given the Breeds when several of them had made hefty donations to his political campaign.

They had learned better quickly.

"I really need to check out the information coming in myself, Jonas." She sighed as she turned to face him, her nervousness gaining in strength the closer they got to the bed.

"Forget it. I'll contact Brim in a few minutes and put him on it. We have a party to attend, and hopefully Drey has indeed managed to pull in some information for us. Now get dressed. I'll see you before we leave for the party."

Rachel chewed at her lip as he left the room, and restrained the need to stomp her foot.

She didn't want to go to that damned party. Not only were there spies, killers and general troublemakers who attended these soirees, but the very ambassador who had tried to force her to whore herself to return home would be in attendance as well. If that wasn't a recipe for disaster, then she didn't know what was.

And if those obstacles weren't enough, there was the fact that she was able to have fun with Jonas now. Perhaps Merinus should have warned him that once she felt her job was secure she could make his life hell? Or perhaps Kane should have warned him?

It wasn't that she caused trouble, or deliberately set out to make anyone crazy. It was simply that she did have rather a smart mouth. She could be quiet and unemotional, or she could be fun and playful. There was no in-between.

And it seemed there was no getting out of this party either. She would definitely have to make Jonas pay for this one.

At least she was able to pander to the girly part of her when she had to attend these events. Merinus always ensured that the Bureau sprang for some really pretty dresses.

The one awaiting her was an evening gown of sapphire silk overlaying a gorgeous slip of silver lace. The skirt was slit to the knee, allowing the lace to spill from the side to the toes of sapphire heels. The bodice was held by narrow straps and cupped her breasts like a lover's hands. It was the most exquisite dress by far that Merinus had provided. With the dress were silver stockings shot with sapphire thread and banded with delicate lace at the thigh.

She had never worn a dress so lusciously feminine in her life. It was enough to make her want to attend that party.

Lifting her hand, she nibbled at her thumbnail as she wondered exactly how she was going to navigate the tricky waters that Ambassador David Slussburg was certain to churn up.

The man was a prick, and on top of it, he hated Breeds. He hated them to the point that he had on many occasions commented that the world would be better off if the Breeds were dead.

He was the type of man who wouldn't care a bit to be snide and mocking in Jonas's presence, and Rachel had a feeling Jonas would be less than charitable once Slussburg got started.

She only hoped she herself could be tactful enough to steer Jonas well clear of him.

CHAPTER 7

Jonas scented Rachel's nervousness as she paused at the top of the stairs, staring down at where he waited below. Turning, he had to forcibly control the animal growl that rose in his throat and the need that had claws threatening to slide from the tips of his fingers.

Had he ever seen anything, or anyone, so damned beautiful? Jonas was certain he hadn't, just as he was damned certain there was no way he was going to make it through the night without taking her.

Hell, he wasn't going to make it from the house before he touched her. He could touch her in reasonable safety, he told himself. But that sounded rather lame even to him. There was no way to truly ensure that the mating hormone didn't affect even the fine hairs that covered his body.

It was damned certainly affecting his tongue. The glands were so swollen they were painful, the taste of cinnamon and cloves filling his senses and reminding him how easy it would be to infuse her with the same arousal tearing through him.

Not that she wasn't aroused. She was. Just not insanely aroused. She wasn't in mating heat, and that was where he wanted her. Now.

Before he realized what he was doing, his foot was on the top step, his intentions clear in his mind. To kiss her. To taste her. To fill her with the hormone tearing through him, demanding sex, touch, taste. Possession.

"Merinus outdid herself." She touched the skirt of the dress self-consciously as she watched him. "The dress is exquisite."

Merinus hadn't arranged for the dress; he had. Jonas kept that information to himself for the time being and watched, waited, as she made her way down the curving staircase.

The dress cupped and hugged her upper body like a possessive lover. The skirt flowed over her legs, lace spilling down the side, the glittering blue threads sparkling through the material.

He wondered if the stockings looked as pretty on her as they had on the mannequin the dressmaker had kept in her shop.

"Are we ready to go?" she asked as she secured the fur-lined silk wrap that went with the dress.

"Not yet." If he didn't touch her, he was going to die. He was going to do something he knew they didn't want to face when the cold light of morning revealed itself.

But did he have the strength to pull back from just a touch.

"Come with me." He didn't touch her, not yet. Turning on his heel, he strode along the short foyer to the receiving room, waited until she entered, then closed the doors securely and locked them.

"Jonas?" The concern in her tone sliced through him as he turned back to her.

Before he could stop himself, and God knew he wished he could have stopped himself, he gripped her shoulders, spun her around and pressed her against the door.

Her soft cry was lost as his lips parted and his teeth gripped the side of her neck in sensual warning. The animal knew what was going on with the man. It knew he was fighting a battle he was going to lose, and he couldn't stop himself.

"Jonas!" Shock and arousal fueled the needy, breathless sound of her voice.

Gripping her hips, Jonas held her still as his knees dipped, his hips pressing against her rear as a harsh growl tore from his throat.

When she didn't fight, when he smelled the soft flavor of feminine juices spilling from the luscious heat of her pussy, his teeth slowly released her.

His fingers flexed on her hips as he rubbed his cock against the cleft of her rear, rotated his hips and imagined the pure ecstasy of sinking inside her.

"Why are you doing this?" she whispered.

"You're my mate." His voice didn't sound like his own. It was rougher, harder, more primal. "Do you know how hard it is not to take you?"

Pressing his lips against the vulnerable crook of her neck, Jonas inhaled the scent of her, tasted her with his tongue, and swore it would go no further.

"I want to taste you," he groaned. "Just one kiss, but I know what just one kiss will do. It will destroy both of us."

Her fingers were flexing against the door, her nails scraping the wood as his hands slid lower, bunched the fabric of her gown and began drawing it upward.

His control was splintering. He could feel it. Every shred of strength he possessed was centered on holding her to him, keeping her locked in place while he touched.

His cock was throbbing as he rolled his hips against the firm muscles of her ass. He imagined pushing her dress higher, tearing her panties from her, spreading the smooth globes and watching as he pressed his cock inside the heated depths of her pussy from behind.

She would be tight.

His fingers met the smooth flesh of her thigh, the material of her skirt and lacy underskirt flowing over his arm as he let them stroke the silken flesh until he worked his way to the tender skin at the crease of her thigh.

"Jonas, if you don't stop now, you won't—" Her soft protest ended with a gasp as the pads of his fingers raked over the silk covering the humid heat of her pussy.

"I'll stop." But he wasn't so certain.

Jonas could feel the hunger rising now, the hormone spilling harder from the glands beneath his tongue and heating his senses with the need to share it.

"Tonight, I have to walk into another of those parties, and I have to see other men watching you, smell their lust and their intent, and know you aren't yet my mate."

"I'm not your mate, period," she argued breathlessly.

His lips peeled back in a furious snarl.

She was denying him, again.

His fingers slipped beneath the elastic leg of her panties and before she could protest, two slid through the slick, hot juices hidden between the soft folds of flesh there.

She was wet. Hot. She was his mate, whether she wanted to admit it or not. *His mate.* God help him, but he didn't know if he could let her go.

◆   ◆   ◆

Pleasure. She had never known so much pleasure in a man's arms in her life.

Rachel fought not to arch against the touch of Jonas's fingers between her thighs, the callused pads rubbing, stroking.

"Oh, God." The words slipped from her lips as heat swirled through her body, built and wrapped around her senses. "Jonas, we have to stop."

He had to stop. She couldn't break away from him, even if he allowed it. All she could do was stand there, her nails raking against the wood of the door as her legs parted further for his touch.

"I want inside you." His voice was so deep, so rough now. "You're so sweet, Rachel, so hot. The thought of how tight and slick you'll fit around my cock steals my breath."

Hearing it stole her breath.

Rachel's head fell back against his shoulder as sensual weakness assailed her. The dangerous, overwhelming sensation of vulnerability washed through her, making her feel feminine, more sexy than she had ever felt in her life.

Jonas did that to her. Whether he was touching her or not, he had the ability to make her feel too soft, too female.

"There, my Rachel," he crooned, a rough, rasping sound that sent shivers of arousal racing over her as his fingers circled her clit. "Just rest against me, baby. I'll take care of everything."

Everything was sliding his fingers lower, pressing two together, and with blunted force thrusting into the narrow, tight confines of her vagina.

"Oh God, Jonas." The words tore from her throat. "It's too good. It's too good."

She was so close. She could feel her orgasm raking at her womb, pounding at her clit. Flames were licking across her flesh, centering between her thighs and causing her abdomen to clench with violent pleasure.

"Think how much better it could be." His fingers bent just enough to caress, to stroke previously hidden nerve endings and tender tissue. "Think, Rachel. I could be fucking you, filling you with every inch of my hard cock instead of my fingers."

She should have been insulted. She had never allowed Amber's father, Devon, to talk so explicitly to her. She had never enjoyed it—until she heard Jonas do it.

Fighting to breathe, she turned her head, her lips glancing the hard line of his jaw as he continued to thrust slow and easy inside her. His fingers caressed with knowing strokes, rubbing, easing through the clenched muscles of her pussy as his other arm wrapped beneath her breasts to keep her on her feet.

Her lips parted, pressing to his jaw, her tongue stroking over his sweat-dampened flesh to taste a hint of cinnamon and cloves. Her hands held on to his wrist, her fingertips rubbing against his flesh in concert with the strokes of his fingers inside her pussy.

"You make me regret," he groaned as he lowered his head, allowing her lips to move as close as the corner of his lips.

"Don't regret, Jonas." Her voice was broken, breathless from pleasure. "You have nothing to regret."

He was a man. A man who had broken rules, one who had done things that perhaps were not even legal. But he had done what he had thought had to be done to save himself as well as his species.

He was a man whose touch was pure pleasure, pure heat. A man who held her with strength and yet a gentleness in the face of overwhelming, animalistic pleasure. And still, he was in control. She could feel him fighting for it. Feel the struggle for it. The intent.

Her body tensed, drawn tight as the pleasure built inside her. His fingers thrust deeper, stroked, firmed, fucked her with increasing speed until she began to pant for air, for mercy.

Her nails bit into his arm, her lips parted against his cheek as a wail began to tear from her.

Rapture exploded inside her. Blood pounded, boiled, erupted. Sensation raged, flaming through nerve endings, racing across her flesh, striking her clit, then deep inside her pussy at the same time, and throwing her into a cataclysm of such astounding pleasure that she completely lost her breath.

Flaming fingers raced up her spine and back again. Her muscles trembled as sensation tore across it and her entire body became a writhing mass of complete ecstasy.

"You're mine, Rachel." The growl at her ear was a snarl, a hard, primal vibration of sound that in no way resembled Jonas's voice. "Remember that when their eyes flame with lust, when the scent of their hunger is like a disease filling the fucking room. Damn you, remember you're mine."

She shook her head desperately and could have sworn she heard him say with utmost softness, "I belong to you."

✦ C H A P T E R 8 ✦

The party for the ambassador to Switzerland was everything Jonas had known it would be: completely and utterly fucking boring and filled with the scent of male lust. There wasn't a second to escape the overwhelming male hunger each time their eyes centered on Rachel.

She was like a breath of fresh air in the room, an oasis of color and sweet ease they couldn't resist. A buffet of sensual pleasure, which they were greedy to partake of.

In other words, a typical D.C. party. Plenty of booze, high-calorie food—there wasn't a steak to be seen or smelled—and enough false joviality to make a saint curse. Enough attention given to his mate that he was on the edge of violence at any given moment.

Drey Hampton's ballroom was filled to capacity. The double French doors on the garden side were thrown open; the band on the patio was smooth and unobtrusive, but it wouldn't have mattered. The noise level inside the ballroom would have drowned the music out anyway.

And then there was the ambassador to Switzerland, David

Slussburg—a fine piece of work. What the hell had ever possessed the president—who seemed to be a fairly astute individual—to assign this man as ambassador to *any* country, Jonas couldn't figure out. He was a cesspool of greed, deceit and lust. Beady eyes, a vain, pinched expression filled with calculating interest.

"So tell me, Wyatt, has Racert managed to convince you of the value of joining some of his pet projects?" Slussburg gave a false little laugh as he asked the question. "Now's the time to get in."

"Actually, he hasn't, Slussburg," Jonas replied smoothly, watching as the ambassador's eyes narrowed at the obvious insult of using his last name only. "Racert and I have a difference of opinion on what constitutes a worthy cause."

He felt Rachel shift nervously beside him.

Glancing over, he nearly caught his breath at the sight of her once again. That damned gown tempted a man in ways that should be illegal. The fall of lace gave the slightest hint of stockings shot with sapphires, while the bodice cupped and hugged what had to be perfect breasts. He thought he might have even glimpsed the hardened buds of her nipples beneath it after they had danced earlier.

He knew her nipples had been hard in his receiving room earlier that evening. Her nipples had been hard, her pussy so tight and hot it had clamped on his fingers like a hungry little mouth.

"That's not a wise move, Wyatt." Slussburg lowered his voice as he moved closer, the scent of greed, lust and hatred pouring from him as he interrupted the pleasant thoughts Jonas had been building in his mind. "Senator Racert could be the wrong enemy to make."

Jonas smiled, careful to ensure that he flashed the incisors at one side of his mouth. For some reason, the sight of those healthy, primal teeth had the ability to fill most men with a strong measure of trepidation.

"Wisdom doesn't seem to be my forte then, does it?" Jonas kept his smile tight, hard.

Slussburg wasn't to be outdone. He turned his gaze to Rachel, the lust-filled scent that emanated from him increasing as his gaze raked over her.

"It seems it's not," he murmured. "I hear our lovely Ms. Broen is learning that as well. Rumor has it that gas explosion in her home was a strike against you. Now you're not just endangering your own life, but your employees' as well."

"Jonas, I see Senator Tyler." Rachel's tone was firm at his side as he and Slussburg locked gazes. "He needed to speak to you tonight."

Tyler was the Breeds' go-between with Drey Hampton, the billionaire whose fingers were tipped ever so tentatively into the Genetics Council sewer due to his family's past relationship with them.

"Ah, Rachel, always the tactful little soul." Slussburg all but sneered in her face, causing the beast in Jonas to awaken with predatory interest.

"As always, Ambassador." Rachel nodded her head regally before turning and gazing up at Jonas. "Are you ready?"

"As you command, my dear." He nodded, though he wanted nothing more than to rip out the ambassador's throat.

Moving through the crowd, Jonas could sense the relief pouring off Rachel in waves. She didn't like being around the ambassador, and Jonas had a feeling he suspected why.

"What did he do to you?" He leaned close and whispered the words at her ear.

"Who?" The tension in her body assured him that she knew exactly who he was talking about.

"I can go back there, lure him outside and rip his fucking tongue out," he murmured in her ear. "Or you can simply tell me what I want to know."

And he had no problem whatsoever doing exactly that. Or at least letting them both believe he would. He was fairly good at that.

"He's an ass," she said quietly. "We've had some run-ins."

And how very tactful she was.

"Did he touch you?" His hand tightened at the small of her

back. If the bastard dared to have touched her, then he was dead. It was that simple.

"He didn't touch me." And she wasn't lying, but there was more to the story and he knew it. Unfortunately, he wasn't going to get the answers he needed at the moment, and he knew it.

"We're going to discuss this later," he warned her. And she would tell him the truth. One way or the other.

"There's nothing to discuss, Mr. Wyatt." Prim and proper, her cool little voice pricked at his anger, as well as his lust.

"We'll see about that." His hand tightened at her hip as they approached Senator Samuel Tyler, Merinus Lyons's uncle and a career senator who had stood by the Breeds from the day he learned of their existence.

Standing with him was Drey Hampton, the current head of the Hampton family and business empire, which stretched across three nations. Tall, blond, with penetrating dark blue eyes and cynically brooding features. Seth Lawrence and his Breed mated wife, Dawn, were part of the group. Dawn had come a long way from the frightened, scared Cougar Breed Jonas had first met eleven years before. Most of that change could be attributed to Seth and his patience and unending love for the woman who had spent ten years denying the bond between them.

Dawn was the only known Breed in the group besides Jonas. There was the son of an African industrialist, Dane Vanderale and his assistant, Rye Desalvo. The Vanderales easily rivaled, if not outpaced, the Hamptons completely in wealth, as well as multinational power. Among the Breed opponents who were a part of the group were Senator Racert, General James Wayne and the man known as the leading contender in the next presidential race, Senator Aaron Bressfield.

The most elite and politically powerful members of society were in attendance, which was befitting any party Drey Hampton threw. This one small group represented both the most powerful support for and against Breed freedom as it stood at that moment.

"Ms. Broen, how charming to see you," Drey greeted Rachel with a quick, brooding charm that instantly set Jonas's hackles to rising. Damn, if he didn't take her soon, then he was going to begin slicing and dicing would-be suitors like the hapless little bastards they were. Drey included.

"Good evening, Mr. Hampton." Cool, yet charming. Rachel showed no personal interest in Drey; there was no scent of sexual allure, no sense of deception or of intent.

Okay, he might allow the bastard to live a little longer.

A thread of amusement lingered in his senses. Strange, never before had he been jealous over another woman. Never before had he thought to kill simply because she may have had the smallest bit of interest in another man. Hell, he'd never given a damn either way before.

"Would you like to dance, Ms. Broen?" Drey's invitation caused Jonas to turn his head sharply, his lips parting on a growl.

"No, thank you, Mr. Hampton," she declined graciously as Jonas felt her fingers against his arm. "It seems my dance card is full tonight."

Possession. Intent. It was there now, directed at him.

Jonas clenched his teeth involuntarily against the surge of need that tightened his balls and throbbed through his cock.

The glands beneath his tongue began to pulse. Emotion fueled the powerful hormone as it spilled to his mouth and entered his system like a tidal wave.

"I would appreciate it if you would excuse me for a moment." She nodded to the other men. "I need to go to the ladies' room."

"I think I'll accompany you," Dawn decided after the quick, commanding look Jonas shot her.

She might be the mated wife of one of the most powerful men in the United States, but she was also still an Enforcer, and under his jurisdiction if she were in the area at the time.

Jonas ignored the quick frown her husband shot him. If worse came to worst and Seth decided to initiate a confrontation, Jonas was confident he could take him. The look he shot the other man was full of that confidence as well.

For the briefest moment, Jonas wondered if he was actually beginning to lose the grip he once had on himself. Once, he would have been actively pursuing a manipulation, a game of words, any way possible to show the bastards here that they weren't better than he, as they believed.

Instead, his mind was on one thing and one thing only: the information Drey Hampton might have, and the difficult job of retrieving Phillip Brandenmore from Iran.

"Gentlemen, if you'll excuse myself and Mr. Wyatt, I believe we have some business to discuss with Seth," Senator Tyler announced as the women moved away. Turning to Jonas, he gave him a telling look. "Seth has an interesting proposition, Jonas. I believe you should hear it."

In other words, Senator Tyler had information he needed to impart. If Drey had circumvented their normal information routes for such events, then there was a problem.

Jonas nodded to Drey cordially before turning and moving to the opposite end of the ballroom and the short, narrow flight of stairs that led to what was supposed to be a secured meeting room.

Jonas rather doubted anything here was too secure. Drey might try like hell to keep his secrets, but that didn't mean he would actually triumph.

◆　　◆　　◆

Rachel entered the ladies' room with Dawn following close behind. Pushing into the powder room designed for several women to use at once—something she rarely saw in a private residence—she wasn't surprised to find Dawn close at her heels.

"Jonas is a bit of a slave driver, isn't he?" Dawn stated as she moved to the wide, tall mirrors and opened her purse to repair her makeup.

Tension didn't often go well with makeup. A fine sheen of perspiration appeared on Rachel's forehead and temples, making repairs imperative.

"He can definitely be a little tense," Dawn murmured as she propped herself against a wall and met Rachel's gaze in the mirror. "But he generally knows what he's doing."

Like sending Dawn to "protect" Rachel in the ladies' room? She'd been to Drey Hampton's parties more than once, and she had yet to run into a rabid human or Breed in the ladies' room.

Finishing with her makeup, Rachel washed her hands, dried them, applied a fresh layer of lotion, then turned to the Breed female.

"He's making me a nervous wreck," she muttered. "Have a talk with him or something." She knew better; he might well return to the subject concerning the ambassador.

"Yeah, I'll get right on that." Dawn gave a short, amused laugh as her brown eyes lit with laughter.

Turning to the mirror, the other woman straightened several shoulder-length golden brown strands of hair that had fallen free of their diamond-studded clip before turning back to Rachel. "Ready?"

"As ready as I'll ever be." Rachel sighed.

Dawn Lawrence gave her a small, seemingly understanding smile before moving ahead and opening the door.

Two women were waiting in the hall, one a small brunette, the wife of a congressman, the other a matronly, pinched-faced middle-aged widow of a former governor. But the women took one look at Dawn, knew her for who she was, and rather than extending a cordial or even polite greeting, turned their noses up and turned away from her. It didn't matter who they were, what they were, they were extending to the Breeds the same disrespect as others whose family members or friends had invested funds in the Genetics Council did. Some had known what the Council was, some hadn't. Yet still, their associates and family members carried the same hatred and disrespect for life that those involved had shown.

Dawn acted as though she hadn't seen the display, but rather walked regally back toward the ballroom.

It happened a lot, Rachel knew. The Breeds were either loved or hated; there was very little in between. But here, amid the glitter, political intrigue, infighting and deals made and broken, she would have thought attitudes would have at least carried a polite face.

As though she had sensed Rachel's thoughts, Dawn began speaking as they reentered the ballroom. "Those two have worked diligently to attempt to ensure that the Breeds go back to the labs. Some people seem to have an instinct for the animals that have been unleashed, wouldn't you say?" The edge of cynicism in her voice was at odds with the happiness Rachel glimpsed in her eyes whenever she was with her husband.

"Humans fear change, or anyone different from themselves," Rachel said as they moved along a path that Dawn seemed to have an instinct for.

The guests they passed smiled and many attempted to engage the two women in conversation, which Dawn effectively fielded.

There was an additional tension filling her body as she began to move through the crowd with an added firmness to her step. Even dressed in a ball gown and heels, Dawn seemed to exude command as her head suddenly lifted, her nostrils flaring.

Rachel was surprised that she noticed the signs of sudden, sharp instinct within the other woman. Something had happened, something that now had Dawn moving through the crowd like a hot knife through butter.

Not that the other guests seemed to be aware of it. What they saw was the woman, sensual and yet predatory, drawing them in even as some human survival instinct warned them to keep away.

The path Dawn was clearing had the women heading straight for the wide double doors that led to the large marble foyer and from there, the front entrance to the house.

"Jonas is waiting on us." Dawn turned back to her briefly before continuing to the exit. "He, Seth and the Enforcers who were stationed outside are in the foyer."

"Ms. Broen, leaving so soon?" Rachel would have ignored Ambassador Slussburg's smooth, sneering little voice if he hadn't suddenly gripped her arm and pulled her to a stop.

Just that quickly, Dawn turned.

Her expression remained calm and poised, but the dark brown of her gaze seemed to flicker with flames as her fingers clamped over Slussburg's arm.

"Ambassador Slussburg," she stated, her voice cordial, even as it rumbled with danger. "I suggest you release her."

His hand was lifting slowly, his fingers uncurling from her arm when Rachel felt the hairs at the back of her neck lift in primal warning. Hell, she wasn't even a Breed and she could feel the violence suddenly swirling in the air.

Her head swung around, and there he was. Silver eyes almost neon, the black pupils nearly obliterated by the swirls of mercury as he stalked toward them.

"Let's go." Dawn gripped her wrist and pulled her quickly from the ambassador. When they were far enough away not to be overheard, Dawn murmured, "Get control of him, Rachel, no matter what it takes. He's lost logic. That's the animal you see, and only you can control it now. We don't have time for this. Trust me."

Rachel's heart was pounding out of control. She had seen the rage in the ambassador's gaze, had felt the pure, violent fury pouring from him as he stopped her. Her arm would hold bruises later from his hold.

That hadn't been frightening. She hadn't been scared of the ambassador, but the man striding toward her now, his gaze reflecting death and pure fury, terrified her.

In a second's insight, Rachel realized that none of the guests around them realized that the man striding through their crowded throng was an animal prepared to kill. That the wrong word, the wrong look, the wrong touch could unleash the very killer they all feared in the darkness of the night.

"No!" She stepped in front of him, unafraid for herself, terrified for the ambassador and anyone who would try to save him or to get in Jonas's way.

He paused, then attempted to move around her.

She couldn't reach him for a kiss; even with high heels she went only to his shoulders. She did the next-best thing. She grabbed his wrist as he tried to pass, lifted it and sank her teeth into his flesh for a hard, quick bite.

That stopped him.

Turning, he stared down at her, the pupil enlarging just enough in his gaze that Rachel could pray there was an edge of sanity returning.

It took precious moments. The prints of her teeth were in his hard wrist; the taste of him lingered against her tongue as she fought to hold him back, to keep the animal inside him leashed.

"We will discuss this." There was more than a rumble in his voice now, there was pure intent.

But sanity was there.

Holding her arm, he turned away from the ambassador and led her quickly to the wide front doors that looked out on the circular drive.

There were six Enforcers standing at the ready, weapons held as he rushed her from the house and into the waiting limo. Something had happened, there was no doubt about that. There was a sense of imminent danger surrounding the Breeds, their hard gazes and savage expressions reflecting a heightened sense of awareness.

Dawn followed, Seth at her side, until the doors closed behind them and the vehicles were speeding away from the Hampton mansion.

Curving mountain roads were the wrong place for the constant switches the limo made in position with the other two that had pulled out behind them. The six Enforcers as well as two drivers in the other two vehicles were driving like kamikaze racers heading for destiny.

"What's going on?" Rachel could feel her throat tightening with fear. "Is Amber okay?"

"Amber's fine. She's currently in a secured room reserved for Sanctuary's children and protected by the Enforcers assigned to give their lives if necessary. The mated parents are with them and looking over them as well as Leo and his entourage of cutthroats."

If those precautions were being taken, whatever had happened was something with the potential to endanger the mated couples as well as the ruling cabinet.

She watched wide-eyed as Dawn and Seth worked on a personal slimline laptop, and Dawn spoke urgently, her tone lowered, into a sat phone.

"Sanctuary was attacked about an hour ago," Jonas stated. "Callan and Merinus's son, David, was nearly kidnapped while on a pre-training exercise with Tanner Reynolds; my sister, Harmony; and her husband, Lance Jacobs. Lance was wounded, which compounded a chest wound he received nearly a year ago."

"The battle in New Mexico." Rachel nodded, fighting to remain calm. "He was shot in the chest."

Jonas nodded sharply. "He took a severe blow to the same area tonight. We have a team tracking the attackers now. I'll be joining them as soon as we arrive."

Rachel clenched her fists in her lap as she stared back at him. First, she had to face the danger to her daughter's life, and now the danger to Jonas. Through the months she had worked with him, he'd kept the more dangerous areas of his life hidden from her. Now there was no hiding it, and it brought to her the realization of how often his life, and the lives of the Breeds in general, were in danger.

"Is David all right?" she asked, knowing what it would do to Merinus if anything had happened to her son.

"Physically, he's fine," Jonas stated. "This is the second attack on the boy in the past two years, though. Each time, a friend has been harmed trying to save him. He's inconsolable."

And Jonas was nearly inconsolable himself.

Rachel stared into the live color of his eyes and saw subtle, agonizing flame. He cared for his sister and her husband, though she knew he often pretended otherwise.

Merinus had warned her that Jonas was cold and hard, and if he didn't thaw, if he didn't relent in the constant games he played with his Enforcers, then someone would end up killing him. That or the Breed cabinet would do something themselves to put a stop to his behavior.

Rachel had never seen cold or hard in Jonas, though. She had never seen a manipulator. He was calculating, no doubt; he had to be to survive. He had to be, to maneuver the people he loved into the lives he knew would benefit them.

He was a lover, a leader. He was a man who used the training he was given—to kill, to destroy, to sabotage—to build and to nurture instead.

He just had a rather unique way of doing it in an ass backward sort of way though.

"Jackal has landed the heli-jet one mile from our location," Dawn stated, her voice calm, though her dark brown eyes raged with anger. "We also have two pickups filled with armed assailants bearing down on us. Prepare to run."

Jonas snarled.

CHAPTER 9

The three limos pulled into the clearing, sliding to a stop within sight of the heli-jet. From the backseat, Rachel swallowed tightly at the sight of the armed men standing outside the pickups that were parked in a diagonal angle to the superfast helicopter assigned to Sanctuary.

Dressed in jeans, T-shirts and dark masks, they held their weapons in a relaxed, nonthreatening manner, but there was a tension there that assured Rachel that the nonthreatening part could change in an instant.

There was also a familiarity to them. Rachel leaned forward, staring out the window, her gaze narrowed as she fought to pinpoint exactly what she recognized about the men.

"Jonas, a message just came through on the sat channel." Lawe turned in the driver's seat and stared back at Jonas. "They're refusing to identify themselves but they're saying the way is clear. They're here for security and we need to hurry because the real bad guys are only miles away with rocket launchers."

The Enforcers from the other two limos were moving

from the vehicles, surrounding the one they were in as the two Enforcers from the heli-jet joined them.

"We have a message to tell Rachel to giddy up and go." Jonas's gaze sliced to her as a gasp fell from her lips.

"It's Diana," she whispered, her eyes widening as she stared back at Jonas. "She left that code for me when she left, just after Amber was born. It's safe, Jonas. And that code means it's imperative we go now."

"We can't be certain." Jonas was checking the rifle he had jerked from a panel beneath the seat as Seth and Dawn followed suit.

"I can." Rachel jerked open the door and all but fell out, the heels she was wearing making it more difficult to move.

"Rachel!" For all his reflexes, Jonas managed only to grab the skirt of her dress.

"Let me go, Jonas!"

"Like hell." He was out of the limo, his weapon held ready as a single figure detached from the group.

A gloved hand reached up and peeled the mask off to reveal the delicate, if stony, features of her beloved sister's face. A face she feared daily she might never see again. The life of a female mercenary wasn't exactly an easy one, or one with any amount of security.

"Wyatt, get my sister the hell out of here now or I'll take her myself," Diana called out, her tone furious. She meant it. Diana was a protector, and she had decided early in life that her baby sister had to be protected.

"Fuck!" Jonas turned back to Seth and Dawn. "Go. Move."

He gripped Rachel's arm as she stared back at Diana.

"Come with us, Diana," she cried, her tone desperate as Jonas pulled her to the heli-jet.

Her sister stood still, her gaze narrowed in the bright lights cast by the limos and the heli-jet. She didn't move, nor did the six men standing behind her, their weapons held ready.

"Vehicles moving in," Jackal yelled out as the door slid open. "Sensors show firepower, Jonas. Let's fly."

Jonas all but threw her into the seat of the heli-jet as the others rushed in behind her, blocking her from calling out to her sister once again.

Her heart was racing, fear overwhelming her as she fought against Jonas.

"Diana!" She screamed out her sister's name as she glimpsed her racing—not for a pickup to escape in but for a defensible position to fire on the arriving attackers.

"Get her." She turned to Jonas, wild-eyed, terrified. Her sister was there because of her, to protect her. If something happened to her, Rachel didn't know if she could bear it. "Make her go with us."

"She'll blow my head off," Jonas snarled back at her, and even though she knew it was true, Rachel fought the need to beg him to do it. "If she wanted to be here with us, that's where she'd be, Rachel." Turning to Jackal, he gave the order to fly.

She hadn't seen her sister since Amber's birth. A few quick moments, and Diana had been gone again. What she did and why she did it, Rachel didn't know. All she knew was that whenever she was in trouble, no matter the trouble, Diana was there. There had been only a moment in their lives when she hadn't been there: the months Rachel had spent in Switzerland, fighting to try to get home, her passport stolen, her money depleted. Diana had been nowhere to be found, and Rachel had been alone.

The heli-jet lifted off, powerful jets kicking in and holding Rachel back in her seat as it turned and headed the short distance to Sanctuary.

"Diana's group is moving out with time to spare," Jackal called out. "Hell, Jonas, you need to recruit her."

"She would kill us all," Jonas muttered as the heli-jet streaked through the sky. "Contact Sanctuary; we're flying in. I want Alpha Team One ready to move."

"Alpha Team One assembled and ready," Jackal called back. "We have sporadic fire on the estate house. Vanderale Team Two has taken to the mountains. We have two prisoners, six enemy causalities, two Breed causalities and nearly three dozen wounded."

Rachel wrapped her arms around her stomach as information was reported. So many hurt or dead. In the years since the revelation of the Breeds' existence, they hadn't known a moment's peace or true safety.

Breathing in roughly, she tentatively laid her hand on Jonas's hard thigh. Tension held his body tight, invading every cell as he watched the screen of the small communication and information device an Enforcer had handed him.

Entering the secure code, Rachel watched as the black screen flickered, cleared, then showed the image of the Breed known as the Leo.

Gold eyes flamed with fury as he stared back. The two men had some uncannily similar features. It was rumored he was Jonas's father as well.

She didn't doubt it. Both men were arrogant and calculating enough to be fully related.

"Status," Jonas snapped.

"All secure," Leo snarled, strong, sharp incisors flashing at the sides of his mouth. "We still have a few of the bastards to pull in. The main strike escaped, though they left empty-handed."

"How is Lance?" Rachel could hear the concern, as well as the promise of retribution, in his voice.

Leo looked aside for a moment, his jaw clenching, before turning back. "Elizabeth and Ely have him. They're confident he's going to pull through, but he's unconscious now."

"Harmony?" Jonas's voice thickened with concern.

Leo's lips tightened in fury as his eyes blazed. "She's gone after them, Jonas. I couldn't stop her."

Rachel looked into Jonas's face and saw, for just a second, pure, naked fear and pain.

"I'll bring her home," he stated with chilling force. "My ETA is in five."

"Bring her home," Leo affirmed. "But if you'd left her

the hell alone, we wouldn't be worried about her, now would we?"

"No, we'd be mourning her."

Jonas didn't give the other man a chance to respond. The communication device flipped off before his hand clenched around it with enough force that the veins bulged in his hands.

"Harmony's fine." Rachel wanted to console him, wanted to ease the worry, though she knew that wasn't entirely possible.

His head jerked to her. "Harmony will bathe that mountain in blood if I don't rein her in," Jonas snorted. "We need at least one of those bastards left alive. She'll skin them all. She makes your sister look like the tooth fairy."

Rachel frowned. "My sister isn't that bad."

Jonas merely snorted again.

"If Harmony is that dangerous, then she'll be fine," she reassured him again, watching the clenching of his jaw as he fought to rein in whatever emotions were tearing him apart.

"I nearly lost her once." He turned back to her, their gazes meeting, locking as she read the worry in his. "She was on a fast track to suicide, and as much as Leo's family cared for her, they couldn't have stopped it."

"But you did?" She hadn't known this. Merinus had told her very little about Jonas's sister.

His smile was tight but victorious. "When I met her mate, there was a calm about him, a streak of pure peace that seemed to surround him. The second I looked into his eyes I felt my sister's salvation in him, though I swear to God I don't know how. When his cousin mated one of my Enforcers, I was able to use the blood and saliva samples we require for anyone working with Breeds, from him. They matched what I had acquired of Harmony's from the labs we were bred in. I gave her peace, and this makes twice someone has attempted to steal it from her."

Which meant someone was going to pay for it.

"Brandenmore?" she asked. "You think he's behind this?"

"I know he is," Jonas grunted as his hand lifted to rub at hers where it lay on his thigh. The motion was almost unconscious, as though he was doing it by instinct rather than by design. "There's something he's after—something that has to do with the mating phenomenon."

"The information regarding the halt in aging?" She knew what it was. She had known, once she had thought about it, why Merinus and Kane hadn't aged over the years when the rest of their family had.

"Sometimes you're too damned smart." He sighed, but there was a hint of approval in his tone, as well as his gaze.

Sometimes he was entirely too approachable, Rachel could have retorted. Such as now, when he was reaching out to her, amid the danger and the strife of his life. He was still making room for her, finding a reason, and a chance, to be gentle.

He wasn't hiding from her. He wasn't manipulating her. And she knew Jonas well enough to know when he was doing exactly that.

"Sanctuary in sight," Jackal called out. "Prepare to disembark, Director. We have live fire still coming in. Duck and run."

The heli-jet swooped down, its engines powering down, vibrating through the cabin as it set down as close to the estate house as possible.

The door swung open. Rachel found herself held tight to Jonas's side, her feet off the ground as he jumped from the craft, raced across the short distance and toward the opened double doors, which led to the large underground lab network beneath the estate house.

Live fire burst around them from the mountainside. Jonas was shouting orders as Seth and Dawn raced behind them, completely surrounded by a formation of Breeds.

"We're in. We're in," Jonas called out as steel and cement surrounded them.

Jonas still held her tight against him, racing down the hallway and up a short flight of stairs before careening through a maze of tunnels until he reached the door he was searching for.

The door swung open as Merinus stepped out.

"In here." She was wild-eyed, her face streaked with tears. "Callan, Kane and Leo raced out of here minutes ago, after Harmony. A report came in that she was surrounded and Lance's uncles were unable to get to her. Elizabeth and Ely are with Lance but he's not awakened yet and communications can't contact any of them."

Rachel was set on her feet, but she found Jonas's arm still around her, his warmth surrounding her as Sherra, Callan's Pride sister and the woman who'd married Kane Tyler, and head of computer security, handed Amber to her.

Her baby.

Rachel buried her face against her little girl's neck, tears filling her eyes as her fear began to ease marginally.

"Rachel. I have to go."

Jonas was releasing her. His warmth was easing away.

"No. Not yet." She turned, clutching Amber to her. "Wait. Jonas . . ." She knew he wouldn't listen. She knew he couldn't listen.

Staring up into his eyes, she saw the torn loyalties. His need to stay with his mate, his need to save his people.

Swallowing tightly, she forced a smile to her face. "You have to go."

"I have to go." His hand lifted, his fingertips running across her lips. "I'll be back for you."

Fear was a desperate, agonized entity growing inside her. She didn't want to lose him. She'd fought with him for months, ached for him for just as long. She couldn't lose him until she knew where this was going.

"Hurry back," she whispered through numb lips as she fought to hold back the plea that he not leave at all.

"I'll hurry," he promised.

His head bent, his lips feathered over her cheek, and then, he truly was gone.

◆   ◆   ◆

Minutes later, Jonas raced from the estate, dressed in black mission clothes rather than the tuxedo he had arrived in. Surrounded by Alpha Team One, which included Lawe, Rule and Mordecai, he ran for the waiting Raider.

There was no report on Harmony, Leo, Callan, Kane or the team sent in to cover them. They could be deliberately ignoring the calls, or, worst-case scenario, captured or killed.

He prayed, for the world's sake, that the latter was only a personal fear. There were enough Breeds banded together now that it would take more resources than America had to force them back into the labs, or to kill them.

The gunfire had stopped from the mountain above, the Breeds Leo had sent into the wilderness having finally succeeded in taking out the last of the sharpshooters firing on the house. It wasn't the men in the mountains he was worried about. It was his sister.

Harmony.

Her mate had nearly given his life for her once before; now, he had nearly given it for another, the son of a bitch. Jonas was definitely going to have to have a long talk with him about the proper way to take care of himself. That, or assign a damned detail to keep his ass out of trouble.

His sister Harmony, once known as the Breed assassin Death, didn't need more heartache in her life. She needed time to laugh, to love, to heal from the horror she had been trained within. A horror Jonas had unknowingly contributed to. And a chance to raise her infant son and watch him laugh, live, love and grow. A chance for more children, a life for herself that didn't include blood.

Death had been forced to die, and Harmony Lancaster had found a place in life, and in love, in the arms of her mate. Jonas intended to keep it that way.

"Move out!" he yelled to Lawe as they jumped into the Raider.

Immediately the vehicle was thrown into gear and raced

for the compound's wide gates, which swung open at their impending departure.

The Raider was within sight of the gates when another came barreling in. Tires screamed as the brakes were applied, the vehicle shuddering to a stop as Lawe cursed and twisted the wheel to keep from running headlong into the other Raider.

Harmony.

Jumping from the open side of the vehicle, Jonas stepped toward her, only to come to a hard stop when she, Dane Vanderale, Rye DeSalvo and one of Leo's African Breeds, Burke, jumped out to meet him.

Harmony reached in and a second later, tossed a wounded human male to the ground.

The man's knee was shattered. It looked as though it had taken a bullet from the antiquated sniper rifle Harmony still had a habit of carrying. The same rifle slung over her back now.

Blood congealed at his neck from a shallow knife wound, and if Jonas wasn't mistaken, a portion of hair had been scalped from his head.

That matching bloodied portion was stuck in the belt Harmony wore.

"He shot Lance." Harmony glared at him with raging, brilliant green eyes. "Enact Breed Law against me until hell freezes over, you bastard. Anyone that touches what's mine will suffer." She kicked the wounded man as she cast him a scathing glance. "Then they'll die."

Jonas halted in front of her. The pain that raged in her eyes and twisted her expression was one of the hardest things he had ever faced. He also saw the fear that her brother would find a way to enforce his threat to have her charged with Breed Law for the deaths he was certain she had left on the mountain.

"Are there any others living?" he asked her. He knew from the reports that had come through that a four-man team had attempted to capture David Lyons.

Harmony sneered, her green eyes glowing with fire. "They met Death."

Stepping forward, he held his sister's gaze, feeling that shattered part of his heart that had let her go so long ago ache with a fiery pain.

So delicate. She had always been too tiny, too easily broken.

"I would never enact Breed Law on you," he stated softly. "No matter your actions, I would protect you, Harmony, as I have always tried to protect you."

Surprise glittered amid the stark grief in her eyes.

"Liar." The look cleared out a second later, and he couldn't blame her for her distrust.

Jonas shook his head slowly. "Death is gone, little sister. Harmony Lancaster is a mate who deserves the blood she sheds." He reached out, ignored her flinch and rubbed a long strand of dark auburn hair between his fingertips. "I wouldn't have then—and I will not now—see the sister I have always loved suffer. I swear that, Harmony, on the lives I fight to save every day. I swear that to you."

He sensed it then. That grief inside her became an animal, fighting, clawing for release.

Her face crumpled and tears filled her eyes. "They shot him," she whispered, speaking of her mate. "Again, Jonas. They shot him again, and I might lose him . . ."

He had her in his arms. Despite the vague discomfort, he held her against his chest and did what he had never done before. He bent and kissed her gently on the crown of her head before laying his cheek against it while she sobbed in his arms.

Perhaps something had melted inside him as well. Never before had he known the words to say, or how to unlock the emotions he had always kept hidden inside his soul.

Until Rachel. It had happened gradually, he admitted. Slowly. But she had freed something inside him that he hadn't known had been locked away.

Looking over Harmony's head to the men who had

followed her before he had found her again, he finally realized why Dane Vanderale had fought so hard to keep her safe all the years he had.

The son of a bitch loved her. It was there in his eyes, in the twisted, raging fury of his expression. He was in love with a woman who would never consider his touch, his love or his needs.

And he'd loved her enough to let her ago. To allow her to have her mate, to allow her to have her happiness. In doing so, he had lost her forever. But he had given Jonas a gift that could never be repaid: his sister. Jonas had his sister back.

"It's going to be okay, little sister," he promised gently as he stroked his hands down her back and prayed for a way to soothe her. "Ely would have told you if he wasn't going to make it."

She shook her head.

"Leo would have never allowed you to leave the estate if Elizabeth thought he would die," he pointed out, and she paused.

When she pulled back, she stared up at him. And she broke his heart all over again with those tear-drenched eyes, so vivid and filled with pain.

"You hide," she whispered brokenly. "Like I used to do, don't you, Jonas? You hide it all, so you'll never be hurt."

He shook his head. "There's no hiding it any longer, Harmony. Maybe I just needed you to see it without proof." He touched her cheek gently.

She sniffed, like a little girl who didn't know what to do with her tears.

"Go to your mate," he urged her as he turned her to the house. "I have to collect my Pride leader and his stubborn-assed father now."

"His stubborn-assed father is having the time of his life cleaning up the carcasses Death left." Dane kicked at the human cowering at his feet, his expression hardening, filling with fury that came from Harmony's pain as well as the knowledge that she could have died when she went after the men who had attacked the estate. "What are we doing with this nasty little piece of shit?" He hunkered down and smiled in cold anticipation as the other man fought to scurry away while crying for mercy.

There was no mercy. Not in Dane's eyes, nor in Jonas's heart.

"Transfer him to our holding cells." Jonas looked to Burke. "This man is not to be accounted for. Let his boss think he escaped."

Burke nodded, grabbed a hunk of bloodstained blond hair and dragged him, screaming, back into the Raider.

"Lawe, Rule, go with him." He motioned to the two Enforcers before turning back to Dane. "You come with me."

Jonas jumped into the Raider, waited until Dane and Rye moved into the backseat, then took off for the house.

Harmony was racing into the entrance as Jonas drove up, her long, slender legs eating the distance as she moved to join her mate. Pulling the vehicle to a stop, he sighed wearily before jumping out and leading the way to Callan's private office.

Dane. His brother. Hell, sometimes it was too damned easy to admit the tall blond behind him was indeed his relative. They were far too much alike, and yet, too different.

Dane was a hybrid Breed, born naturally, nurtured and loved, held and given security. He had grown to adulthood knowing his place in life, and knowing the parents who loved and shielded him.

There had been danger in his life, but there had been no cruelty from those assigned to care for him. Even now, his parents cherished the ground his feet touched.

"I need a status update on Callan and Leo," he told the other two men as the doors closed behind them and security was engaged in the room.

The Breed society would suffer from the loss of the three Breeds, Callan, Leo and Jonas, who worked so tirelessly to strengthen it, and Jonas knew it. If Leo and Callan were caught unawares, and killed, the Breed society might never recover.

"I told you, brother, they're cleaning up Death's mess." Dane's smile was tight and hard. "You know how bloody things can get when she starts playing with her knife."

Yes, he knew well how bloody she could get. Death preferred a mess. It was her calling card. She was never easy when she killed and she never gave a damn what others thought or how they saw it.

"What did she learn?" She wasn't a stupid woman; she knew how important information was now.

"Brandenmore hired them to kidnap David," Dane revealed. "They have more spies here, Jonas. They knew about the training maneuver David was on with Tanner, Harmony and Lance, and exactly how to get into the compound. Brandenmore ordered the kid brought in alive too. No exceptions."

"Why?" Jonas snapped. That was unusual. They didn't need a live subject for the tests Jonas suspected they needed.

"It got fuzzy there." Dane shifted his broad shoulders as a frown worked over his brow. "It seems Brandenmore believes the child has mated and that the answer to the problem he's looking for in the decreases of aging can be found with him. What the hell is going on with that?"

Jonas shook his head. Dane's confusion stemmed from the fact that there were absolutely no variances of mating hormones in the children born to the Breeds. "We don't test the children, Dane. You know that."

"You can't test children. Hybrid Breeds don't hit puberty until they're near eighteen, and most don't become sexually active until they're in their twenties," Dane snarled, his South African accent slipping with his anger. "The fuckers have lost their minds."

"That, or do they know about you?" Jonas posed the question.

Dane snorted. "Not a chance. Brandenmore so loathes Leo that if he knew, the world would know. Trust me."

"Perhaps he's found himself another hybrid," Jonas

thought aloud. "Whatever the answer, we have a more serious problem."

"Your spy," Dane pointed out. "I know for a fact how secretive David's training is. Whoever knew is close."

David Lyons was nearly thirteen years old, and despite Elizabeth Vanderale's claims that Breed males hit puberty late, he seemed to be hitting it exceptionally hard. His temper, as well as his animalistic nature, was becoming impossible to hide. The training maneuvers were designed to help ease the primal awareness beginning to grow inside him, as well as to teach self-defense.

"Or lucky," Jonas bit out. "I want to question the captives myself. Let's see what I can get out of them."

"The Breed bogeyman." Dane's smile was cold as he referred to the nickname the press had given Jonas. "If what I saw outside is any indication though, your reputation is going to suffer. First Ely calls you a fucking sissy girl pussy; now you're petting your sister. Breeds and humans alike might start believing you're not a robot after all."

"Fuck off, Dane," he snarled and headed for the door. "And get your father and brother back on the fucking estate. I'll be damned if I need to deal with their deaths. The paperwork alone would make me fucking crazy."

Jonas made his way from the office directly to the secured rooms below the house. He needed his mate. He couldn't possess her, but the touch of her, her warmth, the gentle sound of her voice was another hunger he craved as well. He'd never considered that with mating heat. None of the other mated Breed Enforcers had mentioned it in their reports: that the need to simply *be* in the presence of their mates was so overwhelming that it was impossible to stay away.

Passing security, Jonas paused outside the secured safe room and waited until Merinus opened the door once again.

Rachel's scent hit him immediately. Her head turned from where she had been watching her child sleep in her arms, then she stood quickly and moved toward him.

She still wore the evening gown, minus the shoes. Her hair had slipped from its upswept style, and heavy strands fell to her shoulders.

Her face was pale, tearstained, the baby clutched in her arms. She had never looked more beautiful, or as sexy.

"Callan, Leo and Kane are cleaning up," he told Merinus and Sherra as he passed them to meet Rachel in the middle of the room. "They'll be returning soon."

He felt their relief, felt the love that seemed to fill the room. The children were all here, along with Leo's specially trained Enforcers, Breeds trained in the care and protection of the children should they have to escape with them.

The children themselves were calm. At eleven, Kane and Sherra's son appeared much more mature as he kept an eye on Leo and Elizabeth's newborns while Dawn talked to two of the Breed guards.

Tanner and Scheme's twins, ten months old, were playing quietly on a specially designed floor mat that held a variety of activities to entertain them. Merinus's newborn lay sleeping peacefully in one of the cribs set up in the room.

Only David, Callan and Merinus's thirteen-year-old son, appeared less than peaceful, and who could blame the boy?

Jonas would have approached the child, and had all intentions of doing so, until Merinus moved closer to him, blocking him from David.

"David asked to be left alone until he could talk to Callan." Her dark brown eyes were filled with pain. "I don't know what to do, Jonas."

This wasn't the Prima; this was the mother. She was uncertain, fighting to make sense of the danger this world provided and how best to protect her children.

"Then I would suggest respecting his wishes," Jonas stated quietly as he glanced to one of the Breed guards closest to David and gave him a silent nod toward the boy.

The Breed would be available if he felt David was becoming overly distressed.

"He needs to talk about it," she whispered as she crossed her arms over her breasts and tried to calm herself. "David doesn't do well when he broods over things."

"Sometimes a man has to brood," Jonas answered her, knowing the boy could overhear their conversation well. "He's being forced to grow up, Merinus, and as sad as that is, it's not something we can halt. David is well-adjusted, and he knows his father is willing to listen to whatever problems he wants to bring to him. Give Callan a chance to help his child the proper way."

The message was for David as well. He could discuss the issues with Callan, or Jonas would ensure the boy discussed them with his father. And David rarely liked Jonas's forced discussions.

"Rachel and I will be returning to the cabin now," he told the Prima. "If you need me, you have only to call the sat phone."

"Is the cabin safe?" Merinus asked worriedly as she glanced at a sleeping Amber. "Stay here, Jonas. One of the lower-level suites can be prepared quickly."

The lower-level suites were beneath the house, part of the design of the labs and taken for couples in mating heat that were forced to stay at the estate house for safety's sake.

Jonas shook his head. "I have adequate security, and it seems the danger has passed, for tonight. Besides, I know Rachel will be more comfortable with time alone with her child."

Rachel remained silent, thankfully. Jonas had no desire to stay there, where he could and would be disturbed at every chance. The animal inside him was already pacing in impatience to, at the very least, be alone with his family.

His family.

As they left the house, Jonas couldn't help but be amazed at the thought. He had been created to father children, and had been considered a failure by the scientists. Jonas knew what they didn't: He wasn't a failure, he just hadn't found his mate.

Now that he had, he feared the results.

Nothing mattered but protecting his mate and the child he had claimed as his own. The problem with that was, any child he would sire would be in even greater danger. He would be the child who would truly bridge Breed and man, to create a being that both races would ultimately fear.

A fire was burning brightly in the fireplace when Jonas escorted Rachel into the cabin. Mordecai sat on his haunches in front of it. The four-legged Coyote that traveled at his side was lying in front of it, black eyes watching as Jonas and Rachel entered the room.

Amber was sleeping peacefully after the formula Rachel had given her before they left the estate house, yet still, the Coyote Mordecai called "Cote" came to its feet, narrowed his eyes on the child and tilted his head as though attempting to figure out exactly what it was.

"The perimeter of the cabin is secure." Mordecai came to his feet as he wiped his hands down the front of his jeans, his blue gray gaze meeting Jonas's before he shrugged his broad shoulders.

There was an edge of discomfort whenever he was around Rachel, which Jonas hadn't yet figured out.

"Contact me immediately if you so much as sense anything," Jonas ordered him. "I'll be working tonight, then Rachel and I have to fly back to D.C. tomorrow afternoon for a meeting with the House Appropriations Committee concerning satellite usage. I want the heli-jet and Alpha Team One providing security for the trip and the meeting, as well as the return."

Mordecai gave a sharp nod as Rachel moved toward her and Amber's room. As Rachel's door closed, Mordecai turned back to him.

"What?" Jonas questioned as Mordecai stared at him silently.

"Merinus was forced to leave the safe room just after the male mates left. She was in the hall for long moments. While there, David became very agitated. He was pacing the room, and though he was fighting to hold them back, I could hear the tiny growls rumbling in his chest. He had all the appearances of adolescent feral fever, Jonas."

Jonas's jaw clenched. "I'll talk to Callan and Ely and see what they think."

Mordecai nodded. "He's a good boy. I'd hate to see his head messed with feral fever."

As Mordecai left the cabin, Jonas blew out a hard, silent breath. Feral fever had caused the scientists to kill too many young Breeds while they were still in the labs. Jonas had hoped the hybrid Breeds would be immune to it.

Moving to the kitchen, he quickly pulled a prepared meal from the freezer and shoved it in the oven. He hated damned microwaves.

Setting the temperature, he moved to the coffeemaker and flipped the switch to start the brewing process for the already measured grounds of coffee, then set out two cups, bowls and spoons.

Chili was one of the few things he could prepare well. That and coffee.

Turning at the sound of the bedroom door opening, he watched as Rachel reentered the room. She had taken off the exquisite dress and replaced it with soft cashmere lounging pants and a top. Her feet were covered with pristine white socks, her long red hair brushed until it fell down her back in a soft, satiny ribbon.

Seeing her dressed more comfortably, her face devoid of makeup, her demeanor softer than it was in the office, gave her an even more delicate, petite appearance.

She barely cleared his chest at five foot six inches. In heels, she went no taller than his shoulders. She was so damned tiny he was almost scared to touch her.

Fear was something he wasn't used to feeling either, not in any regard. Confidence was, at times, a fault where he was concerned, and he knew it. When it came to Rachel though, confidence was something he invariably found himself lacking.

"Is Amber sleeping comfortably?" he asked as she made her way into the kitchen.

"Like a baby." Her lips tilted up in amusement. "That child could sleep through a bomb, I believe. As long as her diaper is dry and her belly is full."

She was an unusually peaceful child, Jonas had to admit. Even for her young age, Amber was content to watch everything and everyone when she was awake.

"I'll have something ready for us to eat in a few minutes," he promised as he poured the coffee. "You have to be hungry."

"Starved." She leaned against the counter, staring up at him, her gaze quiet, intense.

Jonas could almost hear trouble brewing in her mind. The woman had more questions than China had rice at times.

♦   ♦   ♦

Rachel watched as Jonas moved around the kitchen, still dressed in the mission uniform, a weapon strapped to one thigh, a knife to the other.

He was the badass he was rumored to be, there was no doubt. But there was a softer part of Jonas that few people saw, that he took great pains to hide. A part that she had often glimpsed, even when she knew he would prefer no one see.

It was the same part that had him fixing her coffee, and long minutes later preparing her meal before he set it on the table. She had never had a meal prepared for her, that she could remember, by anyone other than herself or her sister. Even Devon, when they had lived together, had never bothered to fix her so much as a glass of water.

But here was Jonas, tough, hard, coming down from the surge of adrenaline that she knew came from battle, and he was fixing her coffee, chili, a salad. There were crackers and fruits and bread. Everything laid out on the table for her to tempt her appetite.

"I'll get fat at this rate." She moved to sit in the chair he pulled out for her, and felt a start of surprise as he helped her adjust it.

"Your metabolism is too well-adjusted and you're too physically active to get fat anytime soon." He took his own chair and began digging into his own food.

Breeds consumed vast quantities of food to power those gorgeous, powerful bodies.

There had actually been a television special concerning Breed eating habits. It had amazed her that producers would even think of such a thing.

The meal progressed quietly. As she finished, Jonas removed the dishes, stacked the dishwasher, turned it on, then moved to the doorway.

"I need a shower and I have some papers to go over before the meeting tomorrow. I'll see you in the morning."

He left her sitting in the kitchen, alone.

Rachel stared at the doorway incredulously. He had just walked out, moved across the living room and entered his own bedroom as though she were no more than a guest.

She blinked as she fought to grasp this new attitude.

She would have expected to be fending him off tonight, not wondering why the hell he hadn't at least given her the chance to do so.

The knowledge that she wouldn't have minded the chance

to do so had her lips quirking in a smile. The arousal that had slammed into her body the second she had seen him in that mission uniform hadn't abated.

When he had walked into the safe room, his tall, corded body outlined in the protective wear, she had nearly lost her breath. The black material only emphasized the height and breadth of his body, as well as the living mercury of his eyes. He looked more a warrior than she had ever seen him before.

Jonas's normal attire was silk suits and conservative clothing. She'd never seen him dressed outrageously, as some Breeds were prone to. No skintight leather or combat boots. He was every inch the conservative politician if one cared to ignore the dangerous aura that surrounded him. Or the gorgeous body. Or the sheer sex appeal.

She breathed, wishing she had better control over her attraction to him. For more than seven months she had fought the heated longing she felt each time she saw him. As she learned more about him, she'd had to fight it even harder.

And what she had seen tonight had made her see even more of the man he was.

The monitors in the safe room covered every area outside the safe house. She had seen him when he had met his sister in the entrance to Sanctuary.

The tenderness he had displayed toward her, the sheer agony on his face as she had cried in his arms had broken Rachel's heart. There were facets to Jonas that would take lifetimes to figure out. And there were others, such as his love for his sister, that were clear to her right now.

So many saw him as manipulating, calculating: A man who deserved little respect because of the pure power he displayed. But Jonas was so much more than that. He manipulated to ensure the safety of the Breeds. He calculated to ensure the happiness of those close to him. He did what he had to do to provide a measure of safety to Sanctuary as well as to Haven, and to bring the Breeds into a cohesive society that projected the appearance of invincible strength.

It was the only way to survive, she knew. The Breeds

were facing an uncertain future in many ways. Laws could be changed on a whim, and what was theirs now could be taken from them tomorrow. It had happened in the past to other races. Rachel had no doubt that the Breeds too faced that threat.

Rising to her feet, she paced to the living room, then to her room. She was looking at a long night. Sleep had never seemed so far away, nor had it ever seemed so unwanted.

◆   ◆   ◆

The rest of the week seemed to progress much as that night had. The day was filled with meetings, wrapping up projects and completing the move of the main office to Sanctuary. There seemed to be very little time to actually talk to Jonas, or to figure out what the hell they were going to do after the move.

It wasn't as though they could go back to the same routine that they had had before. Yet Jonas seemed determined to do just that.

He was more distant that he had ever been, and the time they shared together became few and far between.

She found that by living in the cabin with Jonas, though, there were benefits. He began slipping into her room and taking Amber for her feedings throughout the night.

Not once during the week had she woken to her daughter's fretful whimpers for a meal or a dry diaper. Once, she had awakened to see him bending over the crib, returning her daughter to her bed, his expression caught by the light of the lamp next to the small bed.

It had been a father's face, full of gentleness. The face of a man who had claimed a child—whether by blood or by love— and now carried through with the responsibilities of that job.

For long moments he had stood watching Amber, dressed in nothing more than a pair of soft cotton pants, his chest and feet bare.

Rachel had felt such a surge of emotion, such pure arousal, that for a moment her breath caught.

He had turned then, as though drawn by the power of what she had felt, his gaze locking with hers.

Not a word had been said. He had turned and walked from the room so quietly that she wondered if he had ever been there. She had never caught him again, though she knew he fed Amber nightly. The bottles were always washed and sterilized, sitting on the counter awaiting her the next morning, and diapers were in the waste each morning.

It was a routine they had begun to fall into, and it was one that was wearing on her nerves as she felt his hunger growing as well as the arousal beginning to build within her.

No one could claim this was mating heat, she thought as she watched him carry wood into the cabin for a fire that night. Not that they needed it so much for the warmth. She had learned while living on Sanctuary that the Breeds, for all their technology, preferred classic comforts. A comfortable seat, a fire, steak and potatoes, a cold beer. Many even still carried the outlawed bullet- and shell-loaded weapons from decades before rather than the laser-powered weapons that were more effective when set to stun or wound, rather than kill.

Not that their enemies didn't use the same weapons. Bullets were still preferred by many of their attackers, simply because they did more damage to the body with the same effectiveness of the new weapons being introduced.

Society in general was all about less bloodshed and more humane weapons, or so advertising proclaimed. At least, for those who cared about the damage caused or about leaving others less defended.

"Rachel, before you leave the office, contact Senator Tyler and ask him if he'll move the meeting set for tomorrow in D.C. out here. The Weather Service is calling for heavy snow tomorrow and I'd prefer not to get grounded by a blizzard."

He moved from his office into hers, a frown edging at his brows to indicate his irritation as he faced her. Jonas didn't mind the snow unless it ended up delaying something he wanted or needed to do.

"Anything else?" She made a note on the electronic reminder she used.

She heard him mutter something—she knew she had. But when she turned back to him, he was merely glaring back at her with the same expression he'd had moments ago.

"Did you say something else?" she questioned him in confusion.

"I said you could work naked, but I doubt you're into that." The glare became more intense.

Rachel just barely kept her lips from twitching. "I could, but don't you think Lawe and Rule might be a little uncomfortable when you start all that growling stuff?"

His expression stilled, no doubt in shock. It wasn't the first time he had muttered something; it was simply the first time she had confronted him over it.

As she watched, the arousal, the pure hunger he always seemed to keep a lid on, flared in his gaze for just a second before he managed to hide it once again.

What she saw stole her breath. The need that reflected for that one second on his face was like nothing she had ever seen or known in her life. It was all-consuming, overwhelming.

Unlike Jonas, she didn't have the self-control to hide her own responses nearly so quickly, and she knew it. Heat surged through her body, raced through her bloodstream, and in less than a second had her clit throbbing and her vagina moist and clenching in need.

She watched as he slowly inhaled, drawing in the scent of her arousal, and thought just how unfair it was that he had that ability.

"You're stepping into very dangerous territory," he warned her as he crossed his arms over his chest, the white silk shirt he wore stretching over his broad shoulders. "If you have no desire to be a mate, then perhaps you should give a second thought to teasing me, Rachel."

Perhaps she should.

"I haven't refused to be your mate. I simply stated that I'm *not* your mate," she pointed out to him. "Just because some hormone in your system wants to turn me into your sex slave doesn't mean I would be anything more than just that."

Perhaps she was wrong. She had spent quite a bit of time watching Callan and Merinus and talking to the friend she had nearly lost contact with. What she had heard hadn't sounded too bad, simply inconvenient. She just didn't have time to be inconvenienced in such a way.

"Keep pushing me," he warned her as he stepped closer to her desk. "You may not like the results."

That wasn't arrogance talking, she realized. It was pure fact.

Shaking her head, she watched him with what she hoped was cool interest. She was actually burning alive for him.

"And here I was actually starting to like you," she told him. "What happened to the man who fixed me dinner, who feeds my daughter at night so I can sleep?"

"I may as well," he retorted. "I'm awake every night, tempted by the scent of your arousal. The walls may be thick, sweetheart, but they're not that damned thick that the scent of your sweet pussy doesn't leave me aching."

She flushed. She hated it when she did that. Damn it, she had red hair; it should be illegal to make her blush. Of course, she should also have hell's own temper, and she was actually rather calm. For the most part.

"I can do without your attitude, Jonas." She stood to her feet, her head held high, and wished she presented a more imposing image. He stared back at her with that small glimmer of amusement in his gaze.

The glare was gone. It was a look she didn't care much for anyway. When he glared, the gentleness that was a glimmer of warmth in his gaze was absent. She rather liked that little light of warmth.

"I could do without your stubbornness," he informed her. "I put up with it anyway."

"My stubbornness?" She propped her hands on her hips and stared back at him with a frown. "How am I stubborn? I am the least stubborn person I know."

His black brows arched as he leaned against the doorframe. "Least stubborn?" His lips quirked. "Let's see, what was your nickname in high school again? I know I saw that on the background check I had run on you."

Her eyes widened. "Don't you dare, Jonas Wyatt." She laughed. She hadn't heard that nickname since she'd graduated.

"I could be bribed to forget it for a minute." He almost grinned. That little twitch at the corner of his mouth was completely charming.

"Just for a minute?" She narrowed her eyes back at him warningly.

He was teasing her. Merinus had stated that Jonas never joked, that he never teased. Maybe it was that no one had ever paid attention to the unique way he did it. Or perhaps, he kept them too angry to pay attention.

"And what would be the price of forgetting?" She just had to push it, she couldn't help it.

The change that came over him was almost frightening. For a woman who had never known a man like Jonas, it could be terrifying.

His expression darkened; sensual, sexual awareness filled every inch of his face, gleamed in silver eyes that seemed to lighten, to burn with hunger.

"Jonas." As though that look alone were enough to weaken her, to turn her legs to jelly, Rachel leaned against the edge of her desk and held on for support.

Predatory awareness transformed his face as sensual hunger flamed in his eyes. Straightening, he moved from the door.

"Get out of here." The order that rasped from his lips shocked her. "Run, Rachel. Get away from me."

She shook her head. How was she supposed to run? She could barely breathe. The look on his face was all-consuming, filled with need—for her.

Had anyone ever needed her? Ever ached for her?

In all her life she'd never truly had anyone but her sister, and Diana had her battles. Danger was Diana's lover, her family, her friend. Amber was Rachel's responsibility. Devon had been a footnote in her and Amber's life, nothing more.

Yet Jonas ached for her. She could see it, she could feel it.

"Jonas . . ." She licked her suddenly dry lips as he moved closer.

"Do you know what I am?" he growled, his tone so rough, so primal, it sent shivers racing down her spine. "You don't even know the beast that draws you, do you, Rachel?"

"Running me off, are you? What about all this 'me Breed, you mate' crap you're always spouting?" She felt light-headed, sensitive. Her flesh was crawling with the need for his touch.

She couldn't blame it on mating heat. Ely had assured her it took more than the few brief touches they had shared to cause the need to rage inside her.

"I was created to be a breeder." He moved to her, his hands curving around her upper arms as she stared back at him, barely understanding what he was saying, her gaze locked on his lips. Lips she needed to taste, a kiss she hungered for in the dead of night and yet continued to deny herself.

"Are you listening to me, Rachel?" His lips pulled back from his teeth in a snarl, revealing the strong, sexier than hell incisors at the sides of his mouth.

"A breeder." She had to fight to breathe now. "I heard you."

"I was created to breed the perfect killer."

She licked her lips again, wondered how he would taste.

"Yeah, well, I guess they had to have an excuse for creating someone so damned arrogant and certain of themselves." It made sense to her anyway, and she had to say something, otherwise he might believe she was as dumbfounded as she knew she was becoming.

A growl rumbled in his chest and vibrated in her pussy.

Oh Lord, what was happening to her?

Should arousal be this strong, this hot? She felt flushed, overheated, oversensitive.

"If you don't get the hell away from me, I'm going to kiss

you." He shook her just a little. "Listen to me, Rachel. You don't feel the heat; I do. You don't know what it does. Trust me." One hand lifted, touched her chin and raised her face until she was staring into his eyes. "Listen to me, baby: You'll regret it."

She shook her head. How could she regret it?

"Just a little kiss," she whispered.

His eyes closed briefly. "A little kiss." When he reopened them, the irises had lightened further, the color swirling, burning.

"I want you," she whispered. "You know I do. Surely there's some way . . ."

"I don't have the control," he snarled.

"The king of control?" She shook her head in bemusement. "What is it, Jonas? All or nothing? You can't let me at least have a glimpse of what I'm getting into without forcing me to accept it all the way?"

She watched his face. His jaw clenched and bunched as rage seemed to flicker in his gaze.

Slowly, so slowly, his head lowered, his gaze holding hers as she watched a battle she couldn't understand flickering in his eyes.

"I would never force you," he whispered.

His lips touched hers. So slowly.

Rachel felt herself shaking from the inside out as she tried to part her lips. She tried to take more of him, only to have him hold her closer. His lips were closed, heated, sending fiery sensations racing through her nervous system as desire began to rage through her.

His hands stroked down her arms, drew them to his shoulders before his hands gripped her hips and jerked her closer.

Her lips parted on a gasp.

Jonas's head lifted, his lips moving to her neck, his teeth raking the sensitive flesh. The feel of his hardened cock pressed tight and hard against her as the position forced her legs to part.

Thin dress pants were no protection against the hardened length of his erection beneath his own slacks.

His cock was hot, hard. So thick and heavy against the overheated, swollen mound of her sex. Rachel couldn't help but try to lift herself closer, to grind her clit against the heated proof of the heavy shaft as the need for release suddenly overwhelmed her.

Jonas's large palm cupped the back of her head as it fell back. His lips stroked along her neck; his teeth raked, nipped. The feel of his incisors, wicked sharp, sent fiery pleasure tearing through her before it struck her womb, clenching it with ecstasy.

"Jonas." Weakness assailed her, yet adrenaline coursed through her. She needed more. She ached for more.

Just as quickly as he pulled her to him, she found herself free. Stumbling against the desk, she stared back at him in shock as he snarled.

"What . . . ?"

"I have work to do." He turned, stalked back to his office and slammed the door. A second later, the lock clicked, informing her with more than words that he wanted nothing more to do with her.

"Jonas." She whispered his name, her hand lifting to her neck and the stinging sensation she could still feel.

Touching dampness, she pulled back and stared at her fingers with wide eyes.

Blood.

"You're playing a very dangerous game, little girl."

Rachel turned quickly, off balance, shocked as she stared back at Dr. Ely Morrey.

Dressed in a heavy sweater, jeans and boots, she didn't look like the genius in Breed genetics that Rachel knew she was.

"How . . ." She blinked, swallowed tightly. "I didn't hear you come in."

Evidently, Jonas hadn't heard either.

"Come with me." She jerked her head beyond the door before stepping into the harsh chill of the mountain air.

Rachel followed, not quite certain why. Closing the

door behind her, Ely glared back at Rachel, her brown eyes enraged.

"I heard more than I probably should have," Ely expressed in a precise, icy tone Rachel had never heard from her before. Anger glittered in her brown eyes, an anger Rachel didn't understand. "You ask that man for the impossible."

Rachel shook her head. "What do you mean, the impossible?"

"To ask him to touch you, to kiss you without sharing the mating hormone, without making you his, is like asking the sun to not rise in the morning or set in the evening. You're asking him to destroy himself."

Rachel shook her head. "You said the hormone had to be shared to produce such reactions. That it was okay . . ."

"For you," Ely snapped. "You walk around him daily, sleep in his cabin, share his day and you don't suffer. Because he respects your desire to wait. Because he will not force this on you, no matter the pain he feels. You do this to him, and you don't even care about the effect on him."

Ely's face flushed with her anger.

"Ely, we haven't shared the mating hormone." Panic was beginning to set in, a fearful realization struggling to reveal itself inside her mind. Her heart.

"*You* haven't shared it with him," Ely snarled back at her. "You haven't tasted what drives him insane with need and pain because he can't have what nature is demanding he take, no matter how it must be taken. You don't suffer into the night, so aroused that it feels your flesh is peeling from your bones. You don't breathe and smell nothing but the scent of hunger and need that clings to the one who desires you, yet refuses you. You, Ms. Broen, aren't tortured with an agony that even the labs couldn't compare because there is no relief, there is no release."

"He has a hand," she shot back, furious. "Don't tell me he can't find relief. What am I asking for? A chance to love him rather than be tied to him without the benefit of a choice?"

"A hand?" Ely's tone was clipped, frosty with disgust. "In

this, my dear, he has no 'hand,' as you so eloquently phrase it. No amount of masturbation will help; it will only make the agony greater. Each time he touches you, breathes in the scent of your desire, touches your flesh. Each time, the hunger is a thousand times worse than starvation. It's like having a limb ripped from his body. What you just did to him is greater disservice than those Council scientists could have ever done to him."

"All I wanted was a kiss," she whispered, horrified at what Ely was telling her. "I would never deliberately hurt him."

Ely glared back, refusing to soften. "You are to him something greater than even your child is to you. If you don't know now that you love him or that you could love him, then the best gift you could give him is to leave, completely. That, or stop being such a child and accept the gift he would give you." Censure glittered in her eyes. "If you're woman enough. Which at this point, I very much doubt you are."

Rachel couldn't imagine the pain Ely had described to her. She couldn't imagine anyone enduring such pain, even Jonas. The man accused of being stone-cold ice inside.

After she returned to her desk, Jonas walked from his office, staring back at her, his expression perfectly calm and perfectly composed.

"I apologize for biting you so hard," he stated, his tone no longer tortured. "It was an accident, Rachel. One that won't be repeated."

She watched him now, trying to see beyond the calm expression to the torment Ely swore was a part of the mating heat.

She should have questioned him more, she thought. She should have taken the time, no matter the danger at first, and the business of their routine in the past week, to learn more about what she was refusing.

"Do you love me, Jonas?" The question slipped past her lips, almost unbidden.

She had always dreamed of love, not mating heat. Commitment. Loyalty. Faithfulness.

His expression hardened, became more stony than before.

"I love you." As though the words were torn from him, ripped from the very center of his being.

"You so obviously didn't want to admit to that," she said painfully. "Why did you?"

His lips tightened, the muscles at his jaw clenched furiously. "You deserve the truth, whether I want to tell you or not," he stated.

"Why?" He was such an enigma sometimes, and at others, she felt as though she had known him forever.

"You're my mate," he growled. "The same as my wife, the other half of me. I won't lie to you, Rachel. You are what I never thought I would have in my life. I don't lie to myself; I won't lie to you."

Nothing could be so simple. So easy.

Shaking her head, she rose from her chair, desperate now to get away from him, to think without him staring back at her with that icy gaze.

"The world was simple to you once, wasn't it, Rachel?" he asked her as she headed for the door. "You had your parents, your sister, the little house in the country, a pet dog named Ruffy, a cat named Kitty."

She stopped, closed her eyes and fought not to remember those days. She didn't want to remember what had been, because it was so different from what it had become.

"Then it was taken from you."

"And your point?" she asked painfully.

"You've run ever since," he stated. "You and your sister both have run from what you lost. A senseless accident, a lack of foresight by your parents to ensure you were cared for if they were taken away and the loss of everything you knew."

Even the dog and the cat had been wrenched from her arms.

"I didn't have to run," she said, holding the pain of the past deep inside her.

"You've run." He stepped closer, blocked the doorway and reached out until his fingers held a thick curl of hair, rubbing against it sensually. "You've made certain nothing could be taken from you again, until you had Amber. And now you hold on to her with everything you have, don't you baby." His voice dropped, softened.

"She's my daughter."

"She's your life."

She stared back at him, not certain where he was going now.

"She's my life," she agreed.

"You live for her. You would die for her."

And she would, so easily.

"Where are you going with this, Jonas?"

"I'm making a point, love," he stated gently. "Imagine the love you feel for your child, and then multiply that by a thousand. Imagine what you felt the first time you gazed upon her, and knew that God had given you the most perfect gift to complete your life, and multiply that again. That is what you are to me. That is what I felt the first moment I saw you. Unlike humans, Breeds live for the small gifts, the little kindnesses fate would hand to us. We search for them. We cherish them. The moment I saw you, the animal inside me roared in triumph, the man melted in the face of the woman who stared back at him.

"That was love, Rachel. It was the acceptance, the knowledge that what I feared the most, what I ached for the most, was now standing before me, and reaching out for it, claiming it, could destroy everything I am."

She shook her head desperately. "Love doesn't happen like that. It takes time. It builds."

He nodded slowly. "It can happen like that. It can build slowly. It can come like a gentle rainfall, or it can slam into you like a tsunami. You are my tsunami, love."

She couldn't accept that. Staring back at him, she saw his understanding that she refused to accept his logic.

"Racert left a message while I was in my office." He changed the subject coolly. "He's decided that the decision the appropriations committee made needs to be reviewed. He believes the amount awarded initially to Sanctuary and Haven were well above what we deserve. He's moving to have the funds reduced."

"Stop." She lifted her hand in refusal. "You can't just switch that way."

"Of course I can." He shrugged as he moved away from her, dropping the curl he had been caressing. "As you stated, you refuse the mating. My control isn't inexhaustible. I have my limits. And I'm drawing close to that limit. I need you to pull the information we have on Racert and bring it to me. We need to find a weakness."

She inhaled slowly. "Jonas."

"Do it." His voice was like a lash of ice now. "Questions are for later, when I can handle what you do to me. That isn't something I can do at the moment."

He turned and stalked back to his office. The way his body moved had little to do with simply walking. The Lion his genetics came from was too close to the surface now, too much a part of him.

She had seen that before, she realized. In Callan, in Sherra, and in Taber and Tanner. Merinus's family, the ruling Pride. The animals that were so much a part of them were often close to the surface in the presence of their mates, when they were forced to control more than simple arousal.

Turning away, she moved to the computer and began pulling together the information they had on the senator.

Unfortunately, from what she remembered, there was very little they could use against him. Racert had kept his nose clean. He hadn't done drugs; he had conducted his shadier dealings under the auspices of legitimate actions. There was no way to prove he had done anything illegal. He had a wife, no mistress. One child, a daughter, widowed. A granddaughter still in high school.

She finished the file, sent it to Jonas's computer, then left her desk to check on Amber.

She was still sleeping. At three months old, she was only now beginning to fill out. She smiled and laughed often. She was the greatest joy in Rachel's life.

Rachel couldn't imagine that Jonas could take one look at her and feel more, love more, than she had felt or loved the first time she'd held her child.

Lifting her from the crib, Rachel cuddled Amber close to her heart, reached out and stroked the tiny strands of red-gold hair from her brow.

The soft blue dress and little stockings she wore had been bought by Jonas. The clothes, tiny shoes, everything Amber now possessed had been provided for by Jonas. Everything Rachel now owned, Jonas had given her. He provided everything. And he did so without demanding payment. Without asking for the slightest thing in return.

Had anyone besides her sister ever done that?

"You were born to be a mother."

Jonas was behind her again. She had felt him before he spoke, and that amazed her.

"You don't make sense to me, Jonas," she whispered. "What are you trying to do to me?"

"Complete you. Protect you." His voice deepened as it speared through her heart.

Rachel kissed Amber's forehead gently, smiled as the baby pursed her lips as though to kiss her back, then laid her back amid the incredibly soft blankets that covered the mattress.

Turning to Jonas, she passed him, moved back into the office and felt his presence as he followed.

"I have to return to D.C. tonight," he told her as she moved back to her desk.

"Running away?" She stopped at her chair and turned back to face him. "Isn't that what you accused me of, Jonas?"

"My running is the only thing that will save you," he informed her, his voice turning to ice once more. "Never doubt that, Rachel. If I stay here tonight, I won't have the control not to take you. Now get everything ready—"

"No." Adrenaline raced through her as though she were facing losing something, someone. Jonas would be back, she knew he would, but something inside her couldn't bear to see him go.

Reaching out, she gripped his arm and held on tight. "You wouldn't let me run, you won't let me hide. Why should you be able to?"

"Because of this." His finger touched the mark he had left on her: the small scratch his incisors had left on her neck. "I drew blood, and for a second, love, I nearly licked over the wound. Do you know what would have happened, what I would have done to you, had I done that?"

She shook her head as she fought to control the pain that tried to twist her expression.

"The mating hormone would have infected the wound. Within hours, it would have moved into your system. A few more hours and you would be begging me to fuck you. Screaming for it. That's what's going to happen if I stay."

Rachel jerked away from him. Raking her fingers through her hair, she fought to make sense of her emotions, her needs, her confusion.

What was he doing to her?

She remembered, so many years ago, seeing his face on a news interview. She had watched his eyes, the swirl of color, and had felt her heart clench. Over the years, nothing had changed. Each time she saw a glimpse of him in the news, she had watched, absorbed by the sight.

Meeting him had produced a stronger reaction. It hadn't been simple attraction. It hadn't been mere interest or even absorption. From that first face-to-face meeting, Jonas had inspired emotions inside her that she hadn't wanted to face.

"Rachel." His voice rasped across her senses as he moved behind her.

His hands gripped her hips, held her to him as he laid his cheek against the top of her head.

"I don't sleep because I can do nothing but hunger for you," he whispered. "I smell your scent, heavy with arousal, and it burns inside me. I see you and I want nothing more than to taste you, every inch of you. I'm a strong man, baby, but I'm not that strong."

His hands stroked up her side, moved around, cupped her breasts.

She breathed in sharply and arched into his touch.

"I sat in that office, fighting for control, and the scent of you drew me back. Do you know I can smell the wet heat of your pussy clear into that fucking room? All I can think about is spreading your legs." His fingers found her nipples, stroked them, gripped them between fingers and thumbs before rolling them firmly.

Her head fell back against his chest as her back arched in pleasure.

"I can't keep my hands off you."

Did she want him to keep his hands off her?

She didn't.

Her breathing roughened as sensation sizzled across her nerve endings. His hands moved, his fingers flipping apart the buttons that held her blouse together.

"Do you know what mating heat does?" he growled.

She shook her head. Merinus had evidently neglected to give her a lot of information.

"The pleasure is unlike anything you could imagine," he whispered at her ear as he parted her blouse, his fingers moving to the clasp of her bra between her breasts.

The pleasure was unlike anything she could have imagined. Rachel lowered her head, watched as his large hands cupped her breasts, caressed them, his fingers stroking across her nipples.

Biting her lip, she fought to hold back the whimpers of pleasure that fell from her lips, and failed.

This was incredible. It was unlike any pleasure she had known in her life.

"All it takes is a kiss," he whispered. "Or a lick. I could taste the sweet heat of your pussy, push my tongue inside the tight little muscles there, and you'd go crazy for the pleasure, Rachel. You'd beg, but you wouldn't have to beg. I'd give it to you. All night, all day. Over and over again while your body begs for more, demands more."

His hands slid from her breasts, down. He flicked open the button to her pants, slid the zipper down and pushed his hand inside the silk panties beneath.

"Is this mating heat?" she gasped.

She could feel her juices spilling over his fingers, the swollen folds of her sex parting beneath his fingers. The sensations were exquisite, heated, rife with such longing that she wanted to beg for possession.

"Not yet." He breathed out, his chest laboring at her back as they both fought for air. "Not for you."

But it was killing him. She felt it now. The tension in his body, the primal rasp of his voice. This wasn't the cool, logical, in-control Jonas that she knew.

His breathing was heavy at her ear, a groan tearing from his chest as his fingers met the swollen bud of her clit. A groan that mingled with her whimper of need.

"Then something's wrong." Her hand moved to her thighs, pressing against his as the need for a firmer touch surged through her body. "Jonas, this is killing me."

Then what was it doing to him?

According to Ely, it was thousand times worse for him.

He growled behind her. A sound so reminiscent of the animal he shared his genetics with that she shivered.

"Tell me . . ." She had to swallow tightly to continue as his fingers eased through the lush collection of heat between the folds of her sex. "Tell me, Jonas, what this does to you."

His head buried against her neck as his large body seemed to shudder behind her.

"Heaven and hell," he groaned. "I want to go to my knees and beg, Rachel. I would beg for just a taste if I knew you wouldn't hate me once you realized you were tied to me forever. And from all we know, mating is a long, long time."

The Leo was more than a century in age.

Her lips parted, her eyes closing as she tried to force herself to move away from him.

His fingers moved again. They curled, two pressed together, and a heartbeat later they were thrusting inside the tight, clenched depths of her vagina.

She went to her toes. The pleasure was so extreme, so intense, a cry tore from her lips.

He didn't stop. His fingers moved fast, hard, thrusting inside her, fucking into her with smooth, sure strokes and throwing her over the edge of completion.

Rachel clamped her thighs on his hand, her entire body tightening as ecstasy raced through her body over and over again. She didn't want it to stop. She wanted to feel this forever. She wanted to lock the sensations inside her and never let them go.

"I love feeling you come for me." His voice was barely recognizable now. "The way your pussy clenches on my fingers, sucks at them. I would die to feel it around my dick, sucking me in, pulling my release from me."

His fingers were still buried inside her, locking her into the pleasure swirling through her as it slowly, so very slowly and yet too quickly, began to ease inside her.

"I have to get away from you." He kissed her shoulder gently. "If I don't, Rachel, one day, my control will snap. The animal that wants nothing more than the promise of what it knows belongs to it will accept nothing less. I'm not just a man, baby. I'm a Breed. Animal and man, and the animal isn't nearly as patient as the man wishes he were."

He was going to break behind her, his body was drawn so tight.

"It hurts," she whispered. "Ely said it hurts."

"Ely has a big mouth." He drew his fingers from her, released her slowly.

A second later, Rachel opened her eyes, stared up at him and watched as his gaze held hers while he tasted the fingers that glistened with her juices.

His silver eyes turned nearly colorless. His face tightened until his cheekbones seemed to push against his flesh, his lips tightening, his brows lowering.

The animal was there, close to the skin, fighting to be free as he tasted the release that had poured from her body.

"If you need anything, Harmony will be here for a while." He pulled from her as though he had to force himself to do so.

Then he was gone.

He didn't go to his office. He left the cabin entirely. The door slammed behind him, something that had only happened once before in all the months she had known him. Jonas didn't make noise, until now. And he'd nearly slammed the door off its hinges.

Stumbling to the bathroom, Rachel cleaned herself, repaired her clothing, then stared at the woman gazing back at her from the mirror.

Who was she?

She touched her perspiration-damp hair back from her face and stared at the stranger she had suddenly become. The stranger who was suddenly wondering what in the hell she was allowing to happen here.

She shook her head. Jonas wouldn't be gone long, and she knew it. She rather doubted he would make it to D.C., despite his claim to be heading there.

He was too protective. He had claimed her, even without the mating. She was his mate, despite the fact that he hadn't possessed her.

He wouldn't leave without her, and he had no intentions of risking her by taking her and Amber from Sanctuary until he managed to capture Brandenmore.

Moving back to her desk, she sat down and stared at the computer. They needed information against Racert. Something that would force him to back off and to stop his attempts to destroy the Breeds.

She pulled up her email, located an address and typed in the message she knew would produce results.

Racert is a threat. Diana would know what she meant, and she would know what to do. If there was information to find, then Diana would find it. If there was a weapon they could use against the senator, then her sister would ensure that Rachel had it.

Rachel had never asked Diana to help her. The one time she had tried, her sister had been impossible to locate. Diana had sworn she would make up for it. That all Rachel had to do was ask.

She would have never asked for herself.

For this, for Jonas, for Merinus, for the Breeds who now stood between her and whatever plans Brandenmore had had in store for her and Amber, she would make the request.

◆   ◆   ◆

Jonas strode into the estate house and moved directly to the labs below and Ely's office.

Pushing into her office, he watched as she lifted her attention from the samples she was studying, her gaze clearing as she watched him enter the room.

"Damn, she's killing you." She moved back from the bioscope, a computerized biological scanning machine that she used to detect anomalies in Breed fluid samples, and crossed her arms over her breasts as she glared at him. "You touched her again, didn't you?"

"Give me a break, Ely," he growled before staring around the room. "Where the fuck is Jackal?"

He'd assigned Jackal to her security months ago. The other man was only to leave her side in the most extreme emergencies.

"The man has to sleep sometime, Jonas." She rolled her eyes at the question. "He has someone else on duty outside." She waved her hand to the door. "I don't want them in here."

She had been endangered. The protection he'd arranged for her hadn't been good enough; her assistants had nearly killed her, slowly poisoning her body and her mind in their attempts to betray the Breeds. It had nearly destroyed her.

He sat down gingerly on the stool she pushed toward him. He felt as though he had been through a war. Hell, he'd been through wars and hadn't hurt so damned much.

His cock throbbed worse than any bullet he'd ever taken; his flesh was so sensitive that the air around him was painful. This mating shit was about to kill him.

He held his arm out to Ely.

She shook her head. "More samples aren't going to help, Jonas. It's only going to show the same thing. The hormone is getting stronger. There's nothing I can find to stop it."

"Something's happening to me, Ely." He shook his head. "I haven't slept in days, and it's not just the arousal. I can't keep my claws sheathed." He showed her the deadly sharp claws, which had retracted beneath his nails. "My incisors ache and the barb is trying to emerge without sex. This is killing me."

Picking up the pressure extractor, the slender, wandlike needleless instrument used to take blood, she pressed it to his vein. The flesh was so tough from the tension inside him that nothing filled the vial.

"I'm going to have to use the needle." She sighed as worry filled her expression. "I've never had to use a needle on a Breed before, Jonas."

Moving to a cabinet, she pulled a sterile needle and vial from the supplies stored there and moved back to him.

Minutes later, two vials filled, she returned with a swab.

Jonas opened his mouth, grimacing at the swollen condition of the glands beneath his tongue as she swiped the swab over them, producing a heated ache as the hormone pulsed from overly filled glands.

"Kane didn't have these symptoms, but he's not a Breed," she stated as she began to make notes on the electronic pad she pulled from another counter. "Your genetic and biological makeup is so different from other Breeds that I don't know how to help you."

He was in agony. He was so close to losing control of the animal pushing at his mind that he could barely function now.

"I have to leave," he growled. "I'm going to end up raping her, Ely."

Ely turned back to him, sympathy and aching affection reflecting in her gaze now.

"I need samples from her," she told him. "The only chance I have at developing anything to help you will have to come from her."

"No." He had been refusing that idea since bringing her to Sanctuary. "I don't want this for her. I don't want her to see this part of the mating, Ely. The constant tests, the embarrassment of them. Hell, she's wary enough as it is."

He ran his hand over the back of his neck and fought to hold on to the furious lust raging through him. It was worse than feral fever, and he should know—he'd been there, done that.

"She's destroying you." There was an edge of anger brewing in Ely now.

Jonas shook his head, forcing himself to stand. "Do you need semen samples?"

She breathed out roughly. "Can you produce any?"

It hadn't happened yesterday. He hadn't been able to masturbate, to find release. Nothing worked, and he'd been trying for days.

"Is there any other way to get them?" Hell, he'd try for the needle if he had to. Anything to help Ely find a way to ease the agony washing through him in fiery waves.

"There's no other way, Jonas." She shook her head. "I need the semen samples. The blood and saliva isn't enough."

He grimaced, feeling the tightness of his expression as he tried to think of a solution.

"What about Amburg?" he asked. "Does he have any ideas?"

"Amburg always has ideas," she snorted rudely. "Unfortunately, he hasn't come up with anything to help with this."

Jeffrey Amburg was strange as hell, but if he said he had no solution to this problem, then he had none. He was a master geneticist, a third-generation Genetics Council scientist, and once considered the scourge of the Breed labs. He lived for his research and for his granddaughter. Nothing else mattered to the man. When Jonas had extended the option of living and serving the Breeds versus dying, Jeffrey had actually smiled.

Seeing the evolution of the Breeds, even if he couldn't share it outside of Ely and Elizabeth, was worth more than gold to the man. It was almost worth more than his grand-daughter's life at times.

"Looks like I'm screwed then," he grunted as he headed to the door. "Let me know if you figure anything out."

"Jonas." She stopped him as he gripped the doorknob.

"Yeah, Ely?" He was certain he didn't want to hear what-ever she was getting ready to say to him. There were times when she was a little too honest.

"Kiss her."

Jonas clenched his teeth at the overwhelming urge to do just that. He'd nearly taken the choice out of her hands earlier. The only thing that had saved her was the fact that he had managed to keep her back to him.

And still, he'd nearly kissed her. When her head had lifted back, when she had watched him taste the sweetness of her pussy, he'd almost taken her lips and spilled the hormone into a kiss that he knew would have burned them both alive.

"Let me know what you find out after you've finished with the tests." He opened the door.

"You're going to let her destroy you," she stated, her voice painfully low. "If she does that, Jonas, then she will destroy all of us."

Jonas shook his head. "No one is indispensible, Ely, even me. I've ensured that."

"You think you have," she said, her voice trembling. "But you haven't, Jonas. What you do, no one else can."

He almost laughed at the statement. "Ely, every Breed alive can manipulate and calculate until hell freezes over. Brim, Del Rey, Callan, Wolfe, any of them could do what I do and not cause nearly as much trouble doing it. You're just prejudiced because I don't let you sit around and feel sorry for yourself when others do."

He teased her. He refused to let her sink into despair of the lapse she'd had when the drugs spreading through her system had eroded her judgment.

Ely was a fragile little thing, despite her façade of strength. She had seen too much in the labs at too young an age, had been forced to harm too many Breeds while there. She lived with the nightmares of those years, and now she lived with the nightmare of nearly being forced to do it again.

"No, you don't allow me to feel sorry for myself," she agreed quietly. "But I should stand aside and watch you allow this woman to destroy you. Would you do the same, I wonder, if the tables were turned?"

He pursed his lips and stared back at her for long moments before saying, "I've been allowing it, little cat. Do you think I haven't figured out who your mate is, and that you know it as well?"

She blanched, her brown eyes skittering away from him as fear flashed across her face.

"Do something about it soon," he warned her.

"As you are?" she shot back, anger filling her voice now.

"I think I'd try a different venue there if I were you," he retorted as he left the office. "A far different one. Kiss him. I really don't think he'd object."

Closing the door behind him, he moved through the hall, back to the flight of stairs that led to the main level of the house.

He was trying to force himself to leave Sanctuary. Leaving was the best thing he could do for Rachel. If he didn't get the hell away from her, then he was going to end up taking this decision out of her hands.

"Jonas." Mordecai met him in the hall as he reached the main level, his expression hard. Several Enforcers followed him.

"What now?" he growled, sensing the trouble that was sure to follow.

"You have a problem."

It wasn't "we," as in the Breeds had a problem; it was "he," as in shit was about to hit the fan.

"And that problem is?" He propped his hands on his hips and regarded the Enforcers with a frown.

"Devon Marshal," Mordecai sneered. "He claims he's the father of Rachel's child. He's at the gates with his lawyer as well as a county official. They have papers signed by a judge out of D.C. demanding Amber be relinquished to Child Protective Services until the matter of custody can be resolved. The papers state Amber's safety is in danger due to Breed carelessness." Mordecai slapped the file into Jonas's hands. "I don't know about you, but I say we shoot the fuckers, bury the bodies and deny they were ever here. Because trust me, you don't want to turn that baby over to him."

Jonas stilled.

He was aware of the Enforcers backing away, even Mordecai, and glancing at each other as though uncertain about even their own safety.

Jonas grinned. He knew it must have been a frightening sight; the scent of nervousness began to pour from the three Enforcers, who watched him with varying expressions of concern.

"Well, then, Mordecai, perhaps you should appraise Callan, Kane, the Leo, of course, and the rest of the Pride that we're about to have a burial. I'll see you outside when you've finished."

With that, he moved toward the main doors, distantly aware of the growls vibrating in his throat and the rage tearing through his body.

Devon Marshal was a dead man.

Jonas had made a claim on Rachel's child before she had even drawn her first breath. Sheltered in the womb, her senses much like that of an animal's, reaching out to him and her mother, the animal inside him had accepted her as his own.

The man who claimed paternity had deserted Rachel in Switzerland, stolen her passport and what money she possessed when his parents had cut his funds when they learned Rachel hadn't aborted the child, and left her stranded.

Throughout the pregnancy and Amber's birth, Devon Marshal had been absent from her life.

Jonas had a feeling he knew exactly why the other man was standing at the gates of Sanctuary with a team of lawyers, Child Protective Services and Buffalo Gap's sheriff.

Devon's parents, Greg and Marsha Marshal, were opponents of Breed Law and critical of the world's acceptance of the Breeds. They had poured huge amounts of funds into the legal teams that had worked to fight against Breed freedom, and even now used their vast influence to attempt to halt the growth of Breed society.

They were there for that child, but not because she was part of the Marshal legacy. News reports of the explosion of Rachel's house had stated that she and her child were now residing in Sanctuary, along with the director of Breed Affairs. There was speculation as to their relationship, as well as a story that had claimed there was proof that Rachel and her child were now living in his cabin.

As he drove the Raider toward the security checkpoint, he came to a stop as another pulled into the road ahead of him.

Eyes narrowed, he watched as Cassie Sinclair, dressed in her best conservative lawyer's outfit, a slim below-the-knee skirt, white blouse, black jacket. Her long hair was pulled back into a neat, low ponytail, and she carried a bulging briefcase.

He'd known she would be there. With Cassie, he could always be certain she was where she needed to be.

The door of the Raider opened and she stepped in.

"They have papers signed by the magistrate," she stated as she pulled a folder free of her briefcase. "What the magistrate is unaware of is that we have the papers Devon Marshal signed just after Rachel began working for you, where he signed over all rights of the child to Rachel. I was there, if you remember." She grinned precociously. "I bet he remembers too."

Jonas put the Raider in gear as her driver ahead moved the other vehicle out of the way.

"How much trouble are we going to have?" he asked her.

Cassie shrugged. "They won't get her out of Sanctuary legally, I can tell you that much. I have all those bases covered, in triplicate. I also have the papers you signed accepting Amber Broen as a part of Sanctuary, with all the rights that entails." She pulled free the papers he had signed just after Amber's birth.

"I also have the papers signed by the Breed ruling cabinet, accepting her as a part of the Breed community, and Jess Warden is standing by to fly out of D.C. if we need her."

Hell, he hoped they didn't need the Breed's head legal

counsel. Jess was still pissed over Amburg's disappearance after he was captured. She was certain he was being held by Jonas, and refused to believe otherwise. She harassed him every time she saw him.

"What's going on here, Cassie?" he asked her.

Cassie was different; that was the only explanation Jonas could give for it. Some people swore she talked to ghosts; when she was smaller, she claimed to have a fairy that warned her of impending danger.

She was considered a psychic by others, while still more simply called her a freak.

"What's always going on?" she retorted absently as she set a pair of glasses on her face and arranged the papers she had brought with her. "I have the investigative report on Devon that we had done just after we hired Rachel, along with pictures and detailed reports of many of his associations with several drug dealers. I also have the reports of his contacts with known terrorists against Breeds. I have enough to keep him away from Amber for the time being. We'll just have to see what they come up with next."

Jonas pulled up to the security post, exited the Raider, then walked to the side and helped Cassie out. Another vehicle rolled in behind them.

Jonas wanted to curse. He stood still, watching as Rachel jumped from the Raider, her green eyes narrowed on Devon Marshal as he stood at the gates.

"Hold on, Cassie." He strode to Rachel quickly, gripped her arm and pulled her to the back of the Raider.

"He is not getting my baby," she snapped furiously, staring up at Jonas like an enraged mother lioness as Lawe stepped out of the driver's seat and walked toward them.

"No, he isn't. I took steps to ensure he couldn't when Amber was born. Just keep quiet, Rachel. Let Cassie handle this, and I'll explain everything when we're finished here."

"What do you mean, *you took steps to ensure it*?" Despite the low pitch of her tone, Jonas flinched at the undercurrent of violence it carried. It was a damned good thing what he had done would benefit her; otherwise, he might have been wondering if he should be frightened.

"Rachel, calm yourself immediately." The order was given in a tone just as low, but rumbling with the power of the animal inside him. "You will stand quietly, lend the power of your support behind Cassie and we'll discuss the specifics later."

Her gaze flickered, but only for a moment before her eyes narrowed once again. "If you try to give him my child . . ."

"I would die before I would allow him to take that child," he snarled back at her, furious that she would ever consider that he would do such a thing. "If you want this to go smoothly, without Child Protective Services having Sanctuary surrounded by state police, then do as I say. Lend your support rather than your panic."

Rachel was in shock as he gripped her arm and led her back to where Cassie stood by the side of the Raider, watching calmly as reporters began to arrive at the gates as well.

"Ready?" she asked gently as she met Rachel's gaze, her neon blue eyes seeming deeper, darker than before.

Rachel nodded sharply. "As ready as I'll ever be without preparation."

Cassie smiled back at her. "Everything would have been explained once I finished the paperwork. I would have met with you tomorrow had both our schedules allowed it. But have no fear, Jonas had your back."

Jonas had her back? She prayed to God Cassie knew what she was talking about. Devon's family had power and influence. She'd prayed they wouldn't come after Amber, had done everything to ensure they simply forgot about her. And now here they were.

Devon stood in front of the gate, a glare on his too handsome, darkly tanned face. His blond hair was thick, waving back from the sculpted features of his face, while his blue eyes narrowed in dislike.

He had stolen from her, left her stranded in a strange country, and he was watching her as though he disliked her? There was something wrong with this picture.

More reporters were pulling up as she stepped into the guards' shack with Cassie and Jonas. The small building boasted a large table for just such preliminary meetings, a refrigerator, microwave, weapons locker and an array of electronics carefully protected behind heavy steel-, cement- and blast-resistant glass.

"Crank." Jonas nodded to the guard on duty, a less-than-sociable Coyote with shaggy black hair and gray eyes.

"Director." Grating and rough, his voice sounded torn from his throat. "Can I shoot the bastards?" He nodded toward the reporters gathering outside.

"Not yet, Crank," Jonas drawled. "But if you could escort Mr. Marshal and his attorneys inside, perhaps we could get this over with."

"I say we set them loose in the woods and use them for the babies to hunt," Crank grunted. "Bastards ain't good for nothin' else."

"Crank, please." Cassie shot him a disapproving frown. "I know how you love intimidating the masses, but let's see about making a nice impression today."

The Coyote sighed but cleared his expression as he moved to the door, stepped out and met with Devon, Buffalo Gap's district magistrate and the three attorneys, all dressed in their finest, most intimidating suits.

They stepped into the security shack, the attorneys staring down their perfectly straight noses as Devon lifted his lip in distaste.

Rachel stood next to Jonas, taking comfort from the strength and complete assurance he projected.

"Director Wyatt." The lead attorney nodded in Jonas's direction, and Rachel could have sworn she glimpsed an edge of respect in the lawyer's gaze before he turned and nodded at her as well.

"Mr. Edgewood." Jonas shook hands with the attorney

before turning to Rachel. "This is Miss Broen, and accompanying us as legal counsel today is Ms. Cassandra Sinclair."

The three men glanced at Cassie. Only Edgewood was aware of the perceptive young woman he was now facing; the other two, by the condescension on their faces, didn't have a clue.

Cassie was considered one of the foremost authorities on Breed Law, and was currently in her final year of law school. At nineteen, she had excelled far beyond what even the Breeds had anticipated.

"My colleagues, Ryan Former and Daniel Frost. And may I introduce Ms. Blanchard, from Child Protection Services."

The CPS agent nodded with a faint smile, her brown eyes gazing around in concern as she felt the tension in the room.

"Ms. Broen, a pleasure." John Edgewood maintained a respectful, cool manner as he shook her hand.

"Mr. Edgewood." She fought to keep her voice cool, to keep her voice from shaking with fear.

"Gentlemen." Jonas nodded when the other two stepped back, refusing to partake in a handshake with either Jonas or Rachel.

"And may I introduce my client, Devon Richard Marshal." The attorney turned to his client as he stepped back as well, his arms crossing over his chest as he glared back at Jonas, then at Rachel.

Jonas's eyes narrowed before he turned back to the lead attorney. "I believe you remember that this area is monitored by video as well as audio on a continual basis." Jonas looked around the room to the eight cameras that kept the inside of the shack covered. There were even more outside.

"I do remember, Director Wyatt." The lawyer nodded. "I may have neglected to mention that." He turned to the other lawyers. "Gentlemen, all meeting areas within Sanctuary are recorded continually for your protection as well as for the protection of the Breed society."

The two attorneys, who had deliberately snubbed Jonas, were now well aware of the fact that their recorded reactions would be used against them. Each of them had varying expressions of displeasure and concern now.

"Would you like to have a seat, gentlemen, Ms. Blanchard?" Jonas waved his hand to the table where Cassie was pulling files from her briefcase.

"Rachel?" Jonas's hand tightened at her back. "Shall we take a seat?"

Her knees were shaking as she sat. She was terrified of what this meeting would result in, but not for a moment was she frightened that Jonas would allow anyone to take her baby.

Rachel clenched her hands in her lap as Edgewood and Cassie spent a moment talking in low tones before Cassie took her seat with a murmured assent.

"Director Wyatt." The attorney nodded to Jonas once again before turning to her. "Ms. Broen. Ms. Sinclair. As we informed your guard, we have papers here signed by Judge Joseph Markham. You're ordered to turn over the minor child Amber Diana Broen immediately to Child Protective Services until custody can be decided and the complaint brought against Ms. Broen in the neglect and deliberate endangerment of the child can be decided."

The attorney handed Cassie the papers before laying out a copy for both Rachel and Jonas.

Rachel couldn't bear to read them. She glared at Devon instead.

"The grounds this is based upon?" Cassie asked coolly. "There has been no neglect or endangerment of the child. As you know, according to Breed Law, no child can be demanded or removed from Sanctuary or Haven without irrefutable proof of any charges."

Edgewood's gaze was sympathetic as he glanced at Rachel before turning back to Cassie. "I'm sorry, Ms. Sinclair, that law applies only to Breed children."

Devon's smile was a slow curl of triumph. The arrogance and superiority he showed now was something she hadn't seen in Switzerland. Or had she not wanted to see it?

God, how had she so lost her mind to have actually slept with this man, let alone believe she loved him at one time? But she couldn't make herself regret it. Without Devon, she wouldn't have had Amber, and her child was more than worth every moment of hell he had put her through.

"I'm sorry, Mr. Edgewood, but that's not precisely true." Cassie's voice was soft, cool, assured.

Edgewood frowned. "I checked this law just to be certain, Ms. Sinclair."

Cassie shuffled through her papers, pulled a file free, then handed it to the attorney.

"As you'll see, Breed Law in many areas has stipulations that must be addressed in each situation." She handed out copies of the particular law.

Edgewood read, frowned, then stared back at Cassie.

"This isn't entirely legal," he stated. "This law is not in an accessible area . . ."

"Had you done as you were advised when you checked the statutes and laws that apply to the Breed society, you would have read the clause on addendums and notations attached to it. Many of our laws have such addendums, Mr. Edgewood. Our country, those elected to protect and preserve all human life, were involved in our creation, our imprisonment and the torturous deaths of our children before they had a chance to consider escape. Because of that, any question in regard to child welfare or extraction of a child from Sanctuary can and will be known and understood before any such action is taken. The Bureau of Breed Affairs was not notified of this complaint, nor of any accusation of neglect or endangerment. Added to that, Mr. Marshal relinquished all rights to Ms. Broen's child at the child's birth." She flashed him a sunny smile. "You do remember me, don't you, Mr. Marshal?"

His jaw set as fury shimmered in his blue eyes.

"What is she talking about, Devon?" Edgewood questioned him.

"Here's what she's talking about." Cassie laid out another

paper. "Signed, notarized and filed with the Bureau of Breed Affairs. Mr. Marshal signed away all parental rights, as represented by his legal counsel at the time, one Mr. Claude Desmond of Nevada."

Edgewood's look was one of ice as he stared at Devon.

"That's not legal," Devon stated. "I didn't fully understand what she intended to do with Amber. And that's besides the fact. Child Protective Services is to have the baby until the charges have been decided anyway."

"It doesn't work that way, Mr. Marshal," Cassie said sweetly. "Child Protective Services has no jurisdiction here."

"Amber is not a fucking Breed brat," Devon snarled, his tone nasty, his expression filled with disgust. "That fucking law doesn't apply to her."

"A fucking Breed brat. What an interesting choice of words," Cassie stated succinctly. "As though our children have no worth. Is that how you see it?"

"Shut up, Devon," Edgewood warned him.

"Don't tell me to shut up," Devon snapped. "And hell yes, that's how I see it. Amber is a Marshal. She's human, not a damned animal or an animal's whelp."

Jonas tensed. Rachel felt the dangerous tension that slowly tightened his body.

"Do something with your client, John," he ordered the attorney. "Before I do."

Whether it was the sight of the incisors flashing at the sides of Jonas's mouth or the look of murderous fury in his gaze, Devon subsided with a childish pout and glared at Rachel once again.

"This changes things, Mr. Edgewood." The mayor lifted his head from the document before glancing at the Child Protective Services agent. "Ms. Blanchard? Do you see anything I don't?"

"I agree with your assessment," the kindly middle-aged child services representative stated as she too closed her file. "The child can't be taken from Sanctuary."

"Sanctuary has no rights over non-Breed children," Frost defended their position.

"Read your file, Daniel," Edgewood advised him. "Mr. Wyatt himself has signed the documents necessary to incorporate Ms. Broen's child into Sanctuary, which has been written into Breed Law and signed by our president as well as by Congress. She doesn't have to be a Breed; her mother merely has to be considered a Breed's mate, which by her presence, I assume she's agreeable to?" Edgewood stared back at her.

Jonas's tension ratcheted by several degrees.

"I'm agreeable." There was no way she couldn't be. She couldn't lose her child, and she was well aware she was fighting a losing battle where Jonas was concerned.

"Whore!" Devon sneered, a long, drawn-out hiss of viciousness.

Rachel's hand tightened on Jonas's thigh as she felt him move. The insult was designed to draw a reaction from Jonas, one Devon and/or his lawyers could use against the Breeds and Rachel in a battle to take possession of Amber.

He didn't move. He sat still, silent, his full attention locked on Devon as Rachel felt the promise of retribution pouring from him.

"Daniel, Ryan, please take Devon back to the limo," Edgewood snapped as Cassie rose slowly to her feet, centering an imperious, icy glare on the other man.

"Mr. Edgewood, before you file any motion with any court, or attempt to take one of our children from Sanctuary, perhaps you should do a full investigation into Breed Law and all the steps necessary to so much as file an intent to file," she informed him. "Mating laws are complicated, exacting and, trust me, created to be unbreakable for the next two centuries. Think of that before you attempt to have Ms. Broen's child placed with anyone other than her mother."

Edgewood grimaced before gathering together the files and documents Cassie laid out for him and storing them in his case.

"I apologize for my client, Director Wyatt," Edgewood expressed as he snapped his case closed and prepared to leave.

"No apology necessary, John," Jonas drawled as he too moved to his feet. "Think nothing of it."

Rachel shivered at the sound of intent in Jonas's voice, and Edgewood was no man's fool. His sharp glance settled on Jonas before he nodded slowly and turned back to Cassie with a muttered, "I'll be in touch."

The room cleared, and seconds later the dark blinds over the windows slowly eased up once again.

"This isn't the end of it," Cassie informed them both. "And a piece of advice to both of you: Marshal could demand proof of the mating, which unfortunately you cannot provide until you actually mate."

"How long do we have, Cassie?" Jonas asked, his voice tight.

Cassie paused, glanced at Rachel, then smiled gently. "Enough time, Jonas. I don't think we need to worry." A small frown edged at her brows then. "At least, not yet."

Rachel rubbed her hands together, still feeling chilled and frightened.

"When did you do all this?" she whispered, turning to Jonas. "The paperwork, accepting Amber into Breed society, declaring me as your mate?"

There was a hardness to his face that was almost frightening.

"I declared you as my mate before her birth. Once she was born, I filled out the paperwork to accept her as my daughter."

"You *adopted* her?" she asked incredulously.

He shrugged his shoulders before rubbing at the back of his neck. "I didn't adopt her, I accepted her. There's a difference. A Breed isn't required to adopt a child. Once he or she is accepted as the Breed's responsibility, then it's his child, whether that child lives in Sanctuary or in Haven, or not. It's simply a part of Breed Law to ensure that a mate cannot be governed by society's laws any more than a Breed can be. We're self-governed, completely, unless we declare aggression against the nation itself, not just its laws or law enforcement agencies."

Rachel knew Breed Law was deliberately complicated, and much of its explanations left out unless one were given permission to see a particular law in full. The red tape required to do so was lengthy and expensive.

It had been done in such a way as to remind the nation and the world that they were paying for the hell the Breeds had endured. For two centuries, they were given rights and allowed a leeway that was inconceivable at any other time or with any other race.

"You should have asked me." Pushing her fingers through her hair, Rachel fought to get a handle on her emotions and her fears.

Stepping into a mating was a hell of a lot different from deciding to sleep with a man, or agreeing on marriage.

"Why?" He motioned Cassie and Crank from the shelter as he closed the automatic shades on the windows once again. "What would telling you have accomplished?"

"I would have known."

"You could have protested and therefore delayed paperwork that would have protected Amber," he informed her matter-of-factly. "My main objective was protecting you and your child, Rachel."

"My God, you act as though she belongs to you," she burst out, wondering at his motives.

"You belong to me, therefore Amber is my responsibility," he stated. "I knew you were my mate. In accepting you, I accepted your child as my own."

"That doesn't make sense." There was no way a man could simply accept a child as his own without knowing the mother or loving her.

She didn't understand.

Jonas could feel the confusion that swirled in her, part anger, part fear.

"It's part of Breed genetics." He sighed, wishing he could

make her understand, wishing she could accept this as easily as Elizabeth Sinclair had accepted it.

But then, her mate, Dash, had come for her because of their correspondence. It hadn't come like this. A bond had developed with the child before birth, because her mother was his mate.

Animal genetics were a bitch.

He watched as she breathed out roughly, raked her fingers through her hair once more and stared at him as though she weren't quite certain she knew who he was.

"Male lions kill the young when they take another male's pride," she muttered in exasperation.

"Human males love the children of the women they love," he completed for her. "We're not just animals, Rachel. We're men with a few added genetics. Nothing more, nothing less." Which wasn't a lie, but wasn't really the truth either.

"Devon isn't going to let this go this easily." She moved away from him, staring at the darkened windows. He felt her fighting to make sense of what her life had become.

"Devon has no choice." It was that simple. "All the money in the world, all the lawyers he could buy can't change Breed Law, Rachel. We ensured that."

A mocking smile twisted her lips. "You act as though the Marshals will play fair after this."

"You act as though Breeds will." He chuckled, though the sound was tinged with a warning of danger. "Come on, let's get the hell away from here and those damned reporters out there."

He touched her again. His hand pressed against her lower back, steering her back to the doorway, where Enforcers waited to escort them away from the entrance and the reporters who could just as easily shoot with bullets as with flashbulbs.

The ride back to the cabin was made quickly, silently.

Rachel kept her arms wrapped across her chest as she fought to hold in not just the questions that raged through her mind but also the emotions that tore at her control.

She was falling in love with him, and she couldn't help it. There were just so many ways Jonas had proved his complete dedication to her. His hunger for her. His need. His determination to protect her.

He didn't call it love. To him, she was his mate, pure and simple. The one gift God had given him that could never belong to another man.

But he didn't call it love. He didn't recognize it as love.

Moving into the house, she walked into Amber's room, informed the young Breed female watching the baby that she could leave, then lifted her daughter from the crib.

"Cassie's on the sat phone. She needs to talk to you." Jonas stood at the doorway, his gaze dark. "Would you like me to hold Amber while you talk to her?"

Silently, she handed Amber over to him, watching as he cuddled her close to his chest, his eyes still watching her carefully.

That look. There was complete arrogance in it, yet a vulnerability that tugged at emotions she didn't want to admit to.

She lifted the phone to her ear. "Cassie?"

"Go to another room, Rachel. We need to talk." Cassie's tone brooked no refusal. For a teenager, she could sound amazingly mature. "And don't bother to make excuses to Jonas; we both know he just heard every word I said."

She rolled her eyes as she glanced at Jonas, noticing how well he pretended he wasn't hearing every word Cassie said.

Breeds were a pain in the ass.

Shaking her head, she moved from the bedroom, through the living room, then into the kitchen.

"Good," Cassie expressed as she stepped into the far room. "So how are you feeling?"

How was she feeling?

"Cassie, are you doing drugs?" she asked carefully.

The young woman laughed lightly. "I don't do drugs at all, Rachel. I simply wanted to assure you that the legalities of Amber's acceptance into Breed society has no loopholes. There is nothing the Marshals can do to break that clause."

"What they can't acquire legally, they'll acquire illegally." Rachel sighed. "Amber will never be safe."

"No adult or child within Sanctuary is safe, Rachel," Cassie said softly. "No Breed mate or friend is safe. It's simply a part of our world."

A part of their world. And it didn't matter if they were child or adult, friend or mate. Anyone associated with the Breeds came under fire at one time or another.

She had known that, Rachel told herself. She was aware of it from the beginning, but until now, it hadn't truly hit her. She and Amber had never truly been safe; they had been living merely on borrowed time. Sooner or later, she would have been targeted because of her job, her friendship to Merinus and Kane, or simply because she believed so deeply in the freedom of the Breeds.

"I'm fine, Cassie," she finally told the young woman. "I just need some time to think."

"Thinking is perhaps what you don't need to do, Rachel," Cassie said gently. "Maybe now it's time to simply feel. Good night, Rachel."

The line disconnected, leaving Rachel staring into the kitchen with a vague sense of impending anticipation. Nervousness.

Disconnecting the phone from her end, she turned and headed back to the bedroom, only to come to a stop, once again amazed by the man, the Breed, who claimed her.

He was diapering Amber as though he had done it many times before. And he had, while Rachel slept.

"Cassie likes to poke her nose into things when it's not needed just as well as she does when it is." Jonas fixed the undershirt Amber wore before pulling her gown back around her feet.

The baby kicked, gurgled, her fists flailing as she stared up at Jonas with childlike wonder.

"She worries, I think," Rachel whispered.

Jonas nodded, picked Amber up from the bed, held her close to his chest and reached for the bottle he had obviously prepared earlier.

"Go bathe, Rachel." He watched her, his silver eyes calm rather than raging as normal. "Relax for a while. The next adventure will come soon enough."

The next adventure.

She almost smiled. That was similar to many of her sister's views. And it was nothing less than the truth.

Hopefully, the next adventure wouldn't be quite so hard on her nerves.

· C H A P T E R   1 3 ·

The bath helped, but Rachel found herself not quite as sleepy, nor as tired, as she should be. Pulling on the long, warm gown that had been provided for her and a matching robe, she took a deep breath before leaving the bathroom.

She found Amber's crib empty when she reentered the bedroom. She touched the ultra-soft comforter on the mattress and felt her heart clench in something akin to panic.

Jonas was drawing her in. He was tying her to him in ways she wasn't certain she wanted to be tied to him.

Love.

She had thought she loved Devon. Those months in Switzerland had been incredible even though the job she had gone there for hadn't quite worked out.

She had thought it fate when she met Devon.

He had been bright, funny. She hadn't even known who his family was for months. Not until his father had arrived, dour, disapproving, and informed her that she wasn't good enough to marry into the elite Marshal clan.

Her confusion had been almost comical.

He'd looked Devon straight in the eye and disowned him until he decided to get some balls, as he called it, and ditch the dumb bitch he had knocked up.

He'd thrown a clip of money on the floor, ordered her to get an abortion and left.

Devon had sworn he loved her. He had contacts, he'd claimed. He would get a job; he loved working.

She snorted at the memory. That night he had disappeared. Not just with the money clip and Rachel's money, but also her passport and credit cards as well. She had been stranded; the rent and utilities were due. There had been no food.

He'd left a letter, short and to the point. He would contact her when the doctor he directed her to called and informed him the abortion had been performed. She could go home then.

The embassy had refused to help her after firing her. Of course, Devon's father had ensured that. She hadn't been able to get a job. Every time she secured one, something happened and she was fired within hours.

She'd called Kane out of desperation when she couldn't reach Diana.

And now, here she was.

Perhaps Devon had been fate after all, she thought. That road had led her to Merinus, and then to Jonas.

Or perhaps she was simply being as fanciful as Diana had always accused her of being.

Either way, here she was, and she was learning that love wasn't as tidy, or as sweet and easy, as she had once thought it should be.

It came with complications, and it came with a hell of a lot of questions.

Turning, she strode to the doorway, and for the second time, came to a stop. In front of the fire, on the large, soft rug before it, Jonas lay with Amber.

He'd changed clothes. Dressed in loose sweatpants, bare feet and a bare chest, he lay next to the baby as the fire flickered in front of them.

Amber was watching the flames with the drowsy wonder that only a baby could show. Her lashes lay low, sleep edging her expression as Jonas softly hummed a lullaby.

The dark rhythm of the sound lulled her as well, but it did nothing to cause drowsiness. Rachel felt her entire body flushing with arousal instead. The sensation was deeper, stronger, than it had ever been, fueled by emotions that tore through her, that left her aching for his arms around her, or a glimmer of warmth and amusement in his gaze.

Was it mating heat, or simply an amplification of the emotional and physical response to the person she was meant to love anyway?

Society had created a world where commitment to a relationship, to marriage, didn't mean what it had once meant. Marriages broke up over money, family, petty arguments and jobs that left individuals tired and searching for peace. A peace that wasn't often found when they walked through the doors and met screaming children, endless chores, and phone calls from demanding relatives.

Had nature decided to circumvent the ability to ignore the relationship and the commitment to one person?

What she felt wasn't a forced seduction or hunger. This was natural. What she would feel once she took the kiss she knew was awaiting her was another thing. That kiss would tie her to one man for more than a normal lifetime. And it would make her a part of something she still didn't understand, but found she didn't want to miss.

And her sister, Diana, said she lacked a sense of adventure. She was about to go on an adventure that even her sister would hesitate to face.

"She's almost asleep." The soft hum stopped to be replaced by the rich, dark sound of his voice. "She loves watching the flames."

And watching him with her daughter was breaking her heart. The man lying on the floor was nothing like the Director of Breed Affairs that he had been when he walked out of this cabin.

This man was meant to be a father. He was meant to cherish and to love everyone who came under his protection.

"It's the flickering light she loves," Rachel told him as she watched her daughter's lashes lower farther.

His fingers gently stroked the baby's arm, her tiny fingers. Amber looked so tiny next to him that Rachel wondered that he wasn't frightened to touch her. At times, Rachel was terrified of breaking her.

"She looks like you," Jonas said, his voice still soft. "A living beauty."

Rachel's breath caught as his gaze lifted from the child, to her. For once, the living mercury of his eyes wasn't raging. They were calm, glowing in his dark face with power and promise.

She couldn't speak. The words felt locked in her throat, the power to pull them free lacking inside her. He stared at her as though he truly adored her, as though she was perhaps perfect, beautiful, a woman well worth desiring.

No man had ever stared at her in such a manner before. No man had ever made her feel as though she was the center of his hunger, and only she could relieve it.

Jonas rose to his knees then, picked the baby up and straightened before moving across the living room to the smaller crib, which he must have placed there while she was showering.

Rachel closed the bedroom door and stepped into the living room.

He was putting the baby closer to them so they could hear her from his room, separated by the open fireplace. Private, yet accessible should Amber need them.

"I thought you would want to hear her if she fussed tonight." He laid Amber in the crib so she could continue to watch the flames, before drawing a light blanket decorated with tiny pink teddy bears over her tiny body.

"I don't understand this," she whispered as she paused before the fireplace and watched as he turned back to her. "And I'm frightened of it."

"Frightened of what?" He moved to her, his long legs eating the distance despite the fact that he was moving slowly. "What's there to be frightened of, sweetheart? More pleasure than you can imagine? A man who would die for you?"

Things women swore they would die for. It wasn't the love, or the devotion, that frightened her, though.

"Of the mating heat." She swallowed tightly. "I don't like not having control, Jonas. I don't know how to live and not be certain of what tomorrow will bring, or how not to control what my own destiny is."

"Did you know what tomorrow would bring when you were with Marshal? And sweetheart, I hate to tell you this, but you have all the control," he told her softly, his hands moving to her shoulders, his fingers caressing the flesh revealed by the loose neckline of the gown. "Whatever you want, I'm here to provide, Rachel," he promised. "Whatever keeps you safe, happy and in my arms, I'm here to give you. Just tell me what you want."

His head lowered, but he didn't kiss her lips. He didn't share the mating hormone that Ely had stated made each breath torturous, the hunger was so intense. Instead, his lips touched the skin just below her ear, where sensations were magnified, where heat built and spread along her nerve endings like wildfire.

Rachel felt her lashes drifting closed as sensual weakness and an emotional overload assailed her. What he did to her, she could barely make sense of. He could break her heart, he could make her want to shoot him, but through it all, she didn't want to miss this chance.

"What are you doing?" Breathing was becoming harder by the second as she felt arousal burning through her, marking her with the need for his touch.

His lips were warm velvet, his tongue, with its slight rasp, a heated roughness that had her eyes closing and her knees weakening, and the hunger to feel more, to feel all of him, nearly overwhelmed her.

"Jonas." She whispered his name, the need building inside

her now, tearing through her and laying waste to any thought she may have been harboring about thinking this step through any longer.

Lifting her hands, she pressed her fingers to his hard, heated abdomen, feeling it flex beneath her fingers as her own stomach clenched in hunger. She loved how readily he responded to her touch. There were no games with it. She gave him pleasure just as well as he gave her.

"Come to bed with me, Rachel," he breathed against her ear. "I promise, there will be no heat tonight. You have all the time you need to become accustomed the idea of it. To decide if the loss of control is worth it."

She lifted her head, staring back at him, wondering at the incredible gentleness in his voice.

"It hurts you," she whispered.

"Like it would hurt any other man not to have you." He cupped her cheek, his thumb running over her lips. "You are an addiction to me, love. But it's not as though I'm going into withdrawal quite yet."

He looked amused, patient. He didn't look like a man in the throes of agony.

"Ely thinks . . ."

"Ely is sometimes a bit overprotective when it comes to mated Breeds, and a whole lot too nosy about the biology of the phenomena," he stated as his hand stroked down her arm, his fingers finding hers as he moved back to draw her to his bedroom. "Don't worry about what Ely says, Rachel. Worry about what you need."

He was lying to her. She could see the lie in his eyes, in the fine film of perspiration glistening along his forehead. He was in pain, and the knowledge of how he held back, to give her the time she needed, had her wondering if holding back was truly what she wanted to do.

He needed to kiss her. The glands beneath his tongue, as Merinus had explained it, could become agonizingly sensitive unless the hormone was shared.

He was protecting her.

She let him draw her to the bedroom as butterflies beat against her stomach and her lungs tightened with nerves.

She had fantasized for so long. So many nights she had imagined what it would be like if he ever touched her. And his touch was more than she had ever imagined.

As he drew her into the bedroom, Rachel stared up at him, seeing in his eyes the incredible control he was exerting on himself now.

Liquid mercury eyes raged with hunger, with need. His expression was tight, savagely hewn. And sexy. The powerful, primal features of his face, the corded strength of his body, were so damned sexy she could barely stand to look at him without needing his touch.

Without needing to touch him.

Reaching to his bare shoulders, Rachel let the tips of her fingers skim across the powerful muscles, feeling the tension in them, as well as the tightly leashed control.

"You are such a liar," she whispered. "Merinus told me all about mating heat, Jonas. And what she didn't tell me, I've guessed or Ely was kind enough to spit out information on."

"Merinus has a big mouth." He grimaced as she let her nails scratch across his flesh.

"Merinus tells me the truth," she stated as he stared down with those oddly colored eyes.

"No. Merinus lies." He jerked as her nails raked lower, glancing over the tight, hard discs of his male nipples.

She wondered how long she could play with him? How far could she push him? Would his control actually break? She had never heard of anyone, man or woman, shattering his much-lauded control.

"I think you like lying." Leaning forward, her lips touched his chest, her tongue reaching out to lick over one of the tight, hard male nipples, tasting it, and then wanting more.

His hand jerked up, tangled in her hair and held her still for long, tense moments before she felt it ease marginally.

"I don't lie," he breathed out, his jaw bunching as she stared up at him before raking across his nipple with her teeth.

"Enough." A groan tore from his lips as his fingers knotted in her hair once again. "Don't tempt me, Rachel. If you think you know fear of the mating heat now, then you will surely understand what true fear of it is if you keep pushing like this."

"Like what?" she breathed out roughly as she kissed the center of his chest. "Like this?" She bit into his flesh, tugged at it, felt his stomach tremble against her own as heat flooded her pussy.

The need for his touch rushed through her like a firestorm, weakening her knees and pulsing through her womb as her breath caught with the sensation.

That smallest indication of her pleasure was nearly enough to break his control. She felt him tighten, watched as his gaze flared, heated, became molten.

A groan rumbled in his chest as he pulled her head back, his own lowering as though in preparation to kiss her.

A kiss that never came. Instead, his lips pressed to her jaw, a muted groan tearing from his lips as he pushed her robe from her shoulders with his free hand before loosening his fingers from her hair, and with that hand, pulled the slender strap of her gown over her shoulder. It was so sensual, so sexual, Rachel couldn't hold back the whimper that tore from her throat.

The bedroom became heated with hunger. Rachel could feel it in the air, brewing between them as she fought to hold on to the shattered senses.

"The need to touch you makes me insane," he growled as the robe and gown puddled at her feet.

She was naked now. Standing before him, her body laid bare for him to see, to stroke, to possess.

"God, look at you." His gaze dropped to her breasts, her nipples tight and hard, so sensitive that the very air moved across them in a stroke of pleasure.

Rachel closed her eyes, lost in the pleasure as his hands cupped her breasts, stroked them. She could feel the imperative need rising between them now, a sense of primal hunger tearing between then.

Rachel felt tremors of need racing down her spine, flickering through her pussy, stoking a flame through it that she wondered if there was any way to put out. Could she ever be sated from his touch, or would the hunger only continue to grow?

As he gripped her nipples between thumb and finger, Rachel promised herself that tonight wasn't just for her. Jonas, she was beginning to realize, would put aside his own wants, his own hungers, for his mate. For her.

Was that fair? So many people took from him; even when he manipulated them into it, still, they took, raged at him for the games he played, the results he achieved, and all he gave of himself. And no one offered of themselves, or of their lives, for Jonas.

And once again, Jonas was willing to give of himself and ask nothing in return.

Was that what she wanted?

Her head tilted back as his lips moved down her neck, rough velvet, stroking pleasure through every nerve ending, yet it wasn't enough.

It was his lips only. No stroke of his tongue, no kiss from his lips. And she wanted it, so desperately.

She was terrified of the mating heat, yet she was just as terrified of never knowing it.

She was terrified, period. Her life was raging out of control in so many ways, and yet in others, it seemed to be exactly where it should be. She was where she should be. Here in Jonas's arms.

And she knew something was missing: his kiss. The feel of his lips moving over hers, his tongue stroking against hers.

His lips were at her breasts, stroking over the flesh, rubbing against her nipple. She arched closer, trying to push her nipple between his lips. She wanted it there, ached to feel it there.

"Jonas." She whispered his name, knowing he was nowhere close to losing his remarkable control.

Should she break it? Could she break it?

She stared down at his dark head, dazed, nearly ready to beg for more.

"Do you think this is enough?" she whispered as his head lifted.

"No, it's never enough." His lips rubbed against her nipple again.

God, it was incredible, just that much.

His hand flattened against her stomach, his fingers edging down, lower, pushing into the curls between her thighs as Rachel felt her juices spilling from her pussy.

She was beginning to lose the train of thought, the determination to make him lose control. Probably because his fingers were working around her clit, stroking her into insanity.

"I want more." Her hands moved from his chest to his abdomen, to the low band of the sweatpants he wore.

She wanted them off. She wanted to feel every inch of his body bare against her. She wanted the feel of his cock, hard and thick, pressing against her, inside her.

First. Oh God, first she wanted the feel of it in her hands, against her lips.

Could she do it?

She'd never done it before because she'd been too embarrassed. Because she'd never understood why she would want to—until now. Now she knew why she wanted to do it. She wanted to make him feel so good. She wanted to hear him growl, snarl. She wanted to know what it would take to make him purr.

The elastic band slipped down his thighs, over the heavy flesh of the shaft as Jonas jerked, groaned and pulled her against him.

His hands were locked on her hips, his head thrown back as he lifted her to him, his cock pressed tight and hard against the mound of her pussy as she heard that hard rumble in his chest once again.

She felt her feet leave the floor and a second later he was laying her back on the bed, coming over her, his lips drawn back in a grimace of hunger.

Incisors flashed, strong and sharp at the sides of his mouth.

She felt his knee press between hers, parting her thighs, moving over her.

"This isn't fair." Weak, shaking, her hands pressed against his chest as he came over her.

She wanted to pleasure him, needed to take him.

"What isn't fair? I'll make it fair. I promise, whatever it takes to make it fair, just sweet God, let me feel you."

"Let me feel you first." She pushed at his shoulders.

His eyes narrowed. "Don't do this, Rachel."

"Do what?" She shifted against him, her leg stroking over his, feeling the nearly invisible, very fine hairs that covered it like the softest down.

Heat prickled the skin where they touched, warmed her flesh.

"Let me control this, Rachel," he breathed out roughly. "I promise, it will be so good."

"Maybe it will be so good if I get to touch too," she suggested, her tone throaty, surprising her, a sense of fun building inside her.

He made her want to have fun. It was as though he challenged her to challenge him. It was that self-control he had. It made a woman just want to crush it.

"I have no doubt it would be." A slow smile curled his lips, one of the rare, true smiles she had seen from him. "But let's see how this feels first."

He licked her.

Rachel froze as his tongue stroked, light as air, over her shoulder, spreading that same sense of heat that feathered over her legs when his had stroked against them.

His tongue rasped, just a little bit. Just enough to feel dark and wildly primal. Enough to send a forbidden thrill racing through her mind.

He was good at keeping the upper hand: the stroke of his

tongue, the twist of his body, the way he pulled her against him, his hand curving around a soft mound of her rear to tuck her hips against his.

His teeth nipped the lobe of her ear. Lightly. So very lightly. His hands stroked over her, the pad of one finger rubbing against her nipple as she felt the slightest pinch.

A scrape, like his nail against the areola, sent a bolt of heat racing across her nipple to her clit.

She twisted beneath him. She wanted so much more. Heat was building between her thighs, washing through her body. The feel of his cock pressing against the mound, blazing against her clit, was making her insane.

His hips rolled, thrust, slid from side to side, stroking the hard, heated shaft through the heavy, slick moisture. The folds of her pussy, swollen and sensitive, parted beneath the pressure. Her clit was in agony, release held just out of reach as she arched beneath him.

She had to see him, watch him.

Opening her eyes, she stared above her. Sweat beaded on his forehead, his shoulders. A rivulet ran down his chest, slow and easy, rolling with lazy sensuality as her lips parted, her head lifting as her tongue peaked out to catch the little droplet of moisture.

Cinnamon and cloves. A rich, dark storm. Midnight and madness. The tastes infused her senses as she felt him move. Her thighs were parted farther, a hesitation as he rolled a condom over the hard length of his cock. There was something wrong with that. She knew she should protest it, but before she could form the words, before she could remember why, he was pressing inside her.

Fiery, intense, pleasure-pain washed through her. The stretching of delicate, tender muscles, the stroke of his thick, hard flesh easing inside her. It was exquisite. It was like burning alive inside a fiery storm that she couldn't control or escape.

For the first time, he wasn't behind her as he gave her

pleasure. He was staring down at her, his silver eyes darkening, turning into a storm of mercury, a heated conflagration that matched the wildfire surging through her senses now.

Bit by bit, one agonizing inch at a time, his hips rolled, pressed and worked the hardened flesh deeper inside her.

She had to look. To watch. Staring between her thighs, she could see the latex-sheathed erection glistening from the dampness that he was pushing through. It was broad, dark, parting the folds of her flesh and disappearing inside her.

He was taking her.

Her head flung back as he pushed in deeper, a hard, demanding thrust followed by a groan of pleasure as she arched beneath him and the length of his cock disappeared fully inside her.

Heat, ecstasy, the feeling of complete surrender, total freedom, infused her. She felt as though she were flying, as though they were locked in a flight of complete rapture, racing toward the sun.

Light and color exploded behind her closed eyes as Jonas began to move. He fucked her as though each stroke were to be relished, remembered, forever imprinted in both their minds.

His hips thrust, rolled, shifted from side to side, causing his erection to stretch her farther, to reveal previously hidden nerve endings and erogenous zones in their climb to release.

She couldn't breathe. She was gasping for air, certain she was going to pass out. The pleasure was so intense, hunger so deep and strong inside her, she couldn't get enough. She would never get enough. She would always need more.

No wonder his lovers were so hard to get rid of in the past, she thought hazily. This was why. Because he fucked like a dream, like a dark fantasy come to life to possess her very soul with no more than this. This possession.

Lifting her legs, she wrapped them around his waist and fought to hold on to him as the pleasure began to spiral out of control.

Control was lost. Above her, Jonas's thrusts were becoming harder, faster. She could hear the growls coming from his chest, animalistic, feral, as his cock plunged inside her, fucking her with a furious pace as she began to tighten beneath him.

Sensations raced through her system, poured through her bloodstream. The brush of the air against her flesh was exquisite; the feel of his body thrusting inside hers was rapture.

Her hips lifted, her head arched back into the blankets and the cry that spilled from her lips was barely muffled by the hard, calloused palm that suddenly clamped over her lips.

Rachel exploded. Her orgasm tore through her mind and body, reaching clear to her soul as she pierced the blazing, white-hot center of fire awaiting her.

She was dying in his arms. She lost her breath, her will, the very heart of who and what she was, as ecstasy climbed inside her, exploding over and over again, pulsing in fiery bursts through her body.

Above her, Jonas thrust in one last time, hard, deep, holding still as she felt his erection throb and pound with such fierce motions that a part of her wondered if he felt pleasure or pain from his own release.

That part was distant though, shielded by light and color, by sensations that never seemed willing to stop but vibrated inside her again and again.

She couldn't stop coming. Each time he moved, each time his cock throbbed, another explosion detonated, another pulse of pleasure tore through her.

Until finally, he was jerking free of her, still hard, his breathing still rough as he collapsed beside her and pulled her gently into his arms.

Soothingly, with the utmost gentleness, his hand stroked down her back, easing her until her breathing finally slowed and a measure of normalcy returned to her limbs. She no longer felt too weak to move, too weak to breathe.

Her hand lay against his chest, feeling his heartbeat as the fierce, hard pounding eased to a measured beat and assured her that they would both survive the experience.

For long moments, Rachel had feared that wasn't going to happen.

"Sleep with me," he murmured, his voice drowsy as he shifted them both against the pillows and pulled the sheet over their bodies. "Right here, Rachel. Let me feel you against me through the night."

She didn't have a problem with that. Settling against his chest, she exhaled tiredly and slipped into sleep.

◆ ◆ ◆

When he was certain she slept, Jonas slipped slowly from the bed, pulled the blankets around her body, then rolled the broken condom from his cock before pulling a sterilized baggie from the drawer by his bed and dropping it in. It was a damned good thing Ely had thought to supply him with them, just in case something unusual happened. Something had damned sure happened, just as something else hadn't: He hadn't come.

He was as hard as forged iron.

His mouth burned from the taste of the hormone in his mouth, its properties obviously intensifying as he defied the demand that he share its taste with his mate.

He was losing control. He had never bitten her. It would have taken no more than the slightest break of her skin to give the hormone the chance to mark her, to throw her into the mating heat. And nature was damned determined to do it too. Lust was an insanity pounding through his blood now, raking sharpened claws over exposed nerve endings. Wanting her was hell. It was destroying his mind, because he couldn't take her. Not yet.

Holding back was his only option. It was the only way to ensure that she fell in love with him. He couldn't bear to feel as though she were being forced into his arms and into his bed.

Striding through the living room, he pulled the sat phone from the charger on the kitchen counter and moved to the far end of the room.

"Jonas, what's wrong?" Ely was on the line instantly.

"The barb breeched the condom." It was unheard of for a mated Breed to use a condom. Just as it was unheard of for the barb to extend without a mutual mating. Not that anyone had tried it as of yet.

"I need the condom," Ely stated brusquely. "The barb has minute hormonal properties. If we're very lucky, then the condom might have caught some of it."

"Quite a bit of it." He grimaced. "I didn't release, but the barb did."

"What the hell is going on with you?" Ely snapped. "Mate her already."

"Not yet, Ely." He shook his head as he rubbed at the back of his neck. "I want her love. Rachel won't trust what she feels for me if she doesn't realize she loves me before she's tied to me for the rest of our unnatural lives."

Hell, who knew how long a mated Breed could actually live?

"Besides," he sighed, "there's still the truth to tell here. I won't mate her without it."

Silence filled the line. He knew Ely didn't agree with him. The truth, she claimed, would only be proven if it happened; until then it was no more than a supposition.

He'd been created to sire a creature unlike any that the scientists had created. A true animal in a man's body. How could he tie his mate to him without first warning her what she would be giving birth to when that day came?

"I need the condom," she repeated. "And I need you in here ASAP. Leave your Enforcers to watch Rachel. I'll be waiting in the labs."

The line disconnected. Bringing the phone down, Jonas stared at it with a sense of amusement. Damn, Ely was getting bossier than she had ever been. That wasn't a good thing.

But she was right. She needed whatever he could give her now. Soon, there would be no chance for tests, examinations or nosy doctors. The animal inside him was raging out of control, the mating urge was tearing at his mind. And he knew, once he had Rachel, once he completed the mating cycle, he would become the most possessive son of a bitch ever known.

He was afraid he would make her hate him.

⋄ CHAPTER 14 ⋄

Jonas strode into his office the next morning, aware of the taut expression on his face and the tension that filled his entire body stretched tight. It was hard to miss the toll the mating heat was taking on him. And if he had missed it, then Ely was quick to point it out each morning.

Hours in the labs with Ely hadn't produced any answers, only more questions. Questions such as what the hell was the hormone in his mating semen?

Mating semen came from the barb only, ejaculated after the main release, and mixing with Breed semen, which held just a few human sperm. The mating semen seemed to strengthen the human sperm as well as laying in important Breed DNA and a hormone that eased the mating heat for a short period of time.

The mating hormone Jonas had ejaculated had held all the same biological components as any other Breed mate's, but it had held a few additions as well. Additions that Ely was still frowning over when he'd left an hour before.

Returning to the cabin, he'd found Rachel in the office,

right on time, Amber in her crib in the room beside her and everything running with the same efficiency that it ran with in D.C.

The only thing not running right was Jonas.

"Lawe, Rule, with me," he snapped to the two Enforcers waiting in Rachel's office as he strode through it.

Lawe and Rule followed him into his office, closed the door behind them, then stood and watched him silently. He could feel their readiness, their tense preparation for what they sensed.

Jonas was a man running on borrowed time, because the animal inside him was growing stronger by the day.

"I want a complete investigative profile done on Devon Marshal," he ordered. "Go deeper than we went before. I want to know who breathed the air that son of a bitch has breathed before he did. I want to know every strand of hair on his head, and who the hell is supplying his drugs. And I want to know why I smelled the scent of Brandenmore on him when he arrived yesterday evening."

It had taken Jonas a while to figure it out. His senses were so screwed up with Rachel right now that he was dangerous.

"Crank said the bastard stank," Lawe grunted.

"Of Brandenmore," Jonas agreed. "My guess is the son of a bitch was in the limo. Attempts had been made to diffuse the scent, but it was there. If he was that close, it was only because they were certain they would get Amber out of Sanctuary. I want to know why he wants her, and what he's after, and I want to know now."

Rage was eating inside him at the thought of what Brandenmore, a genius in pharmaceuticals, could have planned for such a small child. Especially a child he knew Jonas would never allow him to take.

"Jess Warden is trying to reach you as well, Jonas," Rule informed him quietly. "The lawyers for Horace Engalls have filed a protest with Sanctuary against the Enforcers we placed on surveillance to keep him from leaving the country as well. They've demanded we stop following him and have also demanded an immediate hearing with the ruling cabinet to hear their arguments."

Which meant, according to Breed Law statutes, Engalls was pretty much fucked. It would first have to go to the pre-cabinet, six Breeds and three humans who would decide if the ruling cabinet needed to hear the arguments. Then, and only then, would it go to the ruling cabinet, of which Jonas was a member. Once the request was kicked back and vetoed, only then could it go to court, where at least five or more Breeds had to sit on the jury.

Sucked to be Engalls this year.

"Not happening," Jonas growled. "Have the Enforcers appear to back off. Let's see what he has planned. If he attempts to get on a plane, then I want them there as well. I want to know what he's doing, where he's going, and what the hell he's doing each time he goes to the men's room. And I want to know before he does it."

Engalls would try to run next. So far, Brandenmore was having incredible luck with his little escape to the Middle East. The country that had taken him in was also providing lawyers and financial resources designed to buy Brandenmore out of his current predicament.

"Dog's been trying to reach you as well." Lawe kept his voice low. "Seems Brandenmore has a nice little lab where he's staying. He hasn't left the royal palace yet that they can see, so there's been no chance to grab him, and Dog hasn't found a way to slip into Brandenmore's suite yet."

Jonas lips thinned. "Tell Dog he has forty-eight hours to capture Brandenmore, get him on a plane and be headed my way. I have a feeling we don't have much longer here."

Pulling up his email, he began to sift through it quickly, his eyes scanning each subject header as his lips thinned further.

The Breeds were either loved, or hated, according to which story was hitting the gossip rags and who liked them at the time. At present, several of the world's largest box office draws thought it was cool to have Breeds for friends.

Tanner Reynolds made a great movie star groupie, though his wife, Scheme, was a bit more standoffish. There were other Breeds, trained in the art of endearing trust and friendship, who were working the same angles under Tanner's careful eye.

The groups opposing the Breeds were looking for a war though, believing there were no more than the thousand or so accounted-for Breeds that they would have to face.

How wrong they were, and Jonas wondered the panic many governments would feel to learn just how wrong they truly were about the Breeds' actual numbers.

"Dog will try, but I'd bet against it happening," Lawe stated as he moved closer to Jonas's desk. "Just as I'd bet for Engalls attempting to run in the next forty-eight hours. The protest and filing with pre-cabinet is just an attempt to divert your attention and force you to travel to D.C. to handle it yourself. Which would either leave Amber and Rachel here, where a spy could get to them; or in D.C., where they would be more accessible to a well-planned abduction attempt."

Mates rarely traveled alone. If Jonas went to D.C., Rachel, and possibly Amber, would be accompanying him. And there was no way that would happen without a full unit of Enforcers covering them.

Jonas would have to pull back the unit covering Engalls, pull a team from a mission, or pull in one of the units he kept in the shadows, revealing there were still more Breeds who had remained hidden thus far.

A straggler here and there didn't hurt the society one way or the other. But if units started popping up, they were going to be in trouble.

"Keep Alpha Team One on standby," he ordered Lawe. "Inform mission control they're at my command."

Lawe nodded quickly. As a member of Alpha Team One, he knew exactly how often they were needed and how many missions they could be sent out on in any given week.

"Rule, I want you talk to Sherra. Pull in the two female units we have here at Sanctuary. No one is used to seeing us use the female units. Let's see how pretty and defenseless we can make them look, if you don't mind. I'd prefer they not be seen as a threat unless we have no other choice."

That "no other choice" was only a life-or-death situation.

"I want more teams added to the mountain patrols as well." Jonas frowned over the map of Sanctuary that he brought up. "So far, each time we've had an attempted kidnapping from Sanctuary they've used the ravine here, where Mordecai found evidence of a watcher, or the ravines here, farther up." Jonas pointed out the weak areas. "Hidden sensors are in place now, but I want several teams patrolling each of those areas from here on out. If Kane has any problems with it, then please have him contact me."

Kane Tyler was head of Sanctuary's security, and a damned good man for it. But Jonas could feel the edge of premonition pricking at him now. There was going to be trouble, and he had no idea from which direction it was coming. And neither did Cassie.

"Callan and Leo have requested that you come to the main house, along with your mate and child, tonight for dinner." Lawe seemed hesitant to relay that information. "I believe it might have been the Leo's idea."

The Leo. His father.

Jonas rubbed at the back of his neck. They wouldn't have asked just for the hell of it.

"Find out what time," he growled, feeling his tension ratcheting higher now.

Lawe nodded. "By the way, congratulations."

Jonas looked up from the computer and frowned. "For what?"

Rule and Lawe both stared at him as though he were crazy. "You're mated. Congratulations. We scented the proof of it the minute Rachel opened the door and allowed us in. It's particularly strong . . ." Lawe trailed off as Jonas stared back at him in surprise.

"There has been no mating," he told the other man.

There hadn't been. If there had, Jonas wouldn't be in the physical hell he was in.

Lawe scratched at the side of his cheek. "Well, there's no scent of crazy lust coming from her, I admit." He cleared his throat nervously. "But the mating scent is there, Jonas. There's no missing it."

Unless you were the mate. His own scent was so familiar to him that he wouldn't have detected the mating scent itself on Rachel. That scent was for other males, not for the mate.

Ely was right; he needed to get Rachel to the labs for testing as soon as possible. If he carried the mating out, then the examination would be painful, too painful. Though according to his Enforcers, the mating had already been completed.

Which he knew for a fact wasn't possible.

"Has anyone else been in here?" he asked the two men, wondering how many others would be aware of that scent.

Lawe shook his head. "Just us. We were here when she unlocked the office doors waiting on you."

Jonas rose from his seat, his teeth clenched. He had to get Rachel to the labs for tests, there was no other way around it. But in doing so, he was opening himself up to a vulnerability he wasn't ready for anyone else to know, especially the Vanderales.

If Rachel was indeed displaying the mating scent, then that particular hormone would display variances that would reveal the DNA used in Jonas's creation. Elizabeth Vanderale's DNA. It would also show that his creation was far different than his files stated. He wasn't created to be simply a Pride leader, and commander. He had been created to breed the very animal that Breeds and humans alike feared the species would eventually become.

He couldn't ignore the fact that others knew this information. Scientists that had been at the labs and had escaped Breed justice. There was a slim chance Brandenmore at least suspected he was the Breed scientists still searched for. The one designated as Alpha One.

He was one of a few male Breeds given a unique designation during creation. He was created not to be the ultimate Breed, but to create the ultimate killer.

It was a hell of a legacy, he thought savagely.

"Get Dog in gear and oversee Alpha Team One," he ordered Lawe. "I'll contact Callan to see what time we're needed for dinner. Assign a Breed to Marshal, while you're at it. Make it a female Breed. Someone nonthreatening."

"Ashley," Rule murmured. "She at least appears non-threatening."

She was a killer in heels. As one of the Coyote Breeds, and exacting of her privacy, there were no tabloid pictures of her, and even less information about her.

"Put her undercover," he ordered Lawe. "A little rich bitch looking for fun. That should be right up Devon Marshal's alley right now. Give her backup. Her sister Emma should work."

As a team, Ashley and Emma were hell on wheels.

"I was going to suggest both of them." Lawe nodded. "We'll have an update for you on Dog as soon as we speak with him, and I'll let you know when Ashley and Emma head out."

Jonas nodded shortly, waited, then blew out a hard breath as the door closed behind the two men.

Fuck! He jerked from his chair, his hand clamped to the back of his neck as he paced across the room. This was the last fucking thing he needed. A mating that wasn't a mating. Unknown hormones in his semen, and a variety of protests and actions being filed against him, the Bureau and Sanctuary at a time when he didn't know his ass from a hole in the ground.

To add to those particularly irritating problems was the nearly mindless lust tearing at his mind and tearing at his control. The past months had been hell, and it was now multiplying daily to the point that he hadn't even recognized Brandenmore's scent on Marshal's body last night.

How the hell had Phillip Brandenmore managed to get out

of the Middle East without Dog's team being aware of it? To fly out, and then back in, and no one being the wiser was a hell of a feat to accomplish. Especially considering the fact that Dog would have been watching for it.

But as the Breeds had been trained, there were few things that were truly impossible.

He truly hoped that getting Rachel in for those tests before a true mating didn't prove to be one of those "impossible" things. If she was displaying the mating scent without a mating, then Ely needed to know why. And she needed to know why *now*, before any more surprises were thrown at them.

◆　　◆　　◆

Rachel finished the report logs Jonas was required to submit to the Bureau of Breed Affairs Oversight Committee, a panel of several senators, Breeds and foreign ambassadors. The oversight committee was tasked with keeping an eye on the running of the Bureau, Jonas's actions as Bureau director and the official missions the Breeds participated in for the American and allied countries.

Each day, a report log was filed for the day before and sent to the secretary of the oversight committee. At the end of each month, Jonas met with them for any outstanding questions.

There wasn't a lot of factual information per se that went into the reports. But as Rachel read them, she was always amused at the inventiveness Jonas displayed in twisting many of his more calculated schemes and making them appear perfectly acceptable and logical.

The man had to have the DNA of an Irishman well versed in kissing more than one Blarney Stone.

Her head turned as his office door opened. That familiar little catch of her breath was stronger now. The memory of the night spent in his arms, her body humming with pleasure, caught at her senses, whipped across her flesh with ghostly fingers of sensation and had a smile tugging at her lips.

"Your report logs are getting better," she told him as she sent the file to his electronic notepad for his signature.

"Callan still gets a laugh out of them." He shrugged as he moved to the desk, his gaze hooded as he stared down at her. His nostrils flared as though searching for some scent he couldn't quite put his fingers on.

Rachel tilted her head as she stared up at him quizzically. "Is something wrong?"

"Many things," he told her. "Are you feeling okay today?"

Propping her hand on her fist, she let her gaze lock with the liquid silver of his eyes. "I'm feeling fine. You?"

"I've been better." That undefined emotion in his eyes that had always drawn her raged now.

A frown pulled at her brow. He was unusually tense, and for Jonas, that was saying something. He gave tension a bad name. The man was normally drawn as tight as a bow string. For him to be more tense than normal was something to worry about.

"Is there anything I can do to help?" She was willing to try many things. The thought of going to her knees in front of him, her lips caressing the straining length of his cock, had her mouth watering.

"Actually, there is." As though he had made some decision within himself, his shoulders straightened and his gaze narrowed as he stared down at her. "I'm making an appointment for you with Ely this evening. We need to get started on the examination and tests you'll be required to participate in once full mating occurs."

Rachel stared back at him silently. She had determined, once, that she wouldn't be his mate. That she couldn't be unless she decided she was.

Had she made that decision?

She knew she had.

There was a part of her that knew she belonged to him, longed for him. There was a part of her that knew the mating heat was coming, it was simply a matter of time.

"So soon?" she asked, rather than refusing outright. "I thought, after the mating . . ."

"We need to get started now, Rachel." His tone was harder

than it had been in past days. She was so used to him using the softer, gentler tone of voice that the normal tone was like a slight dash of cold water across her flesh.

She nodded though. "Ely will be doing the examination?"

She liked Dr. Vanderale but the other woman had the power to intimidate her. Rachel didn't like acknowledging that power where anyone was concerned.

"Only Ely." He nodded as though he understood her hesitation.

"Very well." She drew in a hard breath, mentally preparing herself for the coming tests. "I can do that."

He nodded sharply. "We've also been invited to dinner tonight with the Leo, his family and Callan and his. I'm sure you'll enjoy some time with Merinus."

His voice was oddly cool, even though she had agreed to what he'd asked of her, which indicated there was something more going on. She'd learned many of Jonas's ways, and one of them was that the more he expected a complication or a problem from one of his requests, the cooler he would become with whomever he was dealing with.

Rachel nodded again. "I'll check with Erin to make certain she can stay with Amber." The young lynx Breed had taken to Amber with surprising affection.

Jonas frowned at the statement. "Erin and Amber will be going with us. Socialization begins as an infant, Rachel. You want her to know how to deal with others, and how to interact, even as a toddler."

Her brows raised. Jonas's frown deepened.

"She's my baby, Jonas," she reminded him. "I appreciate what you've done to protect her . . ."

"She is *our* baby." He leaned forward, his hands planted on her desk with a suddenness that had her staring up at him warily. "Never doubt that I don't claim that child as my own. We will raise her together, we will protect her together. If you have other ideas, then perhaps you've been right to deny the mating."

He straightened as quickly as he'd leaned forward, his

shoulders straight, his expression forbidding as he seemed to glare at her.

"Don't imagine you can demand those rights." Rachel was out of her chair immediately.

"I don't demand them. I have taken them," he growled, bending again until he was almost nose to nose with her. "Raising a child is a partnership, mate. Don't imagine otherwise."

"You're pissing me off." Her hands went to her hips. "Asking for something is a hell of a lot nicer than demanding it. What the hell is wrong with you, and since when did you decide you could arbitrarily decide that you have any rights over me or Amber?"

"When I knew you were my mate," he snarled back at her. "And why have you decided to suddenly become so damned difficult? I do know a few things about children. Cassie didn't turn out so bad, and all of Sanctuary has participated in raising her."

"Cassie has an excellent mother," she pointed out, exerting effort to be calm, her eyes narrowing. "And likely had a father who understood not to speak to her mother as though she knew nothing about raising a child."

Jonas was fighting for control; Rachel could sense it. She watched him, her heart racing, a sense of impending doom rising inside her as his eyes flashed from silver to mercury and back again.

He was testing boundaries he didn't want to tempt, not now, not yet. Likely, never.

"Amber has an excellent mother," he growled, obviously pushing the words past clenched teeth. "I never implied otherwise, Rachel. You have turned a simple discussion into a conflict that should not exist."

"Or perhaps you have." They were still nose to nose, eyes narrowed, the tension stifling. "Now that we've agreed Erin and Amber will accompany us, you can see about becoming prepared for the telephone conference you have with Senator Tyler in exactly one hour. After that, you have a meeting with the pre-cabinet concerning the latest attempt by various groups to gain access to a hunting permit for Sanctuary's northern boundary. You don't have time to stand here growling and snarling at me."

He flashed his incisors at her. She crossed her arms over her breasts and stared back at him with steely resolve.

"Mating heat is coming, mate." His voice lowered, rasped, stroked along her senses like dark velvet. "Let's see where all that anger gets you then."

Turning on his heel, he stalked from the ante office back to his own, and closed the door quietly behind him.

Very quietly.

Rachel flinched, then blew out a soundless breath.

Now, there was an attitude she hadn't seen from him before. If she wasn't mistaken, he had been seconds, inches, one last thread of control from kissing her.

For one wild, exciting moment, she had nearly kissed him instead.

And she'd had fun.

Smiling, Rachel took her seat and returned to the computer and her own work.

Not many people could say they had faced the bogeyman of the Breeds in a screaming match and came out unscathed. Rachel was betting she was the only one who could lay claim to that particular talent. And she looked forward to the next round.

She paused at the thought.

Hell, she knew she was in love with him now, because the only other person she would dare to yell back at was her sister. She and Diana had gone nose to nose many times over the years, and Diana hadn't always backed down, but she had always ended up laughing at Rachel's particular manner of "handling" her, as she called it.

She glanced at the door again.

She should stalk right in there and kiss him herself. She had no idea why he was holding back now. No idea what demons were shadowing him that he hadn't claimed her.

She knew he wanted to. She knew it was going to happen. Yet, he was fighting it with every breath he took.

◆   ◆   ◆

He was drowning.

Jonas sat at his desk, glared at the wall, and felt the stifling tightness in his throat, his chest. The taste of cinnamon and cloves was choking him; the need for her was stealing his breath and his control.

He parted his lips to breathe in roughly and a growl tore from his lips despite his attempts to hold it back.

His hands lay flat on the desk, claws extruding, digging into the wood. The glands beneath his tongue were so swollen, so sensitive, he was in agony. He felt as though his tongue were being ripped out.

He lifted the comm link from a drawer, attached it to his head and pressed the direct secured line to Ely's office.

"Jonas," she answered immediately.

"Rachel will be in this evening for the examination and tests," he informed her. "Get whatever you have to have while you can."

Silence filled the link for long seconds.

"I'll be waiting for her," she stated. "Amburg was in here earlier. He's asking for more blood from the baby. He found a slight anomaly in the last test he conducted and wants to investigate it further."

"I'll discuss it with Rachel."

"If you're bringing her this evening, then whoever is watching Amber can oversee my assistant extracting the blood," Ely suggested. "There's no need to tempt her refusal, Jonas."

He shook his head. "You've learned too well." He sighed. "She's my mate, Ely, not a particularly stubborn Enforcer. I won't go behind her back."

There had been a time when Ely would have never suggested such a thing; to the contrary, she would have protested it had Jonas made such a suggestion.

"Perhaps I didn't learn fast enough from you," Ely murmured. "Whichever, I'll be waiting for you this evening. Let me know by then how to proceed."

The line disconnected, leaving Jonas to stare broodingly into the dark room as he reflected on games, machinations and his past calculating attempts to ensure that his Enforcers met, mated and lived, if not happily ever after, at least with a measure of softness in their lives.

He didn't regret a moment of it, but damned if he wasn't paying for it now.

CHAPTER 15

The tests weren't so hard, definitely not the hell Merinus had warned her that they would be after mating. Rachel consented to allow the blood to be taken from Amber, more concerned with the fact that Jeffrey Amburg felt he'd found some "anomaly" in previous tests.

The Breeds had more anomalies going on in their lives than a gardener had seeds to plant.

Once the tests were finished, Rachel had re-dressed a sleepy Amber and handed her over to the lynx Breed assigned as caretaker. Then the real problems of the evening began. And they began with the Leo.

Moving into the large family room of the estate house, Rachel followed the subtle directions of Jonas's hand against the small of her back as he led her to a settee to the side of the large fireplace, across from a matching settee shared by Leo and his wife, Elizabeth.

In the two large chairs next to Leo and Elizabeth, Leo's son, Dane, and his bodyguard, Ryan—or Rye, as they called him—Desalvo sat, with Callan and Merinus in a sofa facing the fireplace and Kane Tyler and his mated wife, Sherra, in a matching sofa beside them.

Dinner had been filled with discussions of the latest protests against the Breeds, the surge in protestors at the gates of Sanctuary, and a future still uncertain where Breed peace was concerned. It was a discussion still under way.

"The Congo has a lot of hiding places, Callan." Leo sat in the corner of the settee, his arm thrown over the back behind his wife, his gold eyes fierce as he stared into the identical ones of his son. "My compound there is completely secure and not so damned easy to get to. The mates there live in relative peace. The tribes surrounding us are loyal to us. It's a good place to raise and train our children to meet the future."

"Virginia's a good place to raise and train children as well," Callan argued.

"My grandson has nearly been kidnapped twice now," Leo argued. "Each time, David has had to face the death or injury of a friend entrusted to protect him. It's beginning to affect the boy."

The light chastisement wasn't lost on Callan or Merinus.

"David has to learn to accept the dangers in his life." There was a note of regret in Callan's tone. "There is no utopia for us, Leo, you know that. He's in danger, no matter where we are, just as our twins are."

"They'll be in less danger there."

"This argument is moot," Kane interjected, his tone brooking no refusal. "We've set our course here, Leo. We're not willing to change it, and this argument grows weary."

Leo didn't so much as look in the other man's direction, his gaze staying on Callan, his expression demanding.

Callan shook his head. "Kane's right; our future is here."

"Your people are dying daily," Leo argued. "Three Breeds were beaten to a bloody pulp in California last week. You want to pretend you're safe here, and you're not."

"We prefer not to bury our heads in the sand and pretend that hiding is the same thing as freedom," Jonas spoke up then. "We've given the Breeds here the option of joining you in Africa, or staying. They choose to stay."

"They follow Callan," Leo snapped back at him. "They'll go where he says to go—we all know that."

"Leo, let it rest." Elizabeth laid her delicate hand on his knee as she looked up at him, her expression disapproving. "Each visit is filled with this argument and I grow weary of it. We hid because we had no choice, and we've built a society we're very happy with, and a life that holds a measure of safety. Callan has simply chosen the path you would have chosen then if you had had that option."

He grunted at the statement before his eyes turned to Rachel. She watched his nostrils flare, the narrowing of his eyes. He'd done that often throughout the evening, just as the others had in a less direct way.

"Ms. Broen, what's your opinion of safety for your daughter? If she were a Breed child, would you prefer life here, or one where she would be allowed to blend into society and to live without the threat of capture and torture?"

Which would she choose?

"I have to agree with Callan," she stated sadly. "Better that they know the price of freedom and what they're fighting for than to learn to hide and to lie. The battle isn't one that will be accomplished overnight. Just as it isn't a choice one man or Breed can make for many."

"But you agree that this life," he waved his hand to include the room as though it were the entire Breed society, "is one far less safe for your child than the one I propose."

Rachel frowned. "I agree with nothing of the sort. I simply believe it's a choice as individual as the man or the Breed making it."

He stared at her as though she should be squashed beneath the heel of his very expensive boots. No doubt, that was exactly what he felt as well.

"I've had enough of this conversation." Jonas rose to his

feet, the tension that had burned inside him most of the day shimmering around him now. "Are you ready?"

It was asked politely enough, but Rachel saw his face. Being ready wasn't an option; it was time for Jonas to leave.

"You're not one to heed anyone's opinion but your own, are you, Jonas?" Leo rose to his feet as well, his gaze going between Jonas and Rachel, that quizzical look in his eyes making Rachel intensely nervous.

"Leo, I'm not in the mood for your demands tonight, or your views on how your way is the best way and the only way to proceed. In my opinion, we were far better off when your wife was sneaking and helping Ely rather than having your arrogance infect Sanctuary on a regular basis." The statement was made calmly, even politely. The tension filling the room was anything but polite or calm.

"Leo, take your seat," Elizabeth ordered softly. "Now isn't the time for this."

He glared back at his wife. "The whelp has ignored every suggestion I've made for months, gone out of his way to ignore and avoid each of us, and tries to pretend he has no responsibility to the future of the Breeds in any way."

"If I felt such a way, then I wouldn't be busting my ass to keep our Breeds out of your path and off your radar when they try to make a life for themselves here," Jonas snapped back, his tone icy now. "You can't force them to duck and hide in a jungle while you play the innocent benefactor and pretend to age at a normal rate." Jonas sneered in contempt, his gaze encompassing the temporary wrinkles around the Leo's eyes, the artificially gray streaks in his hair. "You're not human, Leo, and all the wishing in the world isn't going to make it happen."

Lion's eyes narrowed as Elizabeth stared at Jonas in shock and surprise.

"Jonas, enough." Callan finally felt the need to intercede, far too late by Rachel's estimation.

"Suits me." Jonas shrugged as he laid his hand at Rachel's back and began directing her from the group once again. "I can always find something better to do than to argue with a man whose superiority far exceeds his logic."

Leo growled. A low, commanding snarl, a sound that demanded instant respect.

Jonas chuckled mockingly. "I can do that too, Leo. Mine sounds better though."

"Leo, no!" Elizabeth's cry was the only warning they had. A second later, Rachel found herself pushed back from Jonas as he flew across the room, landing on his back with a thud while Leo began to slowly advance.

Jonas rose slowly. "Callan, please excuse our father's manners," he requested snidely as Callan and Elizabeth both moved in front of the Leo. "I'm certain he must have forgotten to pack his manners when he made his hasty exit from Africa."

"A hasty exit to ensure you didn't fuck up any worse than you already had," Leo snarled as Callan grimaced. "Just as you're fucking up now, you manipulating little . . ."

"Whelp?" Jonas sneered. "A misgotten batch of DNA that should have been drowned at birth?" He was obviously repeating someone's words. Rachel prayed they hadn't been Leo's. "Been there, Leo, died without the T-shirt."

They all froze. Elizabeth turned around slowly, staring at Jonas in shock as Rachel's lips parted in horror.

Surely such a thing hadn't happened.

"Surprised?" Jonas's voice dropped, became so dangerously soft Rachel flinched. "Don't be. The scientist knew whose DNA I carried. One little zap to the heart and I was back again." His smile was pure ice. "And I died again. And again. And again. To prove I was the Leo's whelp." His gaze drifted to Elizabeth before jerking back to her mate. "Get fucked, old man. I haven't needed you since the day I was created and I sure as hell don't need you now."

Jonas stalked across the room only to stop in front of Rachel, his hand lifting as he held it out to her. She took it immediately, allowing him to draw her to his side as they began moving from the room.

"I didn't mean those words," the Leo stated harshly as they passed him, his golden gaze locked on Jonas now. "They were said in anger, Jonas. We both know why. It's just I'm willing to admit to it; you're not."

Jonas froze for a second before continuing from the room. He pushed through the double doors, his stride easy, matched to Rachel's, but quick enough to take them from the house and into the chilly night air.

"Jonas!" Leo's voice stopped him once again as they reached the Raider that pulled into the drive.

Rachel turned with Jonas, staring back at the proud, fiercely stubborn Breed watching them.

"I've given you every chance," Leo called out, his face filled with regret now. "Do something about it, or I'll take matters into my own hands."

Jonas was aware of Rachel standing at his side, her confusion mounting as he faced the man whose DNA he carried. He didn't dare call him his father. God only knew they couldn't be in the same room for more than five minutes without coming to blows.

"Hit me again, Leo, and I'll return the blow," he stated rather than answering to the other Breed's accusation. "I may be a whelp that should have been drowned at birth, but you content yourself with the fact that as far as I'm concerned, I was never your whelp."

He turned, opened the door to the Raider and helped Rachel into the seat as Erin and Amber moved around the Leo. Opening the back door, he waited, took the baby from Erin's arms and buckled her into her infant seat as Erin returned to the estate house.

Moving to the driver's side door, he couldn't help but look back at the man still glaring at him from the entrance to the house. Elizabeth and the others had joined him, all watching him with quizzical surprise.

"Show's over, Prime," he called out to Callan. "My apologies to your Prima as well as your family."

"You're family as well, Jonas," Callan answered clearly, reminding him they were bound by blood.

No, it wasn't blood; only DNA bound them.

Jonas shook his head before moving into the vehicle and sliding it into drive.

The ride to the cabin was made quickly. Darkness surrounded them as they reached the tree line and Jonas headed the Raider to the cabin above.

"What was he talking about?" Rachel finally asked as he pulled the vehicle into the small attached garage and shut the engine off.

He stared into the dimly lit interior, wishing that just once, the past could be forgotten.

"We have a lot to discuss," he finally said quietly. "Things I'm certain you need to know."

Things he had swore he would never tell anyone. The truth might be told, but he had promised himself it would never be told by him. He had no desire to destroy himself in his mate's eyes, or in anyone else's.

"And it's something you think that will change what's between us?" she asked.

A mirthless laugh escaped his lips. "I've lived in a fool's paradise since bringing you here. Perhaps in a way, I've lived in one since the day I allowed myself to become the director of the Bureau. Your past always returns, Rachel."

He turned to her as he felt her hand touch his jaw, urging him to look at her.

And she was much too close for his self-control. Her lips were too close. Her deep, dark green eyes stared too deeply into his. For a moment, just a moment, he allowed himself to sink inside her, to feel the peace, the contentment he should have been able to find with her.

"And you think it changes the man you are now?" Her question threw him off.

"Nothing can change who I am." The arrogance in his tone nearly had him wincing in self-disgust.

Rachel only smiled. "I didn't think so."

Then before he sensed what she was about, before he could counter the mouth, her lips were touching his, her tongue flickered past his lips to the hormone-rich interior of his mouth. And she freed the animal raging inside him.

· **C H A P T E R   1 6** ·

Logic. Sanity. They fell by the wayside the moment her tongue touched his. So sweet and cool, tempting, stroking against the tortured flesh of his own, Jonas lost what little control he had been hanging on to.

He felt that final thread snap as the man was pushed aside and the animal he'd sworn he would never become took over.

There was only the most distant awareness of the baby sleeping peacefully on the other side of the room. Just enough awareness so that when his hand clamped on the back of her head to hold her to the kiss, the other arm wrapping around her hips, lifting her, he knew he had to get her to the bedroom.

The journey there was endless, torturous. It was hell trying to stumble to the next room, his senses, his entire being focused on the rush of adrenaline-spiked pleasure tearing through his body. His leg caught the corner of the chest. He banged against the dresser. He kept his mate carefully sheltered from harm as his tongue pumped in her mouth, his harsh, "Suck it," a rasp of demented hunger before he filled her mouth with the mating hormone.

He was known as a graceful, predatory lover. A man who knew all the right moves. A Breed with the patience and experience to drive a woman wild for hours at a time.

That was the man.

The man wasn't in control now.

The graceful, predatory lover of the past was now primal. Possessive. It was starved for the mating, obsessed with the taste of this woman's kiss, the stroke of her hands over his body.

He was the animal that even he feared.

The glass doors on the two-sided fireplace had been secured from the bedroom earlier, but the fire blazed warm and bright, sending flickering fingers of red-gold over her face, along her body. The room was quiet, cool, but nothing could pierce the haze of fiery heat raging through his body.

A heat he knew he would regret, come morning. A pleasure that overshadowed anything that had come before it. Jonas knew there was nothing in his life that would ever compare to the complete, sensual bliss to be found in Rachel's touch. In touching her. Stroking her. In pumping his tongue in her mouth and feeling her suck at it lightly, tentatively.

Tomorrow, she would regret it. She would regret him, and he knew it. For now, his tongue was thrusting into his mate's mouth, fucking it with wild, primal hunger. The hormone spilled freely from the glands beneath his tongue now, as though the warmth of her mouth, the touch of her tongue, the gentle, pulsating sucks as she tried to capture it, had been all that was needed to end the agony he'd suffered for months.

There was no pleasure so great as holding her to him, feeling the soft, hesitant little licks and sucks against the agonized flesh of his tongue. As though each small stroke touched more than those swollen glands. It touched his soul, warmed it. Built a fire inside him where once there had been nothing but cold emptiness, a hollow, haunted shell of a man.

The more she gave him, the more he wanted.

His hands stroked down her back, over her hips and up again. As the soft material of her blouse caressed his palms, he felt the claws tucked beneath his fingertips slowly stretch forward, revealing themselves, reaching for the cool pleasure of her flesh.

Licking at her tongue, holding her close, Jonas felt the claws as they suddenly sliced through her soft white blouse.

He wanted to apologize. Ah God, he wanted to go so easy. He wanted to show her he could be a man, that he could touch her, love her, as he had so longed to do. But he had waited so long. The mating hormone had taken too much of a toll on his natural restraint. He didn't want to smell her fear. He didn't want to tear her from the arousal the hormone would ignite inside her.

But he couldn't wait. Even the few minutes it took for the hormone to react on a female's system was too much time for the animal. He needed her now. He had hungered for far too long.

He pulled the shreds of her blouse from her body, tossing them to the floor. The soft skirt came next. The feel of it was exquisite against his palms. The black velvet stroked over his flesh as his claws ripped through it, drawing a gasp from her as she pulled back, fought to free herself from his kiss.

"Rachel." His voice was fractured, more animal than man now, a harsh, primal sound that had him fighting to hold on to the restraint needed to not harm her.

As though the animal part of his genetics was a separate beast inside him, his mind railed at the thought, that even amidst this singular impulse of total sensation, he could never harm her.

"Let me breathe." She was panting for air, her hands gripping his wrists as his fingers fought not to clench at her hips. He could feel the silkiness of her flesh, knew how fragile it would be beneath the razor-sharp points of his claws.

Turning his hand, he stroked the backs of his fingers up her back, down. He needed to touch her, needed to experience the warmth and softness of her flesh without terrifying her.

He gave her a moment. His lips moved along her jaw, his

incisors scraped against her flesh as his tongue lapped at her flesh, infusing each touch with the potency of the hormone spilling from the glands now.

He could feel her beginning to heat. Sensed the fires already igniting inside her body as they began to slowly, seductively, burn hotter.

The scent of it, the sweet rush of feminine lust and need, tore through his senses with the power to splinter his senses. He was losing all sense of place and time. Nothing else mattered—just this touch, this woman, nothing else.

His lips covered hers again, his tongue pushing into her mouth once again as he tore at his own clothes, desperate to meet her flesh with his own. He wanted her breasts bare against his chest, her hips silky and sweet sliding against his, her thighs parting, spreading for his.

Pumping his tongue past her lips, he growled again when she tried to pull back. Gripping the hair at the back of her head, Jonas held her still. One more minute. Just another second to relish the sweet, cool relief as the glands beneath his tongue began to ease marginally.

But with that relief came a stronger, more overwhelming urge. The urge to finally, fully, possess her. To mark her. To ensure that she was his mate, that no other could ever have the chance to take what belonged to him.

Pulling back from the kiss, he stared down at her, knowing he should force himself to show some restraint over the animal clawing to take it all at once, rather than relishing the sweet, supple taste of her.

The backs of his fingers traced down her spine, then up again to the middle of her shoulders. Watching her, seeing the heat that burned in her eyes, he let the smooth edge of his claw stroke over the curve of her breast, wondering if she could know, if she would feel the danger inherent in the touch. Claws that could rip, could shred, he swore would do nothing but bring her pleasure.

It was sure as hell bringing him pleasure. Jonas's entire

body was blazing with fiery pleasure as he pulled her tighter against him, feeling the smooth, silken flesh of her belly cushion the hard length of his cock.

Warm, soft flesh.

He wanted to groan, but he growled into their kiss instead. His hands, both turned, the blunted side of the claws raking over the sides over her plump breasts as he felt her whimper, and her body weakening in need.

Pulling back, Jonas felt his own breath shorten as he stared down at the ripe mounds, tight, hard cherry nipples topping the firm flesh.

God, he couldn't resist.

Grimacing at the hunger inside him, he lifted his hand until he could touch the hardened tip with the back of a claw. Stroked it, fed the need ripping through his balls as he slowly began to realize that like the man, the animal overpowering him had no other thought but to protect the mate he had waited so long for as well.

Staring at the pale rise of her breast, his fingers stroking over it, shadowed by firelight, the image was a fantasy. It couldn't be real. Nothing in his life had ever looked so beautiful. Even freedom hadn't been as imperative to his life as this woman was.

"Jonas." Her gaze lifted, an edge of shock shadowing her darkened green eyes as she glanced back down at the claw that continually stroked against the tender, vulnerable flesh.

The slight curl at the tip of the claw eased over her nipple as she trembled before him. Jonas could feel the warmth of it brushing against the tip of his finger, the silken feel of it softer than anything he had ever known in his life.

Lifting his eyes, he gazed into her vulnerable green eyes, and knew he would give his life if he could ensure no more than her pleasure. She was worth more to him than his life, his freedom. And more surprising, she was worth more than the lives of those he had fought for all his life.

She was his world.

"I won't hurt you." He wanted to still the agonized sound of hunger in his voice, but found it impossible to do so.

She shook her head as a slow tremor raced through her body and the smell of her heat rushed through his senses like wildfire.

She wanted him. The silky heat of her juices was spilling between her thighs, preparing her for him.

He felt his nostrils flare. His body tightened further. His cock jerked, throbbed, and he hungered for more than just the scent of her. Sweet Lord, he hungered for the taste of her.

He wanted, and he didn't dare lay her across the bed. He didn't dare tempt himself so far, so soon.

He had to close his eyes as he lowered his head once more, his lips stroking down her neck, moving to the plump, ripe fruit of her nipple.

It beckoned. It tempted.

He stroked his tongue over one and had to fight to hold back because it tasted as sweet, as perfect as it looked. Curling his tongue over it, man and beast merged, melded, and as a single entity strove to pleasure the only mate he would ever know.

Rachel shuddered in Jonas's arms, the feel of his tongue, roughened just enough to rasp, to further heat the tight sensitivity of her nipple, was enough to send her head spinning.

Her hands tightened on his shoulders as her head fell back, her knees weakening. She wasn't going to be able to stand much longer. She couldn't bear pleasure like this. She didn't have the strength . . .

Her knees weakened further, causing her to stumble as his teeth raked against her nipple and caused a cry of incredible pleasure to tear from her lips.

"Jonas." A strangled cry tore from her lips as she felt herself falling, her legs refusing to hold her weight.

"I have you, baby." And he did. Shifting, moving, his lips still at her breasts, his tongue stroking from one nipple to the other as she felt herself lowering.

He moved, bent, knelt. Rachel felt the cool wood of the night table beneath the silk of her panties and the bare flesh of her thighs.

The small lamp tumbled to the floor. A harsh, ragged growl filled the fire-lit shadows of the room as her thighs were pushed apart. One foot she quickly placed on the edge of the bed, the other on the cushion of the chair beside the table. She was spread, opened; she was laid out for the hunger that flickered in his eerie, glowing gaze. Need, raging desire, emotions she was afraid to define, and a pleasure he did nothing to hide warred with something akin to fear in his gaze.

Rachel stared down at him, shaking like a leaf. Firelight flickered over him, painting his bronzed features in gold and shadow. Silver eyes glowed in the darkness as his hands lifted to her thighs, his claws raking down them, gently, so gently.

Lightning-fast, prickling sensations raced from that vulnerable area straight to her pussy and struck through it like a sensual blow. Her muscles clenched, desperate to be filled. Her clit throbbed, aching for touch.

"Oh God." Violent sensation tore through her vagina, burned with such amazing ecstasy that she found herself breathless, reaching, longing. The shards of pleasure were so intense, so incredible, she fought to close her thighs, to hold on to it forever.

She got a growl in return, a flash of strong white teeth as he pushed her thighs farther apart. Before she could protest, those claws hooked in the band of her panties and the sound of rending cloth echoed around her.

"Oh my God, Jonas." Her head fell back against the wall as she felt his breath against the heated folds, a whisper, a breeze of sensual, erotic hunger, a second before his tongue swiped through her pussy. Like a loving, luscious stroke of hunger, it delved through the juice-laden slit.

Friction. Just the smallest bite of sandpapery roughness and it nearly sent her over the edge before his head lifted again.

"You taste sweet, so sweet and soft." His voice rasped over her senses.

Lowering his head again, Rachel felt his lips bestow an intimate kiss. He sucked her clit just past his lips, flicked it with his tongue before releasing it. Soft, sucking kisses moved lower. His tongue emerged to tempt and tease, to taste with every little thrust into the folds of saturated flesh.

"I can't stand it," she panted.

She couldn't. Those erotic kisses were making her crazy, making her desperate to feel his cock press inside her.

Sliding his hands up her thighs, he gently parted the folds with claw-tipped fingers. So gently. The pricks of the sharp tips were another pleasure, a slice of exquisite sensation as he opened her farther, and licked.

He licked her like a treat, relishing every taste he found of her and throwing her senses into chaos.

He growled, the sound vibrating over the entrance to her pussy as she fought to memorize each touch.

Licking, stroking, his tongue worked through the curl-shrouded folds with hungry demand. It dipped into the entrance, thrust and flicked along the sensitive walls. It drove her into a maelstrom of fiery pleasure so intense she feared she would drown within it.

Returning to the distended, sensitive bud of her clitoris, his tongue curled around it, drew it between his lips and kissed it with slow, devastating movements of his lips as his tongue laved and stroked.

She couldn't believe the complete abandon in his expression, his pleasure as he ate her with decadent hunger. His claws stroked her thighs, giving a hidden element of danger, a reminder of the creature he was, man and animal, and completely devoted to her pleasure. A pleasure so destructive to her heart, her emotions, that she found herself reaching out to him with everything inside her.

She feared she couldn't survive it. Need was such a driving, deepening hunger that it overrode every thought, every instinct other than the one for his possession.

Looking down between her thighs, she watched as his tongue distended and slid through the glistening flesh. Probing, flicking around her clit, a cry tore from her throat at the sensation. Pleasure raced through her. It tingled up her spine, through her nerve endings, sped through her bloodstream until every cell of her body felt flushed with it.

It was too much. She arched, fighting to get closer, her hands gripping her knees as he pushed her legs farther apart and began to devour her with an intensity that hinted at his own desperation.

She hadn't thought it could get better. It did. His tongue pushed inside her, suddenly fucking her pussy with a demand that kept her poised on the edge of bliss. Each stroke was white-hot; each thrust rasped, tingled, sent a flush of agonizing pleasure tearing through her as it built the ever-increasing fire burning for complete possession.

She needed it all. She needed all of him.

"Jonas, please," she whimpered as she felt his claws stroking up her thighs once again.

Sweat glistened on his brow, his shoulders; a rumbling growl vibrated against her flesh. He drew her clit into his mouth again and began to suckle it. Silver eyes filled with living hunger lifted to hers and threw her over the edge.

It was an edge of complete release. A firestorm swept through her, hurled her through a kaleidoscope of color and had her screaming his name with what little breath she had left.

She was shaking, shuddering, aching, reaching for him. She watched as he rose to his feet, his hands gripping her shoulders to lift her to him.

She wanted more. He'd had his taste of her, devoured her until he destroyed her mind.

It was her turn.

The heavy, thick length of his cock was before her, the flushed crest dark and broad, branded with firelight, tempting her lips.

Drawing closer, she let her tongue swipe over the head as he tried to pull her to her feet.

He seemed to freeze. As though that lightest touch held him suspended, locked him into place.

He tasted wild, like the mountains themselves. Fresh,

invigorating. The dampness of pre-come exploded against her tongue, and with that taste of the mountains was a hint of the cinnamon and cloves that filled the taste of his kiss.

It was an intoxicating elixir. It fed the need already burning inside her; like gasoline to flames, it exploded through her senses and sent fiery lashes of exquisite pleasure ripping through her.

It wasn't a gentle thing. The need that arose inside her wasn't tame or calm, it was as wild as the hunger that raged in his eyes, in his expression. As wild as the animal whose genetics he shared.

A moan of pleasure left her throat as her lips parted and she drew the engorged head into her mouth.

What had she unleashed?

Jonas's head fell back as his hands flew to her head, his fingers gripping it, holding her still, everything inside him fighting to pull free of the wicked grip of her lips.

Damn her. He was holding her still to keep her from moving on his cock, but she was still destroying him. She was suckling at the engorged head with greedy flexes of her mouth, licking over the crest of his dick as though he were a favored treat.

He couldn't resist. His hips flexed, shifted. He watched as the flushed, wide crest slid just to her lips, then he pressed inside once again.

Again. He did it again, and again. It was a pleasure so intense, so violent, he swore he felt his knees shaking for a moment before he tightened them. His entire body was taut, tense with lightning-fast, erotic fingers of sensation.

He was fucking her mouth with slow, easy strokes. The tight, wet grip, her flickering tongue drove him crazy with need, with hunger.

Ah God, he couldn't bear it. He fought it. He couldn't come like this. He couldn't risk whatever unknown results . . .

His hands locked on her head again, stopping the rapid strokes of her mouth. Not that it stopped her. Once again she sucked, her tongue flicked, rivulets of heated, pulsating pleasure wracking his balls as he forced himself to pull back, forced himself from the ecstatic grip of her lips.

Snarling, he fought to restrain the hunger racing through him and lost.

"I needed to tell you . . ." He turned her, pressed her hands to the wood table and urged her to bend over.

Like this. The wildness inside him would have it no other way. Only here, only behind her, could he grip her as he needed, could his teeth lock into her shoulder and the hormone in his tongue spill to her system with maximum results.

Gripping the shaft of his cock, he pressed it against her, grimacing at the feel of her juices lubricating the crown, slickening it to allow for easier penetration.

The tiny entrance of her vagina parted, sucking at the head as he pressed it closer, clenching, urging him inside.

Her back arched as the scent of her pleasure whipped around him. He had to fight to hold back a roar as she cried out when he pressed the head of his cock tighter against the slick, fiery portal of her sweet pussy.

Bending, he pushed inside, felt the tight gripping muscles as they began to part for him, his cock bare as he began to forge his way into the sleek heat of her pussy.

"I'm sorry, Rachel." He felt the sweat drip down his face, watched as it fell to her shoulder a second before his lips moved to the vulnerable bend of her neck.

He was going to bite her. He could feel it. Animalistic, pounding, the strident demand of the animal was impossible to ignore.

Right there. Close to the heavy vein that meant life or death.

She was shaking. He felt her shuddering even as he felt the snug, wet heat of her body gripping him.

He was losing all restraint. He was losing his grip on what little awareness he had. There was nothing but the woman, nothing but the pleasure. Nothing but the fist-tight grip enveloping his cock as a snarl tore from his lips and he powered inside her.

Rachel's back arched.

Pleasure-pain streaked through her as she felt the sudden, fierce thrust that parted the tender tissue and filled her with exquisite, blinding heat.

She couldn't hold on. Her nails dug into the edge of the table as she began to move, her hips thrusting back, her muscles clenching on him as he began to move behind her.

His hips rolled, knees bent. She felt his claws at her hips, digging in with stinging heat, a pleasure-pain that added to the deep, driving thrusts inside her body as he fucked her deep, hard.

With her back to him, she had no choice but to concentrate on the pleasure. There were no distractions. She couldn't see his eyes, couldn't watch his expression, and it combined to send pleasure screaming through her system.

She was flying through ecstasy. She was thrown past reality into a world where nothing but the blistering, driving hunger existed. Where nothing mattered but this moment, this man. This pleasure.

It built inside her, tightening, tensing, burning. Wracking shudders raced up her spine. Agony gripped her clit as she felt the world beginning to unravel around her.

The explosion that resulted had her gasping his name. Nothing had ever been like this. Nothing had burned with such heat, stroked with such pleasure, or exploded with such shattering results.

Jonas felt it. The clench, the fist-tight grip that only became snugger, hotter. The rush of liquid heat, the shudders that raced through her body.

The pulsing, suckling grip she had on his cock was too much. Pleasure conflagrated. A fiery storm of sensation tore up his spine, tightened in his abdomen and exploded in his balls.

Before he could stop the impulse, his teeth locked in that sweet, soft area of her shoulder. The sharp tips pierced the flesh, the iron-sharp taste of her blood exploding against his rapidly licking tongue.

As his release tore through him, the barb emerged from beneath the head of his cock, extended, locking him inside her milking pussy, and began to heat his entire body with the powerful, minute release that detonated inside it.

His body was a mass of ecstatic pleasure. Powerful, brutal, primal in its intensity, building and burning inside him until his head jerked back from her neck and a hard, strangled roar left his lips.

His mate.

His.

His gift. His life.

He had betrayed her the moment that he had allowed her kiss. In this second, now, spilling his seed inside her, he had the horrifying realization that without Rachel, without her touch, her laughter, her warmth, his life held no meaning.

With that thought came the understanding, the knowledge, that when morning came, he might lose her warmth as well as her laughter.

What woman would welcome being mated to a monster?

• CHAPTER 17 •

Rachel awoke in Jonas's arms, her head cushioned on his chest as his fingers stroked along her spine. Fingers that lacked the lethal, strong claws they had displayed the night before.

She'd seen the dangerously tipped extensions before, but had never had the nerve to actually explore the long, broad fingers to find out if they worked as a cat's would. She had to admit though, the feel of them stroking down her thighs had sent arrows of sensual excitement shooting straight to the core of her sex.

Her gaze dropped to the strong, broad hand that lay across her bare stomach. Reaching down, she lifted his index finger, stroked it for a second, marveling at the strength of it. Did she dare, she wondered? She knew she didn't dare look at him as she did it. Biting her lip, she pressed firmly just beneath the broad, well-manicured nail and watched as the lethally strong claw emerged.

His entire hand flexed then, and slowly, each finger sported the well-manicured, lethally sharp tipped claws she had felt across her thighs the night before. Her lips quirked. Only

Jonas would have his claws manicured and honed to dangerous points. When it came to the idea of Breeds being civilized, Jonas gave an Oscar-worthy performance.

He was silent as she ran her finger over the sharp tip, his silver eyes watching her with quiet intensity as she lifted her gaze back to him.

She wished she could decipher the emotions that roiled in his eyes. She wished she could understand why the sight of them bit at her heart with aching sadness.

"Can all Breeds do that?" she asked as she flicked the tip of a claw with her finger.

His head shook. "Only a primal."

"A primal? I haven't heard that designation before." She thought she had heard all of them.

The color in his eyes flickered momentarily. "It's a sub-designation and kept carefully quiet. Many Breeds aren't even aware we exist. We are truly the monsters of the species. Primals are bred to be less merciful and compassionate. Our animals are closer to the skin, you could say, and the human instinct for cruelty and egomania was bred to be uppermost in our human genetics."

"The perfect soldier," she murmured, remembering the news releases that had accompanied the Breed rescues.

"No, Breeds are the perfect soldiers," he amended. "Primals are the perfect killers. We were created to work best alone, to never be able to be a lover or a friend, and to kill that person on command, or as needed. We were created to have no heart, no mercy. And we were created to breed hybrids that were animals walking on two legs."

Something more flickered in his gaze then: apprehension, perhaps? Did he expect her to feel fear at this point? As far as she was concerned, it was a little too late for that. She was in his bed now, she was truly his mate. Fear at this late date would have been drama. And Rachel seriously didn't believe in drama.

"What happened with the breeding part?" Her heart was breaking at the knowledge that they were created to never love, to never laugh. What a weight it must be to know they had been created to destroy, to kill, and that the world knew why they had been created. So many hated and feared them for their very existence. They had no idea how much the Breeds regretted that reason as well.

A short, bitter laugh escaped his lips. "They could never get that part to work so well. For the most part, the scientists were unaware of the need for mating. But the groundwork was laid for the creatures they eventually wanted to produce, though."

The creatures, not the children. Rachel had to force back her tears at the words he used. Jonas wasn't much on sympathy. He preferred reality and honesty above all things. She'd heard him say once or twice that sympathy was an empty emotion for those who had no desire to expend the effort to actually fight against an injustice.

"It doesn't matter if it's human or animal," she said softly as she stared back at him. "I don't believe anyone is born or created to kill. It's taught to them. You can use all the genetics you want, but it comes down to what you teach your children. Just as it comes down to what that child wants to be once you've taught it all you know. The knowledge of right and wrong is inherent, Jonas. The Breeds have proven that."

She saw the indecision in his gaze then, or perhaps disbelief.

Lying in his arms, his body warm, hard, tense against her, she finally broached the subject that had bothered her the previous night.

Jonas and the Leo had such a conflicted relationship as it was, but last night, they had both been more on edge than normal.

"What is the issue with Leo? He's been picking at you for as long as I've worked for you, but he was worse last night."

"He's been picking far longer than you've been with me," he grunted.

"Why?"

"Who knows why the Leo does what he does, or what

he hopes to achieve from it." There was genuine confusion in his expression. "He keeps pushing for something that he has no desire to explain, and I refuse to ask for that explanation. I'm simply the whelp I'm certain he wishes they hadn't created."

His tone was matter-of-fact, accepting, but Rachel saw the hint of betrayal in his eyes. Leo's attitude pricked at him, and who could blame him? The one dream the Breeds had was that of family. Leo was his father, yet he acted as though he were ashamed, or regretful, of Jonas's existence. His eyes told another story, though, Rachel thought. Like Jonas, the Leo's eyes roiled with emotions.

"You're stubborn," she stated.

"And he's a manipulative bastard," he growled.

"Like father, like son, perhaps?" she questioned him with a smile as she stretched lazily, feeling the tenderness that assailed her body, the proof that she had been well loved the night before.

"My genetics are far different from his," he retorted. "His provided a base, if you will. The scientists then added what they thought would create the animal they wanted. Leo's no primal, but he should have been created as one."

She almost laughed. Unfortunately, she had a feeling that laughter wouldn't go over so well right now.

"I hate to tell you this, Jonas, but you're not that far from your father in genetics," she informed him. "The two of you are more alike than he and Callan are. You even have several of your mother's physical traits, such as the shape of your eyes."

His expression darkened. "Elizabeth isn't my mother. My dam was the Scientist LaRue, who headed the French labs where I was created. I share no genetics with Elizabeth Vanderale."

He was lying to her. Rachel sat up, turned and stared down at him. There was no mistaking the fact that Elizabeth Vanderale was his mother. Many of Jonas's actions mirrored hers, such as his habit of rubbing his neck when he was agitated, or the way he narrowed his eyes. She had seen the woman display those gestures many times over the past months.

Lies and deceit were things Rachel absolutely refused to tolerate. There was no way in hell she would stand back and allow Jonas to practice his less desirable traits against her as he often did in the political circles he moved within.

"Look, I don't know what you think this mating is going to be, Jonas Wyatt, but it will include not lying to me. And don't think I haven't learned by now exactly how to tell when you're lying. Let me guess: Elizabeth Vanderale isn't supposed to be your mother, so you've simply never informed her that she is?"

His jaw tightened. Whatever emotion he was trying to hide from her, whatever knowledge he wanted to keep hidden, was obviously something he had fought to keep to himself.

"How do you know I'm lying to you?" He gazed back at her with an almost innocent charm. It was so obviously feigned that she nearly laughed.

She rolled her eyes. "For some reason my female intuition kicks in. When you lie, it feels like the edges of a panic attack."

If there was one person she thought would understand that, she knew it would be Jonas.

He sighed as he stared up at the ceiling as though that knowledge was an irritant. "Just what I need, a mate who knows how to listen to her instincts."

Rachel gave a light laugh before she moved from the bed, drawing the sheet with her and wrapping it around her.

"The fire is going out. It will be getting chilly soon," she told him as she glanced to the window, where dawn was just breaking over the horizon. "And Amber will be up at any time. Would you listen for her while I shower?"

Jonas watched as she moved from the bedroom into the bathroom, a frown brewing on his brow as he finally figured out what it was that seemed off.

Rachel carried his scent now. He could detect the hormone fusing to her system from the bite he'd given her the night before. He could detect a natural, subtle allure to her. But, she wasn't burning for sex as other mates did. She wasn't close to begging, and it had been six hours at the very least since he'd taken her.

The fire shimmered inside her. She was aroused. He could smell that hunger simmering in the sweet recess of her pussy. But she was controlling it rather than it controlling her as it blazed out of control.

Lying there, he tried to feel the burning, agonizing arousal that he knew affected mates for the few months of mating unless conception occurred. Or unless Ely was able to find the required hormonal dosage for the females to aid in relieving the symptoms.

It was limited, he realized as he rose from the bed and quickly dressed. He was aroused. His cock was as hard this morning as it had been the night before. The need to take her, to spill himself inside her, was still there. But it was no longer agonizing. It was no longer so painful he felt as though he were losing his mind.

Rubbing the underside of his tongue against his teeth, he felt the minor swelling in the glands. The hormone was there, ready to release into her system once again. The glands weren't overenlarged, though neither were they burning as though fevered.

Moving to the living room, he fixed the baby's bottle, then moved to her crib to change her diaper and prepare her for her breakfast.

A small grin tugged at his lips as he met her green gaze and a wide smile split her lips.

"Hey there, little one," he whispered as he moved closer and began the process of diapering her. "Waiting on me, were you?"

It had become his practice to get up before Rachel. He often used those spare moments to play with the baby where no one could see, and to develop the bond he knew would stay with them for a lifetime.

She cooed up at him, which instantly melted his heart

even though he attempted to steel himself against it. This tiny little girl, so vulnerable, had the ability to make him question himself and how his actions would be seen by her as she grew older.

Her mother knew him, perhaps in ways he didn't know himself, he thought. She was definitely stronger than he had imagined. He had expected her to be shocked, horrified, at the knowledge of the child she could conceive. Instead, she had calmly disagreed with his knowledge of what their future could hold, and calmed his fears as well.

Could it be so simple? he wondered. That a child of his could be more than a killer? That there was a chance he could raise it to value life as Jonas attempted to?

Fixing Amber's clothes, he had to grin again as her tiny foot kicked against his hand, her little arms waving in excitement. She knew it was time for him to pick her up, to cuddle her against him, and she was demanding that he hurry.

"You're going to kick ass," he told her as he lifted her from her crib moments later and gave her the bottle. "I can see it now. With an auntie like Diana, all that red hair, and me for a daddy, you won't have a choice."

He would have to teach her to protect herself. The Breeds' world wasn't one where safety was the norm. Danger was the norm, and all their children had to be prepared for it, even those who hadn't been born with Breed DNA.

Sitting in a nearby chair, he rested the child against his chest and held the bottle comfortably to her ready lips as he gazed down at her. She looked like her mother. There was nothing of her father in her. Not in looks, nor in scent.

He tested her scent, and found that Rachel's genetics far overpowered the Marshal genes. Then he frowned and tested the air again.

There was something new there, something he hadn't detected before. But it was as yet so light that he couldn't exactly pinpoint its source.

Of course, a baby's scent changed over the course of maturity, he knew that. Their scent as an infant was far different from their scent as an adult, even though it held that infant scent as a subtle undertone.

But still, Amber's shouldn't be changing so soon. She had several more months before the change would even begin, and slightly longer before it should be detectable.

As she finished her bottle, her eyes drifted shut, and sleep overtook her again as Jonas rocked her gently. Within moments, she squirmed, whimpered and, damn, but he had to grin again.

Easing his restraint, he let the contented purr of a mated Breed rumble in his chest. He'd been purring since the night he'd brought Rachel to his home. Another anomaly, he thought. Most Breeds didn't purr until after the barb had emerged during full intercourse.

Yet, Jonas had. And he'd been very careful not to allow Rachel to hear it. He wanted her comfortable with the mating before he allowed her to see exactly how much of an animal he was.

With Amber, he'd relaxed his guard though. That first night as Rachel slept, exhausted, Amber had been restless for her mother. He'd allowed the purr to escape simply because he had no idea how to hum as he'd heard Rachel when she held her child.

Amber had been immediately captivated by that purr, so much so that now she refused to sleep for Jonas unless he used the unique sound as he rocked her.

He was wrapped as tightly around her little finger as he was wrapped around her mother's.

When he could no longer sense wakefulness in the child, he laid her back in her crib before picking up the comm link he kept close by.

"Command, I need a secure line into lab level two," he ordered the security command center. "I want the channel locked and encrypted."

"Yes, Mr. Wyatt," the control Enforcer answered.

A series of static beeps and pings signaled the secure

line going into place, and seconds later the first ring echoed through the line.

"I've been trying to get hold of you," Amburg answered quickly, his tone distracted. "You should answer your sat phone or comm link more often, you know."

"Really?" Jonas feigned disinterest. "What did you need?"

"I need you and your mate back in the labs together as soon as possible. I'd like to get samples while the two of you are in each other's presence to compare them against previous samples," he informed Jonas. "Ely ran your tests last night and they contained several surprising anomalies. I need to study those further and wanted to see how the added stimuli would affect the tests."

"Hmm," Jonas murmured as he felt his more calculating side overtaking the sated languor he had felt moments before. "Does it have anything to do with the change in Amber's scent as well?"

Silence filled the line for long moments. Jonas felt a tension that hadn't been there before and knew the good doctor's face would be creasing in a thoughtful scowl. Which didn't bode well for the answers Jonas needed.

"Bring the child as well." There was a note of concern in the scientist's voice. "I don't know what the changing scent is, but if it's indeed changing, then Ely, Elizabeth and I need to figure out why."

Jonas's brows arched. When had Amburg, Ely and Elizabeth Vanderale begun working so well together that Amburg felt comfortable enough calling Elizabeth by her given name rather than Dr. Vanderale?

"We'll see you in the labs soon then," Jonas informed him before lowering his voice. "Be careful, Amburg. If I find out you're messing with tests, I promise, you'll regret it."

"You seem to forget, Wyatt, I am a scientist," Amburg stated, his tone regal now. "I may dislike you until hell freezes over, but Breed genetics and evolution have been my life. Messing with those tests never once crossed my mind, simply because it would mess with the results. Can you say the same?"

Jonas's lips quirked. Of course he couldn't. He messed with certain tests of his own every time they were conducted. Any test that would shed light on who his natural mother was, was given a thorough fucking over, though why he bothered, he wasn't always certain.

Wouldn't Leo, Dane and Callan be horrified to learn that the bogeyman of the Breeds was a full brother rather than a genetic by-blow, as Leo liked to call him?

Hell, he didn't reveal it for the simple fact that he knew that damned woman would fucking cry. Son of a bitch, he'd watched her cry over Callan when he was wounded the year before, nearly killed. She had sobbed in Leo's arms, her voice broken, agony tearing through her that she'd not had enough time to love her son. That they'd been forced apart for too long. That she deserved more time, that he deserved more life.

What would she do if she learned that her eggs, frozen by the Council when she had been a part of it, and Leo's semen, had created him? It was only after his creation that his genetics had been manipulated. Manipulated enough that evidently the parental scent had been wiped away. Only the base of Leo's scent had been retained.

"I'm finished." Rachel stepped from the bedroom, her long hair lying damp over her shoulders, her green eyes slightly darker, her arousal slightly hotter. Yet still, he could smell no distress.

He wanted to ask her to return to the bedroom with him first. He wanted to relieve the ache tightening his balls, but she smelled so fresh and soft and appeared anxious to see her daughter.

She strode quickly across the room, smiled down at her little angel, then picked her up gently and cuddled her as she begun to hum.

Jonas rubbed at the back of his neck, the ache there irritating him. Tension activated it. It bred an ache rather like a headache. There were times in the labs when the pain had been excruciating.

"I'm going to shower," he told her, fighting back the lust. He would wait on her as long as he could. "We need to return to the labs as soon as we can. Get some breakfast, and we'll leave once I'm ready."

She turned to him, frowning. "We were just there last night, Jonas. Why do we have to go back?"

"The mating heat is different enough from others that Ely will need more samples now that we've completed the mating," he informed her. He glanced at Amber, wondering how much to tell Rachel, fearing upsetting her. Hell, she'd been through enough, he didn't want to see her worry more. "And I'd like to have Amber checked once again as well."

She stilled. He could smell that edge of fear now.

"Why, Jonas? And don't bother lying to me."

He grimaced. Yeah, it was just his luck that he had a mate with an overdeveloped sense of women's intuition.

Sighing, he explained the scent, and the time line for the changes in the child. She asked few questions, merely watching him, her green eyes large in her suddenly pale face as her hold tightened on her child.

"It's nothing dangerous," he assured her. "If it was, Rachel, I'd know." He prayed he would. As a primal, his sense of smell was off the charts when compared to other Breeds. That didn't make him infallible though, and he knew it.

Rachel licked her lips nervously. "And they'll be able to figure out what's causing that change?" she asked him.

"That's the idea." He nodded. "If nothing else, they can rule out any problems."

"If she were sick, you'd know, wouldn't you, Jonas?" she suddenly asked fearfully. "If she were really sick."

He moved to her then. He couldn't bear to see the fear in her eyes.

Reaching her, he touched her cheek with his fingers before bending his head to kiss her gently. "I would know," he promised, his lips moving against hers. "Any human or Breed disease, both Ely and I can detect, sweetheart, I promise you. And I smell no disease, no sickness, simply a change I want to have checked out."

There was nothing more that he could tell her, but for the first time in his life he wanted to be able to pull the answers out of his ass to ease the fear traveling through her.

Instead, he turned and headed to the shower. There was nothing he could do but take her to those who could find the answers. And pray that he was right.

◆   ◆   ◆

Rachel watched as he left the room, slowly rocking Amber and trying to still the panic that threatened. She was a wuss, she thought, just as Diana had always accused her of being.

She wasn't an adrenaline junkie, and she worried. Rachel was the worrywart, Diana was the daredevil. But the thought that something could be wrong with Amber, that Phillip Brandenmore had harmed her child, was enough to make her stomach roil with fear and rage.

Laying a kiss to Amber's brow, Rachel laid her back in her crib before pacing to the fireplace and staring into the low, comforting warmth of the fire.

She lived for the day Jonas managed to get that bastard out of the Middle East and into Breed custody. She wanted to be there. She wanted to make certain he felt the same fear, the same lack of security and terror her daughter had felt.

She wanted his blood, slowly. She wanted to hear him scream in pain, watch as he begged—the way she had begged while Amber cried and cried for her.

She could still hear Amber's screams as the baby heard her mother's voice, knowing her momma was near, yet a stranger held her without tenderness or care.

Rachel could still remember the way he held her. His hand to the back of her neck braced against his chest.

He had hurt her baby. He had terrified both of them, and she wanted him dead. Rachel had a very bad feeling that once the truth was revealed, she would have no compunction whatsoever about pulling the trigger to take his life. Her female intuition was making her sick now. It had been ever since Jonas had mentioned the change in Amber's scent. As though the very thought of some unknown illness had triggered a knowledge inside her that she couldn't fully decipher.

Moving back to the crib, she quickly undressed her baby, turning her, checking her for any outward signs of problems. She knew Brandenmore had injected Amber with something. Elizabeth Vanderale and Jeffrey Amburg had been certain it had only been a sedative. That had made sense. Amber had been screaming, the sound of it raking across her own nerves because of the fear in her daughter's voice. It would have irritated Brandenmore. He would have wanted her quiet.

So why hadn't he killed her?

Rachel pressed her hand against her stomach at the thought. Brandenmore didn't care about one small child, and he had meant to kill Rachel when she returned anyway. If he hadn't had plans for Amber, then why leave her alive? And if he did have plans for her, then it would be nothing that a mother could find but nightmares within.

Brandenmore was a scientist. He could have created something that hid itself within the sedative. Something that would have begun working long after initial tests were run. That was how he worked, according to the file she had read on him. He was subtle, vicious. Completely and totally deceptive.

She was shaking. She could almost feel her world shattering around her as she stared down at her still-sleeping daughter. Could she survive it if something happened to her baby?

She couldn't. Amber had matured her. Her daughter had given her a reason to live that hadn't existed before her birth.

Biting her lip, she fought to hold back the fear, the tears. Jonas could smell it. He might be in the shower, but who was to say that his sense of smell wasn't strong enough to feel the complete panic threatening to tear her apart?

Amber had known fear much too soon. She'd known pain too soon. Surely that couldn't bode well for the values she wanted to teach her daughter: acceptance, compassion, a small measure of trust that the world could be kind, at least sometimes.

And perhaps the world was trying to show Rachel otherwise.

"It's going to be okay, Rachel."

Jonas's soft voice had her whirling around to meet the dark cloth of his shirt as it stretched over his chest. Lifting her head, she stared into his eyes as he smoothed a tear from her cheek, which she hadn't even been aware she had shed.

"How can you be certain?" she whispered as his arms came around her. "How can I protect her, Jonas, when he's already done something to hurt her?"

Her fingers clenched in the fabric of his shirt as she fought to control the racing of her heart, the shudders beginning to wrack her body.

This was her baby. Her child. So innocent, so dependent on her mother to ensure that she wasn't harmed. She'd already failed her.

"Because I'll ensure it." His tone was so certain, so confident. "We have the finest minds working in Breed research. Scientists that exceptionally intelligent, Rachel, will find out what, if anything, Brandenmore has done. And if they don't"—he gripped her arms, holding her back at she stared down at her, the arrogance and pure determination in his expression brightening his eyes to a neon silver—"if they don't, I'll bring Brandenmore here, and trust me, once I have him here in my territory, he will talk."

That confidence sank into her. She had never seen Jonas break a promise. Even when she had been certain there was no way he could make something he had promised the Breed cabinet to work, he'd still managed it.

He manipulated, he connived. He threatened, he wasn't very good at cajoling, but he knew how to terrify a person. And he always, always did as he said he would.

"She's just a baby," she whispered, trying to explain her fear.

"Shhh." He laid his finger against her lips. "She's our

child. She may not share my blood, Rachel, but she's captured my heart, as you've captured my soul. Never doubt, no matter the cost, I will protect our child."

Not her child. Not his child. *Their* child.

For the first time in Rachel's life, standing there in his arms, she felt that long-buried fear of desertion slowly ease away.

It would never be easy, living with Jonas. It might never be calm. But as she stood there, his arms wrapped around her, his warmth sheltering her, she knew it would always be exactly where she wanted to be. And something that nothing, or no one, could ever steal from her.

The Leo was waiting on them in the labs, along with Elizabeth Vanderale; their son, Dane; Dr. Ely Morrey; and Dr. Jeffery
Amburg.

Rachel had never paid much attention to the labs on previous visits, her attention always splintered by Jonas, that she'd
had no time to consider much besides the danger they were
facing.

That first night, Amber's unnatural sleep had held her
attention solely. The second time she had been there, the
discomfort she had felt during the examination Ely had
performed and Jonas's unnaturally volatile mood had distracted her.

Now she stood holding Amber as Jonas, Leo and Dane
seemed to confront each other.

She saw the lab was now painted in muted greens, tans
and fall reds, rather than the stark white it had been when first
taken over by the Breeds.

The gurney sheets were brightly colored, real pillows laying at one end. There were comfortable-looking chairs, sheer

drapes falling from ceiling to floor in the far corner where a reading chair sat, and heavy, brightly colored screens hiding the necessary equipment needed to aid the scientists.

"You two can bloody well stop getting on my nerves." Dane finally sighed as he glanced from Leo to Jonas, a heavy frown creasing his brow as white brows lowered over his bright, emerald green eyes.

Leo's lips thinned in irritation.

"Leo, I don't have time for this," Elizabeth added weight to her son's disgusted proclamation. "You're here to help, not to make everyone more agitated than they already are."

Leo grunted, but his golden gaze shifted to the child Rachel held. His expression relaxed as his lips seemed to want to tilt into a grin.

"She's a lovely child." He stepped closer as Rachel shifted her gaze to Jonas, her nerves making her ill.

"Settle down now, Ms. Broen." Leo smiled. A faint quirk of his lips, which added weight to Jonas's vow that nothing bad was going to happen here. "May I hold your precious angel?"

Rachel licked her lips before turning Amber over to the tall, roughly hewn patriarch.

Amber whimpered for several seconds before settling back down, her eyes staring up at the unfamiliar male as Leo made a small, almost purring sound as he held her. It was a sound she had accidentally caught Jonas making one night as she pretended to be asleep while he slipped Amber from her crib for a bottle and diaper.

"The purr is distinctive," Leo told her as he glanced up at her. "A mated Breed has many different sounds that they don't make before they mate. The purr they have for their mates. The one they have for their child." He ran his finger over Amber's cheek as his gaze lifted to Jonas. "She's a perfect addition to Sanctuary, I believe."

Jonas shrugged as he crossed his arms over his chest and seemed to wait.

"I'm nearly a hundred and thirty years old, Ms. Broen."

His smile was quick, amused, as he glanced at her. "Can you tell?"

"I thought your arrogance was rather defined for a mere century," she quipped, barely refraining from rolling her eyes.

Leo chuckled, obviously taking no offense. "That comes from being the leader of a Pride of hardheaded, rough-bitten, less-than-congenial Breeds in the wilds of Africa," he assured her. "You develop it better than they do, or you suffer."

"You also learn the fine art of bragging," Elizabeth snorted, though she did so with an edge of pure love as she gazed at her mate. "Get on with it, Leo. I'm certain Rachel would like to leave here sometime today with a knowledge of what's going on."

"The Leo has a hell of a way of wasting time," Dane informed her.

"Watch your language, Dane." Jonas frowned, his brows lowering with dark warning.

Dane's own brows lifted in surprise, though those green eyes held understanding. "Of course, brother. Forgive me."

An apology from a Breed, how interesting. But the bit of byplay helped ease her nerves marginally.

"Come here, little one," Leo crooned, the gentle purr in his chest increasing as he turned and walked to the rocking chair that sat on the other side of the gurney. "Let the Leo get a feel for your scent here. Though my own angels are going to protest a bit when Papa returns with the scent of another babe on him. They're a bit possessive, you know."

He continued to speak to her as he rocked, his head lowered, his nostrils flared, as he obviously drew in her scent.

Rachel rubbed at her arms as she felt Jonas move behind her. His hands settled on her shoulders, his strength and warmth behind her lending her courage.

Leo frowned, then his brow cleared. He smiled a bit, managed to get a chortle from Amber and frowned again as Dr. Amburg watched the scene curiously. Elizabeth moved behind her mate, her hands settling on his shoulders as she watched Amber reach up for the long strands of hair that fell over the Leo's shoulder.

Coarse, a rich tawny blended with black, russet and golden browns.

"Her mother's scent is strong," Leo murmured to Elizabeth.

"I assumed," Elizabeth agreed quietly. "She looks much like her mother. She'll be a replica of her when she gets older."

"The day will come when strangers will believe you're twins rather than mother and daughter." The Leo chuckled as he glanced at Rachel.

Rachel couldn't speak. She knew what was going on. The Leo was using his own senses to draw in the scent of whatever was changing in her child.

"Dane, could you come here?" Leo rose from the chair as Dane moved to him. "Hold her for a moment."

Dane accepted the slight weight as Rachel felt her stomach knot in panic again.

Dane spoke gently, easily, to the baby. He obviously had experience with children. Within minutes, he had Amber cooing, her eyes bright, her lips stretched wide in a smile. Her daughter, even at her young age, was quite content with the male attention she was gaining.

"I can't stand this," Rachel whispered as she felt Jonas's head against the side of hers.

"Easy, love," he whispered, laying a kiss to her ear as though there weren't five others standing there who glanced at him, their expressions registering momentary shock before they returned their attention to Amber.

"There are slight physical changes," Elizabeth remarked, then glanced at Rachel. "May I remove her gown?"

Rachel nodded jerkily.

The examination took a toll on her nerves. If not for Jonas, Rachel didn't know if she could have survived the ordeal. It seemed to last forever before they laid Amber on a gurney covered in a soft russet-colored blanket.

Ely and Amburg moved closer as Elizabeth took several

pressure vials of blood, swabbed Amber's mouth, then, surprisingly, swabbed under her arms, behind her knees and again behind her neck.

"Sweat collects continually beneath the arms, behind the knees and along the back and front of a baby's neck," Elizabeth explained as she stored the samples in sterile containers. "We can use her diaper for a urine sample. That's imperative at this point. We need as many differing samples as possible to see if any changes are occurring in her."

"There's definitely no disease or illness," Leo stated as he glanced back at Rachel. "I agree with Jonas's determination that her scent has changed though. I was here the night you brought her in and took a moment to check her scent then. It's different, and the change isn't natural."

Dane remained silent as they glanced back at him.

"Dane." Leo frowned. "You're often better with the babies than I. What did you sense?"

Dane shook his head. "What you found, Father. I'd be interested in seeing the results of the samples the doctors are taking though."

"Jonas's scent is heavy," Ely stated then, her hand stroking over Amber's head as the baby tried to catch her fingers. "You hold her often?" she asked Jonas.

"Often." Behind her, she felt the slight movement of Jonas's nod.

"Could the changing scent be a marker of some sort?" Elizabeth turned back to her husband and son.

"Of some sort." Dane nodded, his expression too cool, too restrained for the man Rachel had always sensed he was.

"Are the two of you ready now?" Elizabeth turned back to them, a comforting smile on her face. "It will be a while before we have the results back, and we'll need yours as well."

Rachel moved to the gurney, where Amber was once again chortling up at Dane.

"She's physically fine, Ms. Broen," he assured her. "I

promise you, if she stays this healthy, she'll grow up to give
you gray hairs despite the fact that you're barely going to age
a year or two by the time she's mature."

She had to accept their assurances; she had no other choice.
She had come to know Leo and Dane over the months she had
worked with the Bureau. She had spent quite a bit of time in
Sanctuary and had socialized with them often. They were as
bluntly honest as Jonas could be. They were manipulating as
hell; it seemed to be a family trait as well as a Breed trait.
But they wouldn't lie to her about this. Besides, her stomach
was finally settling down, assuring her that there was no lie
to watch out for.

"Elizabeth, please take enough of Ms. Broen's and Jonas's
samples to allow me ample amounts to conduct the tests we
discussed earlier," Amburg asked.

"What tests?" Rachel turned to him quickly.

Amburg smiled coolly. He wasn't a warm man. "Simply
an array of medical tests, Ms. Broen. Unlike the Breeds, I
don't have a sense of smell, and I like to have my own assurances before I begin searching for other answers."

He was lying.

Rachel glanced back at Jonas to see his gaze narrowed
on the doctor. Jonas knew he was lying as well. When he
turned back to her, though, his gaze wasn't concerned or worried. Doctors were always evasive, she told herself, though she
couldn't quite convince herself that everything would be fine.

She knew it had to be fine. Anything else was unac-
ceptable.

◆　◆　◆

The tests conducted on her and Jonas went quickly, smoothly.
Within a few hours, she was back at the cabin, trying to rub
away the discomfort that still lingered on her skin from the
effect of Ely's and Elizabeth's touch as they examined her.

Amber was tucked in her crib, resting comfortably in the
room next to Rachel's office. The sitter, Erin, rested in a chair

next to the crib and read one of the stack of books she kept in the room.

The Breeds were readers. Even Jonas had hundreds of books stacked on shelves throughout the cabin. Sanctuary boasted a well-stocked library, in addition to the extensive collection in Buffalo Gap.

As Rachel paced her office, she tried to ignore the steadily burning ache in the core of her sex. She was becoming so aroused it was almost painful. And the strangest part was the need for the taste of Jonas's kiss. Her mouth watered for it.

She was torn between pacing the floor and worrying about Amber, and walking into Jonas's office, tearing him from the computer and forcing him to fuck her.

Her eyes closed at the thought as she paused beside her desk. She wanted to ride him. She wanted to straddle that hard, muscular body and work his heavy cock inside her.

No. First she wanted to ride his lips, his tongue.

She swallowed tightly. A kiss first.

First she wanted his kiss, his tongue plunging into her mouth, spreading that taste she needed so desperately, then she wanted the rest of it. All of it.

Amber appeared fine. It was her scent, and according to Jonas, Leo and Dane, the change was so slight that it could well be the changes that came from the changes in her body as she grew. It could be an effect of Jonas's scent on her, and the fact that he was now Amber's mother's mate. It could be a variety of reasons.

She didn't have to worry right now. And though she could never put it completely out of her mind, her body was forcing her to concentrate on Jonas.

Her body was demanding her mate now. It was demanding his kiss, his touch. His possession. Mating heat had picked a hell of a time to kick in. She felt besieged on all sides. Fear and worry for her daughter, emotions for Jonas that she wasn't always certain how to handle, and facing a future that had no chance of true peace or safety. At least not for decades to come.

She was trying to decide if the fact that she may be there in those future decades was a good or bad thing. According to everything she had been able to find out, the aging retardation had been tracked at one year per decade. In a hundred years, she will have aged only ten.

Because of the mating heat. Because of the need amplified within her body, digging heated claws into her womb and filling her clit, her pussy, with such raging hunger that it was impossible to deny.

And the urges that hunger fed into her.

She rubbed her hand along her lower stomach, feeling her womb flex, clench. It wasn't just the need for sex. It was a need for complete intimacy. The need was overwhelming, wild. It was as primal as the claws that had retracted from the tips of his fingers.

"Rachel."

She opened her eyes to see him standing in the doorway to his office.

Her breath caught audibly now. She could no longer hide her response to him. Her pussy flooded with her juices, the memory of the pleasure he could bring her racing through her system.

She didn't feel like herself. She felt those urges she had always kept carefully restrained rising inside her, trying to break free.

Rachel had always been perfectly happy being the peace-maker, sitting back and playing it safe while she worried incessantly about her wild sister.

If she had felt a need for adventure, she had always tamped it down quickly. Diana was wild enough for both of them, and she was smart enough, confident enough, to survive those adventures.

Watching him now as he moved slowly across the room, she was once again reminded of the animal he was. So powerful. There were times he seemed invincible.

His eyes were narrowed, living mercury roiling in the darkened features of his face. Hunger and emotion filled that gaze. Emotions she hadn't yet learned to decipher, but felt she was growing closer to the answers.

"You had only to come to me," he growled as he reached her, caught her hand and began drawing her to the entrance of the main house.

Pausing, he turned back.

"Erin, Rachel and I will be unavailable for a while," he called out to the sitter.

"Yes, Mr. Wyatt," Erin called back, no hint in her tone that she knew what was going on, though Rachel knew she must.

When he turned back it was to draw her from the office wing to the residence and then through the kitchen, living room and into the bedroom.

And she followed him. She followed him as her heart beat with a primal, desperate rhythm. As hungers she'd always fought began to tear through her mind and body.

She couldn't get that need out of her mind. The need to go wild on him. The need to claim what was hers.

As the bedroom door closed, he turned to her, his nostrils flaring as he stared down at her with something akin to surprise.

She intended to give him much more to be surprised about.

Lifting her hands, she flattened her palms against his chest, parted her lips and drew in a hard breath.

"You look so civilized in silk," she murmured.

Pushing her hands beneath the charcoal jacket, she pushed it slowly back from his body, her lashes drifting lower as she heard the soft rasp of the material as it slid from his shoulders.

That sound sped through her senses, racing through her bloodstream as it fed a fiery heat straight to her nipples, her clit, the clenching muscles of her pussy.

"Civilized?" He continued to watch her, his nostrils flaring as he drew her scent in. "I don't think I've ever heard that word attached to me, Rachel."

She licked her lips, her hands smoothing down his chest once more to grip the edges of his shirt.

"I didn't say you *were* civilized," she breathed out, her voice rougher, filled with hunger, with a need she didn't want to hold back any longer. "And in a second, you won't look civilized either."

She smiled. Naked. She wanted him naked, wanted him hard and hot and as wild as she was.

· C H A P T E R   1 9 ·

This was the woman Jonas had always sensed inside Rachel. The mate who would shake his world up, who would bind his heart and soul and leave him willing to worship at her feet.

He'd once thought his mate would have to be a female Enforcer. And if human, perhaps a woman like the lawyer Jess Warden, or a fighter like Rachel's kamikaze sister. He'd never imagined his mate would come in a short, calmly quiet, coolly efficient little package. A woman who could handle him in ways that he'd never been able to control others.

He felt her fingers tighten in the edges of his shirt, watched her eyes as she tore the buttons from their moorings and nearly snarled at the raging excitement reflected in the darkening green irises.

She was the perfect lady whenever, wherever she had to be. But now, she was a woman prepared to take her mate.

His hands lifted only to be pushed aside.

"Don't touch me," she ordered as she pushed the tattered edges of his shirt from his arms. "Let me undress you."

Hell. He didn't know if he could do that. He didn't know

if he could stand calmly, idly by and simply watch his world being reshaped by this woman's hands. Hell no, he wanted to participate.

He would give her what he could though.

He stood still, his fists clenching as her hands ran down his bare chest, her fingertips raking over his flat nipples as that seductive, siren's smile shaped her lips.

A second later, her nails were rasping down his abdomen, sending spikes of incredible heat to tighten his balls and throb through his dick.

"This is a dangerous game you're playing," he breathed out roughly. "You may not be able to handle what you unleash, mate."

She looked at him from beneath her lashes as her fingers worked loose his belt.

"Take your shoes off." The commanding tone had his eyes narrowing, the animal raging inside him, demanding that he force her submission.

He had no intentions of making her surrender. Her surrender wasn't what he wanted. This was the woman he wanted.

He pushed the expensive shoes from his feet as he watched her, felt her fingers loosening the clasp of his slacks.

"I want to take you." She leaned forward, her tongue licking over his chest and causing his teeth to clench in furious arousal.

Then he felt the sharp edge of her teeth at the side of one nipple, sinking into his flesh in an intimate, searing little bite.

His body jerked, pleasure rioting across his nerve endings at the feel of her teeth biting into him, her tongue tasting him. His hands came up to touch her, to grip her shoulders, to pull her to the bed.

"No!" Her hands caught his wrists.

She was so delicate. There was no strength in her hold, but clear purpose stopped him instead.

Staring down at her, he had to force himself not to take her, not to dominate the sexuality rising inside her.

"This is mine," she told him, her brow lifting in challenge as he watched her. "Do you really want to miss it?"

Hell no!

He lowered his arms, watching as her small hands went back to the clasp on his slacks and slowly undid it.

His cock couldn't possibly become harder, thicker. Yet he swore as she began pushing the slacks over his hips it did just that.

He wore no underwear. Breeds were created and raised for years without clothes, and adapting to them wasn't easy. Underwear was something they preferred to do without. Now, he almost wished he wore them.

His cock sprang free, agonizingly hard, thick, the broad, heavy crest flushed and damp.

The silk slacks fell down his thighs, his legs, to pool at his feet as he forced himself to stand in place.

Rachel stepped back then.

"I've had the most incredible fantasy since the first time I laid eyes on you," she whispered in a voice so sultry it raked over his senses like pure sex.

"And what would that fantasy be?" His voice was so rough, so dark, he almost winced. Then it was all he could do not to widen his eyes as her fingers went to the buttons on her shirt.

One by one, slow and easy, those buttons slipped free. She pulled the ends from the skirt she wore. A silk skirt. Jonas liked silk. It ended just about her knees, barely covering her incredible thighs.

He did so love his mate's thighs.

Once the blouse was pulled free, with a little shrug and jerk of her shoulders, it pooled to the floor, leaving her clad in a next-to-nothing bra, which barely covered the full, luscious mounds of her breasts.

Tight, hard nipples poked against the sheer lace covering, tempting his lips, the glands that immediately swelled beneath his tongue and the hungers raging through him.

The animal snarled, causing his lips to draw back, the claws to prick at the tips of his fingers, though they didn't retract.

Her hands moved then, too slowly, to the zipper at the side of the skirt. It rasped down, the sound filling the room. A second later it dropped over her thighs, slid to the floor and stole his breath.

Innocent, white low-cut panties matched the bra. Silk stockings ended at those gorgeous, well-rounded thighs. Pretty, cream-colored stockings, which almost matched the panties and bra. But on her tiny, delicate feet were wickedly high black heels.

Her hand stroked over her smooth stomach. There were only a few tiny, almost-impossible-to-detect marks from her pregnancy. They were marks he wanted to kiss, to stroke with his tongue.

"You didn't tell me what the fantasy was." He cleared his throat.

Jonas stood his ground, wondering now what his delectable little mate would come up with.

She stepped closer, her breasts almost touching his chest as her hands stroked up his thighs, those diabolical nails scraping over his flesh once again before raking along the inner thighs and sending flames wrapping around his balls.

His cock felt tortured now, so hard, so desperate for release he had to clench his teeth against the agony.

"You were on television," she murmured. "So handsome, so very civilized." A single nail raked over the tight sac of his balls, causing his breath to break with the extremity of the pleasure. "When the reporter turned to you, your tongue almost licked your lips nervously. It peeked out just the slightest, and I swore I nearly had my first orgasm."

Her fingernails rasped over the shaft of his cock. He was going to die of pleasure before he ever had the chance to come.

"I was a teenager." Her breath blew against his chest. "And I wanted to do something I had heard my friends snicker over. I wanted to sit on your face."

Jonas flinched, a growl tore from his chest unbidden. He was reaching for her, ready to lift her and give her exactly what she had fantasized about.

Before he could grip her arms she bent, licked over his cock, froze him in his tracks, then drew the flushed, straining crown into the heated depths of her mouth.

She licked; sucked. Her tongue swirled and tasted and tightened his entire body with the most incredible pleasure that he had ever known.

When he was certain he couldn't hold back, when he felt the release building in his balls, tightening through his body, her mouth was gone.

She straightened. Her eyes were a moss green, dark, vivid. Hunger swirled in them, flushed her features and gave it the sweetest, spiciest scent. The lush moisture of the juices spilling between her thighs had him jealous of the lace covering the delicate folds.

Before she could demand he stop or evade his move, Jonas had her on the bed, on her back. His tongue plunged in her mouth as he felt those nails prick at his shoulders. He shoved his thigh between hers, pressing hard and tight against the wet mound of her pussy as he pumped his tongue in her mouth, feeling her trying to trap it, suckling the mating hormone from it as his lips moved over hers.

She was his. He would allow her to stake her claim, to have her fantasy. But first, he would stoke that wildness inside her, make her burn and make her take what she wanted.

Rachel raked her nails down Jonas's back, heat and lightning whipping through her, striking at erogenous zones, burning in her blood as she fought to hold on to his kiss and the incredible taste she craved.

He was an addiction, but he had been an addiction long before he had instigated the mating heat between them. He had been an addiction before she ever met him in person.

The taste of cinnamon and cloves filled her senses. Fiery pleasure rocked through her body, but she couldn't get that image out of her mind. She couldn't get that need out of her mind.

As the fires inside her burned, rushed through her, rose

and engulfed the last of any shyness she might still harbor, she struggled in his arms.

Pushing at his shoulders, riding the hard male thigh thrust between her softer ones, she fought the hold he had on her until he rolled to his back.

She was moving as he lifted her. Her leg swung over his head, her knees digging into the mattress as desperation and hunger overwhelmed her.

As she came over him, he was waiting for her. Hard hands gripped her hips, pulled her to him, his tongue swiping through the thick juices collecting there, and driving her insane with pleasure.

Throwing her head back, a low wail erupted from her lips as his tongue curled around her clit. She was burning. She was diving headlong into ecstasy and the ride was both thrilling and terrifying.

Her hands lifted to her breasts, her head tilting, staring down at him as his hands curled around her thighs and his eerie silver eyes stared back up at her.

Her fingers rubbed over her nipples as she felt his tongue flick at her clit, rub it. The raspy texture of it sent the blood rushing to her head, light-headedness nearly overtaking her as she pinched her nipples, increasing the sensation.

He was watching her. A low, growling groan echoed in the room as he drew the little bud into his mouth and suckled at it, his tongue running around it as she began to twist her hips against him.

"So good," she moaned as she tore at the clasp of the bra between her breasts to release it. "Oh Jonas, it's so good. Your tongue's like fire."

That instrument of flaming pleasure lashed at her clit now, stroking around it, over it, as he sucked at it. The hormone in his tongue, it had to be that fiery essence, seemed to sink into the little knot of flesh, tightening it further, throwing her closer to bliss as she began to ride his face. Her hips rolled, twisted, her thighs bunched with the need tearing through her.

A hard kiss vibrated along the ultra-sensitive flesh as he released it, only to lick, stroke, to ease lower. Rachel was nearly screaming with need now, her hands filled with her breasts, her fingers rubbing, stroking, pinching at her nipples as she fought for orgasm.

A second later, his tongue drove into her pussy.

Her back arched, her muscles clenched on the intruder, sucking it, spasming around it as she began to demand to come.

She wanted it now. She wanted to feel that wild ride of complete rapture as it flung her into ecstasy.

His tongue fucked her with hungry strokes, pressing inside her pussy to lick, to taste, to fill her with such desperate need that she could barely breathe for it.

She was dying for more. The overwhelming shards of longing were driving through her clit, her pussy, tightening in her womb as he licked her with an intimacy and abandon that she could have never known to fantasize about.

"No. Don't stop." She was nearly screaming as his tongue slid from her.

Her hips rolled, pressed down, then she stilled in complete pleasure. Her hands fell from her breasts to the headboard of the bed. Her fingers clenched.

His lips covered her clit again, only this time, the pleasure was near agony. He sucked it inside, began to lick, to stroke, to do that rubbing thing with his tongue as she felt her entire body explode.

She cried his name. Her body jerked taut, her thighs began to shudder, tremors raced through her body and the heated tide of her release rushed from her pussy.

And it wasn't enough. She barely had time to draw another breath once the first hard shudders raked through her. She needed more. She wanted him inside her, filling her.

Uncoordinated, so eager to sate the hunger that only grew from the release, Rachel fell to her side, scrambled up and threw her leg over his hips. She wanted him inside her now. She wanted that hard, fiery length of his cock shafting through the tightening muscles that spasmed in longing for his possession.

She had no more risen over him when he filled his hands with her breasts and lifted his head. His mouth sucked one tight, tortured nipple into his mouth, stilling her movements.

She would take him in a minute, she told herself as her hands braced against his shoulders to hold her weight. Just a second. First. This was so good. His tongue lashed at her nipple now, his teeth raked over it, sending those shards of brutal bliss to strike at the heart of her womb before speeding to her pussy.

She needed him. Her head shook. She wanted him now, but she didn't want this to stop. She wanted him to suck her nipples. She wanted his hot mouth on her and his even hotter cock inside her.

Jonas fought to keep the animalistic instincts inside himself from taking over. He fought to hold on to the human parts of himself, to retain just enough of his senses to hold back, to make this so good for her that she would do it again and again.

And damn if he hadn't almost succeeded. He had managed to hold on to that last thread of sanity. Then she moved, her hips slid lower as he sucked at her nipple, loving the taste of it.

Her pussy, so slick and wet, parted over the tight, engorged head of his dick, and he was lost. Hell, lost nothing, he was a madman, pure fucking animal so eager to thrust inside her that his hips immediately plowed upward, driving several inches inside her with no care or restraint.

And she loved it. He felt her pussy clench around him, heard her muted moan of bliss and felt her nails digging into his shoulders as she held on to him.

Her hips were moving, churning. His mate was no easy lover when the wildness gripped her. She was demanding everything he had to give, working herself on the hard shaft, her pussy milking it, stroking white-hot fingers of complete ecstasy over and down his cock until it struck his balls with destructive sensation.

He gripped her hips tight, trying to hold her back. He didn't want to hurt her. He didn't want to take her like the animal he knew he was created to be.

But she wasn't having it. The more he fought to hold back, the tighter her pussy sucked at his dick, the hotter it got. She fought to twist against him, to ride him herself as he fought just as hard to control the desperate lunges of his hips.

He wanted to fuck her hard and deep. He wanted to drive his cock inside her and hear her begging for more, screaming for it.

"Fuck me!" She jerked in his arms as she did just that. "Damn you, Jonas, let me go." She tried to slap at his hands, to force his hold from her.

"Rachel. Baby. Not yet," he pushed out between clenched teeth. "Not yet."

He was fighting to breathe, the pleasure was so intense. He could feel the barb trying to emerge, his release building in his balls.

Then her head lowered, and she bit him. Damn her, her teeth sank into his shoulder as a wild, completely abandoned cry of need fell from her lips and stole his determination to take her easy.

His hands fell from her hips. His palms slapped to the bed, fingers clenching in the blankets as his claws emerged and bit into the cloth, and he let her have her way.

He let her steal his heart, his soul, his very being as he threw his head back and roared out his pleasure. Streaks of intense, volatile sensation wracked his spine, his muscles. Pleasure was a white-hot orb surrounding his body, and Rachel was the center of it.

Rachel had never known anything like the hard, shuddering tremors of bliss tearing through her. The feel of Jonas's cock powering inside her, pushing deep and hard, raking across sensitive tissue and delicate nerve endings, was like a fiery vortex surrounding her body.

She was burning alive. Perspiration gathered along her body, slicking her, creating another sensation to add to the others. Lifting her lips from Jonas's shoulder, she stared down at him, seeing the sweat roll down the side of his face, his silver eyes gleaming back at her, his neck straining as he fucked her with complete abandon.

She had him. Right here, right now. This was the man and the animal, and both were completely focused on her and the pleasure crashing through them.

Her back arched as a particularly intense storm of pure sensation throbbed through her pussy, stroked over her clit, over and over again. She couldn't escape it, she didn't want to. Her head fell back on her shoulders as she lifted and lowered herself, mating the hard, driving rhythm of Jonas's body beneath her.

She could feel the storm building inside her. Like heady whorls of pure fire, it began to stroke inside her body, wrapping through it, around her, circling her in ever-tightening bands of erotic agony as she began to cry Jonas's name.

She had to come. She was going to die if she didn't. And if she did, could she survive it? Her muscles began to flex, her womb convulsed, her pussy began to spasm and clench, tightening and stroking his steel-hard cock as he shafted inside her. Harder, faster. It was building. It was tightening. It was burning . . .

She tried to scream. Was she screaming? She felt it explode with a force that bent her backward, the only thing holding her grounded was Jonas as his hands jerked up, cradled her back, held her to him as the storm ruptured inside her.

Shaking, shuddering convulsions of white-hot sensation raked up her spine. It tore across her nerve endings. She wanted to wail his name but she didn't have the breath. She wanted to scream for mercy, but couldn't even whisper for it.

Her nails bit into his arms as he suddenly jerked her forward, her head falling to his shoulder as his teeth bit into her shoulder, locking in, holding her still as the pleasure-pain evoked another, harder eclipse of volcanic sensation that sped through her.

Then she felt it.

His release was white-hot, spurting inside her as she felt a sudden thickening, a swelling, the emergence of the thumb tip–sized barb as it stretched from beneath the head of his cock and locked into a spot so sensitive, so agonizingly tender, and began to burn it with blistering pleasure.

Rachel lost her mind. Not that she had much left at that point, but that sensation, the white-hot vibration, the rubbing, the tiny, firm throbbing against that center of nerve endings tore her mind free.

She was flying. With his arms wrapped tight around her, his tongue licking at the wound to her shoulder, that barb stroking into a bundle of pure raw nerves, and Rachel felt as though she were flying, totally free. Without constraints, straight into the blistering heat of the sun.

She felt as though she became melded to him. She melted into the pores of his flesh, locked inside him, and knew she could never be the same again.

◆　◆　◆

Jonas had to fight for breath. He had no idea pleasure could tear the world out of his grip, that a release could do more than simply bond him to this woman.

For the first time in his life, he felt a freedom so complete, so vast, that he knew his life was changed forever.

He'd fought giving all of himself to her, and in that moment, he realized he had never had a chance against her.

She was sobbing against his shoulder, the pleasure was so intense. She was whispering his name, begging, shudders still racing up her spine as he felt them digging sharpened talons into his balls.

It seemed never-ending. It seemed as though he had shot straight into the soul of the woman gripping him with a fierce hold, refusing to release him. And he didn't want her to release him. He wanted her to hold him inside her forever.

And she would.

This pleasure would ease, their bodies would separate, but

he knew beyond a shadow of a doubt that he would never be free of her or the effect of this night.

Wrapping his arms around her, he buried his face in her hair and fought just to breathe as he felt the sensations gently easing.

Rationality was returning as the barb slowly receded. His cock softened, but only marginally. Held inside her, the thick width still stretched her. He could still feel the delicate little tremors that attacked the vulnerable tissue every few seconds.

She was relishing this final, unhurried descent, and he wasn't about to disturb her, because he was damned if he wasn't loving the hell out of it as well.

It was like being locked in a well of peace. In all his life Jonas had never known true peace. Not until this moment, not until the pleasure had been agony, forcing him to spill his very soul into the woman who had demanded it.

"I love you." The words rose unbidden to his lips as he whispered them against her ear. "In all my life, Rachel, I have never truly loved until you."

He had sacrificed. He had been responsible. He had led, he had manipulated and he had been driven. But he had never loved a single entity, not truly, not as he should.

He loved his sister, but not enough to open himself to give her the security she had needed, and he was only now realizing that. No wonder Harmony had refused to allow him around his nephew in the months since he had been born. It was no wonder others watched him with fear and loathing.

They sensed it. They had known it. Jonas had been the ultimate master manipulator, and he had manipulated himself right out of the lives of those he had needed most.

His sister.

His brothers.

His father.

His mother.

Those who stood by him despite his failings. Those who watched him with both longing and distrust. Even Rachel.

Until this moment, he realized a part of himself had still been manipulating, searching for an angle to use, a way to control.

He would never control this woman.

"I love you so much. I know I would die without you."

He heard the words, so soft, so weary, whispered against his chest as his mate collapsed against him. Still buried within her, her gentle weight a warmth he never wanted to lose, her words sinking into his soul to hold him a willing captive for eternity.

Emotion nearly overwhelmed him. It clenched his heart, tightened his chest. It rolled through him like a wave of heat, brighter, hotter, than the lust that had fueled them moments before.

No. It wasn't lust. It was pure hunger. A white-hot need to share, and to give himself to the one person, the one woman who been given to him to save him.

He had been on a path of personal self-destruction, a complete isolation from those around him. Rachel and her child had brought him back. Then Rachel had bound his soul to hers with chains forged of unbreakable strength.

Easing from her body, he almost grimaced as her snug pussy tried to tighten on the still-engorged flesh filling it. The stroke of silken flesh across it was a pleasure he was loath to lose.

His mate was exhausted though.

She lay where he placed her, her eyes closed, the strap of her bra hanging from one shoulder. He must have torn her panties again and hadn't realized it, because only a shred of them was lying on her thighs. Her stockings were ruined. She was missing a shoe.

Jonas grinned. She was a wildcat that had turned into an exhausted little kitten.

Carefully, he eased from the bed before striding to the bathroom and collecting a damp cloth and dry towel. Returning to the bed, he undressed her gently, tossing the last remaining articles of clothing to the floor before cleaning her with a tenderness he hadn't known he was capable of.

He had always been gentle with Rachel, but now, he stroked her, petted her, cleaned the perspiration and sensual excess from her body before returning to the bathroom and cleaning himself.

When he collapsed into the bed beside her and drew her against his chest, he couldn't stop the purr. He had managed to hold it at bay until now. It rumbled against his chest beneath her cheek, the pure contentment that welled inside him taking voice despite his attempts to hold it back.

A small hum of satisfaction left her lips as he felt her lay a gentle kiss against his flesh. A second later, his wild little mate slipped peacefully into sleep.

Tangled red hair flowed over his chest as he buried his fingers in it. Silken limbs twined with his, holding him to her even as he wrapped his arms around her and held her just as tight.

And for the first time in his entire life, Jonas truly and deeply slept. For the first time, contentment filled him, warmth shattered the ice in his soul, and Jonas became more than a Breed.

He was a mate.

CHAPTER 20

Dawn was peeking over the horizon and found Jonas standing by the large living room window that looked out over the estate house. It was his early morning ritual. Amber was fed, diapered, wrapped in an incredibly soft blanket and staring out over Sanctuary along with Jonas.

He purred. It was a rumble he found he enjoyed. This was a sound of comfort and security, whereas the purr that vibrated in his chest for the baby's mother was stronger, tinged with passion and spiced with heat.

Here, in these moments with Amber, there was no mating heat. This had been the only peace he had found until he had completed the mating with Rachel. As though the child triggered something inside him that eased the heat and instead flooded him with gentleness and the need to protect.

How his life had changed with the appearance of Rachel and their baby. His entire existence had shifted, gone off balance and righted itself in a way he had never expected.

The fingers of sunlight caressed the third story, glistening across the windows and the widow's walk along the roof. He could barely make out the slightest differences between the roof itself and the four Breeds stationed there. He was going to have to have a talk with Callan and Kane about the guards. They had to be completely invisible, even to Breed eyes.

Perhaps it was time he discussed training a new team with Jag, the commander of Ghost Team. Sanctuary could use a few teams with the talents Jag and his Breeds possessed. Jonas knew they were out there; the four men were spreading themselves between the main house and Jonas's cabin.

Or perhaps it was simply time he began using the abilities he was trained for, rather than playing with the ones he had taken as a hobby.

The Bureau wasn't his passion, it was his game. He amused himself with manipulating the politicians, the bigwigs and financial movers and shakers who could be convinced to contribute so heavily to the Breed community.

It was the reason Jonas had slid into the position. It had been easily done. There had been no challenge. And the amusement value was rapidly wearing thin.

He had found in the past months that the position as Bureau director was becoming something he actually believed in, and that was frightening. There had been very few things that Jonas had ever believed in.

Now, looking out over the community the Breeds had created, that he had helped to create, Jonas no longer felt that hollow ache he had always felt before.

He'd wondered for years what he was truly fighting for, the Breeds or simply vengeance for their creation and the cruelty they'd suffered.

Looking down at the child that slept against his chest, he knew now exactly what he was fighting for: this tiny scrap of humanity and her too-delicate mother. The Breeds were free, that was an unending fact, and they would never allow themselves to be imprisoned again. Their mates and their children were in danger now. They were an endangered species, but they had the will to survive.

Narrowing his gaze against the slowly lightening landscape,

Jonas drew in a hard breath as he realized time was running out in many ways. With the mating had come realization. Realizations he could no longer ignore.

As he stood there, Erin's Jeep moved slowly up the drive until it drew to a stop in the small parking area Jonas had assigned her.

The babysitter jumped from the Jeep, her hand landing protectively on the butt of the laser pistol, her eyes narrowing as she stared around suspiciously.

She did this every morning. Even if she didn't smell or see Ghost Team, she knew they were there. It wasn't an indication of Jag's lax security or abilities. Rather, it was an indication of the strength of her own abilities. She was a Breed he intended to keep careful watch over.

She was still young; she still had much growing to do. Until then, she was the perfect guard for the baby Jonas claimed as his own. Amber would need a diligent, instinctive guard, because as his child, she would be in nearly as much danger as Cassandra Sinclair was.

Still suspicious, and certain something lurked outside, Erin made her way cautiously to the door, unlocked it and pushed it forward.

Jonas stood back and waited.

When she rolled inside it was with a silence that surprised him, and with a quick efficiency and narrow-eyed determination as she quickly recognized Jonas by the window.

The weapon that had cleared the holster was quickly returned; her body became erect as she strode to the door, closing it just as silently and relocking it.

"Windows are secured," he assured her as she began checking the entrances to the house.

She ignored his warning, moving from room to room, even his own, where Rachel slept. The locks were all in place, the house clearly secured, as she made her way back to the living room where Jonas was placing a sleeping Amber back in her crib.

"What did you sense?" he asked her, knowing exactly what lurked in the dark.

"The same thing I sense every morning," she answered coolly as she stood to the side of the room, her gaze questioning. "Someone watches, lurks in the darkness."

"Have you caught a scent?"

She shook her head.

"A sign of a trail or presence?"

Once again, a shake of the head.

"Then you sense nothing," he accused her.

Her lips quirked. "They are there. Are they yours?"

She wasn't assuming they were his, she was asking.

"Intuition can make or break you," he told her. "Find whatever you sense."

She shook her head. "Telling you what I sense is my responsibility, Director. Protecting Amber is my job. Or are you changing the parameters you gave me?"

Jonas paused as though considering her question. "I'll place extra guards outside. As you say, your job is protecting the child. You'll be accompanying Rachel and me to the labs later this morning for more tests. The baby will be seeing the doctors once more as well. Have everything prepared to go."

"I'll make certain you haven't messed with my go-bag again."

Jonas almost grinned. He was prone to mess with the go-bag she had put together when first attaining the position. She was cautious, preparatory. She had placed in a bag a change of clothes, weapons, as well as diapers, formula, bottles, a pediatric first aid kit and warm clothes for the baby. Everything she would need in case of an emergency.

It was very similar to the go-bag Jonas kept prepared as well.

"Once Rachel awakens we'll be leaving." He nodded shortly as he headed for the bedroom. "Inform Lawe and Rule we'll be heading to the main house."

He went to awaken his mate. She slept peacefully, dreamlessly. She slept as a woman in love should sleep, safe in her lover's care.

He only prayed he could ensure that safety for their lifetime, as Leo had managed to ensure his own mate's safety.

As Jonas closed the door to the room, he stopped and closed his eyes. As Leo had protected his mate, his family. He had hidden them deep in the Congo, using an old ancient ruin as a base as well as a home.

He had gathered his "children," those Breeds who had been created using his and Elizabeth's genetics. If there had been other Breeds with them, then they had been rescued as well. But Leo had rarely gone out of his way to rescue those Breeds who had not been created with his and his mate's genetics.

His fists clenched at the thought of that. Harmony had suffered for untold years because Leo hadn't moved on the French labs. His sister had been tortured, punished, beaten and forced to kill because Jonas had been unable to find a way to protect her, when she should have been rescued.

Harmony hadn't been a child of the Leo or of Elizabeth. It was Harmony who had been the true child of LaRue, rather than Jonas. Jonas had been carried by the doctor, he had been claimed as LaRue's "get," but the truth was, he was the hybrid created using the sperm and ovum of a mated Breed pair.

And this was why Jonas hated him. This was why he struck at the Leo with every verbal arrow he could find, and it was why he ignored the mother who watched him with questioning, suspicious eyes.

Elizabeth sensed her child, despite Jonas's denials and icy refusal to relent.

Perhaps, though, Leo hadn't been as wrong as Jonas had believed he was, because as he opened his eyes and stared at his own mate, Jonas wondered if he wouldn't have done the same.

There had been no Breed community a century ago. There had been no nations willing to pay penance for the creation and torture of the Breeds. There had been one man, one woman, fighting to survive.

He would have done the same. He would have hidden his mate, he would have fought to rescue those Breeds he was certain would be loyal to him, as well as those created by himself and his mate.

"Jonas?"

He looked across the room to Rachel, who stared back at him drowsily. Once again, the scent of mating was clear, unmistakable, but the heat had cooled, and there was no biological, hormonal or any other reason to be found for it.

This particular anomaly, as well as the unfamiliar hormone found in Jonas's system, was making the scientists crazy as they fought to figure it out.

"Good morning, baby." He strode across the room, leaned to her and kissed her slow and easy.

The glands beneath his tongue weren't swollen. Their kiss was natural, filled with a different kind of heat, an emotional undertone that at once humbled and strengthened him.

"Morning." Her smile lit up his heart. It curled her lips, warmed her green eyes and flushed her cheeks as the sheet fell away from the gentle curves of her breasts.

He'd marked her shoulder, but he'd also left a mark on the upper curve of her breast.

Reaching out, he touched the small bite mark, at once proud and concerned at the wound he had inflicted.

Rachel glanced down and her lips twitched in amusement. "Do you remember what happened when you did that?"

His entire body clenched. She had tightened on his cock until he had exploded inside her as though he had died.

"Still, I should be more careful." He sighed.

"Yeah, more careful to do it again next time." She slid from the bed, casting a smile over her shoulder as she moved naked from the bed and headed toward the shower. "Do you have breakfast ready yet?"

He stared back at her. "These tests need to be done before

we eat," he told her. "We'll have breakfast with Callan and Merinus."

She paused at the bathroom door and frowned.

"I'm sick of the tests."

She wasn't the only one.

"Hopefully, they'll been finished soon." If they weren't, then he wasn't going to handle it well.

"No, they'll be finished this morning," she told him as she turned and walked into the bathroom. "Because I'm done."

The door closed behind her and Jonas couldn't help but grin. He had to say, he rather enjoyed the fact that his mate wasn't the least bit intimidated by him or his reputation.

She was his lover, his mate. She was his other half and she had no problems whatsoever claiming her place.

◆   ◆   ◆

Rachel endured another examination, more samples being taken. Blood samples, saliva samples, vaginal samples. There were scans this time, old-fashioned X-rays, skin samples, nail samples and hair samples.

It was as though the scientists were well aware that they were never going to get another sample from her.

"Are you certain you're not uncomfortable?" Ely Morrey asked, not for the twelfth time. Perhaps more.

Rachel turned a frustrated look on her. "I'm very uncomfortable," she replied sweetly. "I'm sitting here in a paper gown that shows my ass while the three of you"—she looked at Ely, Elizabeth and Jeffrey Amburg watching her clinically— "talk scientific jargon that makes no sense, and frankly gets on my nerves."

Elizabeth's lips twitched.

"You're showing too many anomalies for mating heat." Ely crossed her arms over her breasts and frowned back at Rachel. "Jonas is showing too many anomalies as well. This is so far beyond normal that we have to be certain to cover our bases."

"Why?" That part confused her just slightly.

"Because it's best—" Ely began.

"Tell her the truth, Ely." Elizabeth moved to Ely's side, her tone firm.

"This isn't information just anyone should have." Ely's lips thinned in disapproval.

Rachel arched her brow at Elizabeth.

"Mating heat is incredibly painful for the females," Elizabeth began.

"I know that part," Rachel broke in. "Painful. Aphrodisiac in the tongue, sperm that stills the heat and a kiss that makes it worse. The mating bite is forever and only after it's given does the heat begin to level off. But still a mate can't bear others' touch, nor can most females function outside the bed." She rolled her eyes. "Sounds like paradise for your men."

"All but Jonas," Ely growled.

Rachel stared back at her curiously. The other woman was angry and trying hard not to hide it.

"You and Jonas have produced a hormone that if we could figure out how it works, could help to ease the heat in our females," Elizabeth told her. "Even I, once every three months, experience that irrational, torturous need as my body attempts to force me to conceive."

"Even when you're pregnant?" Rachel asked.

Elizabeth paused. "The hormones are different then."

"Do you breast-feed? I breast-fed for the first few months, I know I had to be very careful of my diet. Is that a problem with mating heat?"

Elizabeth shook her head. "I thought for years there had to be a correlation. There were only rare times that my desire for my mate was normal, Rachel. But I found nothing unusual then."

Rachel shrugged. "I'm not a scientist, Dr. Vanderale, nor do I pretend to understand what you're dealing with here. But I will tell you, I'm not dealing with it any longer. You have all you're getting from me."

"You're selfish." The accusation from Ely surprised her, and obviously surprised Elizabeth as well. "Jonas deserves better than a mate who refuses to make the sacrifices he's made all his life for his people."

"Exactly," Rachel stated coolly. "He's sacrificed all his life with little understanding and even less consideration from the majority of you. When was the last time Jonas was asked *not* to sacrifice for someone? Not to find a way to manipulate or work miracles? When was the last time he was allowed to be a man?"

"He's not a man, he's a Breed," Ely snapped back.

"And you're in love with him." The knowledge was more intuition than based on evidence. "But you're not his mate."

Elizabeth inhaled sharply.

"Jonas is just a friend," Ely argued stiffly.

Rachel rose from the gurney, gathered her clothing from a nearby counter and moved for the bathroom.

"And I'm finished with this argument. I refuse to argue with you, Ely." She turned back to the doctor, seeing the anger and confusion in her eyes. "Jonas thinks very highly of you, but I wouldn't suggest attempting to try to convince him that I'm not his mate. That friendship could be damaged in ways you don't want to face if you do so."

Stepping into the small bathroom, Rachel re-dressed as she fought to get a handle on her own emotions. Ely wasn't a threat to her relationship with Jonas, she tried to assure herself. They were mates; that was for life. There was no way to break it. And Jonas loved her. He had told her he loved her. She was his life.

Moving back to the main lab, she faced a single person, clearly waiting for her. Elizabeth Vanderale was working at one of the intricate machines that lined a counter.

"Ely sees Jonas as her white knight," Elizabeth said as she turned, propped herself against the counter and watched Rachel. "She's protective of him, Rachel. And perhaps confused by her own feelings."

"He's mine." She wasn't about to let him go.

Elizabeth nodded. "I couldn't have asked for a better mate for him. You'll complete him, Rachel. That's important."

There was something sad, something regretful in the other woman.

"Why is that so important to you? I haven't noticed Leo

caring. The best he can manage is to cut at Jonas each chance he has."

Elizabeth glanced away and drew in a hard breath. When her gaze returned to Rachel, it was filled with sorrow, and longing.

"Jonas knows the answer to that, Rachel," she stated. "And only he can fix Leo's disposition where he's concerned. I've done all I can do."

"Because the boy is too damned stubborn by far."

Rachel whirled around. The Leo stood just inside the main door, a glare on his face as he moved across the room to his mate. "He's trying to throw us out and send us back to Africa," he snapped. "He never misses a chance to remind me that he doesn't want me here."

Once again, that particular flash of pain whipped through Elizabeth's gaze.

"The two of you have no idea how to handle Jonas." Rachel could only shake her head at them.

"And you think you can?" Leo's voice rumbled with irritation. "No one can handle that whelp."

"You don't handle Jonas, exactly. Try being honest with him. And stop calling him a by-blow and a whelp. How insulting can a father get to his own son? It's no wonder he finds every opportunity to remind you that you claim your home is in Africa, rather than here."

Rachel could feel the anger mounting inside her now. For too many months, she had overheard or been forced to watch the confrontations between Jonas and Leo, and for just as long she'd thought how cold and unfeeling Leo could be while his son was watching.

Let Jonas turn his back though. Once he did, Leo's gaze would darken with regret, anger and sadness. He kept a façade, a cold, unfeeling attitude whenever Jonas watched, only to become a regretful father later.

Leo glared back at her. "Think Sanctuary can survive without Vanderale Industries, do you, young lady?"

Did Jonas truly think they couldn't?

Her brow arched. "I have no doubt they could survive, Leo. It may not be as easy, but they would do better than survive. They would thrive with or without your help."

"All because of Jonas?" Leo snapped.

Her eyes narrowed as she took note of Elizabeth laying her hand on her mate's arm in warning. "I never said that, Leo."

"You're his mate. Like all his women, you think the man has no faults."

She turned to Elizabeth. "Your mate is out of control, Dr. Vanderale. When he can be the rational man I know he's capable of, please place a notice on his chest; otherwise, the rest of us may never know." She shot Leo a tight smile. "Excuse me, but I'm sure my daughter needs to be fed soon."

"You should be breast-feeding," Leo snarled as she turned away. "That sissy formula you're giving her isn't nutritious."

Rachel clenched her teeth and continued to the door. Her temper wasn't in the best of states. Whatever mating heat wasn't doing, she appreciated, but it seemed it was triggering reactions in her that she sure as hell wasn't expecting. One of those reactions was the temper she had mastered years ago, when she was far younger.

"There's no way that child will be a fitting mate for a Breed if you're not feeding her properly."

Rachel swung around. Elizabeth was glaring at her mate as Leo crossed his arms and stared at Rachel with that chilling intensity.

"I certainly hope she isn't a fitting mate as far as you're concerned." She advanced a step, temper slowly getting the best of her. "Because your opinion is one I would fully distrust, Mr. Vanderale. And coming from you, any opinion on parenting you would have would be completely hypocritical."

His brows creased into a heavy frown. "I have never been a hypocrite."

"You're definitely a lousy father," she retorted furiously. "I'm sorry, Leo, but if it weren't for your wife, I'd pity your babes."

Fire lit his gaze. "There is nothing more important to me than my children."

"Nothing except your secrecy, your pride and your own ideas of right and right," she stated caustically. "Poor Dane, it's no wonder he's such a manipulator. He has to be to stay under your radar and to keep your love. He's probably had nightmares about losing your regard and suffering the hell of your disinterest as Jonas has."

"Do you have any idea who you're talking to?" he growled, his head lowering, his lips pulling back in what she was certain was intended to be an intimidating snarl.

"An asshole, just to start with," she informed him. "Shall I go on?"

"I've destroyed lesser little upstarts than you pretend to be," he warned her, his expression shifting, turning calculating— just as Jonas's gaze shifted whenever he was playing one of his interminable games. She'd already picked up on this particular game though, as well as the reason for it.

She shook her head, smiling mockingly. "You don't scare me, Leo. You do no more than amuse me."

Surprise almost got the best of him. Rachel watched his eyes widen in surprise, his lips thin as he nearly snarled in frustration.

"Does it work often, Leo?" she drawled politely. "Pissing off your sons' mates to see how they'll respond? To see if they're worthy to be a mate to a Vanderale 'get'?" She sneered. "I don't just feel sorry for your children. I feel sorry for your wife, too. And I must say, she has amazing sons, despite the bastard who sired them."

She turned on her heel, her spine ramrod straight, and stalked back to the door.

"I love all my children, Ms. Broen." Leo's voice stopped her at the door. "And you are more than a worthy mate for my son."

"You're still a lousy fucking father." She jerked the door open and stalked from the lab, her entire body shaking with the anger surging through her.

Manipulating bastard. Jonas had come by it honestly, she had to say, but he was by far kinder about it. He manipulated for the good of his Enforcers. He manipulated and calculated for the good of the Breed community as a whole. Never, at any time, had she seen an edge of cruelty in him.

The Breeds had refined themselves from their beginnings. Leo was still the animal the scientists had tried to create. Jonas was the Breed who gave an air of mystery and romanticism to this savage new race of humans.

Leo still lived in a world where hiding was the only option and games were the only way to survive. Jonas was creating a world where future Breeds had a chance to walk down the street in peace, play cards with neighbors and raise their children as others would.

A world Rachel wanted to be a part of.

◆   ◆   ◆

Ely watched silently from the shadows of her office, her door open as Leo and Elizabeth yelled at one another like combatants set to exchange blows.

She had suspected for the past weeks that there was an edge of conflict between them, but she hadn't been certain until now. Watching Leo's mate as he raged at Rachel Broen, Ely had seen the explosion coming—one it hadn't taken long to blow sky-high.

It would have been amusing if Ely hadn't lost her ability to be amused months ago. Now she was simply clinical, bordering on cold, as she listened, trying to ignore the pain and aching sorrow Elizabeth Vanderale was feeling.

Elizabeth's voice was strong, clear. There was no hint of tears, nothing but anger shading her voice.

"When will you stop?" she yelled up at him, her small fists clenched at her sides furiously. "What the hell is wrong with you, Leo? I haven't seen you like this since we mated. You're like a lion with a sore tooth, and I for one am growing sick of it."

"You're not the one I'm trying to make sick of it," Leo

yelled back. "The bastard ignores us as though we're not blood. He treats us as no more than guests to Sanctuary."

"And what do you expect?" Emotion now entered Elizabeth's voice. "How long, Leo? How long did you ignore the whispers that he wasn't LaRue's son? How long did you put off rescuing Breeds from that lab?"

"Because I knew he was protecting them," Leo charged, enraged now. "You know that, Elizabeth, we discussed it. Others were not so lucky to have a Pride leader such as Jonas. Others were suffering more."

"He's our son!" Elizabeth screamed, filled with pain now. "No wonder he refuses us the courtesy of acknowledging it. Not only did you allow his lab mates to suffer, but the very moment you were face-to-face with him, you did nothing but insult him."

Elizabeth turned away, and Ely watched as she dashed tears from her face. "I can't bear it any longer. That's my son. If I had known the game you were playing with him when it began, I would have instantly put a stop to it."

"We're Breeds, not fucking sissies," Leo snarled. "He's a man, Elizabeth, not a child. Our world is different from others, and you know this. Strength is what matters."

"That's your world." Elizabeth jerked her lab coat from her shoulders and threw it to a gurney. "I'm human, and our children are part human. You can't raise them like animals."

"They *are* animals." Frustration fed Leo's voice now. "We all are. How many more decades will it take for you to see this?"

She turned back to him, the scent of her tears strong now within the lab. "How long will it take you, Leo, to realize that you're not? It's an excuse all of you use for your own prickishness and inability to cope with any emotion. You want freedom. You want peace. But I'll be damned if any of the male Breeds I've met are willing to be human enough to ask what they demand from other humans. You're no better than they are, simply different."

She gave her mate no chance to protest. Instead, she stalked from the labs, the door slamming behind her. Ely slipped carefully back from the door that led into the labs and used the other door at the back of the room to leave her office.

This was something she couldn't keep to herself. A division in the ranks was too important not to report.

"Someone has a big mouth. Should I guess who?" Rachel knew the moment she stepped into Callan Lyons's office to meet Jonas that Dr. Morrey had told Jonas exactly what had happened in the labs.

She should have gotten here first, she thought. She'd run into Merinus as she came to the main floor. Merinus had been carrying Amber, cooing at her, causing the baby to giggle and laugh at the faces she was making.

They had stood and talked before Rachel took Amber and headed to the office. Stepping inside, she saw Jonas's face, and Ely Morrey's cool, composed features.

Ely was half in love with Jonas. A hero-worship that stemmed from the care Jonas had taken of her during a particularly traumatic time several months before. Rachel understood it; she wasn't jealous over it, but she was beginning to see that it could become a problem.

Moving to the small baby bed in the corner of the room, a bed normally used for Callan's own infant daughter, Rachel laid Amber on the mattress, covered her gently and caressed her head before straightening and turning to Ely.

"I'd suggest, Ely, that you find your own mate to cling to while steering clear of mine for a while," she stated. "I do understand that he's been a friend, but you're now beginning to overstep the bounds of that friendship."

Weariness filled her as she stared at the naked rage in Jonas's silver eyes.

"You would have never told him the complete truth." Ely shrugged as she headed for the door, her hand shoved into the pockets of her white jacket. "He deserved to know what happened after you left."

"Very good excuse." Rachel sighed, still staring at Jonas. "And I hesitate to say this, but I will: It was none of your business."

"You believe the insults he deals to my mate are none of my business then?" Jonas growled as he leaned against Callan's desk and crossed his arms over his chest with an air of arrogant assurance and fury. "She was well within her rights to report to me."

"She wasn't reporting to you, she was snitching." God, there were times it was like dealing with children.

The door closed as Ely left the room, leaving Rachel and Jonas facing each other across the room now.

"Snitching is childish," Jonas rebutted. "Her report was logical, concise and to the point. There were no embellishments."

"I didn't say she was lying."

"He insulted you." Jonas straightened from the desk. "Not once, but repeatedly."

"And I insulted him back, not once, but repeatedly," she assured him. "It's over."

Jonas stared back at her, still fighting the same sense of amazement he had felt when Ely had come to him to describe the argument, not just between Leo and Elizabeth, but between Leo and Rachel.

This was his mate, and possibly the only person he knew

who had gone up against the Leo, nose to nose, and called him on his own arrogance and manipulations. She had described the Breed to a T. He was impossible. A gamesman, and so certain he could bring Jonas to heel.

He'd been certain of it since the day he had stepped into that hospital where Callan Lyons had nearly died the year before.

There were so many of them. Breeds who hadn't had the chances others had because they weren't the children of Leo and Elizabeth.

Elizabeth hadn't deserved Jonas's disregard, and that was the conclusion Jonas had come to as the sun had risen that morning. But Leo, well, the Leo deserved far worse simply for attempting to use Rachel and Amber in his battle against Jonas.

"You held your own very well." Jonas turned and walked to the other side of Callan's desk. From there, he stared down at the computer monitor that still showed the deserted lab. "And though I appreciated Ely's report, I had already caught the tail end of it anyway."

He turned the monitor to face her. "Just so you know, when I kill the bastard, it won't be because of anything Ely said. It will be because of what I saw for myself."

What he had seen had filled him with pride. His mate, so proud, her temper flashing in her green eyes, her face flushed as she stood up to one of the strongest males of the Breed species.

And though he had seen something after she left, in both his father as well as his mother, that he hadn't expected, the fact that both of them in some way had been manipulating him didn't sit well with him. By the very fact of her silence, his mother had been playing the same game as Leo.

Bringing Jonas to heel.

Jonas wasn't a dog, and he didn't take commands so well.

Rachel lifted her gaze from the monitor and stared back at him, her gaze tinged with sorrow now. "He does love you, Jonas," she whispered. "Just as she does."

His lips quirked. "It isn't love, Rachel, because they have no idea of the man I am, nor do they respect the man they see. They regret. They ache for what could be but isn't. They hurt for what might never be, but it's not love such as what you feel for Amber, or even as they feel for Dane. Regret can hurt just as deeply as disappointment, sweetheart."

What was she supposed to say to that? She couldn't defend the Vanderales, because in her eyes, they were in the wrong. But a part of her knew Elizabeth loved her child, whether that child had come from her body or been created in a lab.

They left the office and collected Erin and Amber before heading back to the cabin. Amber was fast asleep and placed gently in her crib by Rachel. Jonas gave Erin her orders for the next day before sending the Breed female back to the barracks.

Kissing Amber gently on her forehead, Rachel covered the baby and quietly left the room. Closing the bedroom door, she stood for a moment and stared at Jonas as he gazed into the fire.

As though there were answers in the flames, she thought. He frowned into the newly lit fire with a concentration that hinted at the dilemma roiling through him.

"A mother's love is all-consuming and complete," she stated quietly as he lifted his head. "A father's love is often veiled in the appearance of disappointment, or exacting expectations. It isn't regret, disappointment or whatever else you want to see it as. It's a parent's love, and a parent that even now, despite the veil of civilization, still doesn't know how to handle or to show the emotions that fill him."

His lips quirked. "God made woman to help him come up with excuses for man."

"He made woman to love man," she retorted.

"Yeah, probably because he knew nothing else would," he snorted.

She wasn't going to argue it. Rachel shook her head with a slight smile, watching as he moved slowly toward her now.

There was a new purpose in him, a hunger that had less to do with lust and more to do with pure, confusing emotion.

Like the Leo, Jonas wasn't always certain of the emotions

he felt or what to do with them. These men, Breeds, they loved their women and children with a dedication that bordered the extreme at times, but when it came to loving anyone else, they became contradictory masses of complete denial.

Stopping in front of her, his hands lifted to cup her face as he held her still for his kiss. A long, slow kiss. His tongue touched hers, licked at it, mated with it.

The mating hormone wasn't filling the glands, it wasn't flavoring the kiss, but still, Jonas felt his hunger for her clear to the soles of his feet.

She was his woman. She was his life. Hell, he wondered if he had even had a life before her. Before he saw the innocence and clarity in her eyes, before he'd learned the gentleness and courage that filled her soul.

As he felt her fingers at his neck, sliding around, gripping the strands of hair that grew low along his nape, Jonas knew he had never known a moment's peace until Rachel.

She had the power to humble him, to still his rage, but she also had the power to weaken him.

His knees were nearly shaking at the thought of the pleasure to come as he lifted her against him and moved back to the fireplace.

The flames were blazing, devouring the heavy logs Jonas had placed in the pit, licking greedily at the fuel, consuming it slowly despite the heat pouring from it.

The heavy, incredibly soft fake fur rug spread across the hardwood floor awaited them. He'd had dreams of taking her in front of this fire. Dreams of watching her transform from cool, collected female to the heated, hungry mate he had fantasized about for so long.

She was the perfect mate for him. Strong where he was often weak, understanding of emotions when he had trouble just accepting them. She would keep him warm, keep his heart steady.

He was passing warm now though. As her kiss began to fire the unique Breed mating heat inside him, Jonas felt his cock throbbing in urgent demand.

He was always hard for her, always hungry for her. He swore there hadn't been a day since she had walked into his office that he hadn't been hard for her.

Smoothing his hands down her back, Jonas gripped his mate's hips and pulled her to him, lifting her, finding a ready seat for the brutally hard length of his cock.

"You make me crazy to fuck you," he growled. "There's not a minute of my day that I don't want to be inside you."

His fingers bunched in the short length of the skirt she had worn. She was always dressed so ladylike, so damned buttoned down and proper. The above-the-knee dark skirt was at once conservative and provocative.

He jerked it to her hips, just as it provoked him to do.

The white, long-sleeved black cardigan she wore over the white silk blouse was dropped to the floor. It was all he could do not to rip the blouse from her body.

The sweet swells of her breasts were an enticement; the tight, cherry nipples topping them created a hunger inside him that was both pleasure and pain.

"Leave the shoes on," he ordered, his voice rough as she moved to step from them. "Are you wearing stockings again?"

A siren's smile tipped her honeyed lips. "Would I wear anything else for you, Jonas?"

Something clenched in his gut, some emotion, some over-riding sense of rightness.

"So you wear them for me?" Leaving the shirt hanging from her shoulders, her breasts swelling over the cups of her lacy bra, Jonas went to work on his own clothing.

"I wear them for you," she agreed as her fingers moved to help with the buttons of his shirt. "I never wore stockings until I began working for you."

That was no lie. He could smell the truth of her statement.

"And this." He rubbed his finger over the soft scalloped lace edge of her bra.

"For you," she breathed out, her breathing growing harder, deeper, as the last button released from his shirt.

Jonas shrugged the material from his shoulders as her

fingers went to the closure of his slacks. He could see the hunger heating inside her, smell it burning deeper, brighter, with each passing second.

As his slacks loosened he pushed his shoes from his feet, his fingers still rubbing against the lace of her bra, moving from the scalloped edge to the tight peak of her nipple beneath.

He could feel the heated warmth of her, the throb of blood pounding through her body and echoing in his cock. She was the pinnacle of hunger and need.

The slacks slid down his legs, releasing the torturous length of his cock as his head lowered to her breast, his suddenly sensitive tongue probing at the hard tip.

She stiffened in his arms, her hands going to his shoulders, her fingers gripping tight as he allowed his teeth to rasp the sensitive peak.

"I want to fuck you just like this," he groaned, the need ripping through his balls as he experienced the peaches-and-cream taste of her through the lace.

"Dressed?" Her nails pricked at his shoulders as her voice roughened, a little moan vibrating in it.

"A little dressed." His hand pushed beneath the skirt, gripped the side of her panties and ripped the fragile lace from her hips.

"Buy me panties," she breathed out roughly as the scent of her juices flooding her pussy wafted through his senses with a hint of peaches and heat. Damn, she made him hungry.

He dropped to her knees, his hands holding her hips, the swollen glands beneath his tongue filled with the mating hormone.

Gripping her hip, he touched her with the fingers of his other hand. He parted the glistening, curl-shrouded folds, parted them that tiny bit to see the little bud of her clitoris gleaming within her pink flesh.

The scent of her was addictive.

Kneeling before her, he watched her softly rounded thighs tremble, watched her juices gather thicker along the tiny curls hiding the entrance of her vagina from him.

He would get there. But first, he wanted a taste of her tender clit.

Leaning forward, he flicked the tip with his tongue, felt Rachel's hands grip his head, her nails pricking at his scalp now. Glancing up, he almost grimaced at the flushed, sensual look on her face, the arousal gleaming in her eyes.

He licked around her clit again, felt the flinch of pleasure that rippled through her body, smelled the sweet flush of moisture and felt a purr rumble in his chest.

Fuck, he couldn't stop the sound. She was too good; pleasing her felt too good. He couldn't hold it back. A moan echoed through his ears and her thighs parted farther at the sound.

He let the purr free, let it vibrate, let the sound wash over his tongue and her clit.

"Jonas." She panted his name as her fingers raked over his scalp.

"Shhh, pretty girl," he whispered against her clit as he pressed a firm, sensual kiss on the tiny bud.

"Jonas," she whispered his name again, her tone rife with sensual hunger. "It's so good."

Her legs parted even farther, her thighs opening as he ran his fingers down the slit, parting it, caressing her inner flesh as his tongue licked, stroked the pearly bud.

It swelled with each caress, throbbing in demand as his fingers found the snug, clenched opening to her pussy.

She was tight, silky. A groan rumbled in his throat as the sleek heat of the tender muscles gripped his fingers and they pressed inside.

He knew the grip of that sweet flesh on his dick. It was fist-tight, rippling, flexing. Each tiny spasm of the sleek flesh sent heat driving straight to his balls.

Each small thrust of his fingers into the gripping muscles sent a wave of pure hunger tearing through his senses.

He had the taste of her on his lips, her clit against his tongue, the incredibly tight heat of her pussy gripping his fingers. Fuck, this was good. So damned good.

He sucked fiercely at the little bud, flicked his tongue over it as he let his fingers fuck her with hard demand.

The more he gave her, the wetter she got, the stronger the grip on his hair became, the more her pussy heated, the sweet moisture washing over his fingers, tempting his tongue.

Releasing the tiny bud he'd been suckling, Jonas found himself moving lower, licking, tasting the soft folds as his tongue unerringly found the clenching entrance to her pussy.

It was like burying his tongue in living sensual abandon. Thrusting it deep inside, Jonas moaned at the incredible pleasure, the sweet-spicy taste of her.

He could take her like this forever. He could fill his senses with her and still not have enough. She was addictive. She was lush and sweet and so fucking hot he was going to come before he ever managed to get his dick inside her.

His cock was thick, hard. Throbbing with vicious hunger, the demand that he take her almost painful now.

"So good," she moaned above him, her legs trembling now as sensual weakness rippled through her. "It's so good, Jonas. Oh God. I love your tongue."

He speared his tongue harder inside her, felt the hormone easing from the glands beneath it as the scent of her arousal became deeper, stronger.

Her nails were biting into his scalp now, tremors washing through her. She was close, so very close. He could feel her orgasm building, smell it rushing through her system.

She was becoming immersed in the pleasure, in his touch. Her hips were twisting, pressing her pussy closer.

He was drunk on her. He was dying for more. He wanted more and more of her.

Jonas caught her as her legs gave out and she began to sink to the floor.

She couldn't hold herself up any longer. It felt as though the high heels were suddenly melting rubber, throwing her off balance and pitching her into Jonas's arms.

He caught her, lowered her to the floor, his lips moving up

her stomach, licking, stroking, the rasp of his tongue striking incredible sensations against her bare flesh.

He licked, stroked. The tip of his tongue grazed, his lips kissed, as he lifted himself over her, and pushed between her thighs.

There was no true body hair, only the sparse, silky, almost fur-like hairs that were practically invisible on his body. It stroked against her inner thighs as his hips pressed them apart, sent racing sensations of ticklish pleasure radiating through her.

Her hips arched. Rachel felt a heat stronger than that of the fire burning beside them as his fingers pulled the cups of her bra beneath her breasts, lifted them free, then began to devour them.

His thighs were between hers. The hard length of his cock pressed against her sex, rubbed against the swollen bud of her clit and nearly sent her into orgasm.

Her hands stroked over his shoulders. The feel of his flesh, tougher, harder than hers, was a sensation against her palms that had her moaning in pure bliss. The feel of his tongue stroking over her nipples was ecstasy. Pinpoints of sensation, tiny, striking little shocks of pleasure that raced from her nipples to her clit, to her pussy.

She couldn't believe, each time they were together, how good it felt, how incredible the sensations could get.

"Sweet Rachel." His head lifted from her breasts, his silver eyes glowing with hunger. "I could live on the touch and the taste of you."

Her hips jerked, her fingers flexed against his shoulders as her head twisted against the incredibly soft fur of the rug.

As she lifted against his hips she felt him pushing her skirt from her body. It came free slowly and was then tossed aside as he came back to her.

Heat, incredible, blistering heat seared the tender flesh of her pussy as his cock pressed against it, the heavy shaft rubbing against her clit. The engorged head was a heated brand against her lower stomach as his lips burned hers in a kiss that tasted of pure cinnamon and cloves.

It was incredible. His lips twisted against hers; his tongue twined with hers. His hands coasted over her body, lifted her hips, eased her thigh against his as he shifted again.

Rachel froze. Her eyes flew open as she stared back at him, watching as he raised himself above her. The thick crest parted the dew-laden folds, then pressed against the clenched entrance of her sex.

"I'm going to burn alive," she gasped as she felt the snug entrance part, stretch, for the slow, heavy invasion of his cock.

"I'll burn with you," he groaned. "We'll go into flames together."

Staring up at him as he took her with slow, controlled thrusts, Rachel was caught anew by the savage contours of his face, the glow of his silvery eyes, the bead of sweat that eased down the side of his face.

The vibration of a purr was a steady rhythm that stroked over her senses, amazed her and pushed her arousal impossibly further.

Lifting her legs, she wrapped them around his hips, strained upward and fought to take more of him, all of him. The feel of his cock stretching her, stroking her with short, hard inward strokes as he forged steadily deeper, was almost more than she could bear.

She was flying in his arms. Staring in his eyes, she felt the flames enveloping her, washing over her, through her. She was lost in a wonderland of pleasure she didn't want to lose.

"This." He swallowed tightly, grimaced. "It's the most pleasure I've known."

Her legs tightened around his hips as he drove deeper, harder, inside her. Pleasure-pain erupted inside her as he fucked deeper, his cock pressing, stretching the tender recesses of her pussy as she lifted closer, fought to meld into his flesh.

With a final, heavy stroke, he was buried to the hilt inside her, stretching her, burning her, filling her in ways that Rachel knew no other could ever fill her.

Iron hard, iron hot, he stretched the tender tissue, revealing naked nerve endings that flared in response to the stroke and throb of his cock. Pleasure surrounded her as heat filled her. The incredible mix of emotional and physical pleasure wove together, sending her senses spinning into a neverland of absolute bliss.

Her fingers clenched on his shoulders, stroked down his arms. His back was slick beneath her palms as perspiration beaded on his bare skin.

His knees bent, his hands pulled her closer, lifting her hips as he rose to his knees, staring down at her, his expression savage, tight with lust and amazingly . . . love.

Love filled every stroke inside her body. It filled his gaze, his expression. The bogeyman of the Breeds was the lover she had always dreamed he could be.

Wild. He growled. He purred.

His hands clenched on her hips as he fucked her deep and hard, shafting inside her with a desperate pleasure that rocked her soul and filled her with a wild savagery of her own.

Her nails dug into his arms, her hips writhed beneath his, thrusting against him, taking him as deeply as possible. Her legs fell back from his hips, dug into the rug and lifted higher, taking more of him.

Each stroke dug into violently sensitive flesh. It stretched and caressed and filled her with a power, a bliss she couldn't control. She didn't want to control.

She could hear his growls. She heard his purrs. She felt her body tightening, her pussy spasming. She convulsed, rapture exploding through her. She tightened, on him, with him. She felt ecstasy racing through her body, tearing through his as he gave a muted roar.

His cock slammed inside her, buried deep. The feel of his release spurting inside her triggered another orgasm, this one more intense than the last.

When the barb emerged, locked into the most sensitive

area of her pussy and stroked with subtle, destructive plea-sure, Rachel swore she lost her soul to him.

Her eyes opened, almost unseeing. Her gaze locked with the living silver of his. She felt him, she swore she did, clear to her spirit she felt him locking inside her as surely as he was locked inside her body.

He was a part of her. The other half of her.

"I love you." The words were torn from her, ripped from her heart, locked inside her soul. "Oh God, Jonas, I love you."

She loved him.

Jonas came over her, cradling her in his arms now, his cock still buried deep inside her, throbbing, filling her with his release as he gave every part of himself to his mate.

Hell, he'd already given it to her, he was simply renew-ing it.

He'd feared mating would weaken him. Instead, it had strengthened him, it had softened him, it had made him see some things clearer, and now he was more determined than ever to secure a measure of peace for the Breeds. Because nothing mattered but the safety of his mate and his child.

Nothing mattered but this.

Holding her.

Loving her.

Being loved.

Jonas Wyatt, the bogeyman of the Breeds, was loved.

CHAPTER 22

The next morning Jonas and Rachel walked into the main computer and security control room for the estate house. Set in the far wing with direct access to the labs below, the room was outfitted with monitors, servers and external terminals that housed and stored the guts of Sanctuary's security operations for the house.

All internet, telephone and wireless communications went through the comm center before being routed to the communications bunker outside the house.

Stepping into the small anteroom that held three control computers, Jonas moved past the lioness working them, aware of Rachel following close behind, into the tech room where the technicians took their breaks or the occasional shift nap, then through another door to the heart of the room.

Here, servers maintained the various links to the comm bunker, drove the internet and wireless radios, monitored satellite phones and in-house satellite communications and held a backup security system that notified the comm bunker, the Wolf and Coyote communities of Haven as well as the

Vanderale security system in Africa, in case of emergency. It was a self-contained emergency backup system as well as a last-response notification system.

The main house was powered independently from the bunker, but all systems from the house were monitored by the more advanced network set up in the bunker.

Still, this room was indispensable.

Jonas moved to the back of the room where the brains of the operation worked with a frown on her delicate face, her white-blond hair pulled haphazardly to the top of her head, the long strands falling messily around her face and shoulders.

Dressed in black mission pants and a sleeveless cami top, she cursed like a sailor under her breath and glared at the monitor.

"What do we have, Sherra?"

Jonas moved behind her to stand over her shoulder, his gaze narrowed on the results as he picked out the anomalies of the scan she'd described in her report the hour before.

"We have a bug," she murmured as her fingers flew furiously over the keys. "It activated perhaps a week ago, from what I can determine. It's a silent one; none of the scans caught it. If I hadn't begun the practice of running a deep-level scan in conjunction with full diagnostics and system routing to save time, I would have never caught it."

She paused and sat back before pulling the present screen to the monitor next to her. Within seconds, the five monitors around the main one displayed five different levels of diagnostics as well as the six main results.

"Here and here." She tapped the main screen and the one on the right above it. "The anomalies began here. Once the diagnostics caught the first anomaly, it began trying to hide." She pointed to several other diagnostic results. "At present, it's completely disappeared." Pointing to the screens left and right of the main screen, she hit a command to display the current readers. "Like dust in the wind, my friend. It's gone."

She turned and stared back at him with savage fury

reflecting in her deep blue eyes. "We have a bug, and he's damned smart."

Jonas narrowed his eyes on the screens before turning to Rachel. "Do we have any intel on anything like this?"

The Bureau monitored all new viruses, rumors of nano-viruses and deep-level bugs.

Rachel was watching the screen intently, her green eyes narrowed, her expression thoughtful, before activating the electronic pad she carried. "There's no intel on it, but that doesn't mean anything. For the most part, we only get info on what's been discovered or rumors of what's in the works. There's been nothing like this in the intel we've received of intended attacks against our mainframe or communications network." She frowned at the results of the search she typed in on the pad. "All we have is unsubstantiated intel on one that destroys itself when found and wipes its track to eliminate the chance of identification. Those have to be uploaded manually though." She glanced back to Jonas, concern darkening her gaze as she gave him the information.

"Whoever put the bug in our system would have had to have worked from this room then." Sherra tapped the tips of her well-manicured nails against the table before initiating another search.

"It's not as though we haven't had our share of spies," Rachel reminded her. "The medical assistant we caught several months ago had access to the room during the poker games that were played here, as well as the night he murdered the techs working the room. He could have initiated it at any time."

We. She used a vernacular that placed herself as an indelible part of the community rather than an outsider. It was the first time she had done so, and hearing it sent a surge of satisfaction racing through Jonas.

"Let's not assume it's destroyed itself though," Rachel continued as she turned back to the screens and stared back at them thoughtfully. "We need someone experienced in subversive technology to go through this."

"All Breeds are experienced in subversive technology." Sherra snorted. "It's part of our training. We learn that in puberty."

Rachel was shaking her head as she spoke and typing commands in, one-handed, on the pad she used. Within seconds a list of information began scrolling across the screen.

"You have four Breeds, all rated A-plus in subversive technology, nanotechnology and communications stealth. Those are the Breeds you need."

Jonas lifted his brows. Fuck, where the hell had she gotten that information?

"Since when?" Sherra asked, surprise filling her expression. She looked to Jonas as though wondering why he hadn't known that information. Or, more to the point, why the main Pride wasn't aware of that.

"The information was hidden among some of the Council's more encrypted files," Rachel informed her. "Encryption isn't something that's easy. A lot of information is misread or overlooked entirely because the codes are so difficult."

"And you managed this how?" Sherra turned in her chair and watched Rachel suspiciously.

Jonas bristled at Sherra's tone until he watched Rachel slowly smile. "I like puzzles. I take the encrypted files, the various codes, and when Jonas is away, I play a little bit." She glanced at Jonas. "Sometimes, he's away often."

He wouldn't be away from her any longer.

"And who are our master technology Breeds?" Sherra questioned, still obviously not completely satisfied with the explanation.

"You have a Bengal Tiger Breed of Asian descent, Lee, as the only name listed here." She frowned, her tone becoming quieter, more thoughtful, as she began scanning the file. "There's a Wolf Breed of Scots descent, no name listed, only his file number." She tapped the screen for more information. "He's not registered with the Bureau." But she knew who it was; Jonas could see her expression, the shifting pattern of suspicion as she put together the information on the Breed. "I suspect it's Styx." An amused smile crossed her face. "We're in trouble if it is."

It was.

"We also have two Breeds, lab numbers only, who I haven't yet been able to track any information on or to unencrypt what the information is in the files I found them in. I'll have to work on that."

She lifted her head. "We have no known location or information on Lee. Styx is accessible though."

"Styx is a menace." Sherra rolled her eyes before turning back to the computer. "He'll probably have one of his temper tantrums and destroy every computer we have."

Jonas almost grinned at the thought.

"I'll pull the files I pulled this intel from," Rachel told her. "I'll see if we can find someone quickly. No doubt, we can't let the system go much longer with a suspected bug in it."

"I was able to track its parameters by using the computer logs," Sherra told her. "It's not easy though. Even the logs are trifling." She shook her head. "I don't know what we're dealing with but it's damned smart."

"Isolate the logs and work through them on an independent, unconnected system," Rachel suggested. "That's how they're created."

Sherra turned to her again. "How the fuck do you know all this? You've worked with Jonas for less than a year and you know more than I do."

"I rather doubt it." Rachel's smile was conciliatory. "I'm good at trivia though, so I retain large amounts of unconnected information. It's a talent." She flashed a charming grin Sherra's way.

"A talent, huh?" Sherra glanced at Jonas. "Sounds more like the same coin with a different face. You and Jonas are a better match than I thought."

"I always knew we'd be a good match." Rachel leveled a look up at him that nearly had him grinning. As though *she* had manipulated the entire mating.

"To each his own, I guess." Sherra chuckled before turning

back to Jonas. "Before you leave, Callan needs to see you in Sit Comm One." The situation communications room in the estate house. A room completely secured from any outside electronic or satellite interference.

Jonas nodded. "Could you contact his Enforcer on call and let them know I'm on way?" When Sit Comm One was in use, Callan's personal bodyguard slash assistant was always nearby.

"Contacted." Sherra hit a key on the console, then flashed a smile back at him. "Also, just to let you know, Lance Jacobs is up and moving around. He, Harmony and their son are planning to leave for home within the week."

Jonas nodded shortly. He kept his emotions in check where his sister and nephew were concerned. Harmony had demanded that he stay far away from the boy, and it was a request that tore at something inside him.

He stayed away, though he kept careful tabs on the child. Joseph Leopold Jacobs. They called him Joey. He had just turned twelve months old. He had tawny hair with hints of black and his father's blue eyes. He was a happy child and Harmony was an ecstatically loving mother. She doted on her mated husband and child.

"Ready?" He turned to Rachel as she made a note on her electronic pad.

"Ready." She gave him an absent smile, but her gaze, her entire demeanor as she stayed close to him assured him that she was very much aware of him.

He could sense her awareness, the sensitivity of her body, the arousal that simmered just beneath the surface, ready to burn out of control.

The sweet, soft scent of her body, the easy breaths she took, even her thoughtful attitude as they made their way to speak to Callan, drew him to her.

They made their way from the comm room and to the other side of the house to the newly erected Sit Comm One. The room was in the family wing of the ruling Pride, which consisted of six families, though all were rarely there at the same time, other than the Pride leader, Callan Lyons, and the second-in-command of security, Sherra Tyler.

Callan's personal Enforcer, Fallon, a Lion Breed trained in advanced security and protection, opened the door to the room silently.

Callan; Kane Tyler, who was head of security and Sherra's mated husband; Sanctuary's head of enforcement, Taber Williams; and the head of Sanctuary Public Relations, Tanner Reynolds, were sitting at the long conference table as he and Rachel walked in.

Rachel broke off from Jonas's side, sliding perfectly into her former role of his assistant.

"Good afternoon, gentlemen." Rachel moved ahead of Jonas, poured him coffee and his water and set them at his chair. Jonas almost grinned. She was the perfect mate for him, able to blend in with his business life, as well as the role of mate.

She complemented him at every turn, and had managed over the past months to soothe a lot of the feathers he had managed to ruffle, or completely jerk out, over the years.

"We have files." Callan used the electronic pad to send the file to Rachel as well as Jonas.

She handed Jonas his and pulled up the information on her electronic pad.

"The Senate's Breed Appropriations Committee has called a special session to review the funds already voted on and agreed to for next year's expenditures. The information we have is that they've received information that the Bureau, as well as Sanctuary, has broken the agreement we signed in regards to conducting any military or personal acts of war or aggression toward any of the governments supplying the funds."

Jonas scanned the information before him before turning to Callan. "There have been no acts of aggression or of a military design against any government, period. Their intel is bogus, Callan. As usual."

The Bureau didn't bite the hand that fed it. At least not directly, and sure as hell not without someone or something else to blame it on.

"Senator Tyler is on that committee, as you know," Callan stated. "He sent a heads-up on the information he had; he's requesting your immediate presence before the committee, otherwise funds are going to be held up indefinitely until this gets taken care of."

"We don't need their fucking money," Tanner growled, his Bengal green eyes flashing with ire.

"They owe the Breeds that money," Rachel pointed out, her tone firm. "What you need to do is make a move to keep the money out of the appropriations committee's hands and directly under Breed control at a certain amount per quarter."

"They're too scared we're going to turn on them," Callan grunted as he leaned back in his seat and rubbed his finger along his jaw. "They think halting that money will keep us from taking over their various countries."

"As if we'd want to deal with their bullshit as well as our own." Tanner snorted at the thought. "Hell, just running Sanctuary is enough of a headache, wouldn't you say?"

That was about the truth.

"Rachel." Jonas turned to her.

"A heli-jet is being prepared and I'm having Lawe move ahead to pull mission files," she stated before turning to him, an edge of worry in her expression. "Am I going?"

He nodded abruptly before turning to Callan. "I need preparations made for Erin to bring Amber into Sanctuary while we're gone. Cassie is currently in residence, correct?"

Callan sat up straight, his eyes narrowing. "Cassie will ruin that child. I'll have quarters set up for Amber and her caretaker. She can assume twenty-four-hour detail. I'll assign someone to help her, but Cassie spoils babies worse than their mothers do. You don't want her anywhere near her."

"Wrong." Jonas wanted no one but Cassie near her, actually. "Assign Cassie as backup. I'll accept Erin as primary care."

Jonas rose to his feet, knowing it would be taken care of.

"Jonas, Amber is my child," Rachel stated quietly as

she moved in front of him. "Shouldn't you at least consult with me?"

Ironic amusement filled her tone, although a hint of anger threatened.

"Would you have done it differently?" He tilted his head to the side, wondering if she seriously had a better alternative.

"Doing it differently isn't the point," she told him as she began to pack away their notepads. "The point is," she turned back to him, "consult with me next time. And I will be telling my daughter good-bye before we leave."

She strode from the office with her shoulders straight, her head held high.

"Consider that a warning, my friend." Callan chuckled behind him as he and the others rose to their feet. "Even for the sake of expediency, never, ever make decisions of the family nature without the direct input of your mate. The results could otherwise be fatal."

Evidently they could be. Jonas scratched at the side of his jaw as he gave the other men a rakish smile. Turning to leave the room, he thought the world might be a little brighter today.

He'd watched Callan and the others being gently chastised by their wives on more than one occasion, and he'd always felt an odd sort of envy for it. They'd possessed mates who lovingly guided them in how to be a part of a family, how to be more than a Breed within a unit of Breeds. How to be more than soldiers or killers.

Over the years, he'd seen the results of that guiding influence. Men who had once known nothing but death could laugh; they played with their children; they made silly faces at babies and they moved in a world that included more than blood, death and punishment.

Jonas had longed for that world. He'd longed to be a part of more than the blood and death, the past that haunted him. He had that now. And he intended to keep it. "Senator Tyler has arranged to delay the meeting with the appropriations committee to allow us time to arrive and to gather our information," Rachel informed him as they stepped into the back of the heli-jet. "He doesn't have the details of their supposed proof, but one of the other members who keeps his sympathy for the Breeds secret has advised him to warn us that they have circumstantial evidence at present, and that Senator Racert is working to build upon it."

"Good luck," Jonas grunted as he helped her strap in, before clipping his own safety harness and preparing for lift-off. "Does Tyler have any idea what information we should bring with us?"

She was frowning as she scrolled through the reports she was receiving. "At present his contact is fairly certain they're concentrating on all missions conducted with the U.S. and Israeli military through last year and going into this year," she answered shortly as she began using the electronic notebook's holographic keypad and typing furiously. "We have a total of a dozen missions conducted with the Mossad, Jonas, but nothing that could even come close to providing us with a chance to conduct a military maneuver or act of aggression against the U.S. or any of the other nations that have contributed to the Breeds' funding."

"Start running probables," he told her as he pulled his own E-pad from her briefcase. "I want to know which missions would have come close to presenting such opportunities. Don't confine the parameters to the Israeli missions; branch out to all countries that are a part of the Breed financial accord."

She was nodding as he spoke, working to get the information into the pad as the heli-jet raced for D.C.

"We'll need to stop at the Bureau offices," she told him. "Lawe should have the files pulled by the time we get there. We can head to the Justice Department, where the senators are convening."

Jonas gave a slight nod as he continued to pull up information on his own pad. There had to be a reason for the sudden investigation into their funds. No doubt the reason for it was completely falsified, but even the senators involved with the appropriations committee knew that the Breeds didn't depend on the funds allocated from the financial accord.

"ETA in ten minutes, Director Wyatt," Jackal informed them as Jonas began reviewing missions. "Let's eliminate any chance of a surprise here."

"Do you have any idea the number of missions that have gone out in the past eighteen months?" She stared back at him doubtfully, as though he had somehow lost his mind.

"Exactly three hundred and fifty-four missions; seventeen planning-phase aborts and twenty-six en-route aborts. That doesn't count the four hundred and fifty-seven refusals we gave in the same amount of time. Should I give you the number of privately subsidized missions we've taken in the same amount of time?" he queried.

"One hundred and thirty-six privately subsidized missions, of which there were seventy-two refusals, fifty-three planning-phase aborts and thirteen en-route aborts. Should I catalog them into amounts of kidnappings to extractions to private security?" She glanced back at him with a grin.

Damn if she wasn't good. It was one of the things that had immediately struck him once she began working for him. She knew how to keep track of information as well as the various details of the work he did. That ability, though sometimes irksome in the regard that it limited certain activities, had made many parts of his job much easier.

Shaking his head, his lips quirked at the need to grin, but he was damned if he would let it free. It might not stop at a grin. He might very well end up with a full-fledged fool's smile on his face. And Jackal was already way too attentive to the byplay between them. No doubt, there were bets going on as to the timing of certain phases of their relationship. The most common bets were how long it would take a Breed's mate to make them smile. That, and who would catch him grinning first. Jackal possibly had a bet riding on that smile.

"Lawe will be waiting on us in your office," Rachel told him as she glanced back to the E-pad. He has the files ready in the reader we use for the committees, loaded and unencrypted. Does he need anything else?"

Jonas shook his head. "Have him meet us in the parking garage. We'll take the limo to the Justice Department. How much longer do we have?"

"One hour before the hearing."

There was still had time.

Nodding, he shut the E-pad down, stored it back in Rachel's case, then stared into D.C.'s cloud-riddled sky-line. The weather was calling for a blizzard. He hoped they made it home this evening before it hit. He had planned for champagne in front of the fire, the skylight over the fireplace opened and the blizzard blowing around them as he made love to his mate.

It wasn't a plan that he wanted to cancel.

"Snipers report all-clear," Jackal called back from the cockpit. "All areas secured for landing."

"Take her down," Jonas ordered, his gaze moving over the area as he assessed it for possible threats.

The heli-jet set down within the landing pad on the roof. Jonas quickly released Rachel's flight straps before releasing the catch on his own. Jackal threw open the door and Jonas jumped out, then turned, gripped his mate's waist and set her gently on the floor of the roof, all the while shielding her body with his own.

"Stay here," he ordered as he turned back to Jackal. "We should be ready to fly before dark. I want to get back before the snow hits."

It was definitely going to snow. Jonas could feel the threat of weather in the air, almost taste the ice crystals on his tongue. There was an overwhelming urge to turn around and fly back to Sanctuary.

"I'll be here," Jackal assured him as he reached in and handed Jonas the heavy briefcase Rachel had brought with them.

Turning to the building's entrance, Jonas checked to make

certain the Enforcers were in place before they headed across the roof. They moved quickly toward the pair as Jonas indicated he was ready to leave the safety of the shield offered by the heli-jet.

Surrounded by the three Enforcers, they made their way quickly across the roof and into the elevator.

"Enforcer Justice is waiting in the garage," the Breed at his side informed Jonas. "He asked that you be apprised that the limo is waiting outside the elevator and ready to roll."

Jonas gave a quick nod as he laid his hand against Rachel's lower back and handed her the briefcase, in preparation of escorting her quickly into the limo.

The doors slid open on the basement level. An Enforcer stepped out, opened the back door and Jonas helped Rachel into the limo before stepping in himself.

The door closed behind them, the locks snapping into place.

Jonas jerked alert at the sound, his hand going quickly to the door handle to attempt to jerk it open. With his strength and the rage pounding through him, it would have been no large feat to trip the mechanism in the door.

"Do you want me to kill your mate?" The voice through the intercom system was well-known and filled with amused satisfaction. "Alert the Breeds outside that there's a problem, and I promise you she'll die."

Jonas's gaze sliced to Rachel. She was silent, staring back at him with wide, shocked eyes as her hand slid slowly inside the opened compartment of the briefcase.

She was sitting with her back to the driver's area, the case on her lap, and he knew what she was doing. She was pressing the wipe key to the E-pads and erasing all the information they contained.

As her hand slid back from the case, the partition slid down, revealing Phillip Brandenmore's bodyguard, Josef Svenson. The weasel-faced, dark-haired Svenson watched them through beady eyes, a smile curling his thin lips.

"Ms. Broen, please move to Mr. Wyatt's side, if you don't mind."

Rachel allowed the briefcase to slide silently to the floor of the limo as she moved to sit beside Jonas, facing the bodyguard silently.

"So tell me." He leveled a lethal, black laser handgun at Rachel's head. "Where's the brat? I thought Mommy never left home without her."

CHAPTER 23

Rage was a burning brand thundering through Jonas's veins, ripping through his brain as Jonas stared at the weapon trained on Rachel.

Brandenmore. How had the bastard managed to get through security? What the hell had happened to Lawe? Jonas knew his Enforcers; they would have never allowed anything like this to happen. The very fact that Brandenmore's body-guards had the limo meant Lawe was most likely dead.

Beside him, Rachel sat silently, but Jonas could smell her fear. It ate at his control, enraged the beast inside him and tore at his logic.

He could smell the blood pounding in Svenson's body, could almost taste it, his need for it was so strong.

"How did you manage it, Svenson?" he asked, his voice uncontrollably deeper, rougher. The animal refused to hide.

Svenson smiled again. A slow, cold curl of his lips. "I won't say it was easy, but there's a lot to be said for tranqs, wouldn't you say?"

Jonas hid his own satisfaction this time. Breed Enforcers

were inoculated against tranqs. Ely and the Wolf Breed scientist had come up with that solution years ago when the Council scientists had thought they could recapture their best soldiers by tranquilizing them and bringing them back to their side.

"Yes, there's a lot to be said about tranqs." Jonas crossed his arms over his chest and fought to hold back the growls rumbling in his chest.

The drug would have lasted only minutes. They must have bound Lawe somehow, incapacitated him in a way that had kept the Breed from instantly striking back.

"So, where's the bitch's brat?" Svenson questioned again.

"In Sanctuary," Jonas answered as he felt Rachel trembling beside him. "There's a storm coming in. We felt it best to keep her there rather than taking her on what should have been a rather short trip."

Svenson scowled, his thin, short lips pinching in anger.

"Mr. Brandenmore won't be pleased," he warned Jonas.

"And pleasing him is something that tops my list of things to do," Jonas mocked.

The bastards, all of them, were dead. Anyone who had participated in this little kidnapping plot would pay in the most painful manner.

Svenson glanced at Rachel then. Jonas could feel the slight tremors of her body, smell the anger and the fear burning inside her. She remembered the night Brandenmore had actually managed to get his hands on Amber. That memory still lived clearly within her soul.

"You should have brought the kid," Svenson grunted regretfully. "His displeasure might not worry Jonas here, but it could end up hurting you. Rather painfully. He was none too pleased after you managed to snag the little bitch from him last time."

Her fists clenched in her lap. Fury was a raw, burning scent of maternal rage as the bodyguard insulted her baby.

Not that it was doing Jonas much good, but as long as the other man had that laser weapon trained on Rachel, there wasn't much he could do. It wasn't bullet powered. A killing blast from the weapon he was using would rip through her body, burn and sear and leave damage that could possibly never be repaired.

"Why does he want the baby?" Jonas kept his tone icy, merely curious. There were preconceived notions of Breeds, one of them being that Feline Breed males—and females too, for that matter—were not accepting of any mate's children from previous relationships.

Council scientists cited the fact that lions would kill the young within a Pride that they took over. That they refused to nurture the cubs of other males. The scientists had stated that Breed Feline males would be no different.

They continually forgot that Breeds, no matter their subspecies, were still human.

"He has plans for her." Svenson shrugged, his gaze licking over Rachel in a way that had Jonas biting back a territorial snarl. "Plans that don't include the two of you."

Jonas could feel Rachel fighting to hold back the anger eating at her. Her baby was safe, that was all that mattered to her. She would die for Amber if need be. Just as Jonas would die for both of them. He was simply hoping it wouldn't quite come to that.

"Well, without knowing the plans he has for her, then I really can't help him much, can I?" Jonas sat back in his seat, threw his arm behind Rachel and pulled her closer. "Do I have time for a nap?"

He was known as being uncaring of others' welfare. Could he trick Brandenmore into believing that the mating was only biological? That by holding Rachel he would only incite animal logic rather than debilitating anger?

"He's not getting Amber." Terror was racing through her. "You promised you wouldn't let anyone hurt her, Jonas."

Satisfaction edged through him. He'd never promised any such thing, at least not in that manner. He had staked his claim on the child, and Rachel knew exactly what that meant.

"She doesn't know Breeds very well, does she, Wyatt?"

Svenson chuckled. "You'd sell out your bitch mother if it served you."

"Only if it served me, but as I have no idea who supplied that particular component of my creation, I can't help you much there, now, can I?"

"No mommy, no daddy." Svenson laughed. "You bastards are luckier than you know. Now just sit nice and quiet. We'll be at our destination soon and you can discuss all this with Mr. Brandenmore."

The partition raised, leaving them alone as the vehicle sped through the city.

Rachel didn't speak. She knew the back of the limo was equipped with a two-way intercom, which Svenson would have definitely made use of, as well as a camera that could be activated if needed.

The limo moved out of the city and headed into the mountains, but it hadn't gone far into them when they turned on a small single-lane road, then onto a gravel path for nearly a mile. Finally, it pulled into the front of what appeared to be a small cabin.

Not exactly as grandiose and luxurious as he knew Brandenmore was used to, Jonas thought as he surveyed the outside of the cabin through the side windows.

The woods were thick with sheltering pine, which would work as an advantage for him and Rachel. He glanced down at her neat black slacks, dark gray cashmere sweater and long leather coat. She wore low heels, which were perfect for a business setting, but not so good if they had to run. But he could compensate for that, if it meant carrying her on his back.

"We're here, boys and girls," Svenson announced eagerly as the partition slid down once again. He frowned at them, obviously taking note of the fact that Jonas wasn't cuddling a tearful Rachel. "You sure you two are mates? You act like strangers to me."

Jonas stared back at him coldly, silently.

Svenson grunted before he and the driver stepped from the vehicle and the back door opened.

"Now, let's be polite and not try any of that Breed-going-nuts bullshit, okay?" he warned as he waved them toward the cabin with one hand while he held the gun on them with the other.

Polite? Jonas was never polite.

Rachel fought back a hard shudder of fear as Jonas's hand landed at her lower back while he escorted her to the cabin. His palm was a warm, heavy weight as they stepped up on the rough stone porch and the front door eased open slowly.

She wasn't panicking, Rachel thought. There were no premonitions of danger such as the ones she had felt returning home the night Brandenmore had been in her house.

Stepping into the cabin, Rachel felt nothing but anger, and an overriding fear for Jonas. He would die before he allowed anything to happen to Amber. Though she knew he was attempting to give the appearance of unconcern, she knew there was no way he would allow their child to be harmed.

Their child. As the heat from the fireplace slapped her in the face, Rachel realized that Amber had always been their child.

Then, she came face-to-face with the man who had fathered Amber once again.

Devon sat with Phillip Brandenmore in the cabin's open sitting area. Relaxing in the leather recliner, obviously more than a little drunk, Devon appeared smug, triumphant, as she and Jonas were escorted into the room.

Phillip Brandenmore, on the other hand, simply seemed satisfied. For some reason, he appeared to think he had won. And if his expression was anything to go by, he believed he was being benevolent in his victory.

"Have a seat, Jonas." Brandenmore gestured to the leather sofa across from Devon's chair and parallel to the couch Brandenmore was seated on.

Sitting in the corner, the other man stretched his arm along the armrest before lifting his drink, which had been resting against his knee. He sipped at the golden liquor slowly as he watched Jonas with the careful regard men used when a wild animal crossed their paths.

"Director Wyatt." Brandenmore extended his hand to the sofa. "Thank you for joining us. Can I get you a drink?"

Rachel was almost amused at Brandenmore's cordial tone.

"No thank you." Precise, unaccented, Jonas's tone was like ice. "Shall we get to the point instead?"

Brandenmore sighed heavily. "You moved up my schedule a bit, I must say. I had intended on waiting a few weeks to allow my spy within Sanctuary to be able to gather the information I needed."

Rachel hid her surprise. She knew the tireless search that had been waged for any remaining spies, only to come up empty-handed.

"You mean the bugs you had programmed into our computers?" Jonas's words shocked her even more. She hadn't pieced that together yet.

She knew the virus hadn't made sense. Sherra was diligent about the computers, as were the lionesses who operated them and the rest of their computer security staff, especially after discovering that information had been stolen via a new program that had hidden secrets in innocuous emails.

"Yes." Brandenmore smiled as Devon shot him an irritated look. "The bugs. They were rather ingenious, I must say. I was within days of cashing in on the information they had been gathering when you so obviously found them."

"They were programmed to wipe their tracks and self-destruct." Jonas had already guessed that one.

"You owe me for that one, Phillip," Devon bit out mulishly. "That program was rather expensive."

"I owe your father," Brandenmore shot back in irritation.

There was a tension between the two men, an anger that wasn't entirely understandable, Rachel thought. Then again, she couldn't bring herself to understand what they were doing together in the first place.

"Where's my kid?" Devon turned and caught Rachel's look. His brows lowered ominously. "I told you to abort the little bastard, but you had to make my life hell, didn't you?"

"I've decided to make it my life's goal," she agreed pleasantly as hatred rolled through her. "I so enjoy knowing you're here to make my life hell."

"Smart-mouthed bitch." His lips twisted in a sneer.

Jonas growled. The sound was low, throbbing with power and danger. Enough so that Devon flinched.

"The boy never learned good manners. Although his father often tried to instill them, his mother just undid all the good his father tried to accomplish." Brandenmore gave Devon another disgusted look as he finished the explanation.

"I want the kid." Devon ignored his elder's silencing look.

"Amber is my child," Rachel informed him calmly. She wanted to reach out and rake her nails down his eyes. She wanted to rip out his tongue.

"Enough bullshit. Let's get to the point here," Jonas snapped out, his hand clamping loosely on Rachel's arm as he upheld the appearance she knew he wanted to give: that she was no more than a woman he was now tied to through a biological mating.

Rachel hoped they weren't paying attention to the small, imperceptible strokes of Jonas's fingers against her wrist, or how he kept her close to his own body; otherwise, he had given them both away.

Not that Rachel couldn't hide the fact that she was leaning on his strength. The longer they sat there, the more that gut-deep feeling of dread was beginning to build in her.

"The point is, I want the child." Brandenmore set his glass on the table in front of him before leaning back to watch them with a cold, assessing gaze. "Lions don't enjoy having the young of other males around them," he continued. "I'll do you a favor and solve a small problem I have in the process."

"No!" Rachel couldn't hold back the instinctive denial. Her body clenched, tightened to the point that the warning grip of Jonas's fingers on her arm was barely felt.

"And what problem do you have, Brandenmore, that an infant can solve for you?" Jonas queried, his tone so icy cold that Rachel nearly shivered and almost believed that he was actually considering the proposal.

"Her mother is a Breed mate." He nodded his head in Rachel's direction. "If my preliminary tests are correct, then that would make her child compatible to Breed physiology as well. I'd like to conduct some simple, rather painless tests over the course of her primary years into adulthood. She would be well cared for." He leaned forward, his expression sincere. "She would have a good life and provide an invaluable service as well."

"And that service would be?"

She knew Jonas. Knew his moods, his expressions, the progression of ice in his voice, and she knew that in this moment, the animal inside him was as close to breaking free as she had ever sensed it.

"The Breed mating-age phenomenon." Excitement colored his voice, narrowed his eyes and lent a glow of fanaticism to his expression. "Neither Breeds nor their mates age once mating occurs. We know that now. I want to know why. I could duplicate it, create a serum. All I need is a viable, healthy child whose biology is compatible."

"And how do you know this child is the one you need?" Jonas asked.

"I took blood and urine samples while I had her," he gloated. "I had her for hours—enough time to collect what I needed for the proper tests. Rachel and Devon's child is compatible. Devon's parents have advanced millions of dollars to the project, and my friends in the Middle East have provided the perfect lab to work in."

"You would need a Breed to test her with. How did you achieve that?" Jonas was full of questions.

Rachel had to fight back her horror, her tears, as she stared at Devon's mutinous expression. He and his parents had sold his child to a monster. For what? For an anti-aging serum that might or might not work?

She couldn't hide the fact that she was shaking from

the inside out now, nor could she hide the complete fury beginning to engulf her.

"It was fairly easy to achieve." Brandenmore shrugged then. "We have so many Breed blood, urine and semen samples that have been preserved both by myself as well as the Genetics Council. Testing her against them wasn't that difficult."

"She would have only matched to a specific Breed," Jonas pointed out. "Her mate."

Did Amber have a mate? How could that be possible? She was only a baby.

"Mating tests are unreliable until adulthood, Brandenmore," Jonas continued. "We've proven that."

"A mating test, true." He nodded. "But not a compatibility test, which is what I have created."

He was so filled with self-importance now, so triumphant as he stared at Jonas, certain he would agree to give Amber up.

"Jonas, make him stop with this," she whispered, desperate now to erase the horror of what Brandenmore was suggesting.

Brandenmore shot her a pitying look as Devon glared at her in disgust.

"Shut the fuck up, Rachel," Devon snapped. "She's my kid too. You can have more brats with your lover here. Let me have Amber."

"So you can kill her?" she yelled, staring at him, wondering why she hadn't seen the evil that had infected him while they'd lived together.

"No one's going to kill her. She would be useless dead." Devon laughed in ridicule. "Get a grip. You always overdramatized things to the point of ridiculousness."

"Enough." Jonas's voice was low, a throbbing sound of power that immediately silenced Devon.

"He'll kill you for insulting his mate, my boy." Brandenmore laughed. "He might not love her, she might be a shackle about his ankle, but that animal inside him will protect her with his last breath." He looked at Jonas. "That kid is another matter, isn't it, Mr. Wyatt?"

"So you're suggesting I give you Amber, in exchange for what, exactly?" Jonas asked.

Brandenmore leaned forward again, that fanatic light still gleaming in his eyes. "Well, number one, in exchange for your lives." He smiled. "Secondly though, I will share my research with your scientists. It's my understanding that mating heat is causing no small amount of discomfort, at least according to the medical assistants you caught helping me not long ago. This is a win-win situation for you, Jonas."

A win-win situation? Who lost? Definitely she would lose, her child, the most precious treasure in her life. Amber would lose her life, if not in the first weeks of this so-called research, then in the years following.

Rachel stared at Brandenmore, then at Devon.

"That's your daughter," she whispered, wondering how she could ever face the questions Amber would eventually have about her father now. "How could you do this, Devon?"

He finished his drink off quickly before sneering back at her. "I told you to abort the brat, Rachel. You didn't do it. Phillip can at least use her efficiently."

Rachel flinched. Jonas growled, low and dangerous, as Phillip Brandenmore stared back at Jonas in surprise, as though he recognized the inherent danger in the sound.

"Mr. Wyatt," Brandenmore said carefully, "you want to consider this. We both know the child means nothing to you, but your mate does. You'll call Sanctuary and have the child flown to a location I'll give you. Once I have her, you'll be released."

Rachel heard the low hum of laser weapons powering up behind her.

She was shaking her head. Tears were rolling down her cheeks; she was trembling from the inside out, until that moment.

"No," she whispered. "I won't let you . . ."

"But it's not your choice," Brandenmore informed her.

"It's your mate's. And tell me, Ms. Broen, what do you think that animal inside him is demanding that he do? He wants rid of that kid because it's not his. She isn't his blood, or his species; therefore, she is a hindrance to his Pride, a threat to his leadership and the future leadership of his rightful children."

"This isn't the Middle Ages," she exclaimed.

"Shut the fuck up, you stupid little bitch." Devon's glass flew across the room and shattered on the wall as everyone stared back at him. "You will give him that little brat or I'll have her killed. Take your pick."

"No, you won't," Jonas growled, the hard, dangerous rumble of his voice filling the silence with a bone-chilling wave of vicious intent.

"Of course he won't." Brandenmore was definitely aware of the murderous undercurrents filling the room now. "Jonas, Amber won't be harmed. I swear it. You won't lose in this, and your mate can't hate you. The only way to save her is to trade the kid for her. That simple."

Jonas breathed in slowly, subtly, careful to make certain no one was aware of the scents he was drawing in. There were Breeds outside, more than one. Four of them were from Ghost Team. He'd seen the glow of Jag's green eyes minutes before in the window behind Devon's head.

There were others. Lawe was out there, Rule, Mercury and, strangely enough, Jonas could smell Leo and Dane Vanderale. Not that Dane had much of a scent to him; it was always carefully disguised. But there was the barest familial scent, which Jonas could never have mistaken.

He'd waited, restrained the animal clawing at his insides with brutal, bruising strength to be free. He'd held on to his control, fought the rage, until the others were in place.

The smell of Brandenmore's lies mingled with those of the Breeds. He was a monster. Jonas had no idea what he had planned for Amber, but it wasn't the existence he had described. Amber would know nothing but pain. If reports were correct concerning the rumors of some of the experiments conducted by the man over the years, she would be lucky to live weeks, let alone into adulthood.

"I'll even pacify your mate as best I can." Brandenmore was smiling, his beady eyes filled with malice cloaked by sincerity.

The man should have been an actor. He would have won an Oscar.

"I'll send photos, keep her updated on the kid's progress. Maybe even phone calls for a while." He smiled benevolently toward Rachel.

Horror was pouring from her. Tears stained her pale cheeks; rage ate at her. She was in control. She had, like Jonas, managed to restrain the need to kill.

His hand tightened on her wrist, his fingers stroking a pattern of warning across her flesh until he felt her tense, felt the moment she realized the pad of his finger was carefully outlining the letters to a very short message. *Be ready.*

She was already ready. He felt it. The way she held herself, the sudden smell of the rage solidifying inside her as he tensed and prepared to move.

He glanced to the window, saw the vague outline of a dark hand. Five fingers. Four. Three. Two . . . ONE.

"Down!" He took her to the floor as the window behind the bodyguard Svenson's head shattered and laser fire began to fill the room. It took only a breath to watch blood erupt from the younger man's chest and head, to see his eyes widen and smell the scent of death as it began to fill the room.

Jerking Rachel to the relative safety beneath a heavy coffee table, he went for Brandenmore. Svenson was laid out on the floor, blood staining his hair as Devon Marshal lay on his stomach, his shoulder covered in blood. Brandenmore crawled across the floor at a far quicker pace than Jonas would have expected from a man his age.

Springing ahead of the old man, Jonas caught him by his shoulder, his claws ripping into flesh far more resilient than it should have been, into muscle more powerful than he could have guessed.

But he was still human, and no match for the Breed genetics Jonas possessed.

Jerking him to his feet, Jonas flung Brandenmore to the wall hard enough to daze him before gripping a handful of hair and jerking him back again, placing the older man in front of him.

Alpha Team One and Ghost Team had ended the danger to Rachel's life in seconds. Merciless, quick and efficient. The chilly night air swirled through the room, the scent of blood and death mixed with that of wood smoke, terror and pain as he forced the old man to face the night's work.

"It's over," he yelled, forcing Brandenmore to stare at the results of the sudden Breed attack.

His bodyguards were dead. Blood spilled from their bodies as they lay on the floor, their gazes empty and staring into nothingness.

"It's not over."

Jonas jerked his head to the side to see Devon holding Rachel by her hair, his grip harsh, jerking her head back as the point of a laser pistol lay against her vulnerable head. The younger man looked dazed, furious. The scent of his blood was heavy in the room, as was the smell of his fury and fear.

Jonas froze. The Breeds rising slowly from the floor stared at the scene as though in emotionless interest, but he could smell their sudden intent, could feel them weighing possibilities and considering options.

Rachel was the director's mate. Without her, Jonas didn't know if he could function. His men didn't know if he could function. If she died, there would be no rage as great as what he would feel, forever. Until he killed himself or someone did him a favor and killed him.

"I want that little bastard." Devon pushed her toward the door, his eyes gleaming with hatred as he stared at Jonas. "Let him go. The little bitch is nothing but an embarrassment. There can be no heir to the Marshal fortune, who isn't a Marshal."

And no one considered Amber a Marshal.

There were few options.

"The mother has to live." Brandenmore's voice was soft, so soft. "She will breed a legacy to science."

His child.

Jonas's hands tightened in his hair.

"His gun is empty of power." Almost too quiet, even for his senses to pick up, Brandenmore whispered the words. "I'd never give him a weapon that worked."

Devon was digging the barrel into Rachel's head. The tiny light at the side of the weapon was red. It wasn't powered. Or was it a trick?

"I'll kill you if she dies. So very slowly," he warned the old man. The old man in a much younger man's body.

"Let me out of here," Devon ordered harshly as he jerked Rachel toward the door. "I'll fucking kill her."

Jonas turned his head and gave the Breed still standing in the shadows outside a slow nod. Ghost Team had remained hidden while Alpha Team One had rushed into the room.

Jag had a bead on the back of the bastard's head. He would take him out. It would be messy. Rachel would never forgive them for the mess.

Silence filled the night until a hollow *pop* vibrated through the room and a gush of blood and brain matter exploded from the side of Devon Marshal's head.

Rachel jerked as he fell. She was gripping his hand, trying to jerk his fingers from her hair as she kicked at him, screamed at him.

Tears ran down her face; rage tore through her voice.

"You bastard!" she screamed, managing to loosen her hair as Jonas caught her.

Her foot kicked out, landed in the dead man's gut. "You fucking monster. You bastard. She's a baby. She's a baby."

Jonas jerked her to his chest, his hand covering her head, his eyes burning as he stared at Brandenmore, now held easily by Lawe, his hands being restrained.

Jonas turned to the older man and let a slow, cold smile curl his lips. Brandenmore was his now. Amazing how things were beginning to work out. The greatest minds among the Genetics Council were now becoming Jonas's possessions: first Amburg, now Brandenmore.

"Take him to the labs," he ordered the Breed. "He needs to be tested himself."

Brandenmore's eyes widened in horror. "I helped you. But I helped you," he protested as though shocked.

"You helped yourself to your own demise," Jonas swore. "You've just disappeared, Brandenmore. Another casualty to this silent little war you and your friends have begun. And now, you're mine," he promised with a deadly growl. "You fucked up. That's my daughter. Adopted from love, not from duty. Claimed as a daughter, not as a brat. And you'll pay for even daring to consider harming a hair on her head."

He wanted to rip the son of a bitch apart. The last thing he wanted to do was use him to better the Breed community, but he had no choice. Only Brandenmore could explain whatever changes occurred in Amber.

He nodded to Lawe to drag the man out as he turned slowly to the room, his arms still holding his mate close as she sobbed against his chest. Tears of anger, not of fear, or even of relief. They were tears of anger, pain and horror.

"Clean up," he ordered as Leo and Dane stepped from another room, dragging a bodyguard, barely alive.

Then Jonas felt his eyes widen in surprise and utter disgust. Son of a bitch, he couldn't keep them out of his hair for anything anymore.

Leo was tall, proud, exhilarated. His golden eyes glowed with excitement as he held a laser weapon in one hand, and gripped the hair of one of Brandenmore's best bodyguards as he dragged him along in the other hand.

"Mother will know you were here," Dane warned him in amusement. "She'll kick your ass and pout on me for months."

"Wrong, she kicks your ass and pouts on me," Leo argued.

"I'm going to have her kick both your asses." Jonas

snapped, finally at the end of his rope where the two were concerned. In the past months they were like leeches. He couldn't seem to shake them off his fucking back no matter how hard he tried.

Then, they turned to Jonas as though coming up with the same answer at once.

"It was all his fault," they said in unison as they nodded at Jonas. He had a very bad feeling he knew exactly what they were agreeing to.

"Excellent." Leo grinned and slapped Dane on the back. "It's good to have another son to blame shit on. The rest of you are getting damned irritable over it."

He dragged the guard through the room, slapped Jonas on the shoulder and continued into the night as Jonas stared at him in outrage. Suddenly, the cold, hard Leo was gone, and what Jonas smelled rolling from the other man couldn't be true. Acceptance? Why? Why now, and what the hell was the Leo up to this time?

He turned to Dane, though he really didn't expect answers at this point.

Dane sighed heavily. "Your mate," he nodded to Rachel, "evidently chewed his ass and gave him a new lease on life. What is it about you mated bastards that get off on that?"

As though that was an explanation? At least at this point, it made a bit of sense. Rachel was rather good at making man or Breed feel about two inches tall whenever they deserved it.

Jonas blew out a hard breath. "They care," he finally said as Rachel sniffed, her tears easing, her rage lessening. "It means they care, Dane. Only a Breed raised in the labs could understand the power of that ass chewing."

Rachel would do it often.

She would love him often.

She would rage at him often.

She lifted her head, her eyes still wet, her lips trembling.

"I love you," she whispered. "So much."

His head lowered and, amid blood and death, touched hers as light as a feather and whispered, "I live for you."

Dane watched for only a second before turning away. A grimace tightened his features and something ached in his chest. And he wondered if he would ever experience for himself the power of that ass chewing?

· E P I L O G U E ·

It was snowing.

Hours after their return to Sanctuary, Jonas stared out at the snowy landscape through the barred windows of the interrogation center, which sat above an entrance to the underground labs. There were three inches of snow on the ground, and two feet predicted to head their way. Big, wet, fluffy flakes that piled on the ground, the trees, the roofs of the cabins, had turned Sanctuary into a snow-covered wonderland.

How had he never noticed the beauty, the pristine innocence in a snowfall before?

He had never taken the time to see the wonderland, the almost fairy-tale promise that nature lay upon the ground each time it snowed, just as he had never truly realized the beauty in a child's laugher, a mate's smile, or the word "family." He'd never realized what he was fighting for until he had faced losing it that first night Brandenmore had struck against Rachel.

"You don't want to keep me here, Wyatt." Brandenmore's voice was hoarse, choked with terror, as he spoke from his position across the room.

Elizabeth Vanderale, Ely and Amburg, all masked, their identities hidden, had extracted the vials of blood samples needed. Swabs had been taken of the inside of his mouth, as well as from other areas of his body. Urine samples had been forced from him, and an array of tests were taken as he screamed and fought each procedure.

The Leo and Dane stood in a shadowed corner, black masks covering their faces as the scientists completed their work. The air was heavy with Breed rage and human fear.

When the scientists left the room, Jonas turned to him slowly and nodded to Jag, who was masked as well.

Electrodes were connected to Brandenmore's head, above his heart and along the pulsing veins at his temples. The electrical impulses that would surge through them weren't lost on the other man.

"Jonas, please," he screamed. "This is wrong. You have to arrest me. I want to see my lawyer."

"There are no lawyers here," Jonas promised him, his voice steady, cold. "This is Sanctuary, Brandenmore. Here, my word is law. Here, I decide if you live or if you die."

"You can't," the older man cried desperately. "That's not right, Jonas. You're already against me. She's your mate, your child. You can't make this decision."

"You have been tried and deemed guilty of crimes against Breeds so heinous, so lacking in mercy, Phillip Brandenmore, that only death can come close to atoning for your crimes. It is by word, by Breed Law, that you're sentenced to death."

"No." Brandenmore wheezed, his eyes bulging with the knowledge that there would be no mercy to be found, no loophole, no way to escape the pain coming.

"Yes." Jonas crossed his arms over his chest and stared at the Breed behind Brandenmore. "Do you have any last words?" He lifted his hand as though to give the order to electrocute the bastard.

"If you kill me, you'll never know what I did to your daughter."

It was a good thing Brandenmore wasn't a Breed, since

otherwise he would have scented the pure triumph that spilled from the Breeds in the room.

"Nothing is wrong with my daughter," Jonas assured him. "She's been tested completely. Games are over. It's time to die."

"Delayed reaction." Brandenmore's voice was hoarse, desperate. "I know what I'm doing. I knew you'd run every test in the world on her; I hid it. The only way to know how to save her later is if I tell you. If I live."

"You're lying . . ."

"You can smell a lie." Tears poured from Brandenmore's eyes. "You know I'm not lying, Jonas. You know I'm not. And I promise you, without me, she will die. I've ensured it. I made certain I had that ace against you."

He wasn't lying.

"What guarantee do I have you'll tell me anything?" Jonas sneered. "You'll play games, just as you always do."

"I'll be here. Keep me. Just let me live," he cried out.

"Live long enough to see if you're getting younger? Live long enough to see if your aging serum works?" His body was younger than it should be, and Jonas knew his face wasn't nearly as lined as he last remembered it.

"Everything," Brandenmore swore. "I'll tell you everything."

"Yes, you will," Jonas crooned. "Or you'll suffer. Far worse than you would have suffered tonight. Far worse than any Breed ever suffered under you, Brandenmore. I promise you that. You'll cooperate fully, or suffering won't come close to the hell you'll glimpse."

Nodding to Lawe and Rule, Jonas turned and left the room, followed by Leo and Dane. Walking up the short hall to the observation room where Callan and the other members of the Pride family, along with Ely and Elizabeth, waited. Rachel was with Amber at the cabin, the one place Jonas wanted to be more than anyplace on earth.

"Son of a bitch," Callan cursed as the door closed behind them. "What did he do to that baby?"

Jonas rubbed his hand along the back of his neck, the ache there intensifying as he fought against himself. He wanted to go to Brandenmore and rip his heart from his chest.

"Ely, place him on the truth serum you've been working on," Jonas ordered her.

The serum was designed for human as well as Breed biology. It took weeks, sometimes months, to fully integrate into the system and let it begin working. It would work though, and the truth would come from Brandenmore's lips whether he wanted to tell it or not.

"It may need to be refined," Elizabeth stated. "If what we suspect is true, and he's found a serum to reduce aging, then it could change how the serum works with his particular biology."

"It looks like we'll be staying awhile longer then." Leo gave a short nod, his golden gaze locked on Jonas, a message in them that Jonas wasn't certain of.

"I'm beginning to wonder if we'll ever make it back to Africa," Dane stated. "It's a damned good thing I enjoy America."

Jonas rubbed at his neck again. He needed to be with his mate, with their child.

"We'll begin questioning him once the serum has time to initially react," Jonas told them, concern weighing heavily on him now. "I'm heading home now."

Home. He had a home now. It wasn't simply a cabin or a house. It was a place where warmth lived, thrived. A place where peace could be found.

"Jonas, a moment of your time, please." Leo stepped in front of him as he headed for the door. "In private."

"Leo, I don't want to deal with you tonight," Jonas stated wearily. "Let's try later."

"Let's try now." The door opened as Leo gave him a stony look and stepped from the interrogation room.

The room next to interrogation was a file room. Lined with heavy steel filing cabinets, it was cold and silent as the light flipped on and Jonas stepped inside to face the first of their kind. The first Feline Breed to live past the age of five. He had made a way for them all. His genetics had provided a base for every Breed living.

He was the Breeds' Adam, Elizabeth their Eve.

"What do you want, Leo?" Crossing his arms over his chest, Jonas watched the other Breed with weary curiosity.

Leo's chest swelled as he breathed in deeply, his gaze heavy with something—sorrow? What?

"It was years before I knew of the French labs," he finally began.

"I don't want to hear this." Jonas turned to leave.

The hard, furious snarl behind him had him pausing, the animal inside blinking warily as Jonas grimaced and turned slowly.

The animal genetics were too fucking ingrained. Leo wasn't his Pride leader, but he may as well have been. He was the first; he was the strongest. He was his father.

"You'll hear it whether you want to or not," Leo informed him. "By the time I learned of you, you were full grown. Your genetics proclaimed you the child of Madame Scientist LaRue and her consort, with a few of my genetics tossed in. I had other matters more pressing. My son was in danger, my mate was ill, and the Council had hunters in the Congo searching for all of us. I concentrated on rescuing the Breeds I could reach rather than branching out any farther than I had to."

"Unless a child created from both you and Elizabeth was found," Jonas bit out, his voice cold. "You went out of your way, then, didn't you, Leo?"

Leo's head lifted. "I did. Those Breeds are the most dangerous, besides being my children. My God, they were our children." He breathed out roughly. "Once I learned your true genetics, it was too late. The rescues had already begun. You were already free and Harmony was safe. When we received your message that Harmony was in danger, I sent Dane for her immediately. Almost too late, but we got to her."

Jonas tilted his head. "You received the message?" He had been unaware of that.

Leo gave him a hard smile. "Even Dane doesn't know I got the message you managed to send to Africa. I arranged it so he would be there for her, that he would bring her to me. She wasn't my child, but she was a Breed, one far too young for what she faced, and one I had hoped would be Dane's mate."

When Jonas had sent that message so long ago, he had also sent the encrypted, coded file on Harmony that only the Leo could have understood. It had been a test, as well as an attempt to save his sister.

"You never told her you were trying to get her out of there, did you, Jonas?" Leo questioned him.

"I never told her." He shrugged. "It never mattered. She escaped, and she survived."

"She would have died if not for Dane and Rye," Leo stated as Jonas tried to distance himself from the past and the regrets that lay there.

Jonas nodded. "He saved her. I've thanked him."

"And you found her mate for her, and took her from him," Leo said. "There were several times Dane nearly stole her back."

Jonas shook his head. "She wouldn't have stayed."

"No." Leo sighed. "And now, I must find a way other than the one I've used to find the son I fear I lost in the years I remained hidden rather than revealing myself to him. He would never accept the proof that I was watching over him with pride. Nor would he accept the explanation that I'm often simply too arrogant for my own good, and that my sons come by their stubbornness and manipulating ways honestly."

"I never denied that." Jonas stared back at him. "Look, are you seeking forgiveness? Fine, I forgive you."

Leo's gaze was heavy. "Forgiveness? No, Jonas, I'm searching for my son. Emotion comes easy with my mate, with the children I raised, but I've found it's harder with the sons that are grown, who have not been influenced by me or made to understand my ways. I'm searching for the son that is more like me than even those that my mate bore me. One so like me, that even at the best of times, I wonder when he'll challenge me."

"Never," Jonas answered easily as he read Leo's surprise. "I have no desire to challenge you, Leo. Not you, nor Callan, nor Dane, unless you threaten what's mine. Then, I won't challenge you; I'll kill you."

"You could easily claim Sanctuary or my own base," Leo stated suspiciously. "You're strong enough, manipulative enough."

"There's no challenge to it." Jonas faced his father, knowing it was the truth. Knowing that being Pride leader was a far easier job than controlling the Bureau, the humans that were a part of it, as well as the Breeds that served as Enforcers.

"You're joking." Leo grunted. "There is nothing more challenging than assuming leadership of hundreds of Breeds."

Jonas shook his head. "Each to their own, Leo."

Leo shook his head. "And Elizabeth? She's your mother. She weeps for you."

Jonas's eyes widened in surprise now. "She knows?"

Leo watched him curiously. "She's your mother. She's always claimed you. Even when I believed you weren't our child, Elizabeth knew. She knew, and cried for you, just as she left my bed for months when it was proven. She hasn't yet forgiven me, Jonas, no more than I suspect you will ever forgive me."

Hell, he simply didn't have time for this.

He jerked the door open, ignored Leo's suddenly furious growl and stomped back to the observation room. As he pushed through the door, Leo on his heels, he faced Elizabeth as she turned from something Ely was saying.

He gripped her shoulders, bent and kissed her forehead gently. "I'm heading home, Mother. Please get Father off my back and out of my life for a day or so if you don't mind. I do have family matters to take care of now."

Ignoring her surprise, he turned and stalked past Leo, back to the hall, and out of the small building that served as Sanctuary's pre-detaining building.

Calling Leo "father" didn't sit well, but he was a Breed, created, not born, trained rather than raised. He wasn't Jonas.

After tonight, he would never call Leo "father" again perhaps, but he wouldn't deny him any longer.

Mordecai was waiting with the Raider and made the trip home quickly. Jonas needed his mate and his child. He needed to tell his mate the battle they may face, as well as the one their child might face. And he needed to hold her.

She was waiting on him when he walked in the door. Snow swirled inside before he closed the door, locked it, then strode to his mate.

"Where is Amber?" His fingers went to the belt of her robe.

"Asleep." Her breath instantly became harder, her voice breathy and low as he stripped the material from her shoulders.

"I need you." His lips moved to hers. "I love you."

"I love you." Her lips parted for him, his tongue slipped past them, the glands beneath aching, needing the touch of her tongue.

She was there for him. The hormone spilled into her and was taken eagerly as he lifted her in his arms and carried her to the bedroom.

Stripping them both of the clothes separating them took little time. Her gown tore as he jerked at the small buttons at her waist. It pooled at her feet as he worked his pants loose and toed his shoes from his feet. Shedding the pants and shirt, he pulled her to the bed, his lips slanting over hers, his tongue thrusting into her mouth, retreating, filling it again as he moved between her thighs, desperate to have her.

As the touch of her, the taste of her, filled his senses, the ache at the back of his neck began to recede and the heaviness that had filled his soul began to ease.

As he gripped his cock and pressed it against the soft heat of her pussy, he felt renewed. As he began working inside her, he felt the hunger to simply live begin to ease. She was his life, his heart, his soul.

Lifting his head, he stared into her eyes as he took her. Inch by inch, slowly working his erection inside the tight grip of her pussy as he felt her filling his soul.

Never had pleasure been so great. Never had anything in his life brought him peace until this woman—until he looked into her eyes and sensed the woman created for him.

"My heart," he growled as he slid in to the hilt, felt her heated muscles rippling around his cock as her arms tightened around his shoulders and a gasp of pleasure whispered around him. She was burning in his arms now, and nothing mattered but throwing himself into the flames with her.

Gripping her hip with one hand, he began to move inside her. Deep and hard, he fucked her with a desperate, blinding hunger, a need to hold himself inside her forever, to fly with her, to feel her coming apart in his arms.

When the explosion came, it was more than flying. It was floating, surrounded by a sea of such incredible sensation that nothing else mattered. Locked inside her, the barb pulsing, heating, driving her pleasure higher as he watched her shudder, watched her eyes become unseeing and heard her cry his name with such satisfaction that it vibrated through his soul.

This was home.

Where the heart was.

❖   ❖   ❖

Later, as she slept, Jonas pulled on his sweatpants and padded silently to their daughter's room. He had thought to catch her sleeping. She was a baby; if she wasn't eating, then she normally wanted her mother, and voiced that desire loudly.

She wasn't sleeping. She was staring up at the mobile above her crib, her gaze almost thoughtful as the little fairies that Cassie had gifted her with twirled in the slight breeze created by the central air system.

Her green eyes were dark like her mother's, while the shape of her face was more similar to her aunt's. The curve of her nose was pure Rachel.

Reaching in, he picked her up and placed her against his

chest before moving to the living room and standing in front
of the window. Turning the baby, he let her watch the snow as
it piled high beyond the window.

"I'll protect you," he promised as he cuddled her close in
his arms. "With my last breath, I'll protect your mother and
you, Amber."

He felt her then. Her mother. Rachel moved from the bedroom and joined them, watching the snow as it fell in fat, lazy
flakes, piling on the ground.

"Brandenmore did something, didn't he?" she asked softly
as he curved an arm around her shoulders and pulled her
close.

"I'll find out what he did," he swore as he watched her
expression in the window, saw the fear that flashed in her
eyes.

"She'll be okay," she stated. "Cassie's certain of it." She
lifted her face to him. "Is she ever wrong?"

Jonas shook his head. "She's never wrong." But sometimes, she wasn't exactly right.

One thing was certain: The future, and their child's happiness, was now in the hands of one of their greatest enemies.
And Jonas was damned if that sat well with him.

"Jonas?" Rachel turned in his hold and stared up at him,
her hand settling against her daughter's small arm. "Whatever happens, we're together and I love you. Forever."

And suddenly the world was that much brighter.

"You're my treasure," he touched her lips gently, "forever,
Rachel."

Catching her hand, he drew her with him as he laid Amber
in the crib and took his mate back to bed.

No one heard the small sound that was made after their
bedroom door closed: a soft, sweet, kittenish little purr.

Keep reading for a special preview of

The Demon in Me

by Michelle Rowen
Coming May 2010 from Berkley Sensation!

· C H A P T E R I ·

"You're Eden Riley, right? Wow, it's *so* exciting to meet a real psychic!"

Eden cringed and slowly turned to see a wide-eyed man with a receding hairline staring at her expectantly. She forced a smile. "That would be me."

He beamed back at her. "I'm Constable Santos. I was sent ahead to keep you company until Detective Hanson arrives. He's running a bit late."

Since she'd been waiting a half hour already, she kind of figured that.

"I should probably warn you that the detective's a bit of a skeptic. He's not that big on adding psychics to the investigation."

"Trust me, Constable, I'm used to that kind of attitude."

He waved a hand. "Don't let it bother you. You'll just show him how insightful you are and make a believer out of him."

Eden tried to hold on to her smile. "Fair enough."

"So how does this work?" he asked.

"How does what work?"

"The psychic thing to solve our unsolved cases. Everyone's still buzzing about what you did last month."

Eden's stomach twisted unpleasantly. Up until last month, and just before she'd moved to the city, she'd worked at Psychic Connexions, a phone-based service located two hours north of Toronto, meant for entertainment only—astrology readings, love life and job advice. She had a talent for saying the right thing at the right time and keeping her customers happy enough to get them to be repeat callers.

She simply told people what they wanted to hear, helped by some mild insight and a knack for reading tarot cards. Everyone was happy.

But it didn't mean she was really, truly psychic.

Little did she know that one of her regulars was Meredith Holt, the wife of Toronto's current chief of police and a devout believer in All Things Mystical. She'd discovered Eden by accident (or *fate*, as she'd later relate the story) when her usual fortune-teller was away on vacation and she "got a hunch" to call the number advertised in the Entertainment section of the newspaper. Eden simply knew her as Merry, a lovely woman who always ended their daily twenty-minute sessions with a wish of "brightest blessings."

One day Merry called in crying and near hysterical. Her beloved Maltese terrier, Sunny, had gone missing and she was beside herself with worry.

There were . . . *moments* . . . when things just clicked psychically for Eden, even without consulting her deck of cards. As Merry poured out her emotions over the phone at $1.99 a minute, a very clear and precise image of a little white ball of fluff slammed into Eden's head with all the subtly of a Mack truck.

She knew that the dog was locked in Merry's neighbor's rarely used toolshed, living off birdseed and rainwater for two days and was about to be adopted by a family of concerned raccoons.

She made up the last bit to soften the news.

Merry had thanked her profusely and Eden had gone

back to her day, which included assuring a hysterical Aquarius that her Gemini boyfriend was going to pop the question soon. However, she didn't specify exactly what the question might be.

The next day, her boss got a phone call from the chief of police, who wanted to get in touch with Eden because of the grateful ravings of his dog-obsessed wife. He wanted to have Eden on the roster of psychic consultants for future police work.

The man would not take no for an answer.

Eden's boss at Psychic Connexions let her go later that week, explaining that his business, such as it was, would be better off without any close police scrutiny.

If she'd been able to psychically foresee that unfortunate outcome, she would have saved some money for a rainy day.

The first time she'd been called in to officially consult on a police case two weeks ago, it'd been a total bust. Even though she'd concentrated so hard it felt like her head would explode, she'd sensed absolutely nothing useful to do with the missing person. She hated disappointing people, especially when they looked at her with that too-familiar, hard-edged, cynical glare. Most people thought psychics, even mild ones like her, were major frauds, and failing to prove them wrong was even more annoying.

She had no guarantees this time would be any better. The house she presently stood in front of had recently been home to a serial killer and the police wanted to see if she could "sense something" about the killer's current whereabouts.

She wanted to help if she could, but maybe she was in way over her head.

In fact, she was quite sure of it.

Eden cleared her throat nervously. The mid-October air was getting cool enough that she regretted not bringing a light jacket along today. "So . . . how much longer do you think Detective Hanson will be?"

Santos seemed stumped by the question for a moment, but then looked over to his left side. "Oh, here he comes now. But since you're psychic you probably knew he was nearly here, right?"

So very wrong. Eden took a deep breath, held it, and glanced over at the approaching figure.

Detective Ben Hanson was six-foot-two of *gorgeous* with a body like a Greek god and a face like a movie star. There was a reason that his last name sounded like "handsome." She'd noticed that women swooned—seriously *swooned*—when he walked past. And the fact that he was a cop, not to mention an *unmarried* cop, only added the proverbial fuel to the sexy-man fire. Eden had seen him twice before when she'd visited police headquarters at the chief's insistence. When she found out he was the one assigned to walk her through this case, she dropped everything and rushed over.

Did that make her seem completely sad and pathetic?

Yeah, well, Eden thought as she let her breath out in a long sigh. *The truth hurts.*

He approached and her heart did an annoying *ka-thunk-a-thunk*. It wasn't as though she expected them to get married and have lots of babies, but she did like checking him out.

He made her feel like a sixteen-year-old high schooler— geeky and pimply and drooling over the out-of-her-league football quarterback.

Eden was closing in on thirty now. She wasn't pimply anymore. However, the geeky thing was still up for debate. Gorgeous guys had a tendency to make her completely and embarrassingly tongue-tied.

"Is the psychic here yet, Santos?" he asked.

Hello? Had she suddenly become invisible?

Santos nodded at her. "This is Eden Riley."

That finally earned her a glance, but there was zero warmth or humor behind it. "Then let's get this over with."

Obviously, she thought wryly, *he's already fallen madly in love with me, but is having a hard time showing it.*

"Sounds super," Eden said, forcing enthusiasm past her nervousness. "Lead the way, Detective."

The sour-faced look that comment received from him confirmed it was official: She was still a geek.

She followed him to the average-looking house. The front door had some of that police-line-do-not-cross tape on it. He ripped it away and entered the front hallway that led to a small kitchen.

"Here's how this is going to go. The suspect vacated this location about six days ago. Our leads as to where he went have come up dry. The sergeant seems to think you might be able to"—he glanced at her—"work some mojo and tell us where he's hiding."

Eden raised her eyebrows. *"Mojo?"*

He waved his hand in a flippant manner. "Whatever it is you think you can do. Hocus-pocus. Mojo. You know."

He was lucky he was so hot or she might be annoyed by his rude and dismissive attitude. "For the record, Detective, I didn't ask to be here. It was requested of me." She cleared her throat. "If you'd prefer, I can take my, uh . . . *mojo* somewhere else."

"The chief thinks you can help."

"But you don't."

"No, actually I don't."

"Because you don't believe in psychics."

He raised his blue-eyed gaze steadily to hers. "That's right."

"Well, to tell you the truth, I'm not all that convinced, myself." She crossed her arms.

"Excuse me?"

She chewed her bottom lip and tried not to feel like a big, fat fraud. "I can't seem to control where and when I see stuff. It's not a tap I can turn on and get a big glass of sparkling psychic water. I just want you to know that up front so you're . . . you're not disappointed if nothing happens today."

"I won't be disappointed. I'm *expecting* nothing to happen." He tilted his head to the side. "Does the chief know how you feel about this?"

"He wouldn't listen to me." She had explained that it was doubtful she'd be much use to them, but he'd insisted—although Eden suspected it had a lot to do with appeasing his enthusiastic wife. "I figure if I don't turn out to be much help, he'll start to leave me alone. Maybe I only have a knack for finding lost dogs."

Ben looked confused. "So you're a psychic who doesn't believe in psychics?"

"I . . . I honestly don't know." It was the truth, at least. "Feel free to kick me out of here, you know, whenever you like."

Why was she sharing this information with him? She wasn't exactly sure, although sometimes it was better to admit one's weaknesses right away so there'd be no room for later misunderstandings. It might have also had a lot to do with Detective Hanson bringing out the schoolgirl babble inside of her. Once her mouth started spilling words, it was hard to stop the flood.

He studied her for at least thirty seconds before his frown turned into the first smile she'd seen on his face—and *wow*, he had one hell of a great smile. "I think you might be the only skeptical psychic I've ever met."

He scanned her then, from her long auburn ponytail draped over her right shoulder to her green peasant-style silk shirt to the tan leather ankle boots she'd bought only yesterday to go with the dark jeans she wore.

Whatever she'd said—well, *the truth*—was enough to make handsome Detective Hanson look at her a little differently. A *good* differently. She leaned against the kitchen counter and tried to look as alluring as humanly possible, but her elbow slipped so she straightened up. She was more than a little uncomfortable being in the house of a serial killer—although, by the looks of it, a very neat and organized one—but she pretended not to be as she felt Detective Hanson's gaze take her in.

"Huh. Interesting," he finally proclaimed.

She couldn't tell if he meant that in a good or bad way. "I'm sorry if you think I'm wasting your time."

He grinned. "Actually, I already thought this trip here today was a waste of time to begin with. You had nothing to do with it. But I appreciate you being honest with me."

"Honesty is a virtue, Detective Hanson."

"Please . . . call me Ben." He glanced at the clock on the wall that read almost five and then turned his attention back to Eden. "So do you need to be anywhere after this or would you like to grab some dinner?"

Remain calm, Eden, she commanded herself as a flush of pleasure heated her cheeks. Detective Handsome was asking her out. And he wanted her to call him Ben.

Her empty stomach growled its enthusiastic approval.

"That sounds like—" Then she froze as the strangest feeling came over her. A chill that made the hair stand up on her arms. *"Shit."*

Ben frowned. "What?"

She brought a hand to her head as a strange, fuzzy image flickered through her mind. *Damn it, not now.*

She was the "skeptical psychic," as Ben had just described her. But there it was—a feeling crawling down her spine that she couldn't ignore if she'd wanted to. She'd had the feeling many times before in her life, since she was a little girl, but it came and went and was never anything she could channel or control. An awareness that didn't rely on any of her usual five senses.

Suddenly the coat closet just beyond the kitchenette was all she could concentrate on. Something was in there—possibly a clue to help find the maniac the police were looking for.

"What exactly did this creep do?" she asked quietly.

His expression turned grim. "What he did was kill one woman a week by posing as a pizza delivery guy. Eight weeks and eight deaths. Then suddenly he stopped three weeks ago—no more murders since then. It's strange because usually serial killers begin to escalate once they've established a pattern. We don't know when he'll start again, but it's only a matter of time."

A chill went down her spine. If she could do something,

anything, then it would be worth it. She pushed away from the counter and walked directly toward the coat closet.

"I know what I said earlier about not really believing in my abilities," she began, "but I'm getting this weird vibe right now."

"Weird vibe?" The cool, cynical edge was back.

The impulse was too strong to ignore. "This will only take a second. It's probably nothing."

Hell, with her track record, maybe it was the guy's dog.

Eden wrapped her fingers around the handle. The hinges creaked as she slowly opened the door.

She blinked and stared with disbelief at what she saw.

She'd been right. There was a clue inside. A *big* clue.

A clue that was about six feet tall, 250 pounds, and held a large knife.

For a long, frozen second she stared, unable to move or speak with only one thought flitting through her head—

What were the damn odds that the very serial killer they were looking for would be in the house? Hiding in the freaking closet?

Good odds, obviously. *Very good odds.*

Eden shrieked as the large man thrust out his hand and grabbed her. He turned her around and held her firmly in place with one arm. The sharp tip of the knife grazed her throat.

"Shouldn't have done that," he growled. "I was trying to hide all quiet like a mouse."

"Drop your weapon!" Ben had his gun out and pointed at the friendly neighborhood serial killer currently pressed against Eden's back.

The sharp edge of the blade pushed closer against her skin. "I just came back to pick up a few things, not to have a showdown. You should have damn well left me alone."

Eden shot Ben a panicked look and then concentrated on not moving. "Please let go of me."

He dragged her roughly backward into the open archway leading to the living room. The curtains were drawn on the bay window, leaving them in shadows. "I need your help. I heard you talking. You're a psychic. That's how you sniffed me out."

Now that she was really close to him she could *literally* sniff him out. Considering how neat and tidy his house was, the man had obviously been away from deodorant or showers for several days. Her skin crawled and bile rose in her throat.

"How can I help you?" she managed.

"I'm possessed by a demon," he hissed into her ear. "And I want it out of me."

"A demon?" she repeated, trying to sound as if she believed him. "Is that what you think is making you kill people? The devil made you do it?"

She exchanged a fleeting look with Ben, who stood six feet in front of her. He'd be able to hear everything the freak was saying to her. The cop's expression was fierce but a distinct flicker of worry crossed his blue eyes. He was thinking what she was thinking. This guy was insane—even by serial killer standards.

"I can't concentrate." The killer shifted farther back with her. "Can't think with it in my head. I killed a homeless guy a couple weeks ago and the demon's been with me ever since."

"I'm warning you again," Ben snarled. "Let the woman go *right now.*"

The guy tensed. "He's telling me to let you go."

"That's r-right," Eden said, her voice shaky. "Listen to the nice policeman. He wants to help you and so do I. Nobody has to get hurt here."

"No, not the cop, the *demon*. He wants me to let you go."

Okay. "Well, then listen to the nice d-demon. I can help you. I *am* psychic. Very powerful. That's me. I'll be able to talk to your demon and convince him to leave your body and go back to—to *Hell* . . . and then everything will be fine."

"You don't believe me. I can hear it in your voice."

Her stomach clenched with fear. "No, I do. I totally believe."

"The world is full of strange things and strange beings.

They're among us. Walking around, eating, drinking, living side by side with humans. I couldn't see them before but now I can. They're everywhere. Do you see them, too?"

"Of course I do." It sounded like a lie. Mostly because it was. She could be this bastard's next murder victim. Her life might be crappy at the moment, but that didn't mean she wanted it to end. Her legs weakened, and if he hadn't been holding her tightly she would have fallen straight down to the beige-carpeted floor.

She gasped as the knife pressed closer.

"Maybe if I slit your throat the demon will leave," the killer growled into her ear. "He'll see that he doesn't have any power over me."

Eden met Ben's steady but worried gaze. He had his gun aimed at the serial killer's chest, but at the moment she was blocking the way.

"This is your last warning," Ben snapped. "I *will* shoot you."

Suddenly the killer let go of Eden and she spun around to see that he looked extremely upset.

"Shut up!" he yelled, and brought his hands up to his head. "I'm not listening to you, demon. I'll kill her."

His gaze tracked to where Eden stood, his eyes wide and crazed. He raised his knife and lunged at her.

She screamed, staggered back, and tripped over the edge of the carpet, landing hard on her butt.

A shot rang out, then another, and the serial killer crumpled to the ground.

He didn't move again.

"Eden, are you okay?" Ben asked sharply.

Okay? she thought, feeling stunned and shivery. Hell no, she wasn't okay. But at least she was still breathing.

"I'll be fine." Her hands shook so she clasped them in front of her. She decided to stay seated on the floor since she was sure her legs were too shaky to stand on. A line of perspiration sped down her spine. "You wanted me to help find the s-serial killer—" She took a shuddery breath. "Mission accomplished."

Her stomach churned and she was afraid she would be sick right then and there. She tried to focus on something, anything until she could calm down. Her gaze moved cautiously toward the prone body of the dead man she knew she'd have nightmares about for weeks—possibly *years*—to come.

She frowned. "Hey, do you see that?"

"See what?"

"That." She pointed at what looked like a thin, dark shadow emerging from the serial killer's gaping mouth and trailing along the floor like a black scarf.

That is definitely *not normal*, she thought.

Ben shook his head. "All I see is a dead body. It's okay now, Eden. You're safe."

The shadow paused as it moved across the floor between her and Ben. Then, before she could do anything else or figure out what on earth it was, it shifted direction and, in a split second, flew through the air toward her. She shrieked and instinctively put her hands up to block whatever it was, but the moment the shadow touched her . . . it disappeared.

She looked at her hands.

What the hell just happened?

Had it only been her imagination?

Ben held out a hand to help her back up to her feet. "Are you sure you're okay?"

She swallowed hard. "I will be—you know—eventually."

He squeezed her hand in his. "Good."

She definitely needed a drink. A big one. Straight up.

She knew she should have stopped for some lunch earlier. A piece of toast and a glass of juice nine hours ago was not enough for proper mental alertness. She shook away the strange feeling and tried to relax while Ben got on his phone and called for backup.

Constable Santos ran in and swept the room with one look. "Eden! Damn, you sure work fast! You found the killer!"

That she did. And now the killer was killed.

But she still felt like she wanted to hurl. Missing dogs were much easier to deal with than serial killers. That was the lesson of the day.

At least it's over, she thought wearily. She'd be very happy to go back to her regular life now.

No more traumatic experiences for her, thank you very much.

New from #1 *New York Times* bestselling author

LORA LEIGH

NAUTI DECEPTIONS

Caitlyn "Rogue" Walker left her life in Boston to become a teacher in a small Kentucky town. But her dream was shattered when she was framed in a sex scandal. Refusing to be run out of town, Caitlyn shed the identity she had and became Rogue.

Sheriff Zeke Mayes knows there's more to her than meets the eye, though what meets the eye is pretty smoking. He's prepared for a long struggle to get Rogue to drop her defenses—and give in to desire. But soon Zeke will become embroiled in a deadly game that sweeps up Rogue in its wake. And when everything seems to be a matter of life and death, there is no reason to hold back . . .

penguin.com

M592T1009

Deep into a woman's wildest fantasies, deeper still into her most forbidden dreams . . . a place only these bestselling authors would dare to go.

Beyond the Dark

❧

LORA LEIGH
ANGELA KNIGHT
EMMA HOLLY
DIANE WHITESIDE

Lora Leigh does it . . . in the lair of a strange Breed, part man, part wolf, on the hunt for the woman he craves—and needs—to fulfill a hunger clawing at him from within.

Angela Knight does it . . . in the psychic realm of a woman attuned to the touch of strangers—and the powerful temptations of a seductive and mysterious protector.

Emma Holly does it . . . in a fantastic world where a powerful queen rules—until she commits the sin of falling in love with the handsome son of her worst enemy.

Diane Whiteside does it . . . in an alternate universe of Regency magic where two lovers are threatened by a vicious mage and swept up in a turbulent war off the Cornish cliffs.

M527T0709